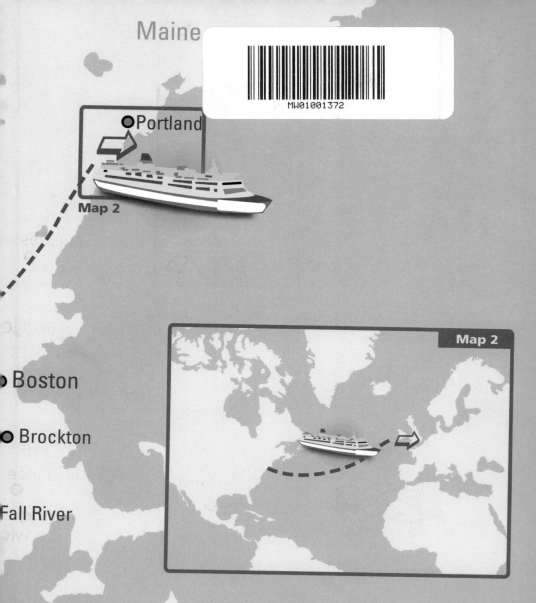

Maine

Portland

Map 2

Boston

Brockton

Fall River

Map 2

A NOVEL BY

ROY S. NEUBERGER

Author of FROM CENTRAL PARK TO SINAI

A NOVEL BY

ROY S. NEUBERGER

Author of FROM CENTRAL PARK TO SINAI

FELDHEIM PUBLISHERS
JERUSALEM   NEW YORK

ISBN 978-1-59826-213-1

FELDHEIM PUBLISHERS
POB 43163
Jerusalem, Israel

208 Airport Executive Park
Nanuet, NY 10954

www.feldheim.com

10 9 8 7 6 5 4 3 2 1

Printed in Israel

In the End of Days, after the Children of Israel have re-turned to their land, the children of Ishmael and the chil-dren of Esau will unite to attack Jerusalem. They will form a world coalition against the tiny nation of Israel. But something will go wrong with their plan. The religious beliefs of the children of Ishmael and the children of Esau will clash, and the two nations will collide and destroy each other. This is what is referred to as the War of Gog and Magog. Following this cataclysmic conflict, the Final Redemption of the Jewish People will occur with the coming of Messiah, the Son of King David.

From the commentary of the Malbim
Rabbi Meir Leib ben Yechiel Michel (1808-1879)
to The Book of Ezekiel 32:17

PROLOGUE

THE ENTIRE WORLD WAS EAGER to ring in the year 2020.

On New Year's Eve, nearly 400,000 people danced and sang in the park near the Eiffel Tower, which had been completely restored since the terrorist attacks of 2012. Revelers jammed Times Square, waiting for the crystal ball to descend.

For months this New Year had been eagerly anticipated. A year like 2020, containing repeated digits, happens only once every century. Virtually every global marketer seemed to have created a special 2020 campaign.

But 2020 symbolized something far more special. This would mark the fifth anniversary of an extraordinary Global Alliance of every nation on the planet. The horrific floods, hurricanes, famines, earthquakes and fires of 2014, followed by the terrifying threat of the PRX virus, had inspired world leaders to put aside their civil wars, nationalistic goals and cultural barriers.

Sharing their brightest talents and pooling huge economic resources, the Alliance had labored feverishly to reverse the environmental nightmare that had gripped the earth. And now, just five years later, there were measurable signs that the earth was responding. Alternative sources of energy were rapidly replacing fossil fuels; non-degradable products had been mostly phased out by manufacturers; there was a new, genuine respect for the wonders of the earth and a realization that only a mutual effort by all nations could protect those resources.

Environmentalism, conservation and the long-term health of the planet were now everyday topics that concerned all citizens as well as their leaders. Green pastures, clean air and quiet pursuits were replacing Hummers, private jets and heated pools as essentials of The Good Life.

It was also noted that 2020 would mark a five-year period in which there had been no attacks by terrorists anywhere in the world. Many observers credited the work of the Global Alliance and its success in bringing together even warring countries for the common battle to save Mother Earth. Cynics, however, believed that the heavy loss of life suffered in the droughts, floods and earthquakes that had hit numerous terrorist strongholds in 2014 had merely delayed their mission.

After the 2020 New Year's festivities, the Global Alliance met to announce a new, five-year plan of environmental strategies. Life settled back to a familiar pace.

Winter waned and spring beckoned. Presidential primaries, the return of baseball and spring cleaning occupied the attention of most Americans. As summer approached, schoolchildren became restless and their parents began planning vacations. Weather forecasters predicted a comfortably warm and calm summer.

It seemed that 2020 was going to be a very good year.

EXPLOSION

Sunday, July 5

NDEPENDENCE DAY WEEKEND, 2020 WAS filled with simple pleasures.

July 4th was on a Saturday. Leah and I spent a quiet *Shabbos* at home. That night, with the cool air washing over us, we sat for a while in our backyard, looking out across the bay at the huge fireworks show on Sandy Beach.

Sunday morning, Leah worked in the garden. Then we rode our bikes through the winding streets of the neighborhood. In the afternoon shade, Leah read and I studied outdoors, both sipping cool lemonade.

Having some time ago quit my Wall Street career, I was enjoying life as an author and speaker, writing books and speaking about our religious transformation. People were interested; there was a huge religious revival going on in the Jewish community. We were proud of our five children and our grandchildren, all of them productive and happy. It was amazing that such wonderful children had come from us. Our life had meaning and purpose.

3

It was late Sunday afternoon, July 5th. The sun was sinking toward the horizon as I sat in front of the computer working on a new book. Leah was at her desk. I thought about the richness of our lives and our many blessings. The President, in his holiday message, had talked about the ideals of the Founding Fathers: free thought, free speech and the right to worship. Over the past fifteen years, our country — in fact, the entire world — had struggled with terrorism, several wars, a divided electorate and environmental disasters, yet somehow on this weekend it all seemed so far in the past as America basked happily in the warmth of its 244th birthday.

There was a time when I couldn't imagine such contentment. Raised in affluent surroundings on New York's Upper East Side, I was privileged to have every material advantage imaginable, including a fine education, cultural enrichments and sophisticated pursuits. Still, as an adolescent and then as a young man, I couldn't shake the feeling that something crucial was missing from my life. But then I had no idea what it was.

By age thirty one, I had explored Buddhism, Hinduism and Catholicism, along with folk music, wilderness hiking and social activism in an effort to find "it." I was married to a brilliant and generous-hearted woman, and we had been blessed with two daughters. I owned the local weekly newspaper in a leafy Hudson Valley town and life seemed full. Yet inside I was empty and miserable.

One day, a friend invited me to a nearby synagogue to hear a speech by Rebbetzin Esther Jungreis, a rabbi's wife who had been widely described as "the Jewish answer to Billy Graham." Although born Jewish, I had never even been in a synagogue. But as I listened, it felt as if her words were marching straight into my heart.

Suddenly my wife and I knew what had been missing.

We began to attend classes and together we eagerly embraced the Torah, the Five Books of Moses and its commentary. Within months, we had completely changed our lives: I sold my business and we moved to a religious Jewish neighborhood, enrolling our daughters in a Jewish religious school. Even our names changed. Linda became Leah and Roy became Yisroel.

Our lives had changed dramatically. In America, no one could prevent us from returning to the ways of our ancestors. That deepened our appreciation for Independence Day.

The sun slipped beneath the horizon and the world darkened. As I switched on the desk lamp, Leah entered the room. An e-mail had arrived from our daughter Tehilla in Israel. We talked and laughed for a few minutes about the exploits of our grandchildren.

Suddenly, the screen flickered and faded to a single dot that slowly disappeared. The house went dark. Before I could get up, the world outside the window turned white, so bright that I had to turn away.

"Yisroel, What's happening?"

I had no idea, no time to think, but my skin became very cold and a flash of fear shot through me like an electric shock. The house shook violently; a crystal vase toppled from a shelf, crashing to the floor. Suddenly the air was punctuated with deep sounds. BOOM!! BOOM!! BOOM!!

For a long moment, we didn't move or speak. Then we groped our way through the darkness, searching for a flashlight. We found the box that held our *Shabbos* candles and a supply of matches. I lit a candle, stuffing the matches and two extra candles in my shirt pocket.

I reached for the phone. Dead.

We found the portable radio. No stations were broadcasting. There was only a faint, scratchy hiss.

BOOM!! BOOM!!

Now the sounds were coming from another direction. We walked to the window and looked towards New York City. Flickering light flashed off the clouds in the darkened sky toward Brooklyn and Staten Island. We could hear faraway sirens. People were gathering in the street.

My insides began to tighten up.

I'm at camp in Vermont, ten years old. I'm wordlessly panicking. What frightens me? The "bad language" of the kids? Their "coolness" and my awkwardness? I'm homesick. Is that it? But when I get home I'm still homesick! Something must really be wrong with me!

My fear is beyond words, beyond explanation. I'm scared of tough kids, violence, cursing. I'm scared of successful kids. I'm scared of drugs. I'm scared of people who aren't scared. I can't put my finger on it. It grips my stomach, my mind. I'm afraid of the dark, but why? It doesn't matter why. Fear is beyond logic, beyond understanding. I'm just afraid! My mind is paralyzed. A lump forms in my throat. I try to swallow, but I can't.

That was then, but now I believe in G-d. I'm not supposed to be afraid any longer. But your basic personality remains with you. What you were when you were a child, you are when you're an adult. Maybe you have different weapons now, but you're still in the same fight. I KNOW that G-d is in charge, but I'm still afraid, the childhood panic seizes me. I can't convince myself to be calm. The world is out of control, and I'm out of control with it. There are no rules. The world is falling apart, and I'm falling apart. I can't deal with it!

9/11/01: white fear grips me. What is "white fear"? Somehow the world goes white; all color is drained. I'm shivering. The world has become cold.

I'm afraid of dying. I'm afraid of being hurt. I'm afraid of seeing people dying. I'm afraid of being alone. I'm afraid of my world disintegrating.

I try to fight the panic, but I don't know how.

Yisroel, control yourself! Bring your mind under control.

Wordlessly, Leah and I walked outside toward Bentzi Stein's driveway. A group of people stood there huddled together, flashlights in hand. No one spoke. As we got closer, we could hear an electronic crackling. Bentzi was a member of the *Hatzolah* volunteer rescue service and had an emergency radio. As we listened to the reports, I felt my heart pounding.

"....multiple explosions in the New York area. Bridges, tunnels, power plants, police stations and military facilities have been hit. We have reports, not yet confirmed, of explosions in other cities....billowing smoke and flames reported at Grand Central and Patrick Moynihan Stations. We've just heard, and this is not confirmed, that some of these explosions may be nuclear. Repeat, we have unconfirmed reports that there may have been a number of nuclear explosions."

Mrs. Kasman, a widow who lived across the street from us, screamed and began to cry. Leah put her arm around her and whispered something. The radio now began to crackle loudly; we could hardly understand the words.

"....traffic lights are inoperative and there is near total gridlock throughout Brooklyn, Queens and Long Island. Our generator is fading; we may not be able to broadcast much longer....CRACKLE.... Good luck and may G-d..."

There was a final, muffled crackle from the radio. For a moment, all of us stood together, motionless. No one spoke. The silence was thick and stifling.

Suddenly, a light burst behind us, high in the sky to the

west. It was so bright that we instinctively shut our eyes tight as the world suddenly went white.

An instant later, a shock wave hit us like a battering ram. There was screaming and moaning and quiet sobbing all around me. Parts of the radio were scattered everywhere. I pulled myself up and looked for Leah, who was across the street, struggling to her feet. We were both a little dizzy and bruised but alive. I am sure that, had we been much closer to the light burst, all of us would have been dead.

Although I didn't understand how it worked, I had read once that an electromagnetic bomb detonated high above the earth's surface could destroy communications for thousands of miles. I was sure that the attacks had been designed to do just that. There was every indication that the terrorists were trying to wreck the emergency communication system. With no telephones, no electricity, no radio and no electronic communications, America's military and civilian defense systems would be crippled.

"Leah, are you all right?"

"I think so, but...where is Mrs. Kasman?" Before I could reply, Mrs. Kasman walked by us slowly, gripping Bentzi's arm tightly. Leah smiled with relief, then immediately started coughing and covering her mouth. Soon I knew why. Dust and grit swirled around us and flew into our noses and mouths; something metallic left a burning sensation in my throat.

Joey and Dina Stein, Larry Kantor, and Harry and Beverly Klaus were standing on the street with us. We were all in a daze. Bentzi came back from Mrs. Kasman's house, his footsteps kind of shaky.

We all just stood there. No one said anything for a while.

Then Larry Kantor said, "Those Moslems. It's unbelievable. We've all known this was coming. We're the stupid ones! We all knew that those livery drivers, those candy store owners, the newspaper kiosk guys, we all knew who they were. They were all just waiting and planning and planning and waiting. And then they became doctors and professors and real estate agents. They were 'just like us.' They were typical Americans, even members of Congress, except they took their oath of office on a Koran instead of a Bible. Just like us.

"I remember the science fiction story our counselor told us in camp around forty years ago. I was just a little kid, but I am still scared from that story! He told it to us at bedtime and I didn't sleep at all that night, or the next... or the next. The Martians were invading earth, and the scary thing was that they looked just like humans. There was only one way to tell that they were Martians: they had a third eye in the back of their head!

"There was only one person on earth who knew the secret, and he was racing around to alert the world. He got to the FBI and then the CIA and then the Joint Chiefs of Staff, and they were beginning to believe him. They had to mobilize the entire security apparatus. But they needed the approval of the President. So finally he gets to the White House. After elaborate security checks he's admitted to the Oval Office. The President walks in.

"'Mr. President,' he begins, 'I want to tell you about this incredible threat to the security of the United States.' He proceeds to describe the entire situation. The President listens with rapt attention.

"'If this is true,' the President says, 'the Nation owes you a huge debt of gratitude. I'm going to call my Chief of Staff into the Oval Office.'

"The President swivels around in his chair to reach for the yellow phone, and that's when the visitor sees the third eye in the back of the President's head!"

Larry looked at us.

"That's what's going on here. They're all around. We let them take over, and now they are destroying America. They're destroying the greatest nation in the history of the world, and, by the way, the kindest to the Jews! Listen, biblically, Ishmael, the father of the Arabs, is called *"pe're adam,"* a wild-man, and that's their nature. And now they're running the world! G-d Almighty! How will we survive?"

Beverly Klaus was shifting back and forth on her feet.

"Larry, you know we love you. We've been your neighbors for twenty five years, but you're a bigot! I can't stand your politics! You're really a bigot! The Moslems are no different from the Chinese or the Irish or any other group. Dr. Chen, who lives over there, is a radiologist. Dr. Ibn Kalil is my radiologist, and he happens to be a lovely man. What's the difference? Stop being such a hateful right winger! You don't know who did this, and the fact is that, if it's Moslems or Iranians or Arabs or whatever you want to call them, you know perfectly well that the crazies, the terrorists are not the majority, and they don't represent the typical Moslem or his religious viewpoint. To say that Moslems are by nature terrorists is like saying black people are by nature thieves. It's not fair and it's not true. You don't know what happened and you don't know who did it."

Bentzi was listening quietly.

"Listen guys," he said, "I don't think we have the luxury to stand here and debate this right now. We'd better concentrate on saving ourselves, whether that means trying to flee Long Island or battening down in our basements. But I'll just tell you both one thing, and I've studied this a little. The Koran is full of hatred, not just against Jews but against Christians and anyone they call a 'Kafir' or infidel. The Koran preaches that Islam is the only religion and that the duty of a good Moslem is to fight what they call 'idolatry' until there is nothing left in the world but Moslems. Period. So no one should be surprised at a Moslem attempt to take over America and the world. It's all there for anyone who wants to see it.

"But now, let's try to save ourselves. We're piling everyone in the boat and heading for New Jersey. I would love to take you, but we don't have an inch of room. May G-d watch over you and all of us, and may we all meet in peace soon again. I hope it will be in Israel. But for now, anywhere there is peace will be a welcome sight.

"Good luck to you, neighbors! May G-d watch over all of us!"

Bentzi turned around and walked quickly to his house.

The rest of us had little appetite for words. We shook hands and exchanged blessings. Leah and I walked slowly toward our house. We were both groping for a way to deal with this rationally.

"Yisroel, now that we've heard everyone else's opinion, what do *you* think is happening?"

"I think we know, Leah. We've been expecting this for years."

She gave me a serious, straight look. No expression; we just looked at each other.

We had known this was coming. Later on, of course, the world found out that the events of July 5, 2020 made 9/11 look like child's play. The terrorists didn't have huge atomic or nuclear weapons. Instead, they had detonated hundreds, maybe thousands, of small, powerful tactical nuclear devices almost simultaneously at targets across the country.

The events of July 5 were the work of skilled and patient zealots, disciplined soldiers who had lived in the U.S. for years. Posing as ordinary civilians who shopped at the supermarket, drove American cars and tended their lawns, they acted just like their neighbors. Organized into individual cells, each cell with a single mission, they had rehearsed for more than a decade, traveling each year to mock facilities set up in places like Azerbaijan, Bosnia, Tajikistan and the Sinai Peninsula. When asked, they would say that the trips were religious pilgrimages.

Somewhere high over the middle of the U.S. they had managed to set off a powerful electromagnetic explosion. This knocked out radio transmissions throughout the entire country, virtually paralyzing police and military communication, and enabling small groups of insurgents to isolate and attack key government facilities, military posts, utilities and transportation systems, pretty much shutting down the federal and local governments.

Before 9/11, America had felt itself to be a fortress, strong and safe from its enemies. We knew there were powerful government agencies, some more secret than others, that dealt with intelligence and counter-intelligence. We didn't really worry about these things until the day that the Twin Towers came down.

In the glow of hindsight, it was clear that a lot had been missed. It's like the world under a rock. One walks by the rock every day, but who thinks about looking underneath? When you lift it, you are always surprised to find that everything under there is moving! It's ugly. Maybe that's why most of us don't look under rocks!

Leah and I used to talk about the changes in our everyday lives after 9/11. We understood why we had to go through airport searches, walk around barricades and show photo ID to security guards. But was it enough? Some people thought there was too much checking and screening, that 9/11 could never happen again. America may have been caught unprepared once, but it couldn't happen twice.

Still, I wondered why only trucks were searched at the tunnels. Couldn't a car trunk carry a powerful bomb? Of course, the answer was simple. Checking every car would have brought America to a halt. We wouldn't have tolerated it. An extra hour at the airport perhaps, but every day?

As it turned out, the tunnels were easy to destroy. It took only four cars for four tunnels. The bridges were not as easy. Six months earlier, a new firm had submitted the lowest bid on a bridge maintenance contract to the New York Department of Transportation. Weeks later, explosive charges were hidden in service channels within the spans. On July 5, two-man suicide subs packed with explosives struck the suspension towers, ramming the bases and blowing themselves up, weakening the structures. In a matter of minutes several huge and vital bridges toppled into the waters. First the Brooklyn Bridge, then the 59th Street, Hell's Gate and MetroNorth bridges, even the mighty George Washington. The Williamsburg, the Manhattan, and the main span of the Triborough were not so easy and the destruction was incomplete. Nevertheless, within a few minutes Manhattan was basically isolated.

Of course, in some ways we had made it easy for them. We had created a society that was dependent on computers. The same computers that made it possible to buy movie tickets online, order groceries, balance one's checking account and talk with strangers, also controlled traffic lights, electricity, elevators, telephones, airports, water and gasoline pumps. Even the police and fire departments were crippled without computers. All systems were paralyzed in less than five minutes.

As Leah and I reentered our home that evening, there was much we didn't understand. But we knew one thing: everyone was on his own. Without communications, there would be no police, no military structures...no government at all. When America realized this, there would be chaos.

How would we function? When Hurricane Katrina had submerged New Orleans back in 2005, the aftermath was more frightening than the storm itself. The police simply disappeared. The most powerful military force in the world went AWOL. Armed gangs looted and terrorized. And that had been when America was fully operational, long before 2020.

As Leah and I walked into our house, we could hear wailing and weeping in the darkness. Then the sound of an agonized, desperate voice, "What am I supposed to do?"

No one answered.

Once inside the house, I closed the door and took a deep breath. Already my eyes were getting used to the darkness, and when Leah drew back the drapes, there was just enough light from the moon to see each other.

I was fighting panic. It would rise up, and then I would try to push it back down. It was an internal as well as an external war. The internal war was to remain sane.

We knew we had to get out. Intuitively, I knew this was a well-planned attack, the product of years of preparation. I assumed it wasn't confined to the Metropolitan Area, nor even to the United States, but rather that it was part of an attempt to establish worldwide Moslem supremacy. After all, the Moslem population had been growing on a spectacular basis, most noticeably in Europe, but also in the U. S. We had seen it coming; all you had to do was look. Anyone could understand who had the courage to see and to think,

So how would we deal with it? We had to be able to run to some place where we could survive until the cataclysm passed. Here on Long Island, connected to the mainland only by crowded, fragile bridges and tunnels, we were especially vulnerable. Long Island had never felt like an island because we had never been attacked before, but suddenly we were trapped. We had to get off the Island.

But where would we go?

And what about our children? We had to find them, or at least try, and they were in New Jersey. So it was clear where we were headed.

There was one small problem: how to get there!

Amidst my mental paralysis, I was doing things. I was moving like a robot. Someone else, it seemed, was grabbing and organizing necessities. It wasn't I, but I was doing it. I felt like an actor in an epic film, acting out our life against the backdrop of a crumbling civilization.

I looked at Leah. I saw her as she had looked when we first met in high school, two teenagers on the threshold of life. Then it was our wedding day. She was never common. She saw beyond the sham. She looked into the distance.

She is a noble person, I thought to myself.

Rumbling in the distance snapped me back to the present.

"Leah, how will we survive?"

"We will survive, Yisroel. G-d will save us. You will see."

I didn't know why, but I believed her.

ESCAPE FROM LONG ISLAND

Sunday Night, July 5

PEOPLE WERE LEAVING.

Not that they knew where to go, but they were going.

Leah and I could hear anxious voices, slamming doors and screeching tires as we carefully made our way, by the light of a *Shabbos* candle, down the wooden staircase to the basement. Years before, in the days after 9/11, we had put together some things we might need if the world blew up.

As I looked at the bottled water, canned food, batteries, candles and first aid supplies, I felt a strong urge just to stay put, at least until we could find out what was going on. I could imagine us hiding in our home, with a mountain of canned goods and vegetables from the garden.

I smiled at the absurdity of it. We were not going to survive by sitting in that house! All my instincts told me we had to leave, to go to a place where at least we would have the freedom to run and hide, where we could take some active part

16

in trying to save ourselves rather than waiting passively until it was too late to run.

Where are our children? Our family? Our friends? What is happening to these beloved people? Mothers and little children? Fathers? Grandfathers? Grandmothers? Were they...?

I had to stop thinking about these things now. We had to keep moving if WE were to survive! Thinking was a luxury which would have to wait. If we didn't survive, then we couldn't help them...or anyone.

We had prepared knapsacks, which we crammed with prayer books, a small Bible, *tallis* and *tefillin*, sweaters, rain gear, flashlights, water, food, clothing and essential medicines, then headed back up the stairs to the garage. As we walked to our bikes, I remembered the day we had decided to buy them. We told the man in the bicycle shop that we were interested in sturdy bicycles that could be used on a long trip. He began to describe vacation destinations. We didn't tell him that we wanted bicycles for the time when the concept of "vacation" would be an anachronism and our survival would depend on the power of our own legs. At first we had stored the bikes down in the basement, but then I started to use mine for local errands. That was one way to squeeze exercise into a busy schedule.

A spring Sunday in New York, our second date. Two young people biking down to Lower Manhattan. We board the Staten Island Ferry. It's still a nickel! You can't get a better sightseeing tour for a thousand dollars! Sailboats; ocean liners; barges, merchant ships; fire and police boats; the Statue of Liberty; Governor's Island; New Jersey; the Brooklyn shoreline; activity everywhere. We spend the day touring farms and countryside in the pre-Verrazano Bridge countryside of this quiet corner of New York City. A picnic on the grass. We sail down hills and glide along country lanes.

Now the time had come again to ride our bikes.

I pushed the garage door button. Nothing! I felt a wave of panic until I remembered...no electricity. Grabbing a flashlight, I found the manual release and pulled the cord. The door freed itself from the electric lift. I pushed it up. We wheeled out our bikes, strapped on the knapsacks, and checked once more to be sure we had everything we needed. I pulled the garage door closed.

My heart was pounding. Could this be it? Could it all end so suddenly? I stood by the front door for a long minute, my hand on the *mezuzah*.

Hamalach hago-el...May the angel who has saved us from all evil up to now accompany us and guard us forever!

We looked at the house, then at each other. This was the moment. We might be back in ten minutes, an hour, a day...or never. We were looking at a lifetime. My eyes got moist. Leah's cheeks were shiny with tears. I wanted an excuse to stay longer, but we both knew we had to move. Even a short delay could be fatal.

Leah and I looked at each other, countless half-formed thoughts moving between our eyes. Then, wordlessly, we mounted our bikes and started down the road, pausing for one last look over our shoulders before we rounded the curve.

I knew in my heart I would never see that house again.

G-d, only You know where this journey will end. Please guard us along the way and bring us in safety to a world of peace along with our family and all those who love You and follow Your laws.

Talking to G-d. Short and to the point, but it was all I had the time and brainpower for. I'm sure that Leah was having a similar conversation.

She was right behind me as we made our way through the familiar neighborhood streets, now alive with activity as entire families prepared to make hasty exits. People were throwing things into cars and yelling at each other to hurry up.

At first, I felt awkward and uncomfortable with a heavy pack tugging me backwards as I tried to lean over the handle bars. After a few minutes, I found the right balance, and the pedaling became easier. I began to look around at the jumbled landscape. It was dark but not pitch black; there was a full moon. The light from dozens and, later, hundreds of headlights illuminated the scene.

The roads were jammed with slowly moving cars, but where were they going? Did anyone know? As we got closer, I could see the faces of people who looked dazed, almost drugged, too confused to be afraid...yet. A man wearing a red baseball cap was driving with his right hand on the steering wheel and pounding the car door over and over with his left hand.

We knew where we were headed. We had children in New Jersey and children in Israel. We had to find our children. Getting to Israel was a bit of a stretch at this moment, but getting to New Jersey was doable...perhaps. It was going to be a challenge, but we were going to try. After all, when everything is falling apart, family is what counts.

Soon we turned right onto a bigger road; my heart pounded as I saw the endless line of cars moving slowly and silently. The silence was strange. People were not honking their horns — yet — almost as though they were in a trance. Since they didn't know where they were going, they were not yet in a panic to get there. After a few minutes of steady pedaling, we reached a four-lane road that would take us to the Belt Parkway.

The idea of riding bikes along the Belt Parkway was a little intimidating, but the alternative was traveling through a tough urban neighborhood. I didn't think we'd fare too well in the chaotic darkness of inner-city streets. Leah agreed. We decided to continue on to the parkway.

At first, we wove closely around the cars, but after a while we veered off to the shoulder, trying to distance ourselves from the roadway to avoid being picked up in the headlights. When the drivers began to panic, someone might try to steal our bikes.

Fortunately, the ground was hard and dry. We made good progress, pedaling mostly in silence. I usually rode first, but sometimes there were wide patches where we could ride next to each other. It was comforting to see each other. We were also able to share our thoughts and encourage each other.

"Leah, I don't want to get us in trouble, G-d forbid, with overconfidence, but it seems as if this could have been much worse, at least up to now. Say they had used huge nuclear weapons, G-d forbid. We would be dead already from heat and radiation. I don't know about fallout, but the air seems breathable. I don't feel sick. Do you? The landscape is basically normal so far. I mean, we're alive! We're breathing. We can move. So far!"

"Yisroel, I think you should stop talking. Save your energy and your philosophy till we're through this mess!"

I was about to make a sarcastic comment, except this voice inside my head said to me, "Yisroel, you know she's right. Just keep quiet for once, OK!"

I kept quiet.

But I couldn't shut off my thoughts. Mental images of city dwellers surrounded by debris and chaos flashed through my brain. Probably in Manhattan, Brooklyn and Queens houses were down, maybe big buildings. How many people were screaming from under tons of debris? How many people were beyond screaming? And if they got out... where was the family? Where were their wives and husbands, their children, their parents? Were there any stores? Was there any food? How would they manage without electricity, phones and email? Babies without medical care, the elderly and disabled — *what do you mean, everyone!* — trapped at home, marauders roaming the streets. It was awful to contemplate. I asked G-d to help them.

The cars inched along, now slowing. Endless gridlock! The drivers seemed to have formed some kind of bond in their desperate plight. At times it was comforting to see other people close to us, the headlights cutting a path through the darkness. We were all in big trouble.

Suddenly the loud shriek of a siren pierced the silence and we looked quickly behind to see the red-and-blue lights of a police car careening along the shoulder, heading directly toward us. That car wasn't stopping for anything! There was only one thing we could do. We intentionally fell off our bikes to the right, away from the road and into the tall grass as the cop roared past barely a foot to our left.

That was so close! Where is he going? Does he know something we don't know?

Ahead on Rockaway Boulevard, we saw flames arching upward near JFK Airport. Thick black smoke was blowing over the road and, as we got closer, we could hear the roar of fire.

"What is it? What's happened?" shouted Leah, pedaling a few feet behind me. I looked up and saw a line of lights in the sky, some far away, others closer.

Were they missiles? Enemy planes?

Then I realized. These were ordinary passenger planes.

They had been heading for routine landings at JFK. But now, without electric power on the ground or radio contact with the control tower, the pilots were on their own, looking for a runway in the darkness below. The pilots must have known that the airport was somewhere near the line of car lights on Rockaway Boulevard, but where exactly was the runway? Was it clear of debris? How could they tell in the darkness and chaos?

We scanned the sky as we rode. I had a sickening feeling. There were hundreds of people in those planes, terrified and desperate. Probably the pilots were both afraid to land and afraid to keep flying. With no radio instructions and no lights on the ground, how could they land?

Suddenly I saw a pair of airplane lights advancing from our right, heading directly at us. The plane was very low, maybe a hundred feet off the ground and wobbling from side to side. It was trying to land and we were right in its path.

"Leah, we've got to move!" I yelled. "Pedal for all you've got!"

The scream of the engines enveloped us and I felt as if my eardrums were exploding. I could see the familiar markings of an American Airlines jet. Until the last second, I thought the wheels might crush us.

We pedaled for our lives, our legs aching and lungs burning. As the plane passed over us, barely clearing Rockaway Boulevard, I was almost blown off my bike by a churning cyclone of wind and the loudest sound I had ever heard. The earth exploded with noise and the entire sky lit up. Chunks of red-hot metal flew past us, setting cars on fire. Windows were smashed and flames jumped into the sky like orange geysers. The swamp grass to our right was on fire. Hot cinders burnt my cheeks.

"Don't stop!" I shouted. "Keep going!"

Our heads down and chests heaving, we pedaled with every ounce of energy. Near us, horns were blowing. Cars were careening off each other as drivers panicked in their frenzied efforts to escape the maelstrom.

We moved away as far as we could get from the roadway, which was bathed in orange light. Behind us, pillars of black smoke pierced the landscape like ugly fingers against the backdrop of flames stretched upward toward the sky.

We kept pedaling, but we had no more strength. Our speed diminished to a jerky crawl. Both of us were panting and coughing.

"Yisroel, I can't go on! I have to stop."

We were now about six city blocks from the crash-site. Metal parts were still flying, but no longer reaching us; the air was beginning to clear. We seemed to be past the danger zone. Leah and I stopped and threw ourselves down on the grass. I was dripping with perspiration and could feel my heart pumping as it used to do during high school soccer games.

"Windsprints" we call them. Rumor was that our coach, a wise guy everybody called "Flip," had been thrown out of high school for standing on a balcony during World War II and imitating Hitler. He's still a wise guy. He suspended me last year because I didn't take a shower after a game! Come on! (I was in a hurry to meet a friend!) A few weeks ago he wouldn't let me play because I had a stomach virus and he didn't want to catch it!

I hate those windsprints! We gasp for breath, but we are in such good shape!

For a few minutes, we lay there, silent, each trying to recover. All I could think was that the world was falling apart. Life would never be the same. I looked over at Leah.

"Are you OK?"

"Yes, thank G-d. I'm one big ache, but I'm OK."

"That was a close shave, Leah. It's a real catastrophe, and this was only one plane. This could be happening at every airport in the country, or maybe the world! Thousands of planes could be crashing. We're still alive, but all those people on all those planes, thousands of people.... It's impossible to comprehend the magnitude of this."

In the glow from the headlights I could see tears rolling down Leah's cheeks. I lay there in the grass, trying to catch my breath. After a few minutes, we turned and looked back. There, where we had just been riding, was a mountain of flame and black smoke.

At that moment, coming from our left, we saw another plane flying very low and heading toward the smoldering wreckage of the first plane. I turned away; I didn't want to watch.

"Yisroel, I think that pilot is trying to use the light from the burning plane to find the runway!"

Leah was right. The plane dipped down, then hit the ground, careening wildly for a few seconds and eventually coming to a stop. There was no explosion, no flames.

"That was a brilliant move by the pilot, Leah, and smart of you to figure it out. It looks like the plane is safe. But now all those people, even though they're on the ground, still have no place to go!"

"You would have done the same thing," said Leah. "It beats running out of fuel and crashing! That would be sure death. Those people are no worse off than we are."

She was correct again, of course. Except for our bicycles, we were in the same mess as those passengers.

"Obviously, you're right. Anyway, we'd better get moving. You reminded me, we've got to save our lives!"

With grim smiles, we picked up our bikes.

I looked ahead toward the Belt Parkway. Something looked strange. In the glare of the headlights, off to the right of the road about thirty feet ahead, I could make out two shadowy figures, hunched over and coming towards us. I felt a cold chill.

"Leah," I whispered. "Don't say anything. But get on your bike right now and move left onto the roadway. Get between the cars; pedal hard and swerve left. Hurry! Don't ask questions. Just do what I say."

We both jumped on our bikes and took off. I stayed to Leah's right, hoping to protect her. Just as we reached full speed, two pairs of hands reached out from the shadows and grabbed at me, just brushing my leg. An instant later, the two figures started running after us.

"Leah," I shouted, "use high gear."

We started to put distance between us and the shadowy figures. Both of us were breathing hard and we were close to exhaustion from the physical and mental strain of the last few hours. My legs were in total pain, but we were fighting for our lives. We had no choice! We pedaled on and soon the Belt Parkway came into sight.

Once again, long lines of headlights were moving very slowly in each direction. But now there were hundreds, if not thousands, stretching endlessly into the night in both directions. Where were they going? Did anyone have a plan? There was no honking or jockeying for position. They probably had no idea that a plane had crashed just a few miles away. Still, I thought they must be starting to feel a little desperate even if the roadway scene hadn't yet escalated into non-stop, horn-blowing, car-crashing chaos. We were close enough to see inside the cars. There were entire families in some of them. I'm sure the parents were desperately trying to keep calm themselves and reassure their children. But what were they telling them?

G-d help all of us!

We slowed down a bit, always looking back to see if we were being pursued. I started to breathe easier and began to think longer term about our prospects for finding a way to safety. We were very fortunate in one way. Two of our children and their families lived in Israel. Another daughter and her family lived about a mile from us but had all gone on a vacation trip to Israel. Our other two children lived in New Jersey. Our first priority was clear; we would try to locate them. Of course, it would take a miracle, but we had seen plenty of miracles, some just in the past few minutes.

Most of all, we wanted the whole family to be together in Israel. It seemed absurd, but I was convinced that "anywhere" on the planet was probably safer than where we were right now. I was always convinced that Israel, with all its troubles, was in the end the safest place. Events right here in New York seemed to prove my point. *"The eyes of... G-d are always upon [the land of Israel] from the beginning of the year to year's end."*[1] We had thought about moving to Israel for years, but some of our children were in the United States.

Enough musing. We needed a plan. New Jersey was the first objective. *We Jews are experts at surviving in impossible situations*, I told myself. We would just take one step at a time and pray as we went.

G-d, You are not any different after a nuclear attack from the way You were before a nuclear attack. You gave mankind free will and now we are millimeters away from destroying the beautiful world that You created. I'm as responsible for this as anyone else. All the times I was praying and my mind was everywhere but on You, thinking about what I was going to eat after I finished praying or all the phone calls I had to make. I wasted that prayer. I could have been crying out to You. Or what about all the lost opportunities for kindness? All the people I snubbed? I know it all counts. I know You examine all these things. I could have prevented this, but I didn't take it seriously.

And now look: the world has been torn apart. Is the entire world on fire? Where are our children and grandchildren? Where are the beautiful and holy families, the idealistic children studying in yeshiva, the great rabbis and leaders who toil in the vineyards of Torah? Where are they all? What are we going to do?

Four years old, I am in the country at the old pond in the middle of the woods. I am lying on my stomach on the concrete walkway, looking at my face rippling in the murky waters. I'm afraid to swim.

"He can swim," a voice says. "The best way to teach him is just to throw him in,"

Suddenly hands lift me up over the water. "NO!" I shout. I see bubbles, then darkness. I gulp water. I'm going to die! It is happening so fast! Panic! Thrashing! Sinking into the black! Choking on water!

Then, strong arms lift me up. Suddenly, I am in the light again. Dr. Haas has jumped in to save me! I am throwing up, but I am alive!

We had to get to New Jersey. And after that? Israel. But how could we do that? Only a day ago, it was so easy. You bought a ticket, boarded a plane and in less than half a day you were at Lod Airport. Today, we weren't sure how to get off Long Island. Israel was like a distant planet.

My thoughts were interrupted by the sound of yelling and shouting coming from our right. What now? About twenty figures were rushing towards us. We had been riding along the grass embankment north of the Belt Parkway near Howard Beach. I didn't think they had seen us yet because they were running directly towards the cars that were inching along the parkway.

"Leah," I hissed, "hide in the bushes! Follow me."

I intentionally fell off my bike and lay on top of it next to some hedges. Leah followed my example. Seconds later, the shadows ran by on either side of the hedges, shrieking towards the cars. Then we heard the sound of breaking glass, people screaming and fighting.

"Let's get out of here!" I whispered. We mounted our bikes and sped westward into the darkness. My heart was pounding again. Another close call. Dangerous characters were on the loose, and there was no one to stop them.

Dialing 911 was no longer an option. It had once been so easy. Three pushes with your finger and the police, fire or ambulance would be on their way. That was all over. Now we were so vulnerable. Funny thing: one "9-1-1" seemed to have destroyed the other "9-1-1." Without the police, we had only our wits, our luck, the cover of darkness and...G-d.

Prayer...constant prayer.

I hoped that G-d would hear our prayers and have mercy on our families and us. Did we deserve mercy? Leah is such an unselfish, kind person. But who am I? What had *I* done to deserve life? Why should G-d save me?

The grass embankment had widened; Leah pedaled up beside me.

"You know, we've never ridden our bikes at night before," she said. "It's really kind of nice—except for the circumstances."

Count on Leah to calm me down. I don't say that it worked, but she had at least tried.

I started to chuckle. We took instant refuge in our laughter, as senseless as it was, enjoying the fleeting escape from worry, fear and stress. Soon we grew quiet again, with only the click of our bicycle chains penetrating the silence.

I thought about the chaos around us. When the forces of insanity take over, it takes miracles to protect you. Now I understood why the rabbis say, "Pray for the welfare of the government, because if people did not fear it, a person would swallow his fellow alive."[2] There was no more government.

A great rabbi is walking alone through Nazi Germany, disguised as a non-Jew. He has no more family. Only he has survived, and now he has escaped from his captors. He keeps repeating to himself, over and over, "Ain od milvado...there is none beside Him."[3] The rabbi walks and walks and finally walks right out of Germany to freedom.

I didn't know how long our journey would last, but I knew that we would have to be prepared to face dangers and circumstances that we had never imagined before. Biblical words came out of my memory and gave me strength.

"Whoever sits in the refuge of the Most High, he shall dwell in the shadow of the Al-mighty...With His wings He will cover you, and beneath His wings you will be protected."[4]

"Those who put their hope in G-d shall renew (their) vigor; they shall rise on wings of eagles."[5]

I remembered hearing that the Jews of Yemen were brought to Israel in a massive airlift. Many had never seen an airplane before. The Israelis sent to escort them were concerned that they would never trust their lives to such a strange machine. But the Yemenites knew that G-d would bring them home "on wings of eagles." They boarded the huge jets without hesitation.

Our pedaling was getting smoother and more rhythmic. At times I felt that I could keep going forever. We glided past

Canarsie. I had taken Exit 13 every day for years, heading to work at Yeshiva Ateres Yisrael. I had spent endless hours in the home of Rabbi and Rebbetzin Abraham Jungreis, whom everyone called Zayda and Mama, our adopted grandparents. As newly "awakened" Jews in our thirties, that home and school had been our own nursery and kindergarten. In Zayda and Mama's living room I had my belated induction into the Covenant of Abraham.

This is scary.

I, a thirty-one year old man, am going to have a bris that is normally performed on an eight-day-old child?

Am I nuts? I know that the Patriarch Abraham had a bris at the age of ninety nine, but he was Abraham! I am just Roy Neuberger! What Abraham did was really brave. I mean, I am not undergoing the entire surgical procedure the way he did. When I was a baby I had a "circumcision" in the hospital because the doctors recommended it. So this is not quite like the bris of Abraham.

But I am still scared!

I am on the old couch by the window. Everyone but the mohel performing the circumcision, and Zayda clear out of the room. Zayda hands me a newspaper.

"Here, Yisroel, read this. Take your mind off the bris. It really won't hurt, but I know you're nervous!"

So I read the Daily News during my bris!

Guess what? I don't absorb a word I'm reading. Handing me the Daily News is a cute idea, very compassionate, but it doesn't work because my mind is totally agitated. When you're eight days old you don't know what's going on; your parents bring you into the covenant. It hurts, but you're a baby. It happens and then it's over.

But I'm thirty one! Yes, I'm nervous!

Today we weren't exiting at Canarsie. The ride over the Mill Basin Bridge was harrowing. With no shoulder, we had to weave around the cars, ready to swerve out of the way. By the time we had passed Flatbush Avenue and were nearing Coney Island Avenue and Ocean Parkway we were grateful to be back on the grass. Riding on the concrete shoulder would have been dangerous. With no cops in sight and people beginning to panic, the shoulder was full of cars.

But the cars were getting nowhere, even on the shoulder. People were beginning to abandon their vehicles and walk up on the grass where we were riding. We could see the panic on their faces as they realized they had nowhere to go. Soon the grass shoulder would be so crowded with people that we ourselves would have nowhere to go. We dismounted and stood to the side. I wanted to think a minute, to assess the situation. Behind us, the horizon was beginning to brighten; I was nervous about riding in daylight. Plus, we needed sleep.

Leah obviously was thinking the same way.

"Yisroel, this is getting dangerous. Maybe we should try the streets. Let's ride to the Ellmans' house. Even if they're not home, we could lock the bikes in their back yard, get into the house somehow, and sleep during the day. We could leave again tonight. And maybe they have some food."

"Great idea, Leah. Let's do it!"

The Ellmans lived about twenty blocks north. Soon we left the Belt Parkway at the Ocean Parkway exit. At the end of the service road, next to Coney Island Hospital, we beheld a sad spectacle. Cars were filling the intersection, with horns honking and drivers shouting. Some were abandoned and others inched forward. A police car occupied the middle of the intersection, lights flashing. Two young cops stood next to their car. Their helpless expression revealed all: they knew they had no ability to assist the shouting throng around them. They were as alone as everyone else. They had no radio contact, no backup, no authority, and — after all — they were just human beings also, with families somewhere.

We shook our heads, moving past the crowd and up Ocean Parkway. As we turned right onto Avenue K, we saw the huge orange ball of the sun filling the width of the street directly ahead of us. To me, it was a sign of hope. We walked our bikes into the Ellmans' back yard and locked them securely to an oak tree.

As we turned toward the back door, Leah tapped my shoulder and pointed down the driveway. Across the street, we could see a man in pajamas nailing plywood boards across his front door. We walked in silence towards the Ellmans' house. I felt a rush of hope and fear as I knocked softly on the glass.

REFUGE

Early morning, Monday, July 6

E WAITED AT THE BACK DOOR, hoping the Ellmans were home. I kept thinking about the man across the street. Were there intruders on the loose? Perhaps the Ellmans' house had been seized and occupied by strangers. I looked back to make sure our bikes were safe. It was possible that the Ellmans had also left their home, just the way we had.

As I was thinking what to do, I saw a face peering out through the curtains. The door opened.

"David!"

"Yisroel! Leah! I can't believe it! Come in."

We sat down around the kitchen table and exchanged emotional greetings. Everyone began talking at once.

"How did you get here? When did you leave? Did you have trouble? Do you know what's going on?"

When we told them about our bicycles, the crowded highways and our adventures on the road, they stared in amazement.

"Does anyone know what's going on? Were you attacked? I can't believe what happened with the plane crash! Are there any police out? Is there poison gas? We didn't leave the house yet, but maybe there's no choice now. How did you think of using bikes? That's so brilliant. What are you going to do about food? Where are you going anyway? Do you have a plan?"

"Listen," I said, "We have no idea what's going on, but we've got to try and save ourselves and find the children, I have no idea what we're breathing or if we're all being poisoned, but we've got to do everything we can while we have the ability. When *Mashiach* comes, G-d will clean up the entire world, but in the meantime we've got to try to survive, right?"

"What's your plan?" asked David.

I told them what Leah and I had discussed.

"Who knows if there's still a Verrazano Bridge, but we're going to try to make it to Staten Island and then over to New Jersey. For one thing, New Jersey is solid ground; it's not an island. If we ever get there, we'll try to find the children. Assuming that we find them, we want to get out of the New York area. I have a crazy idea about getting to Israel. I know it's nuts, but then again I have had a lot of wild ideas during my life. I had this wild idea that Leah would marry me! It came true! So I don't give up on anything!"

David flashed his ironic smile at me.

"And what are *you* thinking about doing?" I asked them.

"We were going to wait awhile to see if Boruch is able to get home from yeshiva, and then we were thinking like you. Go to the other children in New Jersey and then hopefully onward to a safer place, wherever that may be. Somehow Brooklyn doesn't feel safe. The bike idea is good. The only trouble is that we don't have bikes!"

Leah and Miriam reached across the table and clasped hands. As I looked over at my wife, so calm and courageous, I got a little emotional.

"You both must be so tired and hungry," said Miriam. "Please, eat something and get some sleep before you go back on the road."

"Thank you, dear friends. You are so kind to us. May G-d bless you and your family and may we soon all be together forever in peace and tranquility in the Holy Land."

Miriam Ellman just sat there for a minute, looking across the table. Then her face contorted and she started sobbing, sobs that shook her entire body. We watched her silently. My face began to feel warm and wet. I noticed that I was crying too. Everyone was crying. Sitting around the table quietly, it suddenly hit us. It was too big for words, too big for thoughts. All you could do was cry. The whole world was crumbling; everything was out of control. Who knew about parents, grandparents, children, grandchildren, friends? Who knew anything? Who knew where we'd all be in five minutes? What was coming next? We were specks in a global dust-storm.

We sat there for probably fifteen minutes, and then the tears dried up for the moment. Not a word had been said. It was like sitting shiva; sometimes words don't work.

Finally, Miriam shook her head and stood up.

Would you like to get some sleep? I imagine you need it."

"Thanks Miriam," said Leah softly.

Outside we heard sounds like gunfire. We rushed to the front window and peeked outside. A ragtag pack of men walked briskly down the center of the deserted street, shooting guns in the air and screaming something that we couldn't understand. I held my breath, hoping they would keep going. Across the street I could see eyes peering from behind curtains, eyes grim with anxiety.

We had lived in the United States all of our lives, in a land where individuals were subject to the "rule of law." Now there was no law. How were we to defend ourselves?

The gang didn't stop in front of anyone's house. If there is such a thing as a collective sigh of relief, this entire neighborhood must have breathed one. We stood and watched them slowly disappear, the shouting and commotion fading to a faint buzz.

G-d, You protected us in the most amazing ways up to now. When I was a kid I thought I was completely alone in the world. Then, Linda and I were together. At least we had each other, but we were still alone, trying to make sense out of life. Later we realized that You had been there with us all along. The very way Leah and I met, two clueless kids wandering aimlessly in a big world, and You were our Shepherd, unseen, nudging us towards each other and towards You. Now we have to try to remember the reality of Your presence every second, as we make our way through a treacherous world.

The morning light had pushed aside the pink and orange swirls of dawn and I put on *tallis* and *tefillin*. Leah and I prayed, ate lightly and then fell gratefully into the beds our dear friends had provided. We slept the sleep of the exhausted. If anything happened outside during those hours, we didn't know. In mid-afternoon we awakened. We ate lightly, not wanting to deplete the Ellmans' food supply, and then studied maps as we tried to plan the next phase of the journey.

We decided the best bet was to ride our bicycles along the streets of Brooklyn to the Verrazano Bridge and then cross over to Staten Island. Of course, who knew if there was still a Verrazano Bridge? And could we even get there?

The Ellmans loaded us up with nuts, raisins and bottled water.

Summer camp in Vermont. I'm a kid, ten years old, and I'm homesick like crazy! I call my parents constantly. The camp director is kind; he speaks with me every day. But how can he understand a Jewish kid who is sick for G-d, whose soul longs for his Father in Heaven?

The kid himself doesn't understand!

We hike the hills of Vermont. There at least I can be alone with my thoughts. But that's really not good either, because my thoughts are scary. I really do believe that something is wrong with me, that I am controlled by forces that don't permit me to live a normal life.

On our backwoods trips, we eat "hiker's lunch" consisting of hardtack, peanut butter, raisins, oranges and a chocolate bar. By lunchtime we are famished; this restores our strength. Nuts and raisins are easily carried and don't spoil.

At dusk, we headed out the back door and taped over the reflectors on our bikes. The moon would be a little past full tonight and we wanted to be as invisible as possible. As darkness set in, we said good-bye to the Ellmans with hugs and tears.

"G-d bless you and protect you. May He watch over all of us forever, and may we soon dwell peacefully and tranquilly together in the Holy Land. Before that, perhaps we'll see each other again and be able to travel along the way together."

They gathered in front of the house. I had a lump in my throat. Quickly we rode away into the darkness, before emotion could overcome us. If we all made it, there would be time to speak at length "on the other side." In the meantime, who knew whether we would meet again in this world, let alone still be alive by daybreak.

Turning north, as we pedaled up Ocean Parkway, we saw very few cars or pedestrians. Were people afraid? They had good reason to be; danger hid in every shadow. Occasionally we saw other bicycles and sometimes an indistinct moving shape, but we were basically alone in the darkened streets. When we looked towards Manhattan, we could see the orange glow reflected in the clouds.

Our plan was to cut westward through Borough Park on Fort Hamilton Parkway all the way to the Verrazano Bridge, try to get over to Staten Island, and from there to New Jersey. When Robert Moses built the span connecting Brooklyn to Staten Island, it had been the longest suspension bridge in the world. Every autumn thousands of runners would mass on its arching roadway, ready to begin the New York City Marathon. Now we were in our own marathon, a race for life itself.

We pedaled silently along the semi-deserted streets of Brooklyn. Once we reached Borough Park, we began to see small family groups dressed in black, walking together towards Staten Island. Perhaps they had the same idea as ours. As we approached the elevated tracks at New Utrecht Avenue I began to get a creepy feeling, like someone was watching us. It was very dark and lonely under there, so we paused before crossing under the tracks, trying to peer into the blackness.

Suddenly, Leah gasped.

"Yisroel, did you see something flashing up ahead? Look. Over there! Something shiny caught the moonlight. See, between those buildings."

Then, I heard a sharp bang in the darkness. Something flew past my ear!

"Leah, get back on the bike. Bend low and pedal fast. Ride to my right."

We both scrambled onto our bikes and started to pedal furiously. A bang and a whooooosh! Another bullet, maybe an inch from my nose. My arms were getting numb and my tongue was sticking to the roof of my mouth. Just as I was speeding up, I felt a strong push on my left, as though some-one was trying to knock me off the bike.

I tried to pedal even harder but I just couldn't will my feet to move faster. Several more shots were fired, but now they were landing behind us. It seemed we had once again es-caped harm. But what was next?

We decided to switch our route and pedal over to Tenth Avenue until it rejoined Fort Hamilton Parkway a few blocks later. We rode as though our lives depended on it, which of course they did! My legs were aching, my lungs were burning and perspiration was streaming down my face.

Suddenly Leah called out.

"Yisroel, stop! There's steam coming out of your knap-sack!"

"What are you talking about?"

I slammed the bike to a screeching halt and jumped off. Steam was indeed pouring from the opening on the left side of my knapsack. A hot blast hit me in the face when I opened the flap. I dropped the knapsack on the ground.

"Do I smell stuffed cabbage?" said Leah. Then she gasped and started laughing. She laughed so hard that she was crying at the same time. This was surreal. We were running for our lives in the middle of the night on a deserted street in Brook-lyn, and my wife is laughing hysterically.

"Leah, what on earth is going on? What's so funny?"

"Yisroel...this is too much! I packed those self-heating meals and the bullet must have set off the chemical reaction. You've got stuffed cabbage cooking in there!"

I looked at her and my mouth dropped open. Then I started laughing too.

"Welcome to the hottest restaurant in Brooklyn, right here on the pavement of Fort Hamilton Parkway and 60th Street, open all night," said Leah. "Our special this evening is stuffed cabbage."

We ended up laughing together until we ached, from the sheer absurdity of our situation as well as a feeling of relief that we could still laugh.

"Yisroel," Leah began, "I know you won't like this, but I'm not letting this precious meal go to waste. It's cooked and it smells delicious. And we're going to eat it right now."

There are certain things you don't argue about with Leah. In the light of the moon I saw that she was not to be budged, so in the middle of this smoke-filled chaos, surrounded by unknown dangers, we stood there eating stuffed cabbage on Fort Hamilton Parkway. It wasn't so bad.

"That was delicious," I said, "but I think we should skip dessert."

"Very funny, Yisroel. But yes, I agree. It's time for us to go. You know, that guy had good aim. Not only did that bullet miss you, but it made only a tiny hole in your knapsack...just enough to cook dinner."

More laughter. Then Leah and I were back on the road. We had to be close to the Verrazano and would probably have seen the lights on the towers if there had been electricity. Even the moon didn't seem to help, because fog was rising.

The bikes were blessedly silent, hopefully offering protection from whatever lurked in the darkness. We saw more families on the move, walking silently in the direction of the bridge. As we passed them, we gave a silent greeting. They were our brothers and sisters, mother, fathers, grandfathers, grandmothers and children. We were all trying to get to a better place. Would any of us make it? We could not know.

Now there seemed to be a bright glow ahead. As we got closer, we could see buildings on fire. It looked as if flames were coming from Fort Hamilton, a staid sentinel guarding the Brooklyn side of the entrance to the New York Harbor. We pedaled a bit further, crossing over the Gowanus Expressway.

"It's eight-ten a.m. and time for the traffic report: an accident is blocking the right and center lanes of the Gowanus Expressway at Fort Hamilton Parkway. An overturned tractor-trailer spilled a load of oranges all over the expressway. Traffic is backed up for three miles. Cleanup crews are on the scene ...."

Not tonight.

Below us we saw the unimaginable: hundreds of abandoned cars; no movement; no people; no traffic; no more Gowanus Expressway.

NO MORE VERRAZANO BRIDGE!

We gasped and stood there, staring at the void. Gone! It was impossible to comprehend. We cycled up to the end of Fort Hamilton Parkway. We had to be careful not to cycle over the edge into...whatever lay beneath.

The water rippled in the moonlight. Across the Narrows we could make out the silhouette of Staten Island. In front of us was a ghastly sight, a jumble of twisted and smoking concrete and cable, piles of rubble, the burial mound of the colossal bridge that had once been a wonder of the world.

No Verrazano Bridge.

My mind seemed to slow down, reluctant to accept the scene that lay before us. On the shoreline below, others stood looking forlornly into the darkness. I could see families huddled together, some shaking their heads and others weeping softly. We could also see flames across the Narrows. Fort Wadsworth on Staten Island had stood opposite its sister fort on the Brooklyn side. Had Fort Wadsworth also been attacked?

"Leah, let's go down there closer to the shoreline. I want to see what's going on there. You never know. There may be a way across."

Maybe the wreckage of the bridge was protruding above the surface of the waters all the way across. If so, there was a chance that we could just walk across the wreckage to the other side. But the closer we got, the more we could see how thoroughly devastating the destruction had been. The melted mass of twisted steel had disappeared into the dark waters.

From our vantage point we could see huge mounds of wreckage. Dagger-like metal shards stuck out everywhere and steam was still hissing where water lapped up against the metal. Even if the wreckage had reached across the Narrows, there would have been no way to walk our bikes over without shredding the tires and our shoes, not to mention our feet.

Leah looked crestfallen. I felt tired, hot and dispirited. The dream was over. There was no bridge, no passage from Brooklyn to Staten Island. Without Staten Island, forget New Jersey. Without New Jersey, of course, we could forget everything. That crazy idea of getting to Israel was just a pipe dream. We were two worlds away from the mainland and a galaxy away from our dreams.

How frustrating! New Jersey was only a few miles to the west. Our children were there and we needed to find them. New Jersey meant a chance to escape from this poisonous inferno and, hopefully, our unseen enemies. It was only a mile across, but it might as well have been an ocean.

I bowed my head. My hands gripped the handlebars tightly.

It is 2 a.m. I will never forget the date: Monday, January 10. We are living at 606 East Ann Street in Ann Arbor, Michigan. Two kids, recently married, studying English literature at this monster university. To the outsider, everything seems perfect in our world. To the insider, it is hell. Our marriage is falling apart. I can't get my life together; I don't know how to be a good husband, and Leah is getting tired of trying to "understand" me. To tell the truth, I am also getting tired of trying to understand me!

I have tried every trick I know: immersing myself in literature, wilderness hiking, folk music, social activism, meditation, world travel, everything except drugs and alcohol. There's nothing left! My life seems to resemble a long corridor with hundreds of doors. I have opened every door, and every door leads nowhere. NOWHERE! Life is hopeless. There is no truth, no peace, no reality, no hope. Our "perfect" marriage is going up in smoke, and we can't extinguish the fire!

I break down and cry. There's no place to turn. I'm sitting on that old green couch with the stuffing coming out, hopeless and alone in the middle of the night.

There's no hope. No hope. No...

Wait a minute. Hold on. This is the Twentieth Century, right? Nobody normal believes in G-d, right? Of course not. But wait a minute. Could G-d be real? Maybe G-d is real! Maybe that's the problem! Maybe all those "normal" people are wrong. Maybe nobody's normal any more! Maybe G-d is real and the "normal" people are not real! Maybe G-d can help me! Maybe G-d WILL help me! Maybe that's what's been missing my whole life!

G-D! G-D! ARE YOU THERE? HELP ME! HELP ME! HELP ME!

All of a sudden I have hope! There is a way out! It's a way that I always rejected, but I was rejecting my happiness as well! This is amazing! There is hope!

Look, the sun is coming up. There is light in the world. There is hope!

I go to wash my face. I look in the mirror. Who is that looking back at me? Is that me? I look different. My face is shining *like an angel's. Perhaps an angel is here with me. Who am I? Maybe I'm not the person I thought I was. Maybe I could be a great person if I really wanted. Maybe there are holy people who walk the earth.*

"May the angel who redeems me from all evil bless the lads, and may my name be declared upon them, and the names of my forefathers Abraham and Isaac..."[6]

That's when my life changed. I think an angel visited me that night. That angel has never left our side. And now, we stood on the shore of the Narrows, facing Staten Island.

Al-mighty G-d, what are we to do? Now we're really stuck. There's no way out of this, no way to get across those waters. When the Children of Israel stood at the banks of the Red Sea with the Egyptians behind them, and there was nowhere to go, You rescued us. Now Al-mighty G-d, please rescue Your children again. We are also standing at the water's edge.

Was G-d listening? I looked over at Leah and she was talking to G-d also. She looked at me. In the glow from the burning buildings I saw that calm, sensitive face. Right now it was filled with pain, but she is strong, that girl.

After his mother died, our son-in-law Baruch said, "if you have enough faith in G-d you can deal with anything."

We were standing underneath where the huge suspended double-highway-bridge had begun its long arch over the Narrows. To the left, a pile of twisted rubble stretched far above our heads. The ramp that once had carried cars and pedestrians onto the Belt Parkway was still standing. From there, we could make our way to what was left of the shoreline. The footpath along the shore was still visible, although partially buried in debris. The railing between the footpath and the water was broken in many places, and tons of falling debris had created a rough beachhead. Leah and I started moving down the embankment towards the water.

That's when I saw him. A solitary figure stood outlined against the flames on the rocks at the water's edge, holding something that shimmered in the flickering light. Was it a gun? Was he one of them?

"Leah," I whispered. "Look!"

Wordlessly, we looked at each other. Why was he standing there? Should we speak to him? We silently made our way toward the shoreline. Perhaps he knew something. There didn't seem to be anyone else nearby, but still we locked our bikes together for safekeeping. We inched closer to the man on the rocks. Although his face was in the shadows, I could see that he was holding a gun.

"Leah, what should I do? Should I call out to him?"

She answered without hesitation.

"Yisroel, we have no options. There's no bridge, so we can't get out of Brooklyn. And if we don't get out of Brooklyn, we're not going to make it. We can't swim to Staten Island. Let's take a chance and speak to him. Maybe he's a friend and maybe he's not. May *Hashem* help us."

I felt the same way; we had to take a chance. Just a short while ago we had gone to great lengths to escape the bullets of an unknown assailant. Now, unarmed, we were approaching a stranger who was holding a gun. Still, it seemed we had no choice.

I called out softly, in a voice designed to convey peacefulness.

"Hello sir. Can you help us?"

There was a long silence. My heart was pounding.

Finally, he answered. "Who are you? Why do you think I can help you? Nobody can help anybody in this crazy place. Now stand up so I can see you."

A flashlight blazed through the darkness, blinding us in its intense, yellow glare. We stood there like frightened deer.

"Raise your hands high. Do you have any weapons? Walk forward, slowly. Keep your hands way up."

He spoke in a rough voice. Leah and I walked gingerly towards him, our feet slipping on wet rocks, until we were about ten yards away.

"OK. Stop right there. Now, turn around so I can see what's behind you. What's in those knapsacks?"

"Just what we need to survive," I answered, "food, prayer books, maps, clothing. I have a knife, but not to use against you. We rode on our bikes from Long Island. We're trying to get across to Staten Island."

"Hah! And how're you going to do that?"

"We really don't know now that the bridge is gone. But we trust in G-d. Can you help us?"

He paused for a moment, wiping his forehead and pursing his lips. He was an old man, scruffy and weather-beaten but strong.

"How much is it worth to you to get to Staten Island?"

"A lot," I said. "We want to find our children in New Jersey. What do you have in mind?"

He snorted loudly and then shined his flashlight away from us. We followed the beam and there it was, sitting on the embankment, a dilapidated old boat.

"So, how much is it worth for you to go across?"

"Can that boat do it?" I asked.

"I did it twice already. The boat is strong. So, how much is it worth to you?"

"I have some cash. How about $100?"

He snorted again and shook his head, laughing.

"Don't play games with me. Cash is worthless. Come closer."

As we stepped forward, a feeling of queasiness began to

rise in my throat.

He shined his flashlight all over us.

"Let me see that ring, lady." And he took a step towards Leah.

"Listen you creep, don't touch her. Forget about it. You have some nerve..."

"Yisroel, be quiet."

Leah extended her hand towards him.

"You would take us across if I give you this ring?"

"Give it to me."

His voice was barely above a whisper, but there was no mistaking the tone.

"No," said Leah. "I won't give it to you until we get safely to the other side. But I will give it to you there."

Another snort.

"I have a gun. I don't need to take you anywhere to get that ring."

Leah looked at him without a trace of fear, her voice unemotional and firm.

"There may be no more Verrazano Bridge, but there is a G-d. G-d is watching you and you will have to answer for everything you do. But I know you are a G-d-fearing man. Will you take us across for this ring?"

He sighed and raised his eyebrows.

"Get in the boat."

"We need to bring our bicycles."

"Bikes? Get out of here. There's no room for your bikes."

"We need them," I insisted. "They're our only way to survive."

He kicked a stone towards the water.

"Where are they?"

"Back there," I said, gesturing up towards the embankment behind us.

"Go get them, but leave your packs here."

"No," I said. "We will not leave our packs here. We're going to get our bikes and then come back. You know you can trust us. We fear G-d."

He was silent. I thought that it was a sign that we had won. Still, when we turned around to head back for our bikes, I wondered if there would suddenly be bullets flying through the air at us. At the same time I felt very strongly that he respected us because we had both mentioned G-d. I hated the thought of Leah giving this animal her ring, but right now there was no choice. The ring was our ticket for survival.

We returned quickly and set the bikes, one atop the other, across the bow of the boat. Then we sat down very carefully on the middle seat. Our scruffy captain pushed off, then jumped aboard. The creaking boat tipped wildly and the bicycles began to slide off the bow, but we managed to grab them just before they hit the water.

We watched as he grabbed the greasy cord and gave it a yank. The engine sputtered. He yanked again. Another sputter.

Hey, I thought to myself, *we're never going to leave Brooklyn, let alone get to Staten Island. He's just a crazy old man.*

Then, another yank and a roar. He pushed the gear lever and the boat jumped forward.

"Wow, this thing's alive!" I shouted above the din.

Leah looked at me and smiled. We both were awash in hope. The boat moved into the dark channel next to the wreckage of the great bridge.

G-d was parting the waters!

GIL

Late Monday night, July 6

MY MIND RACED AS WE glided across the dark waters of the Narrows.

Just a few weeks ago I had driven a powerful car over the beautiful, arched bridge and used a computer chip to pay the toll. Tonight, we were lurching precariously, next to the jutting wreckage of that same bridge, in a greasy boat belonging to a bushy-haired, unshaven stranger with whom we never would have associated in the past. We regarded him — despite his slavish greed — as an angel sent from Heaven. His form of transportation was primitive, but it was all that was left in our humbled world. His services were worth a fortune.

G-d had made so many miracles for us already. We were alive even though New York City was in flames. Who and what had survived? Where was our family? What about the rest of the world? Was there still a world?

It is the night of Tisha b'Av, the most bitter day in the Jewish calendar. We sit on the floor crying, trying to feel what we are supposed to feel. On this night our two Temples in Jerusalem went up in flames, attacked by our enemies, and we, the proud nation, were led in chains into exile.

Do we cry? Can we cry? Sometimes I don't feel enough; I don't know how to cry. We have become so hard, so "efficient"; we forget that we have hearts, we forget how to feel, we forget who we are. We forget that we once lived in honor and peace in the Holy Land, gathered around the Temple Mount, a nation of refined and holy servants of G-d. Do we begin to realize what we have lost?

Just one tear is a beginning of understanding. The Gates of Tears are never closed.[7] That entrance to heaven is all we have left, but it is enough if we enter through it. There are those who cry because they don't know how to cry! Even that is a step. There is a time to weep.[8]

Over to our right was a chilling sight. Thirty six hours ago, the Manhattan skyline had reached boldly into the sky. As the flames pierced the darkness, we could see that much of the skyline was flattened. What had once been vertical was now horizontal.

Then, as the sea-breeze momentarily parted the smoke, we saw two huge, jagged structures rising above the flames. I gasped. The new World Trade Towers had been hit! It was 9/11 all over, but this time they hadn't fallen completely. Grotesquely decapitated, they stood there as symbols of a lost culture, standing skeletons, empty shells devoid of life. We could see right through them to the flames on the other side. Here was an immense civilization, the culmination of the Western World, in ruins. I was reminded of the epic words of Daniel.

"You, O king, were watching and behold! A huge statue; this statue, which was immense and whose brightness was extraordinary, stood opposite you, and its appearance was fearsome. This statue: its head of fine gold; its breast and arms of silver; its belly and thighs of copper; its legs of iron; and its feet, partly of iron and partly of earthenware. As you watched, a stone was hewn without hands and struck the statue on its feet of iron and earthenware, and crumbled them. Then they crumbled together: the iron, the earthenware, the copper, the silver and the gold. They became like chaff from summer threshing floors, and the wind carried them away..."9

How many individual tragedies were being played out around us? It was impossible to calculate and dreadful to contemplate. My heart ached at the sight of the Manhattan skyline. How could anyone deal with it?

I couldn't. I looked away, finally, and gazed into the churning water.

A few minutes later, I had the unpleasant realization that our feet were wet. Would we have to complete the trip by swimming? Leah and I are good swimmers, but we were no longer kids. Besides, this was the Narrows, not a suburban swimming pool. The currents were treacherous and stiletto-sharp metallic slivers were scattered under and over the waterline. All of our precious supplies were on the boat, too, and I imagined us ending up — even if we made it to shore — with no food, no bikes, water-logged and exhausted.

Leah lifted her feet up and flashed me a "what else can happen to us today?" look. Just then, I spotted an old coffee can under my seat and starting bailing as fast as I could. Our silent and spooky boat guy just looked at us and continued steering that greasy old outboard motor. All the while that he was steering, he was also constantly jerking his head around, looking out over the boat as though expecting trouble. We were about two hundred feet from the darkened Staten Island shoreline when I heard the sound of a sharp "ping" and then a splash.

"Get down!" said our captain. "Those dirty creeps are shooting."

This was unreal!

Leah and I dove as far down as we could, plastering our bodies against the cold wet ribs of the boat. There was virtually no room for us to move, but we felt safer. I imagine bullets could have penetrated the fiberglass shell, but at least we had the illusion of safety.

"Who is it?" I whispered.

"A-rabs. Now shut up."

He quickly thrust the boat directly at the bridge debris on our left and then cut the motor.

"Ping. Splash."

Another one.

"Ping. Splash."

This is insane. G-d, is there no refuge anywhere? Are we ever going to be able to breathe again? Are we ever going to have a moment's peace in this mad world? Help us. Save us. Please.

I raised my head and saw a tiny flash on shore.

"Ping. Splash."

Another one!

The boatman picked up a rifle from under his seat. Lying on his belly, legs against the side of the boat, he was propped up on his elbows, with his chin resting on the gunwale. After taking a deep breath, he squinted into the darkness and fired.

"BANG!" The rifle flashed and there was an acrid smell.

"AHHH!" from the shore.

"You hit him!"

"Shut up. Don't make a sound."

He reached out and pushed off from the debris with his oar. The boat slowly glided to a different position. Then once again, he balanced himself on his elbows, raised the rifle and fired another time.

"BANG!"

This time we heard a crash in the bushes, followed by the sounds of feet running through the tall grass.

"I got one," he said, almost triumphantly. "They're all cowards. You get one and his friends run. But they're sneaky. These A-rabs been around here for years, waiting for this day. Watch out when you get inland."

This tough guy was the most unlikely of heroes, but I was beginning to have a soft spot for him. This grubby man was saving our lives. Yes, he had taken payment, but he could have robbed us and left us in Brooklyn. For sure, G-d had sent him to save us.

G-d, please help this man.

I wanted to tell him right then just how grateful we were for his efforts, but the words stuck in my throat. Suddenly I worried that any sound from me might draw more gunfire. It could wait.

May You remember him and get him and his loved ones — if he has any — out of here. May he know that he was blessed because he helped Your children, the children of Abraham, Isaac and Jacob. But please let him also complete the job and get us ashore on Staten Island. And please, G-d, let us be safe on the other side, and be invisible to those who hate us.

Our journey continued, the putt-putt of the engine in a cadence with the scrape of the coffee can and the splashing of the waves. Above us, clouds raced across the night sky, dimming our meager visibility, but every few minutes the moon would burst through to illuminate the way. Finally, a steep and wooded bank loomed ahead of us, just north of where the huge bridge had once touched land. We were almost there!

Looking closer, we could see that there was no place to pull in, and once ashore we couldn't have made it up the steep hill with our bikes. Our boatman started up that sickly motor again and this time we headed further right, away from the wooded area from where the shots had been fired and toward a cleared landing area where the street appeared to come right down to the shoreline.

A little beach, basking in the moonlight, awaited us. Under other circumstances, it would have been a picnicker's delight. The boat slid smoothly ashore and Leah and I mouthed silent cheers to each other.

Thank G-d! We made it!

It was a perfect landing place, with sand maybe five feet wide, just enough space for us to walk. There was a rocky embankment above us, but also, to the left, a path from the beach up to the street.

Our man pulled the boat on the sand and unloaded our bicycles. He gave me a hand and I gave Leah a hand. We were standing on the rocky shore of Staten Island.

"Here's what we owe you," said Leah, slowly removing the ring from her finger. "You were as good as your word and we are forever grateful to you. You really saved our lives. We are going to pray for you and may G-d watch over you. Perhaps we will see you in the Holy Land."

"Iz-reel?"

"Yes, that's where we are headed."

He looked at us for a long moment before throwing his head back and laughing.

"Are you two crazy? What do you want me to do, take you across the Atlantic Ocean in this leaky tub?"

"Look," I said, "we didn't expect to get across here, but we met you and here we are on the other side. Jews have a way of getting across waters, you know."

He chuckled.

"Here's the ring," said Leah.

He held out his palm and a little sparkle fell into it. He squeezed the ring tightly in his big, calloused hands.

"You know," he said, "someday maybe there will be an end to all of this insanity and I'll meet you over there in Jeroosulem. I'll give you this ring back and you'll give me a castle there in return."

"You know," said Leah, "I wouldn't be surprised if that happened. What's your name, friend?"

"Gil."

"Gil, I am Leah and my husband's name is Yisroel. I want you to look for us in Jerusalem. There will be many people there, but you will find us, and with G-d's help we will find a beautiful castle for you in the Holy Land. I think it will be on the bank of the Jordan River. You will be the Chief Man to ferry the pilgrims across to the Hills of Jerusalem in the happy days ahead."

"You will have a big job, Gil," I said. "And G-d will bless you forever. We will never forget how you saved our lives. We will meet again on the other side. Now I think we'd better move on, before the sky begins to lighten up."

In the moonlight I could see a tiny tear rolling down Gil's weary face.

"May G-d watch over you until then, Gil."

He nodded and blinked several times, then cleared his throat.

"And you too. You both watch out now. Those A-rabs were scared when I shot that guy, but they're all around. My advice to you is to get inland as fast as you can while it's still dark, and then try to find shelter during the day. Get on the big roads and head west and then south. You may make it into New Jersey. Go for the Outerbridge. It's a small bridge and far south. They may have missed it. You might be able to get over it and get on the mainland. G-d be with you."

"And you, Gil."

I took his hand. Then Gil took my hand in his two rough hands and squeezed tightly for a moment, looking intently at me. He climbed back into his boat, pulled the greasy cord and sped off again into the dark waters.

I looked at Leah: "That man saved our lives. I really do think we're going to meet him again."

"So do I, Yisroel." Her voice drifted off. "I'm happy that we made it here safely, but I keep thinking about the others. How many are stranded back there? All those families we saw. We're the lucky ones... so far. What about them?"

I gave Leah a long look. Her cheeks were moist.

What a privilege to be married to such a noble and virtuous woman! G-d, please answer all her prayers! Please help us and all those good people who are caught in this mess!

It was what you would call a bittersweet moment. We had made it across, but what about the others?

"What can we do for them, Leah?" I said. "We don't have the ability to save them now. We're incredibly fortunate to be standing here, but if we don't move quickly.... We're not helping anyone by standing here."

She nodded and began to pull on her knapsack. Moments later, we were struggling up the embankment, carrying our bikes on our shoulders. It was slippery going, with our shoes already soaking from the boat.

At the top of the embankment we turned to gaze at the incredible tableau before us: the waters swirling below, the Manhattan skyline burning, Brooklyn in its isolation, Fort Hamilton in flames, and the devastated bridge. What a scene!

All of a sudden, I realized something was missing.

"Leah, where's Gil?"

We scanned the waters. There was no sign of a boat and no sound of that sputtery motor.

"That's really strange," I said.

Leah looked at me.

"Yes," she said, "it is really strange."

We stood there in silence for perhaps a minute, our eyes probing the darkness.

"There are some things in this world that I think I do understand," I said to Leah, "but there are some things I just don't understand at all. This has got to be one of them."

"I hear you, Yisroel."

"OK, Gil or no Gil, we've got to move on."

I wasn't sure how to find the Staten Island Expressway, or whatever remained of it. It seemed that we needed to travel away from the shore and towards the left. But we had to be cautious. After what we'd experienced during our crossing, we needed to take every precaution to stay safe. Who might be hiding in the grass or behind buildings? And how would we protect ourselves if we did come across one of these guys? It seemed terribly lonely here; there was absolute stillness and nobody whatsoever around.

G-d, please continue to watch over us. "Ain od milvado... there is no one else beside You." If You want us to live, we will live. That's all there is to it.

Why am I not panicking? It would be so logical for me to panic. I can't understand why I'm not. Logically, our situation is hopeless. I guess I'm just not being logical. I hate to say it, but I feel kind of liberated in a crazy way. I feel as if in some insane fashion we may just make it, even find our children. And I have this wild idea — it's totally illogical, but who knows? — about how we're going to get to Israel.

Come on, Yisroel Neuberger, get your head back on Staten Island. You're not anywhere near safety yet, and the whole world is falling apart. Dream just enough to keep from panicking, and keep your eyes open, because you and Leah are in total danger.

Clouds were racing across the sky. Although moments earlier we had seen the moon, now a light rain began to fall, and I began to worry about the bikes rusting.

Hey man, this isn't the old days, when you lived in a house like a human being. This is after The Catastrophe. Each raindrop is probably radioactive. We're probably going to start glowing in the dark soon.

I clenched my teeth and tried to break away from my internal reverie. But the thoughts kept coming.

Why am I making jokes? Probably the radiation is affecting my brain. We don't know what's happened to the country. We don't have to worry any more if our bikes rust. Just keep moving and trust in G-d. Stop thinking the way you did before the world blew up. Everything is new now. Just keep moving.

Finally, arms aching from pushing our bikes up the path, we could see streets ahead. We stopped in a small overlook near the water. In the drizzle, Leah held a raincoat over my head as I pulled out my flashlight and maps.

"There, I see it. This is the beginning of Hylan Boulevard. Hylan Boulevard leads to the Staten Island Expressway. The Staten Island Expressway leads to Richmond Avenue, and Richmond Avenue leads to Arthur Kill Road and Arthur Kill Road leads to...wait! The Blooms!"

"The Blooms?"

"Leah, don't you remember the Blooms? We met them when we spoke in Eltingville. Maybe we could sleep for the daylight hours at their home the way we did at the Ellmans. From there, I think we can get onto the Parkway that leads to the Outerbridge Crossing."

I felt a surge of hope. It seemed like a good plan.

Leah agreed and we set out again. I figured that we could be in Eltingville by daybreak. The prospect of a bed seemed like paradise, but most of all, I wanted to take off my sopping shoes. They made a squooshy sound every time I pressed on the pedals.

Leah and I made excellent time as the streets got progressively bigger and turned into roads. Finally, we saw the Staten Island Expressway.

Cars, cars, cars. The Expressway, in contrast to the local streets, was jammed. But no one was moving. And for a very good reason: the drivers were gone! It was an asphalt ghost town. Everyone must have left their cars and taken off on foot. It was an eerie feeling, weaving around hundreds of empty cars. One car had a teddy bear and potato chip bags on the rear window ledge, illuminated by a sudden burst of moonlight.

Where had everyone gone?

The Expressway felt safer because there were few places for people to hide. The racing clouds were another ally; there was enough light to see, but enough darkness to conceal our presence.

In a short while, we came to Richmond Avenue. We exited the Expressway, following the service road until we turned left under the bridge. Looking around this new neighborhood, I worried who might be hiding in or between those dark buildings,

Are we selfish trying to make it by ourselves? What about the rest of the world? Do we have the right to do this? But what choice is there? Would we even have contemplated giving up? Of course not. We have to try to survive. "*Yosheiv b'seser El-yon*...Whoever sits in the refuge of the Most High, he shall dwell in the shadow of the Al-mighty. I will say of G-d, 'He is my refuge and my fortress, my G-d, and I will trust in

Him'... No evil will befall you, nor will any plague come near your tent. He will charge His angels for you, to protect you in all your ways."[10]

I wondered what Leah was thinking. We were a good team. I needed to be strong for her, for us. I needed to repeat those words of King David, "G-d is my refuge," again and again. I needed to believe them, to know that they are true.

Suddenly, a whiff of something shot through my nostrils and immediately my throat began to burn. Then my insides felt corroded and everything in my stomach wanted to come up.

"Leah...do you smell someth....?" I could barely get the words out.

She didn't answer. She was wobbling on her bicycle, her lungs grabbing for air.

"Get off the bike and hit the ground!"

We both jumped off — "fell" is more accurate — and put our heads to the ground, hoping for fresh air. But that was worse. The air was thick; my lungs burned; darkness enveloped my brain; I was falling asleep.

Just before the lights dimmed completely, I got a sudden flash: the Bhopal Disaster! Twenty thousand Indians died that night as heavy gas from the pesticide plant rolled through the streets, into valleys and low-lying homes. The gas was heavier than air!

My brain was moving at the speed of molasses, but I suddenly knew we had to get to higher ground!

There was a little park on a hill to our right. If we could make it up the hill .... I pulled Leah up, pushed her up; I don't know what we did or how we did it. Maybe we crawled up that hill. Somehow I dragged myself and held on to her, trying to move faster than the deadly gas. We staggered upward, leaving our bikes behind, desperately trying to breathe as little as possible. It was like pushing boulders up a mountain while all you wanted to do was lie down and sleep.

Just as I was reaching exhaustion level, I felt a wisp of cooler, lighter, cleaner air enter my lungs. I took a slightly deeper breath. Clean air! We kept climbing, the air getting fresher with each step.

Thank G-d!

Leah and I collapsed on the grass like a couple of out-of-shape marathoners. We lay there motionless for a long time, just filling our lungs with the blessedly pure air. After a few minutes a slight breeze brushed over us, the kind of thing we would never have noticed otherwise. But now it signaled that the poisonous air below might be starting to dissipate. This was an island, after all, and ocean breezes were still circulating through this bombed-out world.

Slowly, I sat up.

"Leah, I think we may still be alive."

She nodded. We were both trembling. What had we been breathing? Was it nuclear garbage? Were we radioactive? We didn't have any answers, but we couldn't worry about it. We could only worry about what we could control. When *Mashiach* would come, G-d would clean out the earth completely, and it would return to a pristine state, the way it had been at the moment of Creation. Then all the poison would be sucked away and the world would be new again, clean and pure, as it had been at the beginning of time.

"The day is coming, burning like an oven; all the wanton ones and all the evildoers will be stubble and the coming day will set them ablaze, says G-d... But for you that revere My Name, a sun of righteousness will shine forth."[11]

We had not yet seen the sun of righteousness, but so far we had not been set ablaze either. A faint glow painted the edges of the eastern sky; daybreak was near. We cautiously descended the hill and retrieved our bikes. In the hazy light of early dawn, we sped south on deserted streets. We were nearing Eltingville.

Exiting Richmond Avenue, we turned left onto Arthur Kill, I remembered that somewhere in my knapsack I carried my pocket PC. It worked, although I knew that soon I would discard it when its battery died, but right now it was still very useful. Using the database and my map, we managed to find the Blooms' house.

The sky above us was bright when I knocked on their door.

SOLID GROUND

Early Tuesday morning, July 7

NO ONE ANSWERED. WE CALLED out their names softly, hoping no one was hiding in the bushes. I felt a sense of dread. Maybe something horrible had happened to them. I tried the handle; it didn't move.

"Let's look around the back," I whispered.

Wheeling our bikes as quietly as possible, we tiptoed around to the back. There was a note taped to the door, written in Hebrew. In the early-morning light, the writing was clear.

"We have gone and may G-d help us all. If you need access, the combination is 6-1-3. Use whatever you need and please lock the door when you leave. We are heading for the Outerbridge. May we all meet in the Holy Land."

I was overwhelmed. In the midst of chaos, running for their lives, they had stopped and made sure that their home could be of use to others.

G-d, Your children are so holy! Who else but those who love You would act with such kindness?

I opened the door and we entered the kitchen. Dishes and pots were all over, what you would expect if an entire family had left in a rush.

"Leah, let's bring the bikes inside. I don't think they would mind and then we won't have to worry about them."

Isn't that silly to say "I don't think they would mind"! As if they will ever return! But somehow it mattered. It was still their house, after all!

As we wheeled in the bikes, it occurred to me that the house might be occupied already. Perhaps there were hostile intruders. I whispered to Leah to stay in the kitchen while I checked each room. I walked through the house, quietly opening the door to every room and closet. I found nothing except poignant reminders of the family who had so recently lived there.

I walked down the stairs and back to the kitchen. Leah had opened the refrigerator, which was still somewhat cold despite thirty six hours without electricity. We found some hard cheese and several containers of yogurt, still edible, then added cereal and a banana for a very decent breakfast. The mixture of instant coffee with cold water wasn't too successful. I kept stirring, however, and after a while it almost resembled coffee. I needed caffeine in order to stay awake through morning prayers.

"Won't that keep you up, Yisroel?"

"Leah, nothing will keep me up! But there is a problem."

"What now, Yisroel?" She was slightly worried, but — knowing me after all these years — also a little skeptical.

"We have no vitamins. How are we going to survive?"

She gave me the look. Then we both laughed.

It was good to be inside, with no worries about being drenched in the rain, attacked, or having our stuffed cabbage punctured by bullets.

I put on my *tallis* and *tefillin*. We had a lot to thank G-d for. We were still alive; we had survived explosions, the plane crash, the shadowy figures, bullets, the trip across the water, poison gas. It was amazing, really; so many miracles and we were just at the beginning of our journey.

Even though we had been scrambling from one crisis to another, I was beginning to feel that we had a sense of purpose; we were headed somewhere. A plan was coming together in my mind, although I hadn't discussed it yet with Leah nor thought it out completely. But I couldn't dwell on it now; we had to sleep.

Somehow, with the help of the caffeinated water, I managed to hold my head up over the prayer book. By then, my eyes were literally aching to close. A hazy sun was well over the horizon and the house was already beginning to feel stuffy, but for many reasons it seemed a good idea to keep the windows shut and the blinds closed. You never knew what might come through, whether poisonous air or poisonous people.

Leah and I gratefully eased ourselves onto real beds, covered with smooth sheets and soft pillows. It was utterly calm now, the quiet stuffiness of a closed house in the summer. Our bodies were exhausted, our minds numb. Before we knew it, we were sound asleep.

Leah and I floated across a pristine lake high in the mountains, so high that snow rested on the jagged peaks above. But a warm sun comforted us, and the forests echoed with bird song. We were in a large rowboat, but I wasn't rowing. A young man of beautiful countenance was pulling at the oars, a placid smile on his peaceful face. His entire occupation was to give us pleasure, enabling us to bask in the serenity of G-d's perfect world. The smile on his face reflected his happiness as he con-

templated our happiness.

Suddenly I recognized him. Of course, it was Gil! A young Gil, maybe twenty years old, without a line on his face. His skin was clear and unblemished; his face content in its innocence. He rowed quietly, as if time had ceased to be our enemy.

It was mid-afternoon when I awoke. Although I was sticky with perspiration and the house felt steamy and airless, the sleep had been a gift from G-d. My strength had been restored and I felt ready for our next challenge, crossing the Outerbridge, the final step (we hoped!) before New Jersey and the mainland.

Leah was still asleep. Her face was serene and peaceful, but, as I looked, an expression of intense pain caused her brows to furrow. Then her mouth started to move. Her lips trembled. Suddenly, in the midst of her sleep, she screamed.

"Children! Children! Quick, follow me. It's so dangerous! Where's Abba! They're shooting at us! Children, run into the woods! Ruchoma, hold my hand. Now run! Quick! Follow me! Quickly! Abba, help me. Carry Ruchoma!"

"Leah," I shouted. "Wake up!"

"Oh! Yisroel! What happened? Was that a dream? Where are we?"

"Leah. It's all right. We're at the Blooms' house, in Staten Island. Everything is OK. At least we're alive. Just calm down."

"What a vivid dream! What time is it?"

"Around five in the afternoon."

She sat up and stretched her arms straight out.

"I slept for such a long time. But that dream was so frightening! Thank G-d it was only a dream. When did you wake up?"

"A few minutes ago."

"How do you feel?"

"I feel good, thank G-d. And what about you?"

"Well, now that I know the dream wasn't real, I'm beginning to feel better. Thank G-d, I don't actually feel so bad. What's the plan?"

"I want to look over the maps while it's still light. Then, afternoon prayers. After that, I guess we should have something to eat and then head out again when it's dark. Does that sound reasonable?"

"Yes, it does. Tonight we should arrive in New Jersey, with G-d's help."

"Yup. I plan to take the Garden State to Lakeville. G-d should just help us find the children. It's such a long shot."

"What happens if they're not in Lakeville?"

"I don't know. But that's the obvious place to look for them, right? If they aren't there, then probably they will have left notes telling us where they are. They will know that we're trying to find them, although they may not believe we can pull it off. I can't imagine they would try to come to Long Island to find us."

Not knowing if our children were safe was the biggest burden right now.

"You're right, Yisroel. There's no other plan that makes sense. But it's so unlikely we'll find them. If they aren't home, where would they go?"

"Well, they might head north."

"North? What do you mean by north, Yisroel? Do you have something in mind?"

"It's just my nutty brain. I have this idea ...."

"Yisroel, what are you talking about?"

"Look, let's not even discuss it right now. It's so many steps away that I don't want to think about it. When we find the children, with G-d's help, then we can talk about my musings, but now we should get going."

Leah started to ask me another question and then stopped. She pushed off the bed and took a long stretch.

"Yisroel, do you think we can take a shower?"

"Well, it's not going to be too warm. Are you ready for cold water?"

"At least the house is warm," said Leah. "It may be our last shower for a long time."

"I'm sure the Blooms wouldn't mind."

She stood at the window for a moment, looking out into the summer sunshine. Then she turned to me.

"Yisroel, do you think we'll make it?"

"Do I think we'll make it? You know, Leah, I have this crazy idea that we're going to make it. It's totally illogical, of course, but what isn't illogical about Jewish survival and OUR survival? It's always completely against the odds. I mean, when we were kids we lived in a different world, but G-d gave us this new life when we were thirty. That was illogical and impossible, but it happened.

"When I was a kid in that secular environment, I had this intuition that perfection and spiritual contentment were possible. I didn't know how to pursue them, but all those years alone in that spiritual wasteland, feeling that I was the outcast, I had a sense that some day I would find my spiritual home. Then we met, and we found G-d. My intuition turned out to be accurate. Hopefully, my intuition is still accurate."

I had wanted to reassure Leah, but found myself getting more confident and optimistic as I kept talking.

"Now we're in the next stage. We're wanderers again, and we're not kids any more. We're too old for this, but what are we going to do? We have to survive, right? We knew this was going to happen, and it has finally happened. The world is literally collapsing around us, yet I still have this instinct that we're going to come through it all right and greet *Mashiach*."

"I believe you, Yisroel."

BANG!

What was THAT?

We both stiffened.

BANG!

"Open up!"

The front door was being rattled. We looked at each other and inched towards the window.

"Anyone in there?"

I peered between the blinds. Six shaven-headed teen-agers stood at the door.

"Open up, Jews!"

I gave Leah a puzzled look. Maybe they had seen the *mezuzah* on the front door. Our bikes were inside, so they couldn't have seen them. Perhaps they didn't know if anyone was inside. They may just have been guessing.

CRASH!

Glass shattering downstairs.

"They're coming in," I whispered.

"OW!"

A scream of pain.

"I'm bleeding. I got cut."

"You idiot."

"You're the idiot. At least I had the guts to break the glass."

"So go in there then."

"There's blood all over me! I can't stop it! I'm going to die!"

"Shut up, Larsen. If you weren't such an idiot you would not be bleeding to death."

"Let him die, Hagerty. He deserves it."

"What d'ya mean 'let me die!'"

This tough kid started to cry.

"Hagerty, O'Boyle, let's go. I hate that weakling. Let him bleed to death!"

"No! No! Don't leave me! Help me! Help me!"

I actually started feeling sorry for this pathetic creature. As I squinted between the blinds I saw his cohorts running down the street and laughing. Larsen tottered after them, holding his arm and trailing blood.

The voices faded away. We waited several minutes.

"Leah, I think maybe we should skip the shower and get out of here."

"No, Yisroel. I'm taking a shower."

I knew that tone of voice. There was no sense in trying to dissuade her. Water actually came out of the shower, as though nothing in the world had changed in the last two days. It was cold, but Leah seemed almost relaxed and newly revived.

As soon as night was upon us, we carefully opened the back door and peeked around. Everything seemed quiet. The backyard was tidy, with an assortment of lawn furniture, an outdoor grill and badminton net. I imagined the Blooms enjoying a summer evening. What would happen to them?

We wheeled our bikes to the front and headed for the War Veterans' Parkway. As we looked back at the Blooms' house, with a jagged hole in the front window, we thanked G-d for the respite and for saving us once again from imminent danger. Enemies were everywhere, but *"ain od milvado,"* only G-d runs the world, no other force or power. If He willed it, we would live.

The night was clear and warm. Stars twinkled as we rode southwest, heading for the bridge we hoped would still be standing. Nightfall came around 9 p.m. About 10:30 the moon appeared, huge on the eastern horizon, lighting our way with silver beams.

We weren't alone. Other families, no doubt sharing with us the idea of reaching the mainland, walked in little clusters along the roadway. It was good to see normal families with attentive parents. We were buoyed by a feeling of camaraderie with our fellow travelers. At the same time, one could not help thinking: where would we all be in a day, a week or a month? The more normal the family, the more one worried about their fate.

As we glided along, making our way by the light of the pale moonbeams, I thought again of that second date with Leah, so long ago. There was no Verrazano Bridge back then or now. We were teenagers, but at that moment we knew that our future would be together. Now, decades later, we were back on our bikes in the same place, except that everything was different.

A half hour passed. We rounded a curve and glided onto the West Shore Expressway, probing the darkness ahead. Was the bridge still standing? Suddenly, a glint of steel caught the moonlight. It was there! Hope soared in my heart. Maybe we would find our children! The precious bridge was still standing!

The Outerbridge was nothing like the Verrazano. Narrow and antiquated, it stretched high over the Arthur Kill, separating New York from New Jersey. Without the Outerbridge, I don't know how we would have negotiated the Arthur Kill. You can't really count on having an angel like Gil around.

Up ahead we could hear crying children and muted conversations. As we approached the bridge, we found a steady stream of people walking along the West Shore Expressway from the north, weaving their way around abandoned cars. Mothers wheeled strollers; teenagers pushed elderly parents in wheelchairs; some children skipped along and others walked with wide-eyed looks of wonder.

Just about everyone was marching off the island, over the bridge and on to the mainland. The crush became so great that within minutes we were completely surrounded and had to walk our bikes. It was almost festive, as though the families were strolling on a moonlit evening in an exotic resort.

Of course, that momentary feeling was quickly eclipsed by the inescapable reality. None of us had a safe destination, a place to sleep or much to eat beyond what we could carry. In a matter of days or even hours, this peaceful exodus could turn into chaos and misery. Obviously, people were terribly frightened. Why else would babies and invalids be out in the middle of the night? Clearly, these families were desperate, dragging themselves along on this journey into the unknown.

I'm never in the right place. When I'm at camp I'm homesick, but when I come home I'm still homesick. Where is home? I'm never at peace, forever restless. I travel because my soul has no home.

A plan was forming in my mind. If we were fortunate enough to find the children, we would need a destination, and it was gradually becoming clearer to me. I wanted to talk to Leah right away about my idea, but I hesitated. I thought it better to wait until I had fully thought it through. Yet I was eager to hear her reaction; we were a team.

Then I started to worry about the dangers ahead. It is confusing to imagine future problems that may never materialize. It requires discipline to remember that G-d runs the world in all its details. But we are human beings. I started worrying: what if something happened to either of us?

What would Leah do without me? What would I do without Leah? I hated thinking about it, but these fears kept creeping into my mind. Leah HAD to survive. But I also had to survive, if not for myself then certainly for her. We needed each other, two halves of one entity forever bound to each other. How could one survive without the other? We couldn't afford to lose each other and we couldn't afford to get hurt. This wasn't a luxury; it was a necessity. The only thing I could do was ask G-d for help.

Again!

And again!

And again!

Crossing the bridge, I could hear the conversations around us. Most were soft, but some people were shouting at their families and even at strangers. It was more in panic than anger. They didn't know where they were going once they reached the mainland. What hope did they have if indeed their world was in ruins?

I imagined the horrors of so many people competing for what little food remained. What would happen when blizzards whipped them or torrential rainstorms pelted them in the open countryside? How would parents feel when their children screamed with fever and there was no pediatrician, no emergency room, no medicine?

What if they, or we, were confronted by evil people?

I took a deep breath and looked over at Leah. Her face was calm. I caught her eye and we exchanged smiles.

That look made me feel better. I really don't feel that panicked, actually. OK, maybe a little panicked. But basically I'm calm, right?

I kept talking to myself.

There's clearly a survival gene built into the Jewish soul. Otherwise, how would we have made it through two thousand years of Exile among nations who hated us? Lately, living a comfortable life in the United States, the sense of exile had become latent, somewhat academic. We did not perceive exile as the source of all our troubles. But now I felt it.

I had inherited the ability to survive in an alien environment from my fathers Abraham, Isaac and Jacob. G-d was saying to me, as He had said to my Father Abraham, "Go...from your land...to the land that I will show you."[12]

Our Father Jacob not only had lived decades in exile but he died in exile, preparing future generations for what lay ahead. He made sure his children would bury him in Israel. His children would survive future exiles because they also had a destination, no matter how distant. But in order to walk toward that destination you had to know that you were in exile. People who don't realize they're in Exile, don't realize they have somewhere to go.

A wave of excitement surged over me. We were living the Torah. It had all been laid out in advance. The Biblical wanderings of our Patriarchs and Matriarchs were the pattern for their children in the distant future. That's what kept us going. That's why — in the end — we weren't panicking. We knew in our hearts that, despite the chaos, violence and insanity around us, G-d was in total control. We were playing out the final scenes of the script that had been written at the beginning of time. If we could remember that, then perhaps we could play our parts correctly and make it through to the final scene.

We couldn't know who would survive and who would not. There was no reason to believe that both or either one of us (*Oh G-d, here's that horrible thought again. I can't stand it!*) had been chosen to survive. Still, I kept telling G-d that we wanted to help Him bring about that glorious future world that was promised to us so long ago. I wanted to convince Him that we were BOTH needed! It felt a bit presumptuous, but what else could I say?

I stand alone in the cemetery. It's Mother's first Yahrzeit, the anniversary of her death. As I complete my prayers, I place a small stone on the grave and back slowly away.

"G-d, thank You for taking care of Mother. She had a real Jewish burial. Now I know that her soul is residing in peace in Your eternal world. I realize that this is a little presumptuous, but in reality it was my effort that brought this about. Do You mind if I ask how Mother is doing up there?"

What chutzpa! Come on, Yisroel, don't be ridiculous!

The next morning, our daughter Aliza says, "Abba, I had a dream last night. Grandma came to me and her face was radiant with happiness."

I stare at Aliza.

Yisroel, we're here!"

"What? Oh my gosh! We're in New Jersey!"

Our feet rested on solid ground.

I apologize, Port of New York Authority, that we did not pay the tolls, but you don't seem to exist any longer so there is no one right now to pay. If you still exist, we owe it to you. Thanks for the bridge!

As the crowd surged onto the mainland, I turned for a final look at Staten Island. Funny that the Outerbridge Crossing was named for the engineer who designed it and not for its location at the "outermost" corner of southwestern New York State.

Come on, Yisroel, forget the trivia.

This bridge was a gift from G-d, a bridge to our future. It hadn't deposited us in the Promised Land, but we were that much closer.

Leah and I stood in the State of New Jersey.

NEW JERSEY

Tuesday night, July 7

SOMEHOW, I FELT MORE SECURE.

Of course, we were by no means safe, and the challenge of finding our children was enormous. Yet, we had accomplished something incredible. We had reached the mainland, thanks to a series of miraculous events.

More than anything, we wanted our entire family together in one place. Tehilla and Aliza and their families were living in Israel. Their sister Shira and her family were visiting there. We hoped they were safe. But could we find Shmuli and Ruchoma in New Jersey?

Where would they have gone when everything collapsed? It was unlikely that they would have come in search of us and risk being trapped on Long Island, especially with young children. But locating them would be like finding a straw-colored needle in a moving haystack. First you have to find the haystack!

My guess was that they would have stayed put in Lakeville. The large community of religious Jews there in itself would have offered some protection, or at least a feeling of safety. But the America we had known was gone. Who knew what might have happened in their town. And if they weren't there, where would they have gone? One thing was sure: they couldn't have gone far.

Perhaps toward our son-in-law's parents in the South. But that was unlikely. Not only were they far away but they were deeper into America, and deeper into America seemed like deeper into trouble. We didn't think they would head that way.

No, Israel would be more likely. But what would that mean? How would one get to Israel? I smiled to myself. The idea of finding a way across the ocean seemed so absurd right now. I didn't think our children would have considered that as a realistic option.

But Israel as a long-range goal? I was not ready to give up. When I get an idea, I can be very stubborn. That's what happened with Leah. I decided I was going to marry her. It was an impossible dream, but I wouldn't let go.

The dream came true!

So would this! We were all going to Israel. We simply HAD to.

In this world, G-d helps us constantly with miracles that appear to be "natural events." But one can't rely on miracles; we could not expect to grow wings and fly across the ocean. First, we had to find our children and their families in New Jersey. Then, we would travel northward and eastward toward Israel. That was my plan. I would work out the details along the way. Now that we had reached the mainland, the trek north didn't seem impossible. All we needed was our children. We could follow the west bank of the Hudson Valley and cross the river near Albany, where it's narrow. Then, we would travel east and north. I was focusing on the New England seacoast, which is sparsely populated and therefore un-likely to be the target of enemy attention. Cities were more treacherous than countryside. Although we would stand out in rural areas, where people know each other, there would also be forests in which we could disappear.

Why New England? The water that lapped against the lob-ster boats was the same water that touched the Holy Land. All the years that we had lived on Long Island, I had enjoyed the proximity to JFK Airport, a constant reminder that we lived only a few hours from Israel. Now, if we reached the New England coast, my intuition told me that we could find a way across the water. Yes, New England was far, but the highways leading there were clear and smooth.

Food was a major concern. In the city, the food supplies might already be gone, with stores looted and people fighting in the streets. In the countryside, however, food would be available in the forests and fields. We couldn't be the only people thinking like this, but it's a big country, and at least we'd have a chance.

Radiation might have contaminated the crops around New York and Boston, but all we could do was our best; we had to leave the rest to G-d. We couldn't calculate every pos-sibility; we simply had to do what appeared to be the right thing at every moment.

And we constantly had to ask our Father in Heaven for His help.

But first, always first, we had to find our children. Even if they weren't in Lakeville, they would have left a note. Lakeville was in the opposite direction from New England, but that didn't matter. We couldn't journey north unless the children were with us.

"Yisroel, you don't need your maps here."

Leah, who knew I enjoyed reading maps, was pointing at

the sign for Route 440, which led directly to the Garden State Parkway. It was dark, but there was enough light to make out the letters on the big green-and-white sign. How many times over the years had we driven this route? Happy times, on the way to our children and grandchildren.

Soon, we were gliding south on the Garden State Parkway. The biggest challenge in the darkness, a little like negotiating a slalom, was to avoid the abandoned cars. We breezed through deserted toll plazas, eerie reminders of the recent past. EZ Pass was no longer relevant.

Soon it would be getting light. Here we had no friends along the way where we could stop for shelter and rest. Could we travel safely in daylight now that we were out of the city? It would be hot riding during the day and would take a lot out of us, with little food and water remaining. We decided to stay with our routine and continue to travel only at night. Fortunately, wooded groves lined the Parkway; we could sleep there during the day, invisible from the roadway.

Right now, however, it was still dark. I was looking ahead for road-marks, when suddenly a dark shape appeared directly in my path. I braked and swerved but it was too late. There was an angry yell and my bike slid out from under me.

I had hit someone!

The impact sent me hurtling to the ground with a thud.

"Yisroel, what happened? Are you all right?"

"Why don't you watch where you're goin'!" growled a strange voice.

My side ached and I had scraped my arm on the pavement. My handlebars were twisted out of alignment. I peered into the semi-darkness and saw an old man, wearing a beaten-up hat. He wore a knapsack and carried a long, thick walking stick.

"Are you all right, sir?"

"I'll live, I guess."

"What happened? Are you injured?" Leah was concerned for both of us.

"Well, all of a sudden there was somebody in front of me and I couldn't do anything except swerve. I skidded and this gentleman must have been hit. I'm really sorry, sir. Obviously, I didn't mean to hit you."

"Is it obvious?"

I mean, what was I supposed to say? I was getting annoyed.

"Well, I'm not the kind of person who runs into people on purpose. And, as you may have noticed, there aren't exactly any streetlights around here. By the way, what were you doing walking in the middle of the road in the dark?"

He took a step forward and started shaking his stick at me.

"That's a silly question, sonny. Where d'ya expect me to walk? This ain't a parkway any more and it won't be for a long time to come. So I reckon everyone's got a right to use it, me as well as you."

I struggled to my feet and took a step closer to him.

"Look, I apologize again. I've very sorry. What happened exactly? Did I sideswipe you?"

"Bruised my arm. Who are you, anyway? What are you kids doing out here?"

"Kids?" I had to chuckle. "We're not kids."

"By my standards you're kids."

"My wife and I are from Long Island. We managed to get here thanks to our bicycles and a few miracles. Who are you?"

"My name's Elija Cummings."

"Where are you from, Mr. Cummings, and where are you headed?"

He tilted his head and looked me over. I could feel his stare pierce the darkness.

"Curious fella, aren't ya? Want to know everythin', huh?"

He was acting evasive and ornery, but I wasn't suspicious. There was something about him that I liked, kind of a twinkle in his voice.

"Maybe when I get ta know ya a little better, I'll tell ya more, but in the meantime, I'm much older than you and I still didn't hear your answer. I know you kids came from Long Island, and you had some miracles along the way, but where are you headed? The world's up in flames, so there must be a reason why you two are riding them bikes at top speed in the middle of the night."

I wasn't in the mood for conversation, and I really wanted to get going before daybreak, but, for some reason, I decided to tell him everything.

"The fact is that we're searching for our children. We have a son and a daughter, both married with children of their own, who live in Lakeville. We're worried about them, so that's why we had to get to New Jersey. That's where we figured we would find them. We've been traveling at night and resting during the day because we don't want to meet up with any bad people. It seems safer at night, when we are a little bit invisible."

"Yeah, and when you can run into old men walkin' down the road!"

"Mr. Cummings, I told you that I am very sorry I hit you. It was an accident."

"I know, sonny." His voice seemed to soften a little. "Tell me, what do those children of yours look like?"

I hesitated. Sometimes you don't want strangers to know too much, especially when you meet them in the middle of the night, but my intuition told me to keep talking.

"Well, they're religious Jews. They would probably have black suits on and the women would be modestly dressed, with skirts or dresses and their hair covered."

"Ha! In the dark I knew you were Jews!"

I swallowed hard. Maybe I had said too much. Was this a fanatical anti-Semite? A crazy man with a gun? We stood in silence, waiting.

"Are you afraid of me?"

"No, Mr. Cummings, but some people don't like Jews."

"You're right, sonny. A lot a' people don't like Jews. And it is very, very dangerous out here. But you happened to hit the right guy. I think I can help you two kids. Do you think it's possible your children are maybe on the road somewhere? Maybe this road? Maybe with friends?"

This was strange. What could he possibly be talking about?

"What do you mean?" asked Leah quickly.

"I mean this. About five miles back, south of here, I heard some sounds comin' from the woods off the road. I heard a baby cryin' and a mother tryin' to calm the baby. So I decided to take a look. And I went real quiet up there and saw a little group, well maybe not so little, maybe a hundred people or more. They had a fire in the middle, and parents and children were sleeping near it. Some were up talkin' and this mother with her baby. I could see they were all dressed modest-like, and I figured, these here are religious Jews and they're tryin' to get somewhere.

"I kinda felt sorry for them. These families, on foot, where are they going to go? And I thought, it's hard enough for them Jews in regular times, but what about now? Where will they go and how will they save themselves, with the little children and all? I felt bad for them. But I kept on, because I couldn't help them. But I made a mental note, for some reason, where they were. It was right by milepost 121.8, in the trees on the east side of the road. That's where they are. And here you are. Maybe your children are there. Do you think that could be?"

He looked at us.

I looked at Leah.

"Could it really be? Maybe. It's possible. Mr. Cummings, I know you wouldn't joke about this, would you?"

He cleared his throat.

"Sonny, times like these are not good for jokin'. This is a serious time in the world. The time for jokes is past. The world is burning, sonny. Why don't you go and see if those are your children."

Elija Cummings was facing east and we were looking west. In the first, faint rays of dawn I could see him putting his head to the side and looking at me, just looking. It was a kindly look. My skin tingled with goose bumps. There was something about this man: gruffness with kindness, but something more. As if he knew something. As the saying goes, "There's more than meets the eye."

"Thank you, Mr. Cummings, thank you. This could be very important. Look, I don't mean to be rude, but we need to leave right away. We've got to check this out."

"Sonny, if I were you, I *would* move on right away. By dawn, you should be there because I can see light in the east already. By sunup you'll have ridden five miles. G-d be with you. Perhaps we'll meet again some day and then we'll have a chance to talk."

"Good-bye, Mr. Cummings and good luck to you. May G-d protect you."

I walked over to my bike and started to pick it up.

Leah stepped towards our new acquaintance.

"Mr. Cummings, you have been wonderful to us. You have given us hope. I want you to have this Book of Psalms that was in my knapsack. Please take it. May it protect you on your journeys."

I could see a little sparkle as a tear rolled down the old man's cheek.

"Yes, may it protect me...and you too, children...you too."

There was a long silence. Then he gestured toward the south with his walking stick.

"Check it out, milepost 121.8. By the time you get there, you'll have daylight and you will see. G-d be with you. Good luck."

"G-d be with you, Mr. Cummings."

My shoulder was sore, my sleeve was torn and the handlebars on my bike were off center. But I was energized and eager to get started. Quickly, I straightened the bike with the tools I had brought, and then we pushed off. We turned back and waved. The last thing we saw was Elija Cummings' white hair merging into the darkness. Then he disappeared.

On our way again, we talked excitedly about who the group might be, promising ourselves not to be disappointed if our children weren't with them. And we talked about Mr. Cummings. All the miles we'd traveled; he was the one person I managed to bump into in the darkness. Was it another lifesaving miracle?

The surroundings became more rural and the roadsides more forested as we continued south. As the sky began to lighten, I strained to read the mileposts.

"Leah, can you see the numbers?"

"Not quite, but I'm sure we haven't traveled five miles yet. Let's keep going."

Soon there were densely wooded areas on both sides of the road. Now it was light enough to see the numbers. Mile 122.4 came into view. We were getting close. Then, six more little posts and finally we saw it: milepost 121.8.

Beyond the broad grass shoulder of the parkway to our left was a wooded area, just as Mr. Cummings had described. We walked our bikes across the median and the northbound lanes, leaning our bikes against some trees at the edge of a wooded grove. Inside the woods ahead of us, there was some open ground underneath the canopy of trees, but also enough underbrush to provide a screen. Leah and I peered in.

At first, we heard nothing. A soft breeze rustled leaves. I listened harder. Then, I caught the faint sound of voices from somewhere inside.

"Shema Yisroel, Ado...."

"Leah, did you hear that?"

We both strained to listen. For sure, the sound of morning prayers was coming from somewhere close by. But from where?

Just then, I saw movement off to the right through the trees, shapes moving, silhouetted against the brightening sky. We crept closer. All at once we could see a stroller, a family, then many families. A few more steps and there ahead of us stood a group of men wearing *tefillin*, their heads covered with *talleisim*, a *minyan* of maybe twenty Jews!

We looked all around, staring anxiously at each face.

Then we saw them!

"Shmuli! Ruchoma!" Leah shrieked and ran forward.

"Ima! Abba!"

I started bellowing at the top of my lungs.

"BARUCH HASHEM! BARUCH HASHEM!"

I didn't care who heard me. People turned around. Some started shushing me, then laughing.

"BARUCH HASHEM!"

We gave Shmuli and Ruchoma huge hugs and we stood wrapped together, motionless, for a long while.

"What happened? How did you get here? Is everyone OK? How did you find us?"

We were all talking at once and laughing and hugging each other. Finally, we sat down together in a circle on the cool, lush grass. It was almost too much joy to take in, after so much worry and fear. Living a short car ride away from Lakeville, with instant communication, it had always been so easy to be in touch with each other. These last harrowing days had shown us how dramatically our lives had changed.

We told the children everything that had happened to us since we left home. They listened, enthralled, even gasping occasionally and clapping each time we described an escape from danger. Finally, we told them about Mr. Cummings.

Shmuli shook his head slowly in amazement.

"Abba, that man definitely was meant to be there, standing right in your path."

Heads nodded.

"*Hodu l'Hashem ki tov*," someone said. "Give thanks to G-d for He is good."[13]

"Now tell us how YOU got here."

"Well," Shmuli began, "we knew you would try to reach us, but there were rumors that the Verrazano Bridge was down, so if that was true we didn't see how you would be able to get to New Jersey. Then gangs started roaming around Lakeville, smashing windows, starting fires and making threats. It was getting really dangerous. So a group of us in the neighborhood had a meeting and figured it was best to leave. We decided to find a more isolated location, with woods where we could take refuge.

"We also had the idea of heading toward New England. Any other direction just seemed to be heading deeper into trouble. Plus, the idea of going towards Israel was always on our minds."

Somehow, I wasn't surprised that we were on the same wavelength.

"We started north along the Garden State Parkway, traveling at night, and this was our second night out. We were about to pray and then try to get some sleep in this little wooded area. Afterward, we planned to rest here during the day and then get going again tonight."

"It's unbelievable that we had the same ideas."

Babies were sleeping in their strollers and people were standing around, listening. If all this was happening, perhaps we might get to Israel after all!

Leah and I were overjoyed that G-d had already blessed our quest for the children with success. Incredible! If we hadn't met Elija Cummings....

Now, we could all head north together. Instead of the two of us alone, Leah and I would be with our children as well as a small army of families. All of us would give each other encouragement and advice and, if need be, protection. Plus, we had a *minyan* for prayer.

And pray we did, our hearts overflowing with gratitude for the kindness of G-d. Following morning prayers, Leah and I searched carefully in our rapidly dwindling food supply and ate a tiny breakfast. Afterwards, we joined the group in a strategy session.

First, there were expressions of amazement and thanks to G-d for the many blessings He had bestowed upon us. Then, several people assessed the progress of their journey thus far. There was general agreement that the Garden State Parkway had been a wise choice, with the wide, smooth roadway still intact and its surrounding, sheltering woodlands.

Robert Moses, a visionary and controversial builder, had pioneered the concept of driving as a recreational experience. Now, almost a hundred years later, his "parkway" concept was providing both protection and a path to safety. Had he ever dreamt that his creation would become a ribbon of hope through the Valley of Death? In any case, we had to be grateful to him.

I wanted to start off with some words of encouragement.

"I had an amazing thought a few minutes ago, which I thought you might enjoy. We are now at milepost 121.8. This location has been embedded on my brain ever since Elija Cummings mentioned it to us. Do you know what 121.8 is in the Book of Psalms? Well, I just checked it out. I had a feeling the answer would be interesting, and it is. In Psalm 121, verse 8 you will find these words: 'G-d will guard your departure and your arrival, from this time and forever.'

"Is that *apropos* or not? We all know there are no coincidences. May this represent G-d's blessing to us. May we be worthy of His help. May all our departures and arrivals be guarded by G-d, from this moment until we reach the Holy Land in peace and sanctity."

A big "Amen" from all around.

"Wow," said Ruchoma, "That's amazing. I do feel strength from that! G-d keeps reaching out to us and telling us, 'You will make it through.'"

Now we got down to tactics and plans. It became clear to Leah and me that we would no longer have the luxury of covering dozens of miles a day riding our bicycles. We would walk our bikes (we might need them later), but we'd have to travel on foot with the families.

I took the lead when we began to discuss the route. I had been studying maps for days. Now was the time to "go public" with the crazy idea that I was bursting to share. Beyond New England, beyond reaching the coastline, I had a plan for crossing the sea.

It's been a hectic summer. Most of the children are married, but Shmuli is still single. He's heading back to yeshiva in a few weeks, and we won't see him much during the year. So Leah and Shmuli and I decide to use the last week in August for a little time together. Right after Shabbos, we pack the car and take off for Nova Scotia, still a secluded and isolated island, not so far away but in a different world from New York. It's a long trip if you drive the entire distance, but you can cut off a big chunk by taking the ferry from Maine.

There's an ocean-going ferry operating out of Portland. You board at eight p.m., load your car on the ship and spend the night in a cabin. They have entertainment and food for the hundreds who sail every day, but of course we always bring our own kosher food and we don't need any entertainment. It's beautiful just to walk the decks, with the breeze in your face and the stars bursting out of the black heavens above you. The next morning you land at Yarmouth and drive your car off the ferry. They had to close the ferry service for several years because of a dispute with the city, but it later reopened.

Nova Scotia is a big and beautiful island, with old fishing boats, lighthouses and famously high and low tides in the Bay of Fundy. It played a big part in the Battle of the Atlantic during World War II. Leah, Shmuli and I enjoy quiet days together, rowing boats and hiking.

That ocean-going ferry in Portland, Maine. It sticks in my mind. It's a big ship; it could go a long way, just like an ocean liner. Why, it could sail across the ocean! I can just picture it, sitting there, waiting....

Well, now it was 2020. And that boat may still be sitting there! But that's a crazy idea. We could never get hold of a huge ship like that. Totally illogical! But, then again, since I was a kid I had had crazy ideas.

I am the dreamer, the child with fears and the child with the vision of a new world beyond my fears, a world of noble people who walk with high purpose in the world. As a child I don't know about G-d, but I know there had to be more to life than the G-dless world in which I am growing up. I dream what seem crazy dreams, and there's no one to tell me I'm not crazy.

Years later, we discover the Torah.

I find that my dreams aren't so crazy after all.

In the summer of 2020, after the world had been set on fire, I still had dreams of a perfect world. But now I knew that my dreams weren't crazy, that G-d could pull you out of the bottomless pit if you clung to Him with all your heart and all your intellect and all your strength.

That ship, sitting in the dock at Portland, Maine: I knew it was there. I could visualize it, with silver moonbeams reflecting off rippling water. I knew it was waiting for us....

I took a deep breath.

"Folks, this is my idea. There is an ocean-going ship up there in Portland, Maine. We have sailed on it. I think we should head for it. Suppose that we can somehow arrange to use that boat. It's illogical, of course, but not impossible. Despite our current feelings of joy, our present situation is desperate because the world has gone insane and we are the objects of hatred. Our survival, as it has been for the past two thousand years, is logically unlikely, and yet we have survived as a nation and clung to our ancient bond with G-d. Why should we not consider, when we have done the impossible for thousands of years, something that is, while quite audacious, actually plausible? We need a bold stroke to save ourselves. If we fail, we would be no worse off than we are at present. If we succeed, we shall perhaps before long find ourselves home in *Eretz Yisroel*, the Holy Land."

Silence.

Everyone was listening intently. Everyone was willing to consider something "impossible" because we were desperate. So why not?

I continued.

"I've done some research. Portland is about three hundred forty five miles from here. If we walk an average of three miles an hour for five hours, we cover fifteen miles a day. This seems realistic, taking into account baby carriages, small children and other potential problems like bad weather. We probably could do more, but even at this rate we can cover ninety miles a week. This means we could reach Portland in about four weeks, the beginning of August."

Yaakov Blumenstein stopped me.

"Yisroel, what happens if we get to Portland and there's no ship there?"

"OK. There's a fifty percent chance that ferryboat is sitting there in the harbor. If not, there's a hundred percent chance that there are loads of other boats sitting there that are very seaworthy and whose captains or owners might be persuaded. To me, Portland is the ideal place to go. It's big enough to find what we need but small and distant enough not to be too threatening. It's not an impossible trip and we might just find something there to take us on the next leg of our journey, the trip across the ocean to where we all want to go."

Shlomo Jacobson spoke up.

"Do you really think that the owners of this ship would take us? Forget about 'could' but 'would.' Why would anyone help us even if they could?"

"I really don't know, Shlomo. It's true, of course, that it would be a wild chance. Don't forget, there's something in it for them too. I understand that it's a long shot, but there may be plenty of people who want to get out of here on the chance that life will be better on the other side. But even if that were not true, what I'm saying is that we should go for it anyway, even if we know the chances are slim. What other choices do we have? When the Children of Israel were escaping from Egypt, they had to cross the Red Sea. They didn't have boats, but they went to the seashore to get as close as they could to their goal under the power they had. I think the same is true in our situation. If we use every means that we have to get as close to Israel as we can, then hopefully G-d will help us. But how can we sit here?"

Shlomo persisted.

"I don't know. It's such a long shot. What about heading straight west, away from New York? Or better yet, south."

"Reb Shlomo," I said, "what point would there be? Do you think that these guys who are blowing up everything are confined to New York? The United States is one big Satan to them. All of it. And besides, 'Go West, Young man' was a motto appropriate to the people building the country a long time ago. That was then and this is now. Now the country has been built and is burning. Besides, we are Children of Israel. For us, the direction has always been east, not west. I have no other suggestions. Honestly, I don't know what else to do, but I feel very strongly that we shouldn't stay on this side of the ocean. It's terribly dangerous here. Of course, none of us knows for sure what will be."

Yaakov Blumenstein spoke.

"Mr. Neuberger...."

"Reb Yaakov, we're all one family here. Please call me 'Yisroel.'"

"OK, Reb Yisroel, I have a lot of respect for you. You've been through a lot, so you have the benefit of experience. There's a saying, however, actually a Gemara: we are not allowed to rely on a miracle.[14] Here we are relying on a miracle, and we're not allowed to do it."

"What do you propose, Reb Yaakov? What alternative would you suggest?"

"I would like to see us head into a totally isolated area where we could just disappear into the woods until it is safe to come out, whenever that is. Lakeville is dangerous and every city is dangerous, the bigger the city the more dangerous. I would think that a place like the Adirondack Forest Preserve, which is relatively close and extremely rural in parts, would offer protection. To assume that an ocean-going ship would be available for hire in a time of war to an unknown group of impoverished Jews who look completely alien in a New England town is totally unrealistic. We would look like fools if we even asked for such a thing. That's an example of 'relying on a miracle.'"

"Yaakov," Shlomo Jacobsen answered, "I think you're right and I think you're wrong. It is relying on a miracle even to think of being able to hire a boat to cross the ocean. It's also relying on a miracle to think that we can survive in the Adirondacks for even one winter. Now it's summer and beautiful weather most of the time. In a few months, with or without global warming, the Adirondacks will be covered with snow. Where are we going to live? What are we going to eat? And what makes you think those isolated forests won't be swarming with other people who have exactly the same idea we have? I don't think your idea is any more realistic than Reb Yisroel's. Escape south makes more sense to me, because at least it would be warmer in the winter. But I'm not sure how to get there without exposing ourselves to extreme danger by traveling through heavily populated and dangerous areas. And then what happens when we get there?"

Our son Shmuli waited briefly, looked around to see if anyone else wanted to respond, and then started to speak.

"My father is not a rash person. I think when he speaks, no matter how unusual his proposal may sound, it makes sense to listen. Yes, it does appear that the idea of hiring an ocean-going ship is unrealistic, but I'm not sure that amounts to relying on a miracle. Why? Because we are living in such unusual times that what was considered 'normal' up to now may no longer be normal. Until last Sunday, it was normal to spend the day learning or working, eat three meals, put our children to bed at a certain hour in a comfortable home, and so on. All those expectations have been overturned. What might have been possible in the past is not possible today; on the other hand, what might have been impossible in the past may be possible today. People are thinking differently, because survival has now become priority number one. There may be reasons why sailing across the ocean may be appealing to people who would not have considered it before, if it meant that their own lives might be saved in the process.

"When the Children of Israel stood at the shore of the Red Sea during the Exodus from ancient Egypt, we had arrived there only because G-d had engineered the collapse of the Egyptian civilization. It wasn't an outing; we were escaping to save ourselves and our families. We could have gone in another direction also, perhaps south along the Nile Valley. But that would have been unthinkable for us. Jews in a crisis always look toward Jerusalem and always, if possible, head toward Jerusalem. Here, a civilization appears to be collapsing. When we have a choice of directions in which to flee, it seems to make sense to flee in the direction of Jerusalem. True, we don't know what lies ahead, but neither did our fathers at the shore of the Red Sea. *'Ma'asei avos siman l'banim,'* the actions of the fathers are a sign for the children. The reason the Torah tells us what it tells us is exactly so that we should learn from it.

"I think we all basically agree that we have to get out of the Metropolitan Area of New York. No destination is foolproof or safe. This one at least affords us the possibility that, in addition to being able to lose ourselves in the countryside, we also may have more dramatic options open to us.

"So I would say my father's ideas make sense."

There was a general hush. I felt a huge sense of gratitude to G-d to have merited along with Leah to have raised such a son. Yes, it was partly that he spoke in favor of the ideas I had put forward. That in itself was a sign of honor to his parent. True, he was not required to agree with me. But that he did so, and he spoke up to support me publicly, and that he did so with such dignity and logic.... I thanked G-d at that moment for having given us such children.

At that point, not much more remained to be said.

"Let's sleep on it!" someone said.

"That sounds like a great idea!" came another voice.

No one dissented.

We all milled around for a few minutes. It was such a relief to be with our children and grandchildren.

Leah and I get married at Florival Farm, my parents' country house. It is a perfect June day. The weather is in contrast to my total panic at what I perceive as my complete inability to deal with marriage. After all, I am the same "nebich" who had been unable to speak to Linda Villency at high school, and now I am married to her! What am I going to do? Now I really have to come through!

We drive off in our Land Rover (my father thinks that is the most ridiculous wedding present in the world, but in my brilliant logic that's what I crave!) to the wilds of Wyoming.

This marriage is a lot wilder than Wyoming!

Just the two of us: I, complete with fears and mental somer-

saults, and my wife! Driving off to the wilds. And then, a few years later, there are three, and then four. We still don't know where we're going or what we're doing in this world. We're still in the Land Rover of confusion, cruising down the road to nowhere.

And then we meet this Rebbetzin and learn about the Torah. Everything changes; we have a goal and a reason for being on this earth.

And now...I can't believe it...we have children and grandchildren learning Torah, children of dignity and purpose and nobility of spirit. G-d, how can I ever begin to thank You? "Who is like our G-d?...He raises the needy from the dust, from the trash heaps He lifts the destitute. To seat them with nobles, with the nobles of His people. He transforms the barren wife into a glad mother of children!"[15]

Leah walked over.

"Yisroel, it's a good plan, and Shmuli spoke so beautifully! You've given the group hope and a sense of destination."

"Thanks, Leah."

Leah gives me so much strength! I needed that.

Whatever our decision, we all knew that we faced overwhelming uncertainties that would challenge every bit of our collective brains and faith. More miracles would be needed. How would we eat? What if someone became too sick or injured to travel? Endless questions swirled through my brain, but I was too tired to think or talk or worry any more. One by one, we lay down on the soft forest floor, surrounded by trees and shrubs, and drifted off to sleep.

A few hours later I awoke, drenched in sweat. My first feeling was happiness at having found our children and grandchildren, followed immediately by an overwhelming sense of concern and alarm. I knew I could no longer ignore the question of how all of us were going to eat and drink.

In ancient times, people raised their own food so it was always close at hand. Our contemporary society had learned to depend on a complex system of agriculture and commerce stretching to other cities, countries and continents. But that complex system had now gone up in smoke. The local sources of food were basically nonexistent. Wanderers like us would be competing with millions of others for the same limited supplies. Each would no doubt try to hoard whatever was found, but where would we find any food to begin with?

How would we survive? How would we get food?

Perhaps we could find berries and nuts, but it was still early summer and not much was ripe. Furthermore, sustaining one person on berries and nuts was challenge enough. Our group numbered around a hundred! How would we find enough for all these families to live on as we traveled through metropolitan New Jersey? Even in farm country, would there be anything left for us? Every person in the area would be out looking for food. It would be chaos.

It seemed hopeless.

I took a deep breath. I looked up at the giant trees above and watched their leafy arms swaying in the breeze. Suddenly I had this unbelievable idea. You know, sometimes you go to sleep with an unresolved problem. During the night, your soul visits G-d's realm, the spiritual world. You wake up and you have a totally new perspective. It didn't come from you; it came from Upstairs. I lay back on the grass and tried to clear my mind. What was that wisp of an idea that had floated across my consciousness? There was a thought I was trying to grasp.

I jumped up with excitement. I crept closer to Leah and whispered loudly.

"Leah, are you awake?"

"Well... I am now."

"Oops. Sorry. Go back to sleep."

"Too late, Yisroel. You might as well tell me what you wanted to."

I was bursting to tell her.

"I'm sorry I woke you up, but I've got to tell you something."

She didn't look thrilled.

"OK, Yisroel, what is it? What unbelievable idea do you have?"

"I'm so excited, Leah. I just had an incredible thought."

"I'm listening.

"Uncle Phil."

"Uncle Phil?"

"Phil Feibusch."

"Yisroel, what are you talking about?"

"Uncle Phil is the answer."

"The answer to what?"

"Eating."

"Uncle Phil is the answer to eating? What on earth are you talking about?"

"Serena's Candy. That's what I'm talking about."

"Yisroel, can you speak in plain words?"

"Leah, we're probably about thirty miles from Uncle Phil's candy factory. We could get there in two days, maybe one long day. That factory is an old brick building in a dilapidated neighborhood of Petersonville. It's inconspicuous. If you didn't know it was there, you'd never know that it's filled with tons of candy, chocolate, nuts and raisins, honey, molasses and, well, whatever they put in candy. And, it's all kosher."

Leah looked a little puzzled, but she was listening, her chin resting on her hands.

"I know it's not exactly on your top ten nutrition list, but it's the kind of food that could provide us all with the energy we will need to walk to New England. By then, there will be orchards and farms and we can eat all that healthy stuff right out of the ground and off the trees. But to get us there! We will need to feed the army, and this could be it, enough to feed the army and...it doesn't spoil."

"Yisroel, you're a bit crazy, but maybe...."

"You always tell me I shouldn't say I'm crazy."

"Well, sometimes, you know, you are slightly nutty."

"Slightly?"

"OK, Yisroel, get to the point."

"I woke up this morning and suddenly, this incredible idea came into my head. We just need to find Uncle Phil and Aunt Bessie, who probably are desperate about what to do. Then, we go and open the factory and find enough to live on for the next month. For everybody here. And maybe we'll be saving Uncle Phil and Aunt Bessie at the same time! They'll come with us!"

"What happens if they're not at home? They might have left."

"We'll find that out when we get there. How does 'Yisroel, Leah and the Chocolate Factory' sound to you?"

"Yisroel, you are an interesting guy."

JEFF AND MARGE

UNTIL THE EVENTS OF JULY 5 changed everything, people tended to come up with their own definition of what they needed to survive. How often did someone say, "I couldn't survive without...a cell phone...air conditioning...pistachio ice cream...cable TV...high speed internet."

Now, survival meant food and water.

Not gourmet food and ice water.

Food and water.

I started feeling guilty about the plan to storm Uncle Phil's chocolate factory. There were undoubtedly millions of people out there who were beginning to panic about food. What about them? Still, I felt responsible for the survival of our group of families. We would seek only what was needed for our survival.

There was also a problem with the water supply. Many families had brought bottles of spring water with them from Lakeville, but it was close to running out, despite strict rationing. We had to find a solution very soon.

Leah and I spent the rest of the afternoon resting and talking with our family and the others, enjoying our wooded retreat next to the parkway. As dusk approached, everyone gathered for another meeting and I mentioned my chocolate-factory plan. Coming on the heels of the ferryboat idea, I was apprehensive about how people would react to me.

After I finished speaking, there was a long silence. I looked around, hoping someone would speak up. Finally, Binyomin Feltheimer came to my rescue. He smiled and said, "Hey, it might work; what have we got to lose? Right now we have no solution. Here's a solution. If it works, it's good. If it doesn't work, we keep on looking for something that does work. It's that simple."

Others chimed in. The basic reaction: why not try?

We decided to push hard to reach Petersonville soon, maybe even that night. Our plan was to travel north as far as possible and then find another woodsy refuge off the parkway. Leah and I would leave the group there and ride our bikes to Uncle Phil and Aunt Bessie's house, probably the next night, which would be Thursday. We needed to keep track of the days because we had to know when *Shabbos* was. Our very efficient daughter Ruchoma was recording every day and date on a sheet of paper; someone else had thought to bring a Hebrew calendar as well.

Leaving our wooded retreat was an emotional moment. This was where we had been reunited with our children and had found comfort with a new, extended family. For a while, we had also managed to forget the dangers and chaos ahead.

"I'll always remember this place with joy and gratitude," said Leah. "I think we should name it Reunion Park."

So we scratched the words "Reunion Park" on a large, smooth stone at the foot of the big oak tree that had sheltered us while we had rested so peacefully.

As darkness fell, the group prepared to leave. Now we realized how easy it had been when just the two of us had been traveling together. There were many children in our group and each one seemed to have a different schedule. Some were still asleep, some were wide awake, some were crying and some were placid. Their eating schedules were all different. But we had to move on; survival was at stake. We had to inject military discipline into our schedule. We now had a goal and a timetable. We were fortunate in traveling during this season. Before long, the warm yellow sun of summer would become the white southern sun of winter. We were heading into New England, where the frigid wind roars in from the north. If we were not fortunate enough to find ocean passage, we would have to prepare ourselves for a difficult winter siege.

But our people felt the urgency. Before long, everyone was ready. It wasn't easy, but survival is a strong instinct.

Leah and I wheeled our bicycles out of the woods and onto the parkway, joined by mothers, fathers and teens walking, many pushing baby strollers. We started off at a good pace, striding briskly and energetically, refreshed after having rested all day and still wrapped in the glow of our miraculous reunion. It was a warm, pleasant evening and the sky was clear. I felt cautious hope. As soon as our eyes got used to the darkness, we could see quite well, even though the moon wouldn't appear for several hours. Stars, it seems, also give off light. In fact, the Milky Way was so bright that I was sure it was casting a tiny shadow!

The sky to our right was tinged with a red glow as huge fires burned to the east and north. It was incredibly fortunate that we had been on the fringe of the attacks. Now, we realized, by circling south of Manhattan and then west into New

Jersey, we had been spared not only from destruction but even from the odor of destruction, which the prevailing wind carried eastward.

Joseph is sold to "a caravan of Ishmaelites...bearing spices."[16] Even as he descends into exile, Joseph inhales the aroma of sweet spices. G-d measures every event to a hair's breadth. Joseph's suffering went so far, but no farther. We were also on a journey filled with suffering, but G-d had spared us from the odor of death.

As we made our way northward, endless streams of people clogged the overpasses that crossed over the roadway at frequent intervals. They were headed westward, most likely to rural western New Jersey and Pennsylvania, and perhaps beyond.

How typical. The Jews are always going in a different direction from the rest of the world. Throughout history this has saved us. We've always been alone and we're still alone. In America they say, "Go west, young man," but for us it has always been the other direction, toward the sunrise, toward Jerusalem and the Temple Mount. We are headed in the same direction that Jews have been going for two thousand years, since the destruction of the Temple, still on the homeward path. Just because it seemed impossible is no reason to give up. It has always seemed impossible, but we have never given up. And we are still around.

We walked quietly tonight; everyone seemed lost in his or her own reverie. There was much to comprehend; our minds were working overtime. Even the children were quiet. Darkness invites introspection. I for one was feeling liberated, traveling with no possessions except what we carried on our backs. We had left our entire life behind, the life we had known since our youth. We were following in our Father Abraham's footsteps. "Go...from your land, from your relatives and from your father's house to the land that I will show you."[17]

All of us were leaving the world of money, telephones, computers, salaries, bills, radio and maybe television. No longer would we shop, drive the car, follow the stock market, wonder who would win the election or the World Series. Shuffling papers, catching the train, fixing the roof or buying insurance were obsolete.

I looked over at Leah.

"Leah, why are you so serious?"

She looked surprised by my question.

"What do you think, Yisroel? Don't you feel anything? We're walking along with our children, with a feeling of hope and a goal for the future. We're the fortunate ones. We have so much more this minute than we dared to hope for just two days ago. But I'm thinking about all those people trapped, millions injured and dying, people buried in rubble, overcome by fires and poisonous fumes, babies crying all alone, people screaming for help, husbands and wives separated, homes destroyed... and no one to help."

"Leah, you are so good. That's why people love you so much!"

Amazing lady, my wife! Full of feeling, always doing things for others and yet very practical. My nature was different from hers. I could cry during prayer. I could cry at the destruction of the Holy Temple and the plight of the Children of Israel, our imminent danger in exile. I could cry out to G-d to save us from the destruction that threatened all around. I felt the closeness of danger and a desire to serve G-d. I wanted to do something, to help. That's why I loved writing books and speaking about our spiritual transformation: I wanted to communicate our experience in case it would touch others' hearts. I wanted to give G-d *nachas*. I wanted to say what Isaiah said: "Here I am! Send me!"[18] But I didn't have Leah's heart for people. It bothered me, but no matter what, we still had to try to save ourselves. Whatever my inadequacies, we still had to focus on survival. That was for sure.

Our group seemed determined and hopeful, with that feeling of camaraderie that exists where people are facing a common danger as a family unit. It was good to be traveling together. Thank G-d no one was bothering us so far. After all, a large group of Jews in a world with no government was bound to draw attention to itself.

We didn't try to hide our identity, although our obvious Jewishness might have exposed us to danger. Proclaiming publicly that we believed in G-d and were relying on Him was in itself a kind of protection. G-d had made constant miracles for us; we wanted to acknowledge our gratitude. "How can I repay G-d for all His kindnesses to me? I will raise the cup of salvations and invoke the Name of G-d. I will pay my vows to G-d in the presence of His entire people."[19] We believed — and hoped — that our identity as Jews would be our protection.

Shlomo Jacobson and Moshe Greenberg acted as *shomrim*, guardians, patrolling up and down the line to make sure that no one was having difficulty. They were constantly busy; we were not a small group, and there were many little problems. We could hear them constantly encouraging others, sometimes carrying little children on their shoulders and joking with people as they walked.

"Reuven, you're doing a great job," Yaakov called out to the Steinbergs' son, a skinny boy of nine who was managing to keep pace with the adults despite a huge backpack. "You give me energy when I see you walk!" Reuven broke into an enormous grin, and practically bounced up into the air.

A huge orange moon — about three-quarters full and still quite bright — popped up over the eastern horizon a few minutes after eleven. Encouraged, I guess, by this burst of additional light, we began to walk faster, with a bounce in our step. About an hour later, we came up beside a young couple pushing a stroller. Sometimes you get an intuitive flash about someone, either positive or negative. Someone's booming voice immediately turns you off. Or someone's smile warms your heart. I felt an instant bond with this couple even before we spoke. They seemed very alone and vulnerable, which made them appealingly human.

Leah and I are pushing the stroller in Central Park. Already one can see Tehilla's fascination with G-d's world.

"Look how she sticks her head up out of the carriage. She wants to see everything. She will grow up, with G-d's help, trying to understand what this world is all about."

The young couple seemed a little wary, so I spoke first.
"Hello, how are you?"
He gave me a wave and a quick smile.
"Considering...well...what's going on, OK, I guess. For now."
"Where are you headed?
"We don't know exactly," he said. "My wife's parents — I'm Jeff Klein and this is Marge — live in Westchester and that's where we're trying to go. But after that...we don't know, and we're not even sure we can get there. We really don't know what to do. To be honest, we're a bit panicked. Not much food and water left and we have no idea how to get any. So, who are you and where are you coming from?"
"We're Yisroel and Leah Neuberger. Over there is a big group of friends and neighbors of our children from Lakeville, New Jersey. Leah and I live — 'lived' I guess one would say — in Long Island. We were home when it all started. The first thing we thought of was finding our children in New Jersey.

We had no idea how to get there, of course, because we didn't know if the bridges and roads were OK. But we rode our bicycles all the way through Queens and Brooklyn to the Verrazano Bridge. And then...."

"But wait, we heard the Verrazano Bridge was down."

"Well, yes. It was awful. It took a miracle to cross the Narrows and another miracle to find our children and their friends on the Garden State Parkway. Later on, if you want, we'll tell you the whole story. In any case, we're all headed north, and with G-d's help, out of the Metropolitan area."

"All the way from Long Island! That's incredible. I want to hear the details. By the way, I assume you are Jewish."

"Yes, we are."

"Orthodox?"

"Well, I don't really like that word too much. But yes, that's what you would call us."

"Why don't you like the word?"

"That word came into existence only recently in Jewish history. If 'orthodox' is a legitimate word, it's only because there are other such supposedly legitimate words as 'conservative' and 'reform.' The very existence of the word implies that it's up to us to choose among equally valid lifestyles.

"But religion isn't man voting on Truth; it's G-d telling us what Truth is and how to live, in every detail. So that word in itself creates confusion and polarization among Jews by implying that there are several versions of G-d's law. In my — hopefully humble! — opinion, that kind of confusion helped create the mess we're in today."

We had been walking along at a nice pace, but my remark brought him to a complete stop.

"Wow! Strong words! A week ago I would have said you're a bigot. But in that week the world has turned upside down. Suddenly those words sound a lot more real to me

than they would have last week. We've always called ourselves 'Conservative Jews,' but somehow tonight I like what
you're saying. I don't know why, but it makes me feel better,
more secure, like maybe there's something stable in this jum-
bled-up universe."

Leah tugged on my sleeve and whispered, "Yisroel, do
you have to go into all this now?"

"There's no reason not to talk while we're walking. It's important."

"OK, but remember: we've got to get somewhere tonight
and we have an entire group that can't be slowed down."

"Jeff, the Boss just told me that we'd better keep moving.
Do you think we can have this talk and keep our pace at the
same time? Can you and your wife manage it?"

"No problem for me. Marge, can you keep up the pace?
I'll push the stroller."

Marge nodded. "Do you know, Jeff, how good it is to have
such nice people to walk with? It's a huge comfort. Of course
we're going to walk with them."

"You see, Yisroel, I also heard from the Boss! By the way,
do you mind if I call you 'Yisroel'?"

"No problem. That's my name!"

"Good. Now, may I ask you to elaborate? Please tell me
what you mean by 'polarization'?"

"You know that you just asked for a speech, right?"

"To be honest, Yisroel, we don't have too much else to do
right now!"

"OK. Don't say I didn't warn you!"

"I'm not afraid."

"The blessing upon the Children of Israel has always depended on our unity. Read the Biblical account of our wanderings through the Sinai Desert. Despite all our failings and
weaknesses, we were invulnerable as long as we stuck to-

gether under the leadership of Moses. After all, we Jews are one family; our existence depends on maintaining that family unity and the love that goes with it. Our great Biblical commentator *Rashi*, who lived almost a thousand years ago, tells us that when we stood at Mount Sinai we were like 'one man with one heart.'[20] Our unity enabled us to hear the voice of G-d.

"The flip side is explained by the Talmud, which tells us that the Second Temple in Jerusalem was destroyed two thousand years ago because of gratuitous and causeless hatred among the Children of Israel. Ever since then, we have been suffering from the effects of this divisiveness.

"Actually, our troubles really began with the sale of Joseph by his brothers more than thirty five hundred years ago! This led to our first Exile in Egypt. That disunity among the brothers has never been completely eradicated. Its tragic legacy is still with us.

"The history especially of the past two thousand years is a long tale of varying degrees of vilification, violence and subjugation at the hands of our enemies. The divisions among us have weakened Jews both inside and outside Israel, making us vulnerable for as long as we are divided."

Jeff's eyes were glistening in the moonlight. He was into it; he was absorbing. I could see that he wanted to continue the discussion.

"These divisions among Jews are the reason we are in exile right now and our enemies are strong. Those who are attacking America hate us above all, and their hatred is allowed to prevail, albeit temporarily, because our spiritual strength and protection is sapped by our disunity. It's a matter of survival for the Children of Israel to unite under the banner of Torah. We are a spiritual nation. We and the entire world need our blessing."

"Marge and I are not Orthodox. Are you saying we're partly to blame?"

"Jeff, we're all partly to blame for this mess. Then again, many of us are sincerely trying to clean up our act. I have yet to meet someone who is perfect, although I will tell you that there are some very holy Jews, steeped in the Torah, who are like angels on earth. I have met them. But in today's world many people are trying to find their way back to G-d and would like to attain that level. It's a never-ending process, the fundamental job of life, or at least it should be. The more a person attaches himself to the Torah, studies it and lives it, the more he is going to improve himself and the world. 'I am at fault' isn't such a bad thing to say. That's what we say on Yom Kippur!

"I blame myself somewhat for the thirty years before I became observant, although I grew up not knowing anything about being Jewish. I knew in my heart that I was living the wrong way, but I didn't know how to get out of the maze. However, you can't flagellate yourself completely. We've all been raised to believe that material success was the entire point of life. The Torah lifestyle was totally foreign to us. Now, however, it looks as if the entire cultural and social structure we thought was reality has collapsed forever and there is no place to go BUT back to G-d."

"This is incredible. Honestly, I have never heard anyone put it like this before. Do you think there's any hope? Where will this end?"

"There's no doubt that the end will be completely good. All our prophets assure us with total certainty that Mashiach will come at the end of history and that those who cling to G-d will enjoy a universal era of peace and tranquility in a renewed world. Between then and now I don't think anyone knows how much time will elapse or what events will occur or who will survive, although it is not a stretch to believe that we are very close to the finish line. Our rabbis say that a person shouldn't give up hope even when a sword is suspended over his throat.

"Of course, I'm not immune from worrying. According to the rules of logic, we're finished. But according to the rules of logic we were finished two thousand years ago!

"We're still here!

"Our lives are not governed by the laws of nature; the Children of Israel are attached to eternity. Our rabbis tell us that when the Bible says G-d took Abraham 'outside' and had him 'gaze' toward the heavens, that means G-d was taking Abraham and his children 'outside' nature.[21] Logic would indicate that the Jewish People should not be around at all after two thousand years of exile as a tiny minority amidst powerful nations who hate us. Yet the other nations have disappeared, and we, the tiny, apparently helpless minority, are still here. The Children of Israel are tied to the Eternal. He created time and space, so when we stick to Him, we are above time and space. We are, so to speak, riding His coat-tails through eternity."

"Yisroel," said Jeff, "this is strong stuff, but it makes sense. Maybe it's just the circumstances, which convince me to accept what I never would have accepted before, but maybe this all happened partly so that people like me should open our eyes. What's your reaction, Marge?"

Marge looked at us in the pale moonlight. Her eyes were bright.

"Yisroel is a very smart person, Jeff. I think he and Leah have been through a lot. He's speaking from experience, not theory."

"Well, I've escaped from many things up to now, spiritually and physically. Once I was chased by a bear in Great

Smoky Mountains National Park. As a teenager, I walked across an icy, ten-inch ledge on the Grand Teton in Wyoming with about two thousand feet of frigid air below me. Once our family was lost on Lake Powell in a small boat in the middle of a huge thunderstorm. As a kid, I was caught in the middle of one of the biggest hurricanes of the century on Montauk Point in Long Island. All of these things were physical and I survived them.

"Spiritual dangers are worse because the consequences last forever. I'm probably the biggest worrier you'll ever meet, but I have this underlying optimism that somehow G-d will take care of us. The secret is to stick close to Him. In fact, it was my worrying that finally persuaded me that I HAD to stick close to Him."

Jeff and Marge were silent. Clearly, they were happy and relieved to be with fellow Jews. Meanwhile, we were all moving along at a good clip. The rhythm of walking had taken on its own steady beat. When you find the rhythm, everything gets easier. I remember reading that Harry Truman always walked at the same military pace; people had trouble keeping up with him.

I sit at the piano in the living room at 21 East 87 Street, Apartment 12b ("'b' as in 'boy,'" Mother always says). I like to pick out songs, but I don't like the teacher or the practicing. It's fun just to figure out how to play the melodies; why do I have to work so hard?

You know what I like? The metronome.

It's kind of magic: a shiny wooden pyramid about six inches tall, with a metal pointer like a long clock-hand, that goes back and forth with absolute precision. Mrs. Hansen pulls it out of her bag and carefully opens the case. She places it carefully on the piano, setting the speed and winding it up. Then she pushes the release. It 'ticks' and 'tocks' with perfect regularity. There's something comforting about that sound, and I realize that the music is very organized.

Maybe the whole universe is organized. Maybe there's something that regulates the whole world, sunrise and sunset, the phases of the moon, the march of the seasons. Maybe there's a big metronome somewhere, ticking away and guiding everything.

Later I would learn the words of King David: "The heavens declare the glory of G-d and the firmament declares His handiwork. Day following day utters speech, and night following night declares knowledge. There is no speech and there are no words; their sound is not heard. (But) their precision goes forth throughout the earth and their words reach the end of the inhabited world."[22]

Although it was still dark, we needed to stop so the adults could eat before daybreak. Today in the Jewish calendar was the Seventeenth of the month of Tammuz, on which we fast from morning light to nightfall. On that day thousands of years earlier, the City of Jerusalem and the Holy Temple were attacked. Our ancestors fought for their lives and our entire civilization was threatened with complete destruction. It seemed unbelievable that we were reliving the scene thousands of years later! Would our troubles never end?

The fact that we could look back and remember that ancient day, which might easily have been our last, gave me hope to think that we might survive the current firestorm and see this epic story through to the end.

Just before the sky became light, we paused for food and drink. Obviously, those who couldn't go on without nourishment would take what they needed to survive, but many of us felt strong enough to fast. We then began to look for a place to stop, another forested haven where we could find protection and isolation during the day.

The air was beginning to turn warm and sticky. It was about 4:30 a.m. and we were somewhere near Newark. We thought it unlikely that we would find woods near such a big city, but the Garden State Parkway is beautifully landscaped. Next to a cemetery we found a grove of trees with plenty of space for everyone to disappear and take shelter.

Jeff and Marge and their baby were still with us; our group was growing.

We turned off into the grove just as the first rays began to lighten the eastern sky.

PETERSONVILLE

Thursday morning, July 9

TODAY WAS GOING TO BE HOT. You could feel it in the air and see it in the fiery red sun that was climbing higher in the east. We used to hear the weather forecast on the radio, but "what we used to do" now seemed a lifetime away. We simply watched the sky and became our own forecasters.

Now we were sleeping during the day instead of at night, and we had of course dispensed with sheets, pillows or even beds. There was no fresh clothing, no daily shower. In fact, our clothes were beginning to stick to us. The garments of the Children of Israel had remained miraculously fresh during forty years in the desert. How would ours fare?

Everyone was soon busy at the new campsite. The men said morning prayers; the women set up camp and fed the children. Some adults ate because they needed to do so for health and survival, but most were able to fast. As it was, our eating and drinking supplies had become frighteningly limited, and our rationing rules became ever stricter. We needed Uncle Phil's factory! Hopefully, the plan would work.

All of us had begun to feel the pinch of hunger. Even on a non-fast day, after eight hours of serious walking, people were tired, hot and hungry. But we couldn't take a snack at will, as we had been used to doing all our lives. There was no refrigerator, no cupboard full of snacks, no deli or corner store. I began to fantasize about a glass of ice water. Better yet, iced coffee... or, even better, iced cappuccino!

There was no coffee at all, just a few measured sips of warm water. And today, not even that. How long would it be before we would be in danger of starving or dying of thirst? The possibility was not farfetched.

Leah and I found a shady spot under a maple. We parked our bikes and set down our backpacks. It was our spot, even though there were no walls, furniture or roof. I wondered how much any of us had truly appreciated the homes we had once lived in, with running water and electricity, air conditioning in the summer and heat in the winter.

With G-d's help, we would survive. The forest floor felt soft and inviting. Despite all the problems and worries, exhaustion prevailed and soon we were in the world of dreams.

Around two p.m. I awoke abruptly to the sensation of pinpricks all over my body. Mosquitos?

Rain!

I opened my eyes to a black sky. There was a flash, then a boom. The drops were getting larger. We jumped to our feet and Leah began digging out the raingear. Although I had tried to prepare myself mentally, I don't know if one can ever really feel normal getting drenched. In any case, the children, our *tefillin*, the books, the food and other items had to be protected.

Just at that moment I remembered that I had failed to wash my hands after sleeping. I took a little water and made the blessing. Maybe I was in the woods about to get soaked, but I wasn't going to forget my obligations or miss the opportunity to make a blessing over lightning and thunder. This was a challenge: to remember every detail of the Torah even when we were running for our lives. What in fact saves lives but that? However, the question still is: do we remember?

"Baruch ata... Blessed are You, our G-d, King of the Universe...."

Now it was beginning to pour. There was no protection, so Leah and I just sat there quietly and got soaked. Absolutely soaked! After a few minutes, we saw that the lightning was getting dangerously close, striking ground within a mile of our camp. We started counting the seconds between the flash and the thunder. As a former Cub Scout, I knew that each five seconds is a mile. We counted seven seconds, then six after the next flash.

Cub Scouts also learn that trees are dangerous in a thunderstorm. Civilization might be tottering, but G-d was still operating the heavens and the earth according to the same rules, as far as we knew.

"Hey everyone, let's get away from here. It's dangerous under these trees."

We ran out toward the open roadway, and everyone else in camp followed, mothers with children and fathers with strollers and more children.

I am excited when summer comes: an entire season of thunderstorm weather ahead. Sometimes I could see the massive anvil-tops boiling up into the sky maybe fifty thousand feet above. They're just big cotton balls of wet air, but the turbulence from those clouds can toss jetliners or hatch tornadoes. Frightening, yes, but fascinating.

Thunderstorms offer me a visceral sense of just how puny we human beings are. This demonstration of our weakness gives me solace because human beings can be so arrogant. Of course, I want to watch the storm through a big picture window, not get soaked.

"Blessed are You, our G-d, Ruler of the universe, Who makes the work of creation."

"Blessed are You, our G-d, Ruler of the universe, Whose power and might fill the world."

The rain fell in sheets. I had to do something to take my mind off the drenching I was getting, so I tried to discern individual drops. I once heard that each drop is a distinct creation that has its own specific mission on earth: G-d is sending this particular drop to nourish this particular blade of grass, or to give sustenance to that frog. These thoughts did not dry me out, but my mind was diverted momentarily as I remembered the infinite spiritual world that is the source of this physical one, with all its pain and challenge.

Then I thought about snowflakes. Never since Creation has one snowflake duplicated another. As kids, we looked through a microscope and could see the unique shape of each crystal.

Just as each human face is different, so is each snowflake. Only those who don't acknowledge G-d's existence believe that we are living in chaos. Everything has a reason. "Everything has its season, and there is a time for everything under the heaven... A time to be born and a time to die; a time to plant and a time to uproot the planted. A time to kill and time to heal; a time to wreck and a time to build...."[23] Neither a rainstorm nor a snowstorm is a mechanical event driven by soul-less forces. Nothing is haphazard; everything is under His direction.

"May my teaching drop like the rain."[24] Just as each word of Torah is formulated for a specific purpose, so each raindrop is formulated for a specific purpose.

"Thank You G-d!"

"Let's collect this rainfall! We can drink it!"

With this very practical suggestion, Shmuel Gantz broke through my reverie. The lightning had passed and now a hard, steady rain was falling.

Everyone began scrambling to get pots, buckets, cups, bottles, whatever container was available. This storm became our sustenance; we would be able to drink delicious water from the sky with a heartfelt blessing.

After a while, the downpour slackened and the torrent became pin pricks again. The sky began to clear and soon our steamy clothes and soaking skin began to dry. By dusk, our clothes were merely soggy. As soon as the stars were visible, everybody prayed and ate our modest "dinner." The fast was over.

It was time for Leah and me to set out for Uncle Phil and Aunt Bessie's house. We were glad we still had our bikes; we would need them now. We were scraping off mud from the tires and pedals when Shmuli and our son-in-law David walked over.

"Abba, maybe one of us should go with you instead of *Ima*," said Shmuli.

"That's so nice of you to offer. (Not that you've ever done anything other than 'nice.') What do you think, Leah?"

I couldn't imagine going on the journey without Leah, but we had been through a long, humid walk, a day of fasting and a torrential downpour. Sometimes I forgot that we were grandparents and not twenty anymore.

"Thank you, *kinderlach*," said Leah, "I really appreciate your offer. But I need to go. I'm Aunt Bessie's niece, so it's important for me to be there. We go a long way back; my presence could convince them that this whole idea is legitimate.

It would be great if all of us could go, but we have only two bicycles ...."

Shmuli and David helped us dry off the bikes. They stood at the edge of the camp when we set off, giving us their blessings as we waved good-by and began pedaling north. I turned to Leah.

"I knew you wouldn't let them go instead of you, but they are such wonderful children, thank G-d."

"We are blessed."

It was exhilarating being back on a bicycle again after all that trudging. The wind in our faces refreshed us and evaporated the remaining moisture from our clothing. Although I missed the camaraderie and mutual protection of our lively group, I was able to focus better and concentrate on our mission. We had much to worry about. My thoughts swirled as we glided north along the parkway. Could we find their house in the dark? Would they be there? Would they be able to open the factory? Would they be WILLING to open the factory? Was there anything left in the factory? Was there a truck available? Would we get to them safely? Would we return safely?

Each question was crucial; each answer could be life-altering.

The Petersonville exit was several miles away. As we passed under a number of bridges, I suddenly realized that they were all potential roofs in a rainstorm. We could have avoided getting soaked! Next time a storm threatened, we would look for the nearest bridge.

Just ahead was a sign. We used our flashlights sparingly, but here we needed them. Without the lights, the big signs loomed over us like dark towers; we could see them but not read the words. I aimed my light and the words jumped out at us. Petersonville, here we come!

We took the darkened exit. After several wrong turns, we

were in familiar territory, the comfortable suburban community we had known so well. From the time that we had first met as teenagers, Leah and I had visited Uncle Phil and Aunt Bessie's home on countless family occasions.

My memories of those times were vivid and sentimental. Uncle Phil and Aunt Bessie were sweet people who shared a passionate love for the Land of Israel. She was a warm mother, an affectionate aunt and a very good cook. Uncle Phil was a tough businessman on the outside and a teddy bear on the inside.

After making our way past Maple, Elm and Juniper, we reached Oak Street. A moment later, we were standing in front of Number 32. The entire neighborhood seemed deserted, silent and still. Instead of knocking on the door, I pressed my ear against it and listened.

Nothing. But Leah had her head tilted to the side.

"Yisroel, do you hear that?"

I strained to listen, but heard nothing.

"What do you hear?"

"I'm sure I hear something," she whispered. "It sounds as if it's coming from around back, like people talking very softly, as if they don't want to attract attention."

We locked our bikes to the railing near the front steps. I didn't know what we'd find back there, but I didn't want to be encumbered by the bikes. And if the bikes disappeared, we'd be in big trouble.

UNCLE PHIL AND
AUNT BESSIE

Thursday night, July 9

WE MOVED QUIETLY AROUND THE house, making our way carefully past the shrubs and flowers. Our side of the house was in the shadow of the rising moon, but our eyes were fully used to the darkness and every detail was clear. As we got closer, I could finally hear what Leah had heard before: low, murmuring voices. The backyard came into view in the white light of the moon, a large lawn and a swimming pool encircled by old trees and surrounded by a low, white-painted fence.

We inched closer and stopped. Patches of conversation drifted our way.

"Listen, Phil, we can't just sit here. Even if we were safe, which we're not, we'll starve before long."

"But where can we go? Even if we were kids and had the strength, I wouldn't know where to go. The children are in Westchester, but how can we get to Westchester? There's a big river between us and them but there may not be a bridge..."

"Uncle Phil! Aunt Bessie!" Leah called out to them in a loud whisper.

There was a sound of chairs scraping against stone and several voices rang out.

"Who's there? Don't move. I've got a gun."

"Uncle Phil, don't worry! It's Linda and Roy." Leah, using our childhood names, called out across the darkness.

"What! Linda and Roy! Stand still a minute."

Seconds later, a light beam flashed in our eyes.

"It really is you. What on earth are you doing here? How did you get here?"

"First of all, Uncle Phil, thanks for not pulling the trigger!" I said. "Second, it's really wonderful to see you, and third, it's a long story."

He laughed and rushed up to hug me.

Aunt Bessie began to cry.

"We're so happy to see you," said Uncle Phil. "Come, sit down with us. These are the Frankels, our neighbors. We're all so frightened. We don't know what to do. We have no answers. The world we knew is gone."

Leah sat down next to Aunt Bessie and I took a chair across from Uncle Phil. The moonlight, reflecting off the pool, cast a rippling glow on our faces.

"We're alone," said Aunt Bessie, her voice trembling. "Our children are scattered. We're not starving yet, but we barely have any food. All our neighbors have fled, to the countryside I guess, and we're left here, about to die in our own homes."

The tears flowed again. Leah took Aunt Bessie's hand.

"Linda, Roy, how on earth did you just appear?" asked Uncle Phil. "Did you drop out of the sky?"

"Well," said Leah, we were at home Sunday when everything exploded. We had bicycles and supplies prepared and...."

"Don't tell me that you rode bicycles here," said Phil.

"Well, we actually did."

"What day is today?" asked Aunt Bessie.

"Today, tonight actually, is Thursday, July 9. The attacks were four nights ago."

"Who did it?"

"We really don't know any more than you do. I imagine it was the same people who were behind 9/11. We all knew that we'd hear from them again some day. Anyway, we packed our knapsacks, got on our bikes and headed west."

Leah began to recount our adventures. Everyone listened in silence punctuated by an occasional gasp or exclamation.

"That's our story up to now. Obviously the saga is continuing; in fact we have the feeling that we've got more dramatic moments to come. Roy has formulated a kind of general plan...."

She looked at me. "Do you want to continue?"

"Keep going, Leah. I'm enjoying lying here looking at the moon."

"OK. First, we want to head north, out of the metropolitan area, both for safety and because we think we'll find food in the countryside and farmlands. But also, we've got this dream, the age-old dream which we know you share, to return to Zion, to get back to Israel.

"All Jews live by dreams, right?

"It seems the day has passed when you could board a plane and arrive a few hours later in Israel. So what is one to do? In Biblical times, our ancestors stood at the shore of the Red Sea. Of course, there was no way across. But Nachshon went forward into the swirling waters, at which point G-d opened a pathway for us.

"Well, Roy wants to go up to New England. The same waters that wash the Maine shoreline touch the Land of Israel. Somehow, we think that...well, something will happen. We're hoping to find a way to cross the sea.

"We thought of you as we passed this way. We want you to come north with us," said Leah, "and if G-d will help us, we will all make it. But there's a unique part you could play that could save us all."

Uncle Phil, normally loquacious and animated, had listened in silence. Now he spoke.

"I have a million questions. But let's not beat around the bush. What's your idea? If you have a way to give us hope, we want to hear about it. No matter what, thank you for coming here and offering us hope. We had no idea there was anyone left in the world that we knew, let alone family. I think maybe you are angels from Heaven."

"Uncle Phil," I said, "we feel the same way about you. It's such a comfort to see family in this chaos. We've always loved you and Aunt Bessie and now that we're together it gives us hope too. Do you want to hear my idea?"

"Of course."

"First, a question. Have you been to your factory since the attacks?"

"What's the point? That world is gone. Business is over. That lifetime is in the past."

"Is there any candy in the factory?"

"Candy? It's loaded. It *is* a factory, after all."

"Do you have the key, Uncle Phil?

"Are you kidding? It's my place."

"Do you realize that an army could live on what's inside there?"

"I never really thought about it, but you're right. Sitting here trapped, it meant nothing to us, but it's true there's a lot of food there. And not just candy, either. There's plenty of dried fruit and nuts and bottled water too. We're a distributor for Glacier Springs Water and we have thousands of bottles in the building."

"Uncle Phil! You have water? And dried fruits and nuts? Those are vital foods. This could make the difference between life and death for all of us!"

"I've been a bottled water distributor for five years now; the dried fruit and nuts even longer. I guess all of it would be gone in an instant if people knew what was in there. But it's an old brick building covered with ivy. You can't even tell from the outside that it's a factory. There are no signs, just a number over the entrance. My employees, and there are just a few, live pretty far away. They couldn't have made it to the factory. And Seth, my manager, is...at least was...on vacation in California."

"Well, Uncle Phil, let me explain what we're thinking. I see your truck in the driveway. If there's fuel, we could all ride, along with our bikes, to the factory, then fill the truck with as much candy, fruit, nuts and water as possible and drive back to our group on the Garden State Parkway. Then we'll keep driving the truck northward for as long as it will last. When the fuel runs out, we can divide the food up so that each person and stroller and knapsack is loaded up. This could be just what we need to live on until we're in a place where we can replace it, like farmland, where there are clean lakes and springs, if anything in this world is still clean. You and the Frankels will come with us. You'll ride in the truck and we'll walk.

"What do you think?"

Aunt Bessie and Uncle Phil looked at each other. Her eyes were wide and moist. The fear was not gone, but she had a brightness that had not been there before. Uncle Phil, always the adventurer, was glowing.

"I'm ready," he said, "and all of us are with you one hundred percent. How far north are you planning to go?"

"We are aiming for the New England coastline, probably Maine. I want to be north of Boston. There are big boats up there. The entire world may be in flames, but Israel has always been our home. If we are going to die, then let us either die in Israel or trying to get there. Will you join us?"

"It's a fantastic idea," answered Uncle Phil. "I don't know if it will work, but I'm all for it. We don't have any other hope. Right, Bessie, Norma, Ed?"

Bessie nodded and so did the Frankels. I wasn't really surprised. It wasn't just the idea of trying to get to Israel, which they loved, but also the idea that there was hope, that they were not condemned to sit in their backyard until they died by the swimming pool.

"We're not young, Roy. You're a lot younger, but you're no kids either. One thing I'll tell you, though, is that no one, young or old, wants to die, and you can't live without hope. I guess we're in pretty good shape for old guys, so we're going to throw in our lot with you."

Phil rose to his feet and we embraced. He was fighting to keep the tears back. He and Bessie had lived in this house for over fifty years. They had started the business and raised their children here. A lot of memories floated within those walls.

"Let's not keep Linda and Roy waiting," said Uncle Phil. "Let's get whatever we need: raincoats, hats, you may even need a sweater for New England nights, medicine, whatever we can squeeze in a bag or knapsack. It's 12:07. Let's meet by the truck at 12:15. Eight minutes to pack up a lifetime!"

We watched the two couples disappear into their houses and then saw flashlight beams moving around inside. Leah and I settled back on the outdoor couches, looking up at the stars. At least they were still there! Far away toward the east, we could still see the glow of flames, but around us there was deep, thick darkness. Those very stars and moon had been around since the Creation, but the world under them was in turmoil.

We both lay there, silent and still, gazing upward. The universe rotating above us was no doubt oblivious to the perilous state of the earth that night. The course of the stars was unchanged. We were running in fear for our lives, but they were proceeding as ever in their assigned orbit, following the will of their Creator.

G-d was watching His children.

I felt calm now and eager to get to the factory. I dozed off for a few minutes. Before long, the two couples emerged from their houses, carrying backpacks and duffel bags. Truck doors opened and closed. Even that sound seemed loud, breaking the blanket of silence, a reminder of just how much our lives had changed in four days.

Aunt Bessie, Norma and Ed settled into folding chairs that Uncle Phil had placed in the back of the truck. Phil closed the doors and got into the front of the cab with Leah and me.

"How're you doing back there?" Phil called out. "Comfortable?"

"It's great back here," said Ed. "How long 'til we get to the picnic?"

"Ed," said Phil, "I'm glad you brought along your sense of humor. We may need it."

"I'm just hoping we're not the picnic," said Ed.

"Hush, Ed," said Norma.

Uncle Phil switched on the headlights and slowly backed out onto the deserted street.

THE CANDY FACTORY

Early Friday morning, July 10

UNCLE PHIL DROVE SLOWLY AND carefully through the deserted suburban streets. His LED headlights cut a crisp swath of white light directly in front of us, making the surroundings seem even darker. What lay in the shadows?

After about a quarter of an hour, we entered an industrial neighborhood. Here we began to see small groups of youths congregated at street corners, even though it was the middle of the night. In the orange glow of their cigarettes, I could see eyes staring in our direction. I immediately sensed hostility. We could be in real danger.

Uncle Phil brought the truck to an abrupt halt. He reached over and flipped open the glove compartment. In the dim light from the diode, I could see a gun. He grabbed it and a package of bullets, carefully loaded the gun and put it in his right jacket pocket.

"Just a little precaution," he said.

"Uncle Phil, you actually do have a gun. Leah and I must have had a pretty close call back there."

"Nah, I didn't have it on me then, though I should have. But this is for real. A Glock 9 mm. can make quite a statement."

I always knew Uncle Phil was tough, but I was impressed with this. He may have been a generation older than we were, but he knew how to take care of himself. He hadn't built his business from nothing by being meek.

Suddenly I saw movement in the darkness and the glow of cigarettes moving closer. Seconds later, a shadowy row of figures stood shoulder to shoulder, blocking our way. Phil flashed the lights but nobody moved. He rolled down his window a few inches.

"Excuse me fellas, I need to get through here."

"Get out of the truck, mister."

"I'm sorry," said Phil in an even tone. "I have to get through."

"This is OUR street. Open the door and get out."

Now I was officially worried. I reminded myself that, although we might be outnumbered, we were protected by several tons of heavy machinery, the blinding power of our halogen headlights and, of course, Uncle Phil's Glock. And, they probably couldn't see who was in the truck...a group of older Jews on the prowl for candy and nuts.

Phil turned to me and whispered.

"Roy, can you handle the gun?"

"What? No, not really."

"Well, I can't fire with my left hand and I can't get an angle with my right. Look, just hold the gun like this and pull the trigger. Fire one shot over their heads and then give me back the gun right away. And hold it tight, because that gun will jump when you fire."

Reluctantly, I took the gun from him. My hands were trembling and I swallowed hard. Leah said something but my brain couldn't process it.

"Oh G-d," I whispered, "please get us out of this alive."

Meanwhile Phil was calmly barking orders.

"Linda, please put your head down. Folks in the back, get off the chairs, sit on the floor and hold on. We may be in for a quick start."

Phil handed me the gun. Without wasting a moment, I opened the window and aimed at least fifteen feet off the ground. Then I took a deep breath, gritted my teeth and pulled the trigger.

BANG!

The gun packed quite a punch. It jumped and so did I. Then I practically threw the gun back to Phil.

Meanwhile, the "tough guys" were scattering into the shadows, shrieking and cursing. Phil jammed down on the accelerator. The truck leaped forward and the seats and bikes in the back fell over with a clatter. We left our unfriendly welcoming party in the dust.

Leah, who had covered her face, dropped her hands and exhaled in relief. From the back of the truck came a chorus of cheers. Phil laughed and began to sing "Over the Rainbow" at the top of his lungs.

My forehead was dripping with sweat and I was shaking. I could see Phil's face in the dashboard lights. He looked relaxed but fierce. I got the idea that you don't mess with Uncle Phil.

Our truck now was zooming through the streets at high speed, the headlights on high beam. No more creeping along for us. Whoever was in our path had better get out of the way.

Finally, we caromed around a corner, the truck screeching and squealing, and pulled up to a modest brick building. Phil slowly turned the truck in a circle, using the headlights to illuminate every corner of the street. It seemed completely deserted and ghostly quiet, the only sound being the growling of our engine.

We came to a stop at the roll-up gate that led to an inside loading platform. Phil aimed the headlights on the locks, felt in his pocket for the gun and then climbed out of the cab with his keys. I hopped out too and together we managed to roll up the metal doors so Phil could drive the truck inside. He shut off the motor and then we closed and locked the doors behind us. From the outside no one could tell we were there.

"We made it," I said with a combination of relief and excitement. I was pulsing with adrenalin. We had to work fast. Phil handed out flashlights, put a key in the forklift and turned it on. Minutes later we were loading cartons of candies, dried fruit, nuts and water bottles into the truck.

My spirits soared; I forgot how I tired I was. This was another present from Heaven. Precious water and chocolate, nuts and raisins, dried apricots, peaches, pears, apples, pineapples...and everything kosher! Such a treasure could sustain our group for weeks. It would be easy to divide among many individuals because everything was in small packages. An hour later, we had piled cartons to the top of the truck, leaving just enough room for us to fit in as well.

It struck me as amazing: amidst an apparent breakdown of the entire world, I realized that everything was operating with total precision, exactly the way G-d intended. That metronome was ticking.

"Wait a minute! I think we're entitled to a bonus today!"

Uncle Phil's voice boomed through the cavernous room. He gestured to a far corner where a U-Haul-style trailer stood. We pulled it over, hooked it to the back of the truck, and then loaded it to the top with our bicycles and even more cartons. At 3 a.m. we had finished, all of us dripping wet and exhausted, but exultant.

Phil passed around bottled water and candy; we took a three-minute break. Then he cracked open the street door and peeked outside. He grabbed a powerful flashlight and checked further. Still ghostly quiet. The sky was beginning to brighten a little; we needed to get back to the group before daybreak. We opened the gate as quietly as possible, backed the truck out, then rolled down and locked the gate behind us.

Phil paused to look at his factory for the last time. He had invested a lifetime building this business, which had sustained him and his family for decades. Now, I felt, the final fruition of his life-work would save his and dozens of other lives. Phil patted the side of the building and stood there a minute, saying something to the brick wall. Then he turned back to the truck, rubbing his eyes. As I said, inside Phil's tough exterior was a big heart.

Minutes later, we were zooming once more through the deserted streets, headed for the parkway. Once on the Garden State, Phil had to slow down to maneuver around the abandoned cars. All of us sat in silence as he weaved the little truck through the obstacle course. We had plenty to think about and plenty to thank G-d for. We kept the air conditioning off to preserve fuel, but the early morning air was pleasantly cool and refreshing.

As the sky brightened, I looked closely for signs that we were nearing our campsite. For hours, I hadn't had a moment to think about our group, but now I had time to wonder whether everyone was all right. I hoped they were resting peacefully and not worrying too much about us. It was Friday; tonight would be *Shabbos*. Ideally all of us could spend the next twenty four hours peacefully recuperating from an incredible week. But first we had to find each other.

I had, of course, noted the mile marker, and kept shining the flashlight out the window until Mile 146.7 appeared. Uncle

Phil slowed down. A moment later, Leah and I shouted in unison. There was the cemetery. The pink skies of the emerging dawn cast a rosy glow on the nearby woods. From the road, everything appeared peaceful. Of course, we couldn't see into the woods.

Uncle Phil made a u-turn across the median onto the northbound lanes (somehow, we weren't worried about getting stopped by the cops), then drove off into the woods as far as he could so the truck would be invisible from the road. Leah and I scrambled out first and started walking toward the camp.

As we got closer, I called out softly.

"*Shalom aleichem*. Hello everyone. Are you here? It's Yisroel and Leah. Hello?"

A few heads popped up.

"Hi Abba and Ima."

It was Ruchoma.

"Bubby! Zaydie!"

Little Shaindy and Devorala raced forward and hugged us. What a welcome sight.

Maybe the world will survive after all!

Everyone came up to us, excitedly asking questions about what had happened, if we'd found Uncle Phil and Aunt Bessie, if we had food. We gave a quick thumbs-up, but this was not the time for extended conversation. We had to welcome our new friends, unload the food, say morning prayers before the sun got too high, eat something and go to sleep. On *Shabbos*, there would be time to describe every detail.

Every Thursday, Rebbetzin Jungreis's Hungarian newspaper appears. I know she is anxious to read about all her old friends, but Mama operates with military discipline. During the week, she never stops moving. There are chickens to cook, countless trays of food to carry down the back stairs to the freezer, soup on the stove, endless responsibilities at the yeshiva.

Then there are the Russian immigrants stopping by to pick up old clothes. If you don't watch out, the suit jacket you had just slung over the dining room chair becomes the next hand-out to the Russians. Things happen very fast in Mama's house!

Then a delegation of rabbis comes to visit Zayda. Mama's Hungarian paper is lying on the side table, waiting for Shabbos. Friday night, after the dishes are put away and everyone else is asleep, Mama sits down and reads her Hungarian news. She never allows herself a moment...until Shabbos.

"We need to move quickly, get the truck into the woods and then unload the food and water. It's going to be another hot day and we don't want everything ending up as a mountain of goo."

Leah and I returned to the truck. I sensed that our new foursome were feeling anxious, realizing with a shock that they had left everything behind and nothing ever would be the same.

"Hi folks. Everyone's eager to meet you. Let's see if we can get the truck further into the woods and we'll introduce everyone. Then we can get some sleep."

"Okay, Roy," said Uncle Phil. "But are you sure your group wants us over-the-hill fogies?"

"Uncle Phil, you have saved us all. You and Aunt Bessie and the Frankels are part of our Exodus. May we survive and prosper together! We are one family."

"You know," said Phil, "I'm glad we're here. We're very grateful to you."

"It works both ways, Phil. That's what it's all about. We're saving each other.

"Tonight is *Shabbos*. We'll light candles in the woods, and our *Shabbos* meals will consist of candy, dried fruit and nuts, but we will keep *Shabbos* and *Shabbos* will keep us. If G-d will continue to have mercy on us, we may yet travel onward to the Holy Land and witness the Redemption we've been awaiting for thousands of years."

As we moved the truck over the forest floor, I found myself dreaming about a shower. I was hot and sticky but I knew that I'd have to wait a long, long time. Our clothes were sticking to us, our bodies were layered with grime and this was just the beginning!

I am a kid at the City Athletic Club. Every Sunday morning, you get to go with your father to the Club. I stand under the shower in the big marble-walled enclosure. Those special shower-heads seem to release a soft version of Niagara Falls on you, endless streams of hot water, falling from the top and shooting from the side, delicious on the skin. And that piney green soap, with just a hint of grit in it: you feel as if it is scrubbing all the impurities out of your body. The steam envelopes me and fogs up the shower door. I could stand here forever! On the wall are shampoo dispensers and scented oil, and piled outside are the world's thickest towels.

But we were in the woods, perspiring under a July sun on the Garden State Parkway! Although *Shabbos* was coming, we couldn't wash or change our clothes. No *Shabbos* suit, no *Shabbos* table, very little wine, and no fish or meat.

Every Friday, I enjoy a custom learned from my good friend Avram Gross. Avram was a tzaddik, a holy person. Once I had stopped by on a Friday afternoon. He invited me to sit down. He poured out an ounce or two from an old bottle of bourbon and made a l'chayim. With that taste, I began to feel the weekday load lifting off my shoulders and the restful peace of Shabbos enter my life.

I expand on Avram's custom. Every Friday afternoon, just when Leah's aromatic chicken emerges from the oven, I am awarded the job of checking to make sure it comes out right. Needless to say, I have no objections. That chicken and my own l'chayim always succeed in bringing on the Shabbos mood. I feel my soul expanding, shedding the chains shackling me to the temporal world and its troubles.

But I wasn't at home. I was in the woods by the Garden State Parkway. Actually, even without the chicken and the *l'chayim*, a feeling of peace began to wash over me. *Shabbos* was only a few hours away. Even in a shattered world, running for my life, I could feel *Shabbos* coming. *Shabbos* is woven into the fabric of Creation.

With the truck parked securely in the woods, I pulled out my *tallis* and *tefillin* and joined the other men in morning prayers. Meanwhile, the women started unloading and distributing the food. Whatever couldn't be carried was left in the truck, which was parked under thick pine trees with the hope of keeping it as cool as possible. The food was wrapped up tightly for protection from animals and bugs. We needed to be extremely vigilant; this was our means of survival.

After praying, I took off my *tallis* and *tefillin* and lay back on the grass. Despite the forest cover, the air was heavy and thick. Noise and activity swirled around me, danger lurked everywhere and I had plenty of worries to occupy my brain. But the knowledge that *Shabbos* was approaching and that we had a truckload of food and water lessened the grip of temporal concerns. G-d was around as always. Somehow right now He seemed a little closer.

I slept very well.

SHABBOS AT MILEPOST 146.7

Friday afternoon, July 10

TONIGHT WOULD BE THE FIRST *Shabbos* of our "Exodus," the first *Shabbos* since explosions had rocked the world the previous Sunday. This *Shabbos* was important not just for itself, but also for our group to recuperate from this week and to gain strength for what lay ahead.

Shabbos in the wilderness, or shall we say the "wildness."

We were running low on wine and matzos; there was just enough for a hint of each, hardly enough to taste. But we were alive, and the candy bars had a way of tasting very good. And then, we had our dreams and our hopes. Someday, we would be in our own homes once again, with an abundance of food to sustain us. We were upbeat, reflecting the consciousness that we were part of a new Exodus, that we hoped would lead to our final and complete redemption.

I'm driving on Queens Boulevard. There are a dozen cell phone calls to make, but not today. It's Friday afternoon, not

Wednesday or Thursday.

Organize your mind, Yisroel.

First, my precious CD of Rabbi Mordechai Listman singing "Lecha Dodi" to his own beautiful melody. Ahhh, now I know Shabbos is coming.

I must start thinking about this week's Torah portion. Where's my yellow pad? Leah will be angry if I take notes while I'm driving, so I have to wait for the red lights. (That's another reason to drive on Queens Boulevard; at least there are red lights! Who else ever liked red lights before?)

This week's portion is Teruma, which describes the Tabernacle in the Desert. Now I want to understand something. Why does the Priest enter from the east and go west toward the Holy of Holies? Why isn't it set up from north to south, or west to east for that matter? Let's see: the sun appears to move from east to west, so that means that the earth is really spinning from west to east....

I arrive at home with a "drasha" for the Shabbos table. This has been such a satisfying ride, the best of the week. At home I am greeted by a delicious aroma. Leah is cooking and baking beautiful foods in honor of Shabbos. Now I get to check out that chicken. Considering I've hardly eaten all day, I deserve it, right? In any case, the chicken and the l'chayim are waiting for me.

What else is cooking, by the way? The challah is warming, garlic bread, about twelve different salads, the famous chicken-with-onions-and-gravy, strawberry-blueberry pie... this is unbelievable! The cholent smells incredible this week!

"Leah, I get to eat this, right?"

But first my jobs: I set up the Shabbos candles so they will be ready for Leah to light right before Shabbos. Then I dial the "Eruv Hotline." Is the Eruv up this week?[25] I unscrew the refrigerator lights so that opening the door will not turn them on. Is wine chilling for Kiddush? That chandelier bulb needs to be changed. Up the ladder. Ahhh, now it's time for the chicken and the l'chayim!

Wow! Unbelievable!

"Leah, you outdid yourself this week!"

The doorbell.

"Mordechai and Pinchas, welcome! So glad you could come for Shabbos! Leah, where are Mordechai and Pinchas staying? Ruchoma's room? OK guys, follow me. Do you need a shower first? Here are some towels. How about a little chicken before Shabbos? Yes? OK, please sit down.

"It's great, right? Finished? OK, follow me upstairs. We'll go to shul in about forty-five minutes. Have a great shower!"

Now a shower for me. The warm water is a mechaya!

"Thank you G-d for the warm water."

Shabbos suit, Shabbos shoes. Are they shined? OK, they need a touch-up.

"Thank you G-d, for the clothes. The Shabbos clothes themselves make me feel that I am beginning to be elevated to stand in Your presence."

Shirt, gold cufflinks....

"Leah, does this tie go with the suit? No? How about this one? Still no? OK, you tell me... what works? Now I'm OK? Thank you! See you! Good Shabbos! We're off to Shul...."

Here, at Milepost 146.7, *Shabbos* was going to have to be very spiritual, because we basically had nothing physical. We had candy bars, dried fruit, nuts and water.

I woke up in the early afternoon, just in time to help make the *"eruv."*

An *eruv* is the equivalent in Jewish law of a wall around a given area that simulates an enclosed domain. One plants stakes in the ground, attaching string to the top of the stakes. The area enclosed by the string became our *Shabbos* "home." An *eruv* would allow us to carry objects within the area bounded by the string, to pick up babies and food and whatever else we would have been able to carry inside our own homes. Having thought about this necessity before they left, some of the men in our group had brought along wooden stakes and string for just this purpose. We climbed on each other's shoulders, banged stakes into the ground, then connected the stakes with the string.

It might seem illogical to focus on an *eruv* when we were fleeing for our lives. But this was how the Children of Israel had survived over the ages. Others may have worried about their powerful enemies, but we focused on adhering to our G-d-given commandments. In the end, G-d rewarded our adherence to His laws by protecting us against those enemies. This is how we would face the future. So we constructed an *eruv* next to the Garden State Parkway in the twilight of the world, and we knew that *eruv* would protect us, acting as a spiritual wall separating us from the burning world around us.

As darkness fell, the women asked Leah to represent them all and light the two candles that had been placed on a tree stump in the middle of the camp. We would need to ration our few candles. These two would have to suffice.

Leah looked over at me just before she lit the candles. The prayers at candle-lighting time are very deep. They rise upward with the flames. I knew Leah's great heart was full and that she was conscious of the responsibility of kindling the *Shabbos* lights for all of us. The flames flickered gently in the breeze, a beacon in the deepening darkness. Tears flowed.

Then, the men went over to one side and Menachem Green led us in "*L'chu n'ranena*," the beginning of the psalms which usher in the holy *Shabbos*.

He choked on the words; his voice broke.

"Come, let us sing to G-d, let us call out to the Rock of our

salvation.... Let us prostrate ourselves and bow, let us kneel before G-d, our Maker. For He is our G-d and we can be the flock He pastures, and the sheep in His charge, even today, if we but heed His call."[26]

Shabbos was calming me. Here we were, with no roof over our heads, alone in a burning world. We had no idea where we would be tomorrow or next week, or "who would live and who would die,"[27] who would threaten us or perhaps even help us. Still, we were singing to G-d and welcoming the Holy Sabbath.

That was the only way we could survive.

As soon as we started to sing *"L'cha Dodi,"* the song welcoming the Sabbath Queen, the peace of *Shabbos* settled upon us, a sense of peace that could not be nullified by our physical surroundings. G-d's closeness enveloped us, as if He were nearer than He had been...or maybe we were nearer to Him.

The darkening sky now seemed brighter. You couldn't see it if you weren't accepting *Shabbos*, but it was as if the darkness had light in it. The world brightens up and it's not really physical but you see it; you feel the angels surrounding you. You're not alone; the dark forces have been brought under the control of a Higher Power.

Friday afternoon is sometimes frenetic. Today I just can't do anything right. Finally, every job completed, I jump into the shower and then into my Shabbos clothes. "Oops! This suit has a stain!" I change to another suit and jump into the car. (Driving to the synagogue just before Shabbos saves a few minutes. Saturday night I drive the car home.)

I back out of the driveway. "Whack!" The sound of breaking glass.

Why is that car parked directly across from my driveway on such a narrow street! I am so upset. I jump out, place my busi-

ness card on the other car's windshield, and then take off. I am so agitated that I can hardly pray.

Then we say "L'cha Dodi."

Shabbos enters the world.

Against my will, against my own anger, Shabbos picks me up and deposits my soul in a new place. I know that I have just hit a car, but that knowledge recedes in importance. My soul has been transported beyond this world, beyond damage, beyond pain.

We said prayers by memory because there was no light to read by...and there weren't too many prayer books either. Those who could remember the prayers led the rest.

Then we sang *"Shalom Aleichem"* to welcome the *Shabbos* angels. I felt the presence of those angels as our voices greeted them.

Every Friday night, a good angel and a bad angel accompany each man home from prayers. The angels look inside the house. If it is glowing with *Shabbos* candles, the good angel gives a blessing that the house should be like this the following week, and the bad angel must say "amen." If Shabbos lights are not shining, the bad angel "blesses" the house that it should remain dark next week and the good angel must say "amen."[28]

That night, we welcomed the angels to Milepost 146.7. The glow from those two little candles on the tree stump seemed to penetrate every corner of our camp. For all our extra effort in keeping the *mitzvos*, I felt the angels were giving us extra blessing, perhaps not simply that we should keep *Shabbos* next week, but that we should soon see the day that is "eternal *Shabbos*."

We sang *"Aishes Chayil,"* honoring the Jewish wife and mother.

"Beyond pearls is her value; her husband's heart relies on her....Her children arise and praise her."[29] How much had our wives taken upon themselves, not simply transforming this wooded grove into a dwelling into which we could invite the *Shabbos* angels, but having created the homes we had so much enjoyed in days past.

The group asked me to make *Kiddush* on everyone's behalf, just as Leah had lit the candles. "Blessed are You, our G-d, King of the universe, Who sanctified us with His commandments, took pleasure in us, and with love and favor gave us His holy Sabbath as a heritage, a remembrance of creation." My hand trembled as I said those words. Everyone answered "amen." Someone had remembered to bring a few little bottles of wine; we all had a sip. Then we made the blessing on bread, passing a few crumbs of matzoh around for everyone to eat. I wondered if we would ever again sit at a real table, tasting sweet wine and warm, soft challah.

Actually, the candy bars tasted excellent. But on *Shabbos* everything tastes excellent. After the meal, with its songs and blessings, and some quiet conversation, we all found our spot and lay down under the trees. Tonight, instead of hiking up the Garden State Parkway, we would be sleeping. A normal night! I looked up at the stars shining through the leaves. Since I had slept during the afternoon, I wasn't very tired, so I lay there for a long time, thinking. Gradually the sound of voices faded away. The night became quiet except for the chirp of the summer cicadas. Summer-night noises still existed, even after July 5.

I imagined that some of our group were sleeping and others were probably awake thinking, like me. It had been six days since we had begun our journey. So much had happened; I started to relive some of our adventures.

After a while, I fell asleep.

I am running with a wind blowing at my back. The wind is howling, pushing me forward. I look over my shoulder and see a tornado gaining on me. I can't run fast enough. Then I hear a sound like a mountain exploding.

Still running, I see a wall of fire ahead. I try to retreat, but I can't stop; the black wind keeps pushing me. I am running in front of the wind, but the wind picks me up. I feel the intense heat of the fire in front of me. My heart is racing. My skin feels as if it is peeling and burning, but I cannot stop. The wind is lifting me into the fire.

I am going to die.

The wind is throwing me into the fire.

I AM IN THE FIRE.

But, somehow, I am still alive.

The fire is not burning me.

The fire is warm.

The fire is comforting me.

The fire is warming my soul and my body.

I am alive!

Then, a powerful thrust propels me through the fire. Suddenly before me is the Land of Israel. A spring garden in full bloom, alive with color, filled with parents and children, streaming upwards to Jerusalem. I look around. My family is with me, our children and grandchildren. I am home. We are all home.

I opened my eyes. I was lying on the ground under the trees next to the Garden State Parkway. The sun was shining. It was *Shabbos* and we were still in America.

At that moment I knew I would not let go of the dream.

"When G-d will return the captivity of Zion, we will be like dreamers."[30]

All other dreams fade in the morning light, but when the Children of Israel return to Zion, then the reality will be perfect, just like the dream!

I looked at my watch. It was 7:30, time to pray. Putting on my shoes, I told Leah briefly about my dream. She smiled. It was a good dream. G-d was watching over us.

We men stood there in the woods, with *talleisim* over our heads, facing towards Israel and the rising sun. Shlomo Jacobson had brought a small Torah scroll in his knapsack. Like the Children of Israel throughout our long exile, we were carrying the Torah with us, to guide and protect us.

"Shema Yisroel, Hashem Elokainu, Hashem Echad."

"Hear, Israel, the L-rd our G-d, the L-rd is One."

I stood next to Jeff Klein during our prayers and explained everything to him. We found a prayer book with English and I tried not to overwhelm him with details.

"You know, Yisroel," he told me, "I never did this before. I always thought prayer was some irrelevant canned words some guy wrote, and I didn't want to say his canned words. Now when I look at this, I find that these are really MY thoughts, just expressed better than I could express them. This book enunciates what I want to say to G-d. And to be honest, I really do want to talk to G-d right now. I've got a lot to discuss with Him."

It is a cold night in January, two and a half years after our marriage. We are students at the University of Michigan, living in Ann Arbor. I am sitting on the old green couch with the stuffing coming out. It's 2 a.m. and I am crying. The marriage is falling apart. I am not stable enough to play the role of a husband. I don't know how to fix it; I am trapped inside the maze of my own mind. I have tried everything. I imagine my life as a long corridor, with hundreds of doors opening off it. I have opened every door, and every door leads nowhere. There are no answers; there is no peace in this world; there is no truth; no right way of life. Nothing I do succeeds! I am going to die; my brain is exploding. I am overcome with despair. Our marriage is on fire; my school career is blowing up; all my dreams are over. Will I be condemned to wander alone through life, an outcast and bitter failure? Will I wind up in an institution, banging on my cell walls until my demented existence flutters away?

Hopeless and depressed, I cry bitter tears. Falling through space, like Alice plunging through the rabbit hole, something brushes against my face in the dark, like a feather floating by. It isn't a feather, but a thought.

"No, it can't be. Impossible. No, I can't believe that. Roy Neuberger can't believe in G-d! But, wait…. The alternative is death. Can it be?

"CAN THERE BE A G-D?"

All my life I have never even considered the possibility that G-d exists. I, Roy Neuberger, a sophisticated citizen of the Twentieth Century, a product of the upper classes of society, educated in the finest schools. I know how to think for myself. I would like you to tell me where G-d is! What a joke! In the Dark Ages, of course people believed in G-d, because they were so ignorant. They couldn't read or write; they thought the earth was flat. They were peasants. But we are the most sophisticated society in the history of the world. We have conquered nature. We don't believe in G-d. We can peer to the ends of the universe, and we have not found G-d. So you expect me to believe in G-d?

Good! Logical!

You idiot! What good is logic if your marriage is falling apart? What good are your brilliant thoughts if your life is a failure?

"G-D, I'M SORRY! I NEED YOU! PLEASE HELP ME! I DON'T UNDERSTAND YOU, BUT I NEED YOU! I CAN'T SURVIVE BY MYSELF! I'M PETRIFIED! MY LIFE IS FALLING APART! PLEASE

SAVE ME! ARE YOU THERE? HELP ME!!!

Then I really break down; a river of tears pours out of my eyes, but these are tears of relief! All of a sudden, I realize that I can cry out to G-d. I have no idea Who He is, but I know I need Him; I know I can't survive without Him. This is the greatest relief in my entire life! All those years of agony, which I myself did not understand and could not explain, pour out of me. All those sessions with the shrink, all those conferences with the camp directors, the teachers, all those hopeless attempts to explain what I was feeling, all those moments of berating myself for believing that there WAS something wrong — all that pours out.

I go to wash my face, and I look in the bathroom mirror. Who is that staring back at me?

It isn't my face! I should be petrified, but it is a shining face, clear like the face of an angel! Who is it? Who is here with me?

I believe that an angel has come to me in Ann Arbor, Michigan. An angel has come to save me. When I didn't even realize it, I must have uttered a microscopic prayer, so tiny that even I had not been aware of. But G-d heard it, and He sent an angel to save me!

Jeff was speaking.

"Yisroel, the concept of talking to G-d is mind-boggling. It always seemed to me that we were all at the mercy of forces beyond our control, like robotic pawns in a huge chess game. Now, I find out that I can actually speak to the One Who is moving the pieces on the chess board. Actually He made the pieces. In fact He made the chess board! I really do feel as if I am speaking to Him! It's wild, but there's an emotional bond, a sense of reality to this!"

Our son-in-law Dovid was leading the prayers. His clear voice rose through the treetops with a purity that brought tears to my eyes.

"God save us! Bring us back to our Holy Land. It will take a miracle, millions of miracles. Whatever it takes, Almighty G-d, please save us! *Ana Hashem hoshia na!*"

Suddenly, I began to tremble. I pulled my *tallis* around my head and broke down. I was shaking. I saw the faces of our grandchildren, innocent children who believed in G-d with complete devotion, children without a trace of corruption. Tears poured down my face.

I walked off alone to a spot in the woods where the trees were bunched closely together. The group had asked me to speak before the *Mussaf* service and I needed a few minutes to clear my head. It was important that I find something in that week's Torah portion which would focus on our situation. It had to be real.

A few minutes later, I returned to the group. Everyone was very still. I wiped off my face and took a deep breath.

"In this week's portion, *Pinchas*,[31] the Children of Israel face a crisis in the Desert. Can you imagine? Moses was our leader; we should have been perfect then. And yet, we came close to destroying ourselves, so tempted were we by the material desires that destroy other nations. This foreshadowed our future troubles thousands of years later in Exile.

"The Children of Israel are eternal because we stay connected to the Eternal by living His Torah. Only when we lose sight of our eternal mission do we become subject to destruction.

"Our leaders were paralyzed, but Pinchas somehow was able to act. He killed Zimri ben Salu, prince of the tribe of Shimon, whose personal passion put him directly at odds with the Torah and the authority of Moses, whom G-d had appointed as our leader. If Zimri hadn't been stopped, the entire structure of the Nation of Israel would have collapsed.

"It's against the nature of a Jew to kill. It is, however,

obligatory to kill someone who is threatening to kill you. Under such circumstances, the Torah requires us to go against our nature.

"The Torah commands us to do many things that go against our nature. Giving charity is against most people's nature. Here are some other commandments that are often difficult: honoring a parent, not hating another person, not desiring someone else's property. Many commandments directly challenge our nature. I will give you a personal example: last night, in Petersonville, I fired a gun for the first time in my life. I intentionally aimed high, but I was aiming at people!

"My dear brothers and sisters, just like our Biblical ancestors, we are traveling together in a wasteland, surrounded by danger. Like them, we are traveling toward the Holy Land, although we are thousands of miles away. G-d should spare us, but I can't imagine it's going to be a smooth ride. We will have tests, probably hard tests. Let's remember Pinchas. His zealousness in devotion to Torah saved the Children of Israel. Our zealousness in devotion to Torah will save us. It may seem very difficult now, but this is the darkness before the dawn. As King David said, "When the wicked bloom like grass and all the doers of iniquity blossom, it is to destroy them until eternity."[32]

I stopped and took a breath. A moment passed and then I remembered something else.

"I'd like to add one thought. My wife and I started off from Long Island. We were blessed to meet this beautiful group at a place we have called Reunion Park. A little later in our sojournings, we met Jeff and Marge and Julie. And then, yesterday, Uncle Phil and Aunt Bessie and Ed and Norma Frankel joined us.

"These are all great people. I personally am so happy to

have them with us. They have added so much to our group already. It was Uncle Phil's gun that I fired last night. That gun saved us. Uncle Phil's candy factory is feeding us! May all of us together always be one family, and in our unity may G-d watch over us and bring us home in peace!"

"Good *Shabbos!*"

After prayers, we made *Kiddush* and sipped the wine. Again, we ate a few crumbs of matzoh. In honor of *Shabbos* we allowed ourselves a special treat of dried fruit and nuts. The day continued with relaxation, afternoon services, another small meal and, at darkness, the evening services. Afterwards, we lit the torch — in this case, two matches held together — that signifies the end of *Shabbos* and the beginning of a new week.

CONFRONTATION

Saturday night, July 11

THE DARKNESS DEEPENED. *SHABBOS* WAS over. It was time to pack our belongings and continue our northward trek. I could still feel the lingering glow of *Shabbos* as our group began to assemble on the parkway. The evening was clear; already we could see stars twinkling across the sky.

Leah stood next to me, unusually silent as she gazed into the distance, seemingly oblivious to the bustle of activity around her, with mothers strapping their children into strollers, fathers packing up knapsacks, children playing tag among the towering trees.

"Leah, is anything wrong?"

"I don't know...it's probably nothing. I just feel a little creepy tonight. Maybe I just miss *Shabbos.*"

Leah has good antennae. I got a little chill. In these times, of course, it probably made sense to anticipate trouble rather than tranquility. At any rate, there was nothing to be done at that moment.

Our routine was that the families should walk up front,

and the truck would follow. That way, the truck wouldn't leave us behind in the dark. Also, anyone who was feeling weak could hop on and be carried. At that point we still had a good supply of hydrogen fuel on board.

Aunt Bessie and the Frankels climbed into the truck, which Uncle Phil drove at a deliberately slow speed, not only to keep pace with the walkers, but also because the darkness made it difficult to maneuver around abandoned cars. We kept the headlights off, although we occasionally needed flashlights. We didn't want to attract attention. There was still some light in the eastern sky from the glow of what must have been flames.

I am twelve years old, sitting in that little chair at the shrink's office. It isn't really an office, but an apartment in a fancy Upper-East-Side building, with a doorman and an elevator man. I am sure that everyone there knows I am going to the shrink. It is so embarrassing. My appointment is at 7:45 pm, twice a week. I always have to miss the end of "Highway Patrol"! It starts at 7, but I can never see the ending because I always have to get the bus to Dr. Glumb's office. I never tell Jimmy or the maid or cook where I am going, but of course everybody knows that I am going to the psychiatrist.

Why am I going anyway? What's my problem? It's that nameless fear. Mother can understand, because she is sensitive and introspective. I believe that we communicate so well because she has the same fears; perhaps I inherited them from her. She is a child of the "Salant" dynasty of Lithuanian Jewry, famous for its sensitivity to moral issues. Mother's father was born in Salant, and, although the family completely shed our Jewish lifestyle upon coming to America, we retain the character traits of our forebears. Perhaps these questions bother the Salant family precisely because we have shed our Jewish life-

*style; we still have the questions but we have forgotten the an-
swers. The answer for me lies in the future. In the meantime, I
have to grapple with the problems using the insufficient tools I
possess.*

*Dr. Glumb is an old French lady, an eminent child psychia-
trist. Unmarried, her gray hair tightly bound in a bun, she hardly
says a word. The loudest sound in that little room is her pen
scratching endlessly on sheet after sheet of plain white paper.
What on earth is she writing? Am I a study for a psychiatric jour-
nal?*

*She wants me to tell her all my dreams, and whatever else
is bothering me. I talk; she listens. This goes on for five years.
By that time I have met Leah in high school and it looks as if
my life is becoming normal, whatever that means. So I am "dis-
charged" or whatever you call it. Case closed. I am very excited.
It is wonderful to be "normal." I am now officially free of fear.
There are no more problems.*

*That's on the outside. On the inside, I know the truth. All
those years of pad-scratching mean nothing. I'm afraid exactly
the same way, but I have driven the fear deep inside me, buried
under layers of pretense. It emerges years later like a subterra-
nean nuclear explosion when our marriage nearly collapses.
Dr. Glumb knows nothing more of my soul than the doorman
who ushers me into her apartment building.*

*This is very frightening: you go through life pretending that
you are normal, happy and "well balanced." But inside you are
petrified. What are you afraid of? What is wrong, Roy? What is
bothering your soul? Do you know? Of course you don't. If you
knew, then you could fix it. But you don't even know what
questions to ask. Your soul is sick. You try to ignore it, but you
can't. Maybe that's why you are afraid: you are running from
the truth but you can't run fast enough.*

"The only thing we have to fear is fear itself" touched upon

something, but it's more than that. The only thing we have to fear is running away from G-d. Deep within our soul we know that there is no life without G-d.

I am a summer ranger at Great Smoky Mountains National Park. It's my day off. Leah and I go for a drive. I try to break up a "bear-jam"on the road, but I forget that I am out of uniform. The bear doesn't "realize" that I am a ranger. (Silly bear. Silly me!) What does the bear do? What do bears usually do? They chase people! Leah screams! I am able to put the hood of my car between me and the bear. That's the only reason I escape.

What a fool I am, playing with my life! It's not just the bear I'm running from!

Leah gripped my arm and brought me back to reality.

It was 2 a.m. and we had walked seven miles. A half moon was perched in the eastern sky, casting a pale glow. We were near the back of the group, next to the truck. We were trying to help the Horowitzs with their stroller; the brake was rubbing against a wheel.

There was a commotion several hundred feet ahead of us. Shouts filled the air and suddenly a bright light illuminated the group. Someone spoke in a loud voice.

"Jews! Excellent. We have been looking for you. Such a nice large group. So many beautiful Jewish families."

Loud sarcastic laughter.

Another light flashed on near the first one. Then we heard a different voice. "This is the end of the line, Jews. It's a new world. You're not in charge any more, you and your friends. You tried to run things for thousands of years and you lied about us. But now it's over. We're in charge."

A feeling of dread swept over me. I looked at Leah. My mind raced.

Master of the World, You've saved Your people since the

beginning of time, even when the sword was poised over our necks. Please save us now.

Bang!

A gunshot screamed through the darkness.

"That's so you know we mean business. Now get over here. All of you."

A baby started to cry. There was a rumble of voices, but no one moved.

At our right was an exit ramp. Suddenly, an idea flashed in my head. I grabbed Leah's hand; we moved quietly to the truck. I clicked open the passenger door and we silently climbed aboard. Uncle Phil was behind the wheel, looking ahead intently.

"Phil, keep your lights off; don't gun the engine. See that exit over to the right? Let's just get off the Parkway."

"What do you want to do?"

As he spoke, the truck was already moving up the exit ramp marked "New Jersey Route 3, Eastbound."

"Phil, do you know this area?"

"Whaddya think," he growled. "I've lived here my whole life."

"Okay. Let's speed up now. They won't hear us. Can we make a U-turn on Route 3 and get to the northbound entrance ramp to the Parkway?"

"Yeah, you can."

"OK. Then we'll get back on the Parkway and then do a 180 degree left so that we're going the wrong way southbound on the northbound lanes. We'll come down behind them from the rear, driving without lights. Hopefully they won't know we're there. But everything quietly."

"O.K. Then what?"

"Where's your gun?"

"You think I threw it away?"

"Are you ready to use it?"

Leah looked at me intently, and then at Phil. I wasn't sure if she would approve of my plan, but this was no time for discussion.

"I've never fired it directly at a person. But I will if I have to. It's us or them. Believe me, I'm not giving in to those sub-humans. Bessie and I have a few good years left."

He looked around at her and she smiled wanly. They had been through so much together: the death of a child, building the business from nothing, serious illness. Phil was tough, for sure, and Bessie was always by his side, no matter what.

We reached the northbound ramp, moving quickly and silently in the darkness. Phil slowed and made the 180-degree turn. Moments later we were in the tunnel under the Route 3 overpass. The truck was a hundred feet behind the gunmen, hidden in total darkness.

Looking through the window, I could see three figures silhouetted against the sky, waving rifles. Our people were seated on the ground and the three were running around, trying to make everyone sit closer together.

"Jews, say your prayers!" one of them bellowed. "You have two minutes to live."

I told myself not to panic, just concentrate.

"Phil," I whispered, "do you want to give me the gun or do you want to take it? We have to kill them. There's no other way. One of us gets on the ground and crawls up behind the middle guy; I think he's the leader. Maybe fifteen feet from him we fire at his back. It's a bigger target than his head. As soon as he's hit — with G-d's help — the truck heads for the guy on the right. I'm hoping our people in front will tackle the guy on the left. What do you think?"

At that moment we heard shrieking. It was Ayelet Gruenstein.

"What will you achieve from this? It will do you no good. Soon *Mashiach* will come and then you'll wish you had treated us well."

"Quiet! Stop talking or you'll regret it."

Someone jumped up and started to run into the darkness. A light flashed on and then a shot rang out.

"Ay! No!"

I saw him fall, but I couldn't see who it was.

"Gershon!" screamed Basya Horowitz.

We had just been fixing their stroller! I groaned and Leah began to weep.

"Leave him there to die. That's what happens to anyone who moves."

"Let us take care of him," cried out Devorah Lyons.

"What good would that do? Soon you'll all be very quiet. Now shut up!"

"I represent our group," said Shlomo Jacobson, his deep voice resonating with authority. "Who is the leader here? I want to speak to you."

"Shut up and sit down, Jew. We don't want to speak to you and we don't want to hear you. Understand? You Jews talk too much."

Phil had seen enough.

"Roy, you take the gun and go up there," he whispered. "You're younger than I am. I'll go for the right-side guy with the truck as soon as you fire. There's eight rounds in there. Squeeze the trigger firmly. Don't hesitate. Now, everyone out of the truck, but very quietly. Just stay under the bridge."

Leah squeezed my arm and disappeared into the darkness.

I took the gun in my hand, the second time in two days. But this time was for keeps. My entire being rebelled; I didn't want to kill anyone. Would it stain my soul? Then I thought about King David. He fought the enemies of Israel to sanctify the Name of G-d and save his people. And King David's son, Solomon, said there is a time to kill.

Ribono shel Olam, Master of the Universe, please make my intentions right and my aim accurate. Let me act for Your sake and for no other reason, but let me get the job done.

I slid out of the truck and lay on the ground. Then, I crawled forward, the gun in my right hand. I was in the grass just on the edge of the median, keeping low and moving quietly, about fifty feet behind the leader. He was just under six feet tall, wearing an Arab head-dress and holding a rifle against his shoulder. On the right, a guy was running around shining a light on all the families, making sure everyone stayed in place.

Someone, I assumed Gershon Horowitz, was moaning to my right.

Then, I heard Shmuli's voice from the center of the crowd.

"Sir, don't you know that G-d is watching you. You may think you can do what you want, but G-d is in control of the world and you will be called to account. Let us go and...."

"Shut up! Shut up! Who is that? Ahmed, find who was speaking!"

Ahmed went into the crowd looking for Shmuli. As he did, I quickly crawled forward. Now I was about fifteen feet behind the leader, to his right, hidden in the darkness. I could see him silhouetted against the moon. He watched intently as Ahmed searched the crowd.

It was time.

I raised myself on two elbows and held the gun with both hands. I sighted very carefully and aimed for the middle of his back.

G-d help me.

He stood in the moonlight, motionless.

I carefully squeezed the trigger.

BANG!

He fell straight forward and hit the ground.

I jumped to my feet, ran forward and shot him again, in the head. I didn't think about it, I just did it. Meanwhile, some of our guys grabbed the guy on the right, just as he spun around to look. Ahmed was jumped from behind, also by some young, strong guys.

The truck was roaring forward, but we didn't need it. I signaled Phil to stop. It was all over.

"Is anyone hurt?" I yelled into the crowd.

"We're OK, but Gershon Horowitz was shot! He's over there on the ground."

"I can help him. I'm a doctor."

The voice was right behind me. I turned around and saw Jeff Klein.

"You're a doctor?"

I had never even asked his profession.

"Yes, please give me a light."

We gave him a flashlight and he ran towards Gershon, the rest of us following him. Gershon was lying on the ground, moaning.

Jeff Klein looked as though he knew exactly what to do. He cut away Gershon's shirt and examined him. Blood was everywhere. Gershon moaned.

"I know it hurts," said Jeff. "I'm sorry. Please hold still for a minute."

Turning to the crowd, Jeff asked for a white shirt and antiseptic. In seconds, Devorah Lyons brought over a white shirt.

"I need light," said Jeff. People grabbed one of the Arabs' lanterns; instantly the scene was brightly illuminated.

I didn't like the way Gershon looked. He was gray. He was shivering, but it was a warm night. That wasn't good.

"I think everyone should stand way back from here," I said.

People moved away. Women were sobbing; Basya Horowitz was heaving with emotion. Ayelet Gruenstein was embracing her. Both were crying.

Meanwhile, a half-dozen guys were tying up Ahmed and the other man in their own robes, so tightly they couldn't move. They had taken their weapons. Somebody was shining a light on the leader's face. They checked his pulse. He was dead.

A hush fell over the group while Jeff worked. Shlomo Jacobson, who had been a Hatzalah volunteer in Lakeville, was assisting Jeff. It was all very quiet.

Everyone seemed to be holding his or her breath; people were praying, some in groups and some individually. A group of women started saying psalms. You could feel the ripples of prayer going upwards the way you see the air rippling over a roadway on a hot summer day.

Master of the world, our Father, we are going through so much. Please don't take this fine man, this wonderful husband and father away from us and from his family. Have mercy on us, Tati! There is only so much we can bear. Please allow the doctor's hands to work skillfully and save Gershon the son of Miriam. We are too weak to withstand these trials. Please, Tati. Save Gershon ben Miriam ....

"Yisroel." A voice was calling me.

It was Jeff.

"Yisroel, please come here a moment."

I walked over. I didn't like the sound of Jeff's voice.

"Yisroel, I want to talk to you."

We walked away from Gershon and the crowd.

"What happened?" yelled Basya Horowitz. "What's wrong, doctor?"

"Don't worry, Mrs. Horowitz. Nothing happened. I think your husband is stable now. I just want to speak to Yisroel for a moment."

We walked away from the group.

"Yisroel, he's very bad. He was hit in or near the heart. His vital signs are very low. I really doubt he can make it. He's still alive, but...."

Jeff broke off, and sobs wrenched his body. This guy was a doctor, and he was crying.

"G-d almigh-ty, please make a miracle," I said silently.

"What do you suggest, Jeff?"

"I think we should lift him onto the truck. He really needs surgery. I don't even know if that would save him, but there's absolutely nothing I can do here. All I can do is try to stop the bleeding by external pressure and elevating him, but I really doubt that will be effective. Perhaps we'll get a miracle, but we're really going to need it for him to pull through. The only thing I can think of is to go forward with him in the truck. Maybe the miracle will be that we'll find a functioning hospital. For the meantime, I'll stay with him and do my best. He could hang on like this for a while too. I just don't know what's going on inside him."

"OK, Jeff, let's get Gershon on the truck."

"Guys," I called out, "let's get everyone together so we can lift Gershon very gently onto the truck."

Gershon was tall, and every adult male wanted to help lift him. He was groaning quietly, which I took as a bad sign. If he had been lightly hurt, he would have been screaming. He seemed very weak, partially in another world.

Before we moved out, there was one more piece of business.

"What do we do with these three creatures?" I asked aloud to no one in particular.

"A good question. We can't let the live ones go," said Binyomin Feltheimer.

"This is a very big problem," said Dovid, 'because if we leave them tied up here, they will eventually get free and then they will come after us, G-d forbid. But I don't think we want to kill them either. How could we do that?"

He was right, of course. Nobody had the stomach to kill these guys, even though they had intended to kill us. Shooting each one in the foot so that they couldn't follow us would be tantamount to a death sentence because there was no medical care available.

We decided to use heavy ropes from Phil's truck and tie them up in sturdier fashion. We gagged them with strips of their own robes, so they couldn't yell. Although they squirmed and thrashed, there was nothing they could do. They were completely outnumbered and weaponless.

Our group had made a good haul of very useful weapons, including not only knives, but three powerful Kalashnikov rifles with ammunition. These we might need down the road. For the time being, we stowed them away in the back of Uncle Phil's truck.

Then we carried the Arabs, one dead and two alive, over to the southbound lanes. Shaul Plotsker, who was about six feet, four inches tall and built like a bear, volunteered for the job of knocking the live ones over the head. We figured that when they woke up they would be so confused they wouldn't remember exactly what had happened or where we had been headed. We threw their shoes way off the roadway so they couldn't walk far. Anyway, with no weapons, they would lose their bravado.

We wrapped the dead guy in his robes and left him in the woods; there was no time to bury him. I felt sorry for those who would pass by, but eventually he would turn to dust and become part of the soil, indistinguishable from the forest floor.

"OK, everyone," I called out. "Gershon is on the truck and the three *b'nai Yishmael* are taken care of. Let's prepare now to move on."

Leah's arm was around Basya Horowitz.

"Please save my husband!" she kept moaning.

"Jeff is doing everything he can. Thank G-d we have a doctor with us," said Leah.

Meanwhile I was very upset that I had killed somebody. The logical consolation, of course, was that there surely would have been many others killed or injured if I had not done it. But why did it have to come to this?

I am the lifeguard at East Side Settlement Camp, a summer respite for what we call "underprivileged" kids, poor kids from the Lower East Side of Manhattan who are given a few weeks in the country. We rich kids volunteer for this summer job as a way of trying to feel better about ourselves. It's our way of as-suaging our guilt at being rich. We certainly don't plan to give up our lifestyle, but for the summer we do our part for kids who are being given a vacation from concrete slums, gang warfare and squalor.

There's this camper they call Wingo, a crazy kid, totally out of control. One day, out of nowhere, he comes at me. I don't mean with weapons, but he looks as if he's going to punch me. My reflexes are fast. I'm in a bathing suit down at the pool. Be-fore I can think, my foot is in his face. He falls down, bleeding from the mouth. Later on, he's fine. I mean, a few loose teeth, but they heal after a while.

Meanwhile, I get scared. Am I violent? Am I out of control? The head counselor says I over-reacted. A few years later, Wingo would have dialed 911 from his cell phone and I would

have been arrested and in addition sued by his parents. But so-
ciety had not yet reached that exalted point. In my youth, there
was still a little innocence left in the world.

But the question still bothers me: was I innocent? Why did I
kick this kid? Is there something wrong with me?

I kept saying to myself. "I killed somebody."

I was feeling a little dazed, but now I really didn't have the
luxury of feeling sorry for myself. There was too much to
worry about. With Gershon in critical condition there was no
time to think; we just had to do.

Leah walked over, saw I was upset, and told me to calm
down.

"Yisroel, there was absolutely no choice. If you hadn't
killed him, there would not be one of us left, G-d forbid. Do
you realize that you saved us all?

"You're right, I know. Anyway, I can't think about this
now. We've got to save Gershon."

Uncle Phil came over.

"Are you sure there are no more of them?"

"Who?"

"Arabs."

"Oh, I almost forgot about them. I'm so preoccupied with
Gershon."

"I understand, but we have to make sure we have no
more surprises tonight."

Phil was wary and practical, valuable traits that had
served him well all his life.

"I guess we would have known by now," I said.

"Not necessarily," said Phil. "These guys are tricky... and
patient. I'm just going to make a quick survey before we take
off. He went back to the truck, found a high-powered flashlight, then walked around the perimeter, bathing every bush

and dark spot in high-powered LED light. We didn't see anyone.

I continued to brood about having killed that man. There
was no way I would ever be at peace with it, perhaps even after *Mashiach* came. I remembered the words I had once
heard attributed to Golda Meir: "We may some day be able to
forgive our enemies for having killed us, but we will never be
able to forgive them for having forced us to kill them."

THE HUDSON VALLEY

Early Sunday morning, July 12

AS SOON AS WE COULD pull ourselves together, we started once more on our northward trek. Psychologically as well as tactically, we felt we had to keep going. Meaningful action in itself assists in the healing process, and we all needed healing. Gershon himself, I believe, had he been in a position to speak, would also have said, "Keep going."

The idea that someone hates you enough to try to kill you is in itself traumatic. We felt grateful that we had not all been killed. Once again, we had to thank Uncle Phil and Aunt Bessie. Without their truck, without Phil's gun… where would we have been?

Meanwhile we walked. Those of us near the truck, at the back of the line, could hear Gershon moaning softly and Basya crying from inside. She would not let go of her husband's hand. The Gruensteins had her children. Leah and I were crying. How could anyone not weep who heard and saw these things?

"Over these things I weep. My eyes run with water because a comforter to revive my spirit is far from me.... Arise, cry out at night... Pour out your heart like water.... I am the man who has seen affliction by the rod of His anger. He has driven me on and on into unrelieved darkness.... He has walled me in so I cannot escape...."[33]

We walked through the night, enveloped in prayer. That's all we did. We walked and prayed, walked and prayed, surrounded by the sounds of moaning and weeping. We needed a miracle and we asked for one. No one spoke.

Shortly before 5 a.m. the sky began to brighten on our right, and about a half hour later the sun appeared over the horizon. We stopped briefly to say "*Shema,*" the morning prayers, and have a little refreshment. Efraim Borenstein and some other guys came back to say that they thought we should keep going and try to make twenty miles, even though it was getting light, since we had lost several hours because of the confrontation. Maybe we would be pressing our luck by walking in the daylight, but Efraim said it would be a merit for Gershon's recovery if we kept going toward our goal. Gershon would not fare better if we were stopped as opposed to moving, and each step toward the Holy Land was a step toward healing for all of us. Shmuli and Dovid were with us and we all agreed we should keep going.

Aside from this, there was no discussion. Onward we traveled.

A little after 8 a. m. we heard a scream from inside the truck. It was Basya Horowitz. Then shouting. She was screaming at the top of her voice.

"Do something! Do something! Help him!"

And then the most heart-wrenching cry I have ever heard, a cry of complete agony, a scream so piercing that I am sure it shook the heavens.

Uncle Phil brought the truck to a stop. Tears streaming

down his tough old face, he disappeared into the woods, his whole body shaking. Leah and I walked around to the rear. The door was open. Jeff was inside with Basya. Gershon was lying there, covered with somebody's coat. Jeff was sitting with his back against the side of the truck. He looked completely beaten, in shock. Basya Horowitz was crumpled up on the floor of the truck, sobbing hysterically.

The entire group by this time was standing around the open door of the truck. Not a word was spoken. We all stood there like dead people. It must have been ten minutes, maybe more. Nobody moved. Nobody breathed. There was nothing to say.

At the end of this eternity, Shmuli came over to me.

"Abba, we should bury him now. We shouldn't wait any longer."

I beckoned to Jeff, asking him to come out of the truck. He, Shmuli and I walked away from the crowd. Leah joined us.

"Jeff, there's no doubt, right?"

"There's no doubt, Yisroel. He had a terrible wound. I'm not sure a hospital could have saved him. He had no chance."

"We should bury him now."

"All right."

"I'll speak to Basya," said Leah.

"Oh boy, you are brave," I said. "G-d should give you the right words."

"Someone has to do it, and it might as well be me."

Without another word, Leah turned around and walked toward the back of the truck.

"Excuse me. Thank you."

People stood out of the way for her.

Ayelet Gruenstein and Ariela Greenberg were with Basya inside the truck. Leah climbed in and they all spoke in hushed voices. As Leah spoke to them Basya screamed again.

"Don't take him away from me!"

My heart turned to jelly. I couldn't stop crying. All around me, adults were wailing. Children, seeing their parents in tears, also burst out. I did not think I could live through another minute of this agony. But no one moved. Again, we stood like statues.

Twenty minutes passed. I finally summoned up the courage to step into the truck. Shaul Plotsker followed me, along with Jeff. We didn't ask anyone; we just picked up Gershon's body and very slowly carried him out of the truck. At that point, every adult male in our group gathered around, and every one of us was part of the procession. We carried him into the woods by the side of the parkway, where we had laid out a sleeping bag on the forest floor.

We wanted to perform the ritual of *tahara*, in which water is poured over the deceased. Having hardly any water, we had to content ourselves with pouring several bottles of spring water over Gershon, attempting to fulfill our obligations as best we could. We covered him up in the sleeping bag.

Soon Basya came. She couldn't stand up, but Leah and the other women were holding her. She was devoid of strength. They let her down next to her husband's body. She had no more strength to scream. She just lay there on the ground, sobbing, sobbing, sobbing.

I thought I had no more tears inside me, but they kept coming.

Uncle Phil came up to me and whispered, "I have a shovel in the truck."

"Thanks Phil."

Soon, we heard the sound of a shovel hitting the earth. Shaul Plotsker took the first turn; it was not an easy job; the ground was hard. One hour, one and a half hours... by about ten a.m. we had finished digging Gershon Horowitz's grave. Nobody said a word; nothing could convey the depth of our grief. There was total silence as we lowered his body in the ground. Then we heard our son-in-law Dovid singing very softly the words of King David, *"Yosheiv b'seser El-yon...* Whoever sits in the refuge of the Most High... I will say of G-d, He is my refuge and my fortress, my G-d; I will trust in Him."[34] Sobbing all around. We lowered Gershon's body in slowly; there were no other sounds than the sobbing and the sound of earth falling onto earth as we shoveled the dirt back into the grave and covered over the body of our beloved friend and brother, Gershon Horowitz.

We placed a monument immediately upon his grave. When would we again return to this lonely spot? Basya Horowitz wrote it upon a piece of paper, and we left it there under a rock.

To Gershon ben Hillel, my husband and the father of our children, a man of valor, filled with Torah wisdom and kindness.

May we meet soon again when G-d brings the day of *T'chias HaMaisim*, Resurrection of the Dead, in the Happy World of *Mashiach* the Son of David our King. Until then, may your soul find peace and elevation in The World of Truth. Pray for us there. Until we meet again....

Your wife and the mother of your children,
Basya bas Tzippora
20 Tammuz 5780
July 12, 2020

"Yisgadal, v'yiskadash shmai rabba...." I said the *Kaddish* on behalf of Basya and her young children.

"May His great Name grow exalted and sanctified in the world which will be renewed, and where He will revive the dead and raise them up to eternal life, and rebuild the city of Jerusalem and complete His Temple within it, and uproot alien worship from the earth, and return the service of Heaven to its place, and where the Holy One, Blessed is He, will reign in His sovereignty and splendor, in your lifetimes and in your days, and in the lifetimes of the entire Family of Israel, swiftly and soon... May His great Name be blessed forever and ever...."

No one had strength. We walked slowly over to our spot in the woods next to the parkway. Basya Horowitz sat on the ground. We either stood or sat on logs. Not a word was exchanged, except for the words we addressed to her, "May you be comforted among the mourners for Zion and Jerusalem."

Soon we laid our tear-stained heads upon the ground and slept the sleep of the exhausted. Where would we get the strength to go on?

The day was stiflingly hot and sticky. If we hadn't been so emotionally and physically drained, we might have had difficulty sleeping, but we were beyond tired. By the time I awoke, it was late afternoon and the sky was dark. The air felt heavy; thunder was rumbling to our west. Everyone was waking up. Shmuel Gantz called over to me.

"Yisroel, didn't we talk about taking shelter under bridges during storms?"

"Yes, Shmuel, I had completely forgotten about that. I almost don't care if I get wet after what we've been through, but the rules of normalcy are that we must get under cover in the rain, and we have to try to be normal."

"Well, there's a bridge about a quarter mile back. Why don't we try to get everyone under it?"

"Thanks for your straight thinking, Reb Shmuel." Then, in an urgent voice, I called out, "Everyone, let's try to hurry back to the highway bridge before we and everything here gets soaked in the rain."

People scrambled to gather their belongings. The thought of being drenched again and the danger of a lightning strike quickened our pace. Just as we reached the protected spot, we started to feel the big, heavy warm drops falling from the sky. Thunder was reverberating and lightning hit the ground not far away.

"The angels are crying and wailing for Gershon," I thought to myself.

Huddled under the overpass, we watched the rain blow sideways and then turn to hail, which clattered down, landing with a drumbeat of clicks. Once again, we made the blessings on lightning and thunder.

"Blessed are You, L-rd our G-d, King of the universe, Who makes the work of creation."

"Blessed are You, L-rd our G-d, King of the universe, Whose strength and power fill the universe."

Boom!

Lightning struck a tree less than fifty feet away; the ground shook.

All of a sudden I saw Moshe Greenberg sprinting out from the underpass, right into the fierce winds and pounding rain. What was happening?

An instant later, I saw a tiny figure staggering, windblown, about fifty feet away, in the center of the roadway, with sheets of rain, falling tree limbs, blinding flashes and the dark skies practically obscuring him.

"Yoni!"

Moshe ran directly to little Yoni, scooped him up and raced back to the underpass. The little boy was crying hysterically, but a little TLC from his mommy, magically appearing dry clothes (that was a good trick) and an "emergency" candy bar soon restored Yoni's cheerful smile. Moshe and Rachel were left to figure out how he had dropped behind when they and all their other children had run to the underpass.

The rain began to let up and the thunder and lightning drifted to the east. The air gradually cleared, revealing a magnificent sunset that painted the western sky in vivid hues. This time, we and our supplies were dry.

We ate our usual rations for the evening meal, sitting in silence, said the evening service and prepared to resume our northward journey, even though parts of the roadway were roaring streams. Basya Horowitz had told us that we must not delay our journey on her account. We had asked her permission before preparing to leave. We had to keep going, she said, and her husband's prayers would help us. She told us that she knew, "He wants us to travel on."

Soon we would cross our first state line as a group. We had traveled to the northern terminus of the Garden State Parkway and were approaching the New York State border.

The parkway ends about twelve miles north of Paramus, New Jersey, where it joins the New York State Thruway near Spring Valley, New York. If you turn right on the Thruway, you go south and east toward the Tappan Zee Bridge, Westchester County and New York City. If you turn left, after a short leg westward toward Suffern and Ramapo, the Thruway turns north and begins its ascent of approximately one hundred miles up the west shore of the Hudson Valley towards Albany.

As we crossed the New York border, I felt a certain sense of accomplishment. Our recent tragedy precluded any feeling of joy, but we had overcome a lot so far, including mortal adversaries, crying children, tired feet, aching joints, hot sun and drenching rain. Every inch, every mile we had earned through toil. We had traveled in the dark, hungry and thirsty, and we never knew exactly where we were going or how many of us would make it.

Every landmark, every milestone was proof that we were making progress. As we got closer to where I thought the New York state border should be, I saw what appeared to be a sign of a different shape. I took out my precious flashlight. The beam illuminated the words, "WELCOME TO NEW YORK, THE EMPIRE STATE." The sign lifted my spirits as much as possible under the circumstances. We had hundreds of miles to go, but we were making progress.

I was in favor of following the Thruway northward until just below Albany. There we would find Interstate 90, which cut eastward across the Hudson River and the Berkshire Mountains into Massachusetts and toward the sea.

The route was indirect. We could also have taken the Tappan Zee Bridge into Westchester County and then followed the coast into Connecticut. But what if there were no Tappan Zee Bridge? The Tappan Zee was an obvious target, like the Verrazano. It was very long and therefore relatively easy to damage. I didn't want to trek several miles eastward and find out that the bridge didn't exist.

But that wasn't all.

I also didn't want to be in Westchester County, which was adjacent to New York City and likely to be filled with thousands of people fleeing the city as well as potential enemies.

The west side of the Hudson Valley, by contrast, was mostly rural countryside. I liked the idea of crossing the 100-foot-wide Hudson River near Albany, using the inconspicuous Castleton-on-Hudson Bridge, better than crossing over the three-mile long Tappan Zee at Nyack. Being in a place almost no one thought about had to be better than being in the middle of potential danger.

All of us had discussed it at a meeting. Shaul Plotsker and Efraim Borenstein still wanted to try our luck on the Tappan

Zee because that would have shortened our route, but they were outvoted.

So, we turned left when we reached the New York State Thruway. For more than a century, this had been the traditional Jewish route to the Catskill Mountains. A lot of Jews had passed this way before us.

As we bid farewell to the Garden State Parkway, I once again silently thanked those who had built it. Our brother Gershon was buried alongside that road. We had left our hearts there with him.

With some trepidation, we set out on the next stage of our exodus.

CROSSING THE RIVER

Early morning, Monday July 13

WE CROSSED THE BORDER INTO New York just past midnight.

Then we had a bit of trouble.

I was feeling rather pleased that we had entered a new state. The Garden State Parkway had become the New York State Thruway Extension. In just over two miles we stood at the intersection with the main Thruway corridor. We paused for a moment before turning left.

That's when Efraim Borenstein came over to me.

"Yisroel, I think we're making a mistake."

"What do you mean?"

"I don't think we should go this way. And, I hope you'll pardon me, but I don't really care for the autocratic way that you're trying to run things."

"What does that mean?"

We were all on edge from Gershon's death. I felt a surge of anger.

Who is this guy anyway?

177

We're all trying to cope with life and death issues every second, and he has to start up? We need a confrontation? I don't know if I can hold myself back right now. I'm already up to here with tension... and now this?

"Israel loved Joseph more than all his sons since he was a child of his old age, and he made him a fine woolen tunic. His brothers saw that it was he whom their father loved most of all his brothers so they hated him; and they could not speak to him peaceably."35

Why do we always have to fight?

I'm president of the synagogue. One Shabbos, Harvey Milstein comes over to me in shul and says loud, so everyone can hear, "Who are you, some dictator? Do you have to have everything your way?"

OK, he has a hard life, full of pain. I know he can't bear his pain. And maybe I deserve it. Maybe I AM trying to be a dictator!

"Efraim, nobody appointed me to anything. I'm not the leader here. You don't like the plan? So do what you want to do! Talk to people; take a vote. I'm a nothing, do you understand? But I'm not going to shut up. If I think your ideas are ridiculous, don't expect me to keep quiet. But do what you want.

"I will ask you one thing, though. Don't start with the fighting, OK? We don't need it. And by the way, there was plenty of opportunity to voice your opinion when we discussed this back down the road. Why now, when we're all upset about Gershon and we're having enough trouble putting one foot in front of the other? Why do you think of this now? How come before you didn't say a word?"

Leah came up to me and whispered very softly, "Yisroel, CALM DOWN! Just keep cool and let other people talk. You're too upset to say anything sensible."

By now, of course, there was a group standing around in the darkness.

Efraim continued.

"With all due respect, Yisroel, I don't really have confidence in your opinions. And I don't think that you are giving anyone else a chance to express an opinion either. There are about forty adults in this group and I wonder why everyone just accepts your views. I don't happen to think the idea of trying to cross the ocean in a boat is so nutty, but why go all the way to New England? If we cross the Tappan Zee Bridge we're only a few miles from Long Island Sound, where there are hundreds if not thousands of boats. Why do we have to walk for weeks to get to New England?

"And say the Tappan Zee Bridge is down? So you've walked maybe four miles from here. You could even ride your bike or take the truck. So then you find out in a few minutes. If it's no good that way, so then you turn back and follow Plan B. But we're right here.

"But no, you have this fixed idea in your head that we have to go up the west side of the Hudson to Albany and cross way up there, and spend weeks walking when we could be within a few days of our goal right here. We've had a lot of misfortune with your ideas, and I think you should stop trying to run this show."

"Listen Efraim, go ahead and have your meeting. Do what you want. I never pretended I'm anybody's leader. I have ideas and I'm not afraid to voice them. I happen to believe that you are a hundred percent wrong in wanting to go over the Tappan Zee. And I happen not to like the way you have introduced acrimony into a peaceful, unified, and, by the way, grief-stricken group. That's exactly what we don't need. I don't think you're handling this the right way. But ask everyone else what they want to do. I'm still going to voice my opinion. And keep one thing in mind: there is one thing and one thing alone that will save us, and that is peace among the members of our family. *Sinas chinam*, gratuitous hatred, has brought plague upon the Children of Israel for thousands of years, and we'd better learn how to fix it right here, or we're in big trouble."

There was a long silence. Nobody wanted to say anything. I'm not sure even Efraim wanted to take this burden on himself. He wanted, perhaps, to see if anyone was going to join in his point of view.

Then Shmuel Gantz spoke.

"Efraim makes sense. I would suggest that we send someone ahead, on a bike or the truck, to check the Tappen Zee. If it's clear, then I think we should follow his suggestion. Why should we spend weeks walking hundreds of miles out of the way?

More silence. People were thinking. I took a chance.

"I told you before that I will not be afraid to state my point of view. What you say, Efraim and Shmuel, has a certain logic. But logic isn't always the best course to follow. I'll give you an example. Here is how the Torah describes the Egyptian Exodus: 'It happened when Pharoah sent out the people that G-d did not lead them by way of the land of the Philistines, because it was near, for G-d said, 'Perhaps the people will reconsider when they see a war, and they will return to Egypt.' So G-d turned the people toward the way of the Wilderness to the Sea of Reeds.'[36]

"I am concerned that we will 'see a war' in Westchester. I am concerned that we will become afraid there. My concern is not mainly the Tappan Zee Bridge. Even if it is intact and we cross it, we could end up in the midst of greater trouble than we have already experienced. I would rather go 'the way of the wilderness' if it leads to safety, then go through the near route and by that apparent logic find that we have stumbled into disaster, G-d forbid."

Uncle Phil started to talk.

"Listen for a few minutes to an old man. I'm old enough to be a father to most of you kids. I'm also not as religious as you are. I don't wear a black hat and I can't quote the Talmud like you guys, but I've been around a few years longer than you, and life teaches you a lot. You've got my nephew Roy here. I've known him a long time. He's not as old as I am, but he's older than most of you. He's also been down a few roads, maybe more than you. He's seen things you haven't seen, and he's learned a few things in the tough school of life. I think you ought to listen to him. And I think all of us have got to make sure to be respectful to each other. It's a very tough world out there. There are a lot of people who hate us. Except for the One upstairs, we are all we've got."

Efraim spoke.

"I hear you, Uncle Phil, and I appreciate your words. I respect Yisroel, and I think everyone here does. And I agree that it's vital for all of us to be respectful to each other. But I also think he's wrong in this idea, and I don't think, especially when our lives depend on these decisions, that anyone has time to spend weeks walking out of the way. Yehudis and I are going for the Tappan Zee Bridge. Will anyone join us?"

Silence.

"We'll go," said Shmuel Gantz.

I was concerned. Efraim and Yehudis had no children yet, but the Gantzes had several small children.

"If you two couples go alone," I said, "how will you survive? We need each other. There's so much we can do for each other. It seems that you are the only two who are opting to go across the Tappan Zee. Perhaps my 'fixed idea' is really less dangerous than you two couples and your children separating from the group. I really don't recommend it."

"We're going to go, with G-d's help," said Efraim. "I hope I didn't offend you. You are wonderful people. May G-d help that we should meet again in peace. May you be right and we be right, '*Eilu v'eilu divrai Elokim chaim*.'[37] In the meantime, we will take as many supplies as we can carry and we will do our best. Good luck."

Efraim gave me a hug. I felt a tear dripping down my cheek.

"*Hatzlacha*, success to you. Listen, if you change your mind, you know where we are heading; you know our exact route. You know how we will be traveling. You can probably move faster than we can, so you could always try to find us if you wanted. Hey, I just got an idea. Why don't you take one of the Arabs' guns with you? It might come in handy."

Efraim agreed. We opened the truck and took out one of the Kalashnikovs and some ammunition, as well as a supply of food, which they loaded into a stroller and some knapsacks.

"The gun should help. Hopefully, you will never need it, but carrying it may make you feel better. Good luck, Efraim. May G-d be with you and may angels accompany you and protect you."

I thought I saw him hesitate for a minute, but then he turned and walked away, and the rest with him. We watched them disappear into the night, seven people who had been attached to us until this moment. First Gershon, and then these two lovely families. I had a sense of foreboding regarding them.

Our steps seemed slower now. So much had happened. All the exhilaration and hope that I had felt on Shabbos seemed to be drained. I felt alone and afraid. It just wasn't the same.

Leah walked beside me.

"I know what you're feeling, Yisroel, and I also feel it. But it will be OK for us. G-d will watch over us. I am also worried about Efraim and his group. They are so alone. I agree with what you said. Westchester is just too close to New York City, a little too close for comfort. I like the idea of disappearing into faraway corners. Yes, we will walk a long way around, but perhaps then no one will see us until we want them to see us. That's worth a lot. Don't worry, Yisroel, you're doing the right thing. The group is with you."

Those were kind words, said when I needed them.

The Thruway was littered with abandoned cars just like the Garden State Parkway. From time to time, individuals and families passed us in the darkness, but we kept to ourselves and so did they. People were afraid to trust each other, and you could understand why. You couldn't see faces in the darkness. You had no idea if a person was a predator or an innocent refugee.

Our precious group was a huge source of moral and physical support. I was sad that it was now smaller than before. We relied on each other for comfort, advice and encouragement. More of us could easily have been killed in the confrontation the previous night, but miracles had saved us. Perhaps our adversaries had been too confident, thinking that they had complete control. But they did not have control.

I walked along in silence, thinking about these things. The group was very quiet tonight; everyone seemed absorbed in his or her own thoughts. One does not always need to talk. Sometimes it is best not to talk; silence can protect you.

About 2:30 a.m. several figures appeared in the darkness directly in front of us. I strained to make out who they were, which was even more difficult because they turned out to be black. Leah and I, who were at the front of the group, practically bumped into them—a father, mother and several children who looked to be from about ten to eighteen.

"Hello," I said.

"Hello, friends," said the father pleasantly in a very deep voice. "How are you faring?"

Such a nice greeting, I thought. Someone was actually civilized enough to be polite in this chaos. Although we wanted to keep moving, it seemed rude not to pause for at least a few words of conversation.

"We're doing all right, thank G-d. We've had many adventures and passed through many dangers, but we've also experienced a lot of miracles. For that we're very grateful."

I could barely make out his face, but I could tell that the father was nodding sympathetically.

"I see you are G-d-fearing people. I am sure that is why you have survived. Where did you come from?"

"Most of our group is from Lakeville, New Jersey."

"Isn't that where the great Jewish school of Bible studies is located?"

I thought I heard respect in his voice; my instinct was to trust him. There are some non-Jews who seem to have a great desire for contact with Jews. You sense a realization on their part that we are the descendants of Abraham, Isaac and Jacob, and a desire to receive the Patriarchs' blessing through us. I felt that with this man, even though I could barely make out his features.

"Yes it is. In fact, most of us are affiliated with that yeshiva."

"You are Children of Israel?"

"Yes, we are."

He turned and called out to his family.

"Rachel, Hannah, Robert — please come over here. I want you to meet these people. They are descendants of the

Biblical Patriarchs, holy people. Perhaps they will give us a blessing."

Then he turned back and spoke again to Leah and me and to the others.

"My friends, I believe that my family and I are fortunate to have met you in this howling wilderness. We are wanderers, trying to save ourselves in the chaos. We are also religious people, and we know from our studies that all blessings emanate from the Children of Israel. I would like you to bless me, my wife and our children that we will survive this cataclysm and be able one day to live in a world of peace and proximity to G-d. I would add that we would like some day to visit the Holy Land. Can you give us such a blessing?"

There we were, complete strangers facing each other at 2 a.m. in darkness on a deserted highway in the midst of a crumbling world. Just twenty four hours after being marked for death, we were being asked for a blessing. My voice cracked a little when I answered.

"The blessing, of course, would come from G-d. It is good to try to transmit the blessings of G-d to others. You are correct that G-d said that through our nation others would receive blessing. The fact that you realize that in itself elevates you above other men. I give you the blessing that you should walk in the ways of G-d, always do His will and be a steadfast friend of the Children of Israel. In that merit, may He protect and guide you and allow you to travel in safety until the time comes when the world is ruled by His law and all evil is banished forever. May you and your family live to see that day and may you have a part in bringing it about. Perhaps we will meet again, my friends. Please look for us in the Holy Land, in the good days that are coming."

The father clapped his hands together and called out to his children.

"Ah children, do you see what G-d has done? He has brought us into contact with holy people. This is the first time I have felt at peace since the attacks began. Now I begin to hope that we may survive this chaos."

He turned back to me.

"What is your name, sir?"

"Yisroel Neuberger."

"Is 'Yisroel' the Hebrew version of 'Israel'?"

"Yes, it is."

"See, I've studied a little of the Hebrew language."

"Good for you!"

"We are truly blessed to meet you, Israel, and your group. Is it appropriate for me to give you a blessing?"

"We would be honored. And, what is *your* name?"

"My name is Alexander Coleridge. This is my wife, Suzette, and these are our children. The blessing is for you and everyone with you. May G-d protect you from all danger, whether from two-legged or four-legged creatures or acts of nature. May all mankind respect the sanctity of the Jewish Nation. May you ascend to the Holy Land. And may a king soon arise from your nation who will bring peace unto the earth!"

As his words ended, I heard some people drawing in their breath in admiration for these words.

An enthusiastic "amen" came from many around us.

"Mr. Coleridge, those are truly beautiful words. May G-d grant that all our blessings be fulfilled. We are honored to meet such fine people. Where are you from and where are you going?"

"We come from Newburgh, New York. I'm hoping we can find our close family in New Jersey and then head west to more rural surroundings. We will try to build a new life. I've been worried, but now that we've received your blessing, I do believe that G-d will watch over us."

"May you and your family, Mr. Coleridge, go in peace and arrive at your destination in peace."

"Thank you, Mr. Israel. We do hope to meet you in the Holy Land. May the G-d of Abraham, Isaac and Jacob protect us all!"

A big "amen" resounded through the darkness.

They moved off and soon disappeared into the night. This left me with an inner glow. I was sure that, on the Day when all creation will be judged, this man and his family would stand with those who recognized the existence of the Almighty and understood His unique connection with the Children of Israel.

We were walking past Suffern, New York, near where Leah and I had lived for several years. Shmuli and Orli and Ruchoma and Dovid were beside us, and also, Jeff and Marge. I began telling them about our former life.

"Years ago, we lived near here, over those mountains to the right, in Cornwall-on-Hudson. It was a beautiful place, on the side of Storm King Mountain just north of the United States Military Academy at West Point. I owned a newspaper there. Those were the days before we were religious.

"Even though I myself had not yet comprehended that I actually was a Jew, I received a letter one day saying, 'Jew, you'd better get out of town if you want to keep on seeing your children.' We had two young children then, Tehilla and Shira, who happen to be in Israel right now. Of course, the two of you, Shmuli and Ruchoma, weren't born until after we became religious.

"This incident was very disconcerting. It was, of course, a message from G-d, just like everything else. 'Neuberger, the world knows you're a Jew! Why don't YOU know that you're a Jew?'

"The Cornwall police chief, Sal Triomfo, took me to the local FBI office in Suffern, right around here. He was very excited to be visiting the FBI, but it quickly became apparent that the FBI wasn't too interested in the predicament of a Jewish newspaper publisher. This was a wake-up call: maybe it was time to leave Cornwall. When our lives changed a few years later, we did."

This section of the Thruway was triggering all kinds of memories. Even at night I could make out familiar landmarks.

"About twenty miles north of here is the exit for Route 17. How many times did we speed by here on our way to the Catskills? Do you realize how many millions of Jews in the course of the last century turned off there, how crowded it used to be on a Thursday night or Friday afternoon in the summer, when the fathers who had been working in the city all week rushed to join their families in their bungalows before *Shabbos*. On Sunday night the tide flowed the other way. That world is gone forever. The road is quiet now; these cars will sit here until they turn to dust."

Actually, there were fewer abandoned cars on the road. Little by little, we were getting further away from "civilization."

"There's the Harriman Interchange up ahead, where Woodbury Common was located. That was where you could find the discount outlets for all those fancy stores. Now there are no more credit cards, sales or bargains, just the grass growing higher and higher until someday it will all be green fields again."

"I'm getting depressed," said Marge.

"Yes, Yisroel. It's enough already," said Leah.

"Okay, okay. But really, I don't think it's depressing. I think THAT was depressing, such an unreal world, that world of credit cards and shopping. Hopefully, soon we'll be in Jerusalem with *Mashiach* and then we'll experience reality. Then we'll be living in the real world, the world of satisfaction on every level, a world focused on eternity."

I couldn't help it. Green fields, I would always believe, had to be an improvement over a shopping mall. Why is there a certain level of peace when one looks out over a beautiful landscape? Because at least you're looking at something that was created directly by G-d. When you're looking at a shopping mall you see only the works of man whose purpose is strictly material, and — when you get right down to it — strictly selfish.

Somebody wants to get rich from that shopping mall. Somehow, that's not the purpose of life. No one ever really achieved satisfaction from a shopping mall, not the shopper and not even the owner. That's why, to me anyway, a green field is on a higher level than a shopping mall. On a still higher level than a landscape, however, is something built by man under the direct instruction of G-d, like the Biblical Tabernacle or the Temple on Mount Moriah in Jerusalem.

But we weren't there quite yet.

As we walked further north, the countryside was getting greener, although we had to imagine the greenery in the darkness. It was quieter, too, with fewer people passing in the night. We were now on the flank of Storm King Mountain, just west of where we had lived in Cornwall.

"Over there on the right is the old Mountain Art Center. It's an outdoor museum. You can't see them in the dark, but there are large sculptures out in the fields. We knew the family who created it. They also had a factory, Star King, over on the right. It's that long, low building with big red stars on the side. Oh well, you can't see the stars now, but they're over there.

"Remember that old house in Cornwall we rented from

Ron Ruggles? It was more like a cottage, I guess, but the location was spectacular, on the north slope of the mountain, facing the Newburgh-Beacon Bridge. We would watch the ever-changing sky and the storms heading eastward across the river.

"Remember when Tehilla fell off the swing? She was three and broke her collarbone. The doctor put a figure-eight bandage around her shoulders. Now she's a mommy with wonderful children of her own, living in Israel!

"Somehow, with G-d's help, we were able to forget a lot of tears. So may it be with us!"

I remembered the words of King David: "Those who sow in tears will reap in glad song. He who bears the measure of seeds walks along weeping, but will return in exultation, a bearer of his sheaves."[38]

We continued our journey through the Hudson Valley, reconnecting with our past as we walked into an unknown future. Nearing Newburgh, I heard a loud snarling behind us. I took the flashlight from my belt and waved it around. A pack of six large dogs was circling around two families, the Gruensteins and the Lyons. Like wolves, they arranged themselves in a semi-circle around the parents and small children.

I could hear Shlomo Jacobson.

"Phil! Phil! The guns! Fast!"

The truck headlights flashed on and you could see the dogs coming closer, their mouths dripping and teeth snapping. Phil tried blowing the horn. People scattered as he gingerly moved the truck forward.

"The *possuk*...say the *possuk*," someone yelled.

"*Against the Children of Israel, no dog shall whet its tongue...*"[39] Ayelet Gruenstein yelled out in Hebrew, as she scooped up her children and turned her back toward the dogs.

Blinded by the headlights, the dogs began to back away.

Phil stuck his head out of the door and shouted, "Can't use the gun, too dangerous. Everyone out of the way!"

He maneuvered the truck up close to the dogs. Five of them slinked off into the woods, but one remained on the other side of the truck, snarling and snapping, menacing the Lyons. Little Chaya was crying in her stroller. Other children were screaming. The adults looked on helplessly. To attack might provoke the animal even more.

Phil stopped the truck and carefully aimed his powerful flashlight at the dog, which was about five feet away. It looked like a clear shot, but too many people were within range. Everyone near the dog slowly backed away, but they were still too close.

The dog advanced slowly toward Chaya Lyons, now screaming hysterically in her stroller. Her mother immediately edged forward, now standing between the dog and the stroller. She had absolutely no protection, but she was determined to shield her baby, no matter what.

Moshe Greenberg ran to the back of the truck and grabbed one of the Kalashnikovs we had taken from the Arabs. I had seen him examining the rifles closely for days, learning how to use them. Now the time had come. Phil aimed the flashlight on the dog and Moshe took careful aim. There wasn't a sound except the snarling of the dog and the screaming of the toddler.

Moshe spoke calmly but firmly to the mother.

"Stand back, Devorah."

Moshe squeezed the trigger.

BANG! BANG! BANG!

There was a rapid series of shots, a deafening noise. The dog jumped in the air toward the toddler, but in the middle of the jump, the animal collapsed with a howl, falling on the ground right next to that courageous mother.

Devorah was covered with blood, but it wasn't hers. The dog was dead.

Moshe stood frozen in place, still gripping the rifle. He didn't say a word.

Devorah pulled Chaya from the stroller and wrapped her arms around her baby, sobbing and wiping the blood away.

Uncle Phil got out of the truck and came over to shake Moshe's hand.

"Good job, Moshe, Are you all right?"

"Yeah Phil, I'm fine. Thank G-d it ended like this."

Devorah walked over, carrying Chaya, who had already stopped crying and was just shaking in her mother's arms. Devorah looked at Moshe and tried to speak, but no words came. She just stood looking at him, tears streaming down her face. No words could have expressed her gratitude as effectively.

We were a sober bunch that night, as we cleaned ourselves up and moved on. Another close call. How much more could we take? How far would our protection extend?

A few miles of walking calmed us down. A sign indicating that we were thirty miles from Kingston brought back memories. Kingston was a small city near the town of Woodstock. It was Woodstock that had been enshrined in the annals of American history after a 1969 concert on a nearby farm. The event drew half a million fans, who withstood torrential rain, mud and food shortages for three days. Then, it had been a sensational news story, a cultural milestone. Now it seemed like a dream, not even such an important dream.

Around 3 a.m., just west of Plattekill, we heard many voices approaching. They weren't loud, but you could hear the buzz. As we rounded a curve, we saw a bright glow encircling the approaching group and the nearby road. As they came closer, I could see they were carrying torches made of corn stalks or some similar plant materials tied together. They were singing in soft voices; big crosses hanging from their necks. When they reached us, they stopped. Their leader, in white robes, walked up to our group.

"Greetings, brethren."

Binyomin Feltheimer was up front at the time and replied, "Greetings to you."

"I am Reverend Gabriel Brayley."

"It's an honor to meet you, Reverend."

"We are elated to find Jewish brethren. In fact, you are the ones we most seek. Are you an advance party of a larger group?"

"No," said Binyomin. "Just us."

'Do you understand what is happening?" asked the Reverend.

Binyomin looked at him with a quizzical expression.

"I don't exactly know what you're referring to."

"Then, my dear brother, I will tell you. These attacks have destroyed every government around the world. This is the War of Armageddon. The Millennium will soon be here if it is not already. Our L-rd will soon return!"

His followers began to chant.

"Praise the L-rd! Praise the L-rd! Praise the L-rd!"

The Reverend raised his hands, palms toward us.

"These are the most exalted and dangerous moments in history."

He waited for us to speak, but there was only silence. Our entire group had gathered around, listening to Reverend Gabriel. In the light from the flickering torch, I could see the deep lines in his craggy face. He dropped his arms to his side and continued his speech.

"Only one thing remains now before the Great Coming.

That is the repentance of Israel for your sins. It is no coincidence that we have met you this night. You must understand the gravity of these attacks. Millions are dead. Cities are in flames. Powerful governments have been destroyed, as in Biblical Egypt.

"The flames that are consuming the world will not be quenched until you repent, O People of Israel. Your sin has brought these calamities upon the world. The flames will not be quenched until you accept the savior."

Uncle Phil whispered to me, "These are the weirdest nuts I ever saw."

"Your sins are consuming the world, O People of Israel. You must repent," said the Reverend, his voice rising.

"My brothers, I am ready to accept your repentance. Repent, my wayward children. Accept the supremacy of the L-rd and renounce your misguided ways, your rejection of our savior, which has already condemned you to so much suffering. Repent O people of Israel. The end has come."

It was time to move on. We didn't have the luxury to stand still and converse with these people. I spoke up.

"My friends, we appreciate your heartfelt concern for our welfare, but I don't believe that we can have a dialogue. There's nothing to talk about, really, so we're going to bid you farewell and be on our way. We have many miles to go tonight and young children with us, as you can see."

Reverend Gabriel's face began to contort in a strange way, his eyes narrowing and his lips tightening.

"Brethren, I'm warning you. You face an eternity in flames if you don't heed me. Do not depart, but join the service of our savior."

I wanted to be polite.

"Reverend Brayley, be well. We'll be on our way now. Let's go, everyone! Goodnight friends, and thank you so much for your concern."

"Repent, Children of Israel. Repent before it is too late! The time is nigh!"

"Be well, friends."

"Repent, Children of Israel."

We began walking away, and the light of their torches soon faded into the distance.

The days and nights settled into a routine as we made our way north. Every night we would trek twenty miles and every day we would pray, eat, sleep, pray again and move on at nightfall. We kept careful track of the calendar; each *Shabbos* was its own miracle, refreshing our souls and giving us strength to go on.

We encountered difficulties and setbacks. Children and adults got sick. There were injuries, falls and scrapes, insect bites, hunger and thirst. Extreme fatigue became a condition that a single day of rest couldn't reverse.

The memory of Gershon Horowitz was a constant source of pain, and I could never stop hurting over the decision of Efraim Borenstein and Shmuel Gantz and their families to go their separate way. I missed them, and was worried about them. Also, I never ceased remembering that I had killed someone. Would I once again be called upon to pick up a gun?

One night, near Coxsackie, New York, I was trying to find familiar constellations.

"Leah, look! A shooting star."

"I see what you're pointing at. Actually, that doesn't look like a shooting star. They usually fade in a few seconds, because they're actually meteors burning up as they enter the atmosphere. This has been traveling across the sky now for a while. It's not a comet, because comets don't travel so fast. I suppose it could it be a plane, but that I also doubt, because planes don't trail phosphorescent clouds."

"So what do you think it is?"

I called out to Shmuli and several others who were nearby.

"What do you think it is?"

The object was bright, with a conical phosphorescent tail. For some reason, looking at it made me feel more secure. It made me feel comfortable. I wanted it to remain in the sky, but it was nearing the horizon. Just before it disappeared, it seemed to "wink" momentarily, in other words it disappeared and reappeared. I know it sounds crazy, but I had the feeling that this object, whether it was light years or hundreds of miles away, was sending me a message.

"Abba, that's very strange. I've never seen anything like it. I really wonder what that is."

"So do I, Shmuli. So do I."

We were now able to take advantage of the countryside. We found clear streams and lakes. If the water tasted good, we took a chance. We had survived so far, and we had to trust G-d to protect us. There were even places where we could wash ourselves and swim, a beautiful bonus that reminded us of "normal" life.

One afternoon we were sleeping peacefully near the Thruway, when we were awaked by a child's scream.

"Help! Help! The house is burning! Mommy! Tati! Flames! I can't get out! Help me!

We heard comforting voices murmuring through the trees.

"Shoshana *shefela*! Shhh.... It's only a dream. Wake up, *shefela*. Everything is all right."

Now we heard the mother's voice speaking to her husband.

"Moshe, I feel for Shoshana. Of course she should have

such a dream. The house IS burning. Everything is burning. My own Mommy! My own Tati! I spoke to them twenty minutes before the explosion! Where are they! Is Boro Park also in flames? Are they hurt? Do they have food? Where is Suri? She was supposed to have a date Sunday night! She's such a good girl! I can't stand it! I can't take it! Where are MY Tati and Mommy?"

The sound of sobbing.

"Rivki, what can we do? We have to ask G-d to help and we have to save ourselves. We can't do what's beyond our power. G-d is helping us in miraculous ways. Hopefully all of us will survive this and see happy days. We can't be the only ones seeing miracles."

We were also crying.

On Sunday, July 19, we crossed the Hudson River. This time we didn't need Gil. We simply walked across the Castleton-on-Hudson Bridge, which carried the New York State Thruway extension, Interstate 90, eastward toward the Berkshires and the State of Massachusetts.

On the Berkshire Extension, somewhere around Milepost Fifteen, our beloved truck sputtered out for the last time and died. Whatever makes a hydrogen fuel cell work, stopped working. The food that remained in the truck was divided among the families, filling knapsacks, strollers, bicycle saddlebags and even pockets.

This truck had literally saved our lives. I don't know how our group would have survived without it. Now that we were in the country, we had been able to add wild fruits and vegetables to our diet. We still used supplies from the truck, but it was not our only source of food. In the beginning, however, we had no other food supply beside what the truck had carried.

Of course, the truck had done far more than carry our

food supply. It had carried those who were old or sick or wounded or tired. It had silently traveled around the curve on the Garden State Parkway to allow us to launch a sneak attack from behind against our enemies. It had helped us chase away a pack of angry dogs. And it had carried Gershon Horowitz in his final hours.

We pushed the truck over to the side of the road. It happened to be a beautiful, wooded section and it seemed an appropriate place to leave our precious mechanical friend. It seems silly, but we tend to attribute human qualities to pets or even inanimate objects. Yes, the truck was a hunk of metal, but we loved it. It may not have had any more feeling than a stone, but the truck had been a vital part of our lives when we were in trouble.

Moses had been grateful to the Nile River and to the sand of Egypt, inanimate objects provided by G-d for Moses' protection. It was really a matter of being grateful to G-d and recognizing His "fingerprints" in the material world.

We left a note on the dashboard: "This truck was a means of salvation for a group of the Children of Israel as they made their way northward, trying to save their lives during the Great War in the summer of 2020. G-d sent this truck to help us. We thank Him for His kindnesses to us and all His children. We thank Him for the many signs of His presence during these days of darkness. May you who read this note know that G-d sustains you too, and may we all see a peaceful world soon in our days."

We signed it, "Children of Israel, with G-d's help returning home."

MASSACHUSETTS

Early morning, Sunday, July 19

SOON WE ENTERED THE STATE of Massachusetts, land of the Berkshires. It was a glorious evening, cool and dry, but moonless. The undulating hills are beautiful, but they present a challenge when you're on foot.

Leah and I were walking together with Shmuli and Dovid, Jeff and Marge and their baby. Jeff was like a yeshiva student, full of questions and anxious to soak up as much information as he could about living a Torah life. Tonight, he was eager to discuss the relationship between the chaotic world situation and the Torah.

"Yisroel," he said, "What do you think is the real reason that the world fell apart? I mean, is there a Torah point of view on these things?"

"Well, Jeff, there's a Torah point of view on everything. The Torah has been called the 'user's guide to the world.' The 'Manufacturer' has kindly given us a Handbook on how to live in it. If something appears to go wrong, it is because we are not following the directions correctly. For example, Adam and

Eve in the Garden of Eden did not follow directions. (And at that time, the directions were much simpler!) As a result, terrible sufferings entered the world. Those sufferings have been plaguing Adam and Eve's descendants from then on. If you want to understand what went wrong, you must consult the Handbook."

"I hear what you're saying," said Jeff. "This is going to sound terrible, but I'm secretly feeling a kind of guilty happiness that our entire life fell apart! If things had gone on in that same mundane way forever, I never would have awakened from my lifelong slumber. I am looking at absolutely everything with new eyes. Marge, do you understand what I'm feeling?"

She smiled. Marge was a thoughtful woman; she and Jeff sometimes communicated wordlessly.

"One has to think in life," I continued. "That's why G-d gave us brains, but in general we don't use them. Our society degenerated lately to such an extent that there was a pervasive conspiracy against thinking. Every place you went, from the taxi to the post office to the doctor's office, the TV was on or the radio was blasting (and sometimes both at once). Remember those cars where the sound system was booming so loudly that you couldn't stand the sound even with the windows closed! The entire car would be vibrating. The neighborhood all heard the boom, boom, boom and the meaningless words. No one was listening, but that didn't matter; the idea was to be so distracted that you couldn't think.

"If you look at a Torah scroll, you will see that there are periodic separations between passages. G-d wants us to stop at the end of each section and think about it. Not only should we think about the Torah passage in order to understand the plain and esoteric meanings, but to understand its relationship to our own conduct. The idea is to shine a searchlight on our lives and change what is deficient. But how do you know how to change yourself and from where do you get the strength? All these answers come through Torah study and prayer."

Jeff responded. It was fun talking to him. He was getting excited!

"Yisroel, I like how you try to apply Torah thoughts to life. I totally understand your point about going through life with your brain turned off. From personal experience I know that, just because you have absorbed encyclopedias worth of facts at medical school, for example, doesn't mean that you have learned to THINK! If you're fortunate, however, something may jar you so that you begin to comprehend the meaninglessness of your life. You may then start to change your life for the better, or you may get panicked and just go deeper into your meaningless, brainless existence.

"What happens if you panic? You try to turn off your brain completely, and perhaps you become a workaholic or a pleasure-holic or an alcoholic... or a drug addict. You KNOW that your life is meaningless, but you refuse to get off the merry-go-round. It's all so horrible that you can't face yourself. You're afraid to examine your life because of what you might see there. That's why you turn up the volume and drown yourself in TV and other distractions. It's not just that you don't think... it's that you don't WANT to think!"

Jeff was full of passion. But I wanted to return to his original question.

"Jeff, you asked why the world fell apart. Here's what I think. The Talmud tells us the Children of Israel are in exile because of '*sinas chinom*,' causeless hatred among us. It all started with the Biblical episode of the brothers hating and then selling Joseph, which led directly to the Egyptian exile. This is an eternal lesson: hatred and bitterness among the

Children of Israel leads directly to exile.

"There's a principle called *'ma'asei avos siman l'banim,'* meaning 'what happened to the patriarchs is a sign for the children.' If we want to understand our lives, we have to look at the lives of our patriarchs and matriarchs. Everything that happened to them is a sign for subsequent generations.

"Causeless hatred among us has caused our present exile. If it's continuing, then clearly the condition must still be in effect. If there's hatred between Jew and Jew, then — measure for measure — we experience hatred from the nations around us. That's why we suffer from the hatred of the nations. I'm not exonerating them — they will pay for their brutality, for every action, word and even their evil intentions — but it seems clear that they are able to hurt us only because our protection has been removed. Why? Because of our own actions.

"The emotional separation among the Children of Israel is epidemic. I see it in myself. It comes out in many ways: ignoring others, not greeting them warmly, not smiling at them, feeling superior to them, not feeling their pain. For all these inadequacies, I'm also guilty of destroying the Temple and prolonging the exile."

"Wow!" said Jeff.

Everyone was silent as we walked along in the darkness. I was thinking about Gershon Horowitz, feeling that I had contributed to the tragedy. If I had been good to everyone, if only I had restrained myself on countless occasions when anger rose in me like a geyser, the entire world might have become a happy and peaceful world not just for the Children of Israel, but for every nation. Why should I think I was less guilty than anyone else?

I am nine years old. My Lionel electric trains are my world. I have a huge wooden platform on which I have set up interlocking tracks winding through tunnels, over hills and through the countryside. My freight train has tankers, box cars, log cars — which at the touch of a button can tilt and dump their load onto the siding — and of course a caboose. My passenger train has a beautiful red, yellow and silver Santa Fe diesel engine, a dining car, Pullman sleepers and a rounded observation car at the rear. At night the lights twinkle; trains speed through the darkness. There are signals and crossing lights and stations along the way, not to mention trees and other props. I also have switching engines and steam engines with coal cars and real steam. I have powerful controls that can regulate the speed and direction of two trains at a time, and many switches that I can operate from the control area so that all trains and engines can switch from track to track.

This world I can control. It all responds (unlike my own brain!) to my command. This is my world, into which I constantly retreat. I can pretend this is reality. There is nothing to disturb my fantasy, except the constant ugly intrusion of reality. My world goes round and round like the trains. My greatest joy is to unwrap a new car or engine, signal or switch.

One day when I go out, my brother Jimmy decides to play with the trains.

I return home to find a disaster of elemental proportions, my beautiful trains have crashed, my precious engines and cars are scattered over the fantasy landscape.

My anger knows no bounds. I chase Jimmy into the kitchen. Anna Walsh, the cook, and Bridie O'Malley, the housemaid, look on in horror as I bang his head against the kitchen wall.

Loud sniffing to my left.

Something bumped me...gently but persistently pushing me to the right at waist level.

Something big.

Then I heard a low growl.

I whispered, "*Shema Yisroel, Hashem Elokainu, Hashem Echad...* Hear O Israel, the L-rd our G-d, L-rd is One."

I wanted to scream, but a steely calm took over, perhaps a very deep instinct for survival. I kept walking straight ahead and then said in a flat but very loud voice, "Folks, there's a bear next to me. Let's all move slowly and carefully to the right and just stand there together."

Everyone huddled together on the right side of the road. Someone turned on a flashlight, which caught in its beam a mother bear accompanied by cubs. She began sniffing us out and looking at us inquisitively. The cubs began playing and tumbling around; the mother, who had backed off onto the center median, was still watching us very carefully.

"OK, let's all just move away, very slowly," I said, and we all began, very deliberately and calmly, to back away from the bears and head off, continuing in an easterly direction.

"Mommy, can I play with the babies?"

Nervous laughter.

"Not now, *shefela*," said Kaila Greenberg's mother.

We continued moving and a few minutes later, there was a collective sigh of relief as we regrouped and continued to walk.

"And G-d saves us again," I said.

"But G-d put the bear there also," said Jeff. "So what would you say if, G-d forbid, we had NOT been saved? Say someone had been hurt by the bear?"

"I would say that whatever happens is for our good, even pain. Not that you want to seek it out. We're not allowed to seek to test ourselves against temptation and I am sure that we're not allowed to seek to cause pain to ourselves, but if it comes then it comes for our good. In my own life many things happened that were agonizing at the time, and I now see that they were good. In retrospect I am so grateful that they happened, but at the time I could not have figured a way in the world that they could have been good.

"My entire thirty-one years of life before we became religious were filled with anguish, loneliness, fear, even terror — not to mention obvious mistakes in human relations and many wrong decisions — with no hope of ever finding a way out. But the very hopelessness of that situation forced me to look for G-d. Those horrible times were actually a gift from G-d."

"So, that really brings us full circle, back to my question before, about why the world fell apart," said Jeff. "Are you saying that our own faults cause all our problems, but by working on ourselves and asking G-d to help us we can work our way out of those faults?"

"I think that's a fair statement. I believe that's the historical and in fact the personal role of the Children of Israel. Individually, we are supposed to improve our character, and as a nation, through that constant drive to become better, we are supposed to elevate the world and heal all its pain.

"Big job, right?"

"Yes," said Jeff, very thoughtful, "a big job. And I thought medical school was a big deal!"

Walking fifteen or twenty miles a day, talking with friends and examining the deep subjects of life was more than a satisfying way to spend our time. And yet, with the dangerous conditions of the world and our totally unknown future, our conversations were only a temporary respite from a constant, underlying sense of foreboding.

Along with the possibility of encountering real dangers, life on the road was punctuated with everyday difficulties and setbacks. There were twisted ankles, sore backs, aching feet, blisters; many days it was just plain hard to get moving. Children cried and adults groaned, but we managed to keep moving on.

Then there was the pervasive worry and fear about loved ones. We had all been so used to communicating by phone or e-mail, so that even if someone was sick or in trouble, at least we knew what was going on. We could speak to them, even if they were thousands of miles away. But now, we were in our own bubble. We couldn't reach anyone at all. There was NO communication whatsoever, except among ourselves and through the medium of prayer with our Father in Heaven. It was a shock to a generation that had been raised to take for granted the total ability to give and receive information. We were completely isolated. We all had so many people to worry about! And that's all we could do: worry and pray.

There was no moon these days. On one particularly dark night, Shimon Horowitz badly twisted his ankle when he tripped over a tree root. Within minutes, it had swelled so badly that he couldn't walk. We managed to fashion a litter out of tree branches and clothing. Since we no longer had the luxury of Uncle Phil's truck, the younger, stronger men had to take turns carrying him for several nights until he was healed enough to walk. It was a challenging task, as he was a chunky 15-year-old, but we had no choice.

"How good it would have been," I thought, *"to be carrying Shimon's father like this. But he is lying in the ground next to the Garden State Parkway. Baruch Dayan HaEmes; blessed is the True Judge."*

It was difficult getting used to going without showers and baths. In America, one took a bath or shower every day; indoor plumbing was a given. But what had once been a "given" had now been "taken." Sometimes we were fortunate enough to enjoy the luxurious pleasure of a mountain stream, but in general, our clothes clung to us like plastic wrap. Many had painful rashes and we didn't smell so clean.

I worried about Uncle Phil and Aunt Bessie and the Frankels. That truck had been a source of pride to them as well as a means of transportation. They soldiered on, despite swollen feet, aching knees and back pain. Over time, they began to feel more and more comfortable in the company of our young Torah scholars, brilliant by all measures and most of them at least forty years younger than they were. But the younger people also respected Uncle Phil for his "street-smarts," which had more than once had saved us from mortal danger.

Our Lakeville friends would speak in Torah learning as they walked along, and sometimes offer impromptu lectures and classes for the entire group when we rested and even sometimes while we were moving. Almost everything was from memory, which made it even more impressive. You could learn a lot of Torah passing through the countryside, and we tried not to waste time. This elevated us. We were the descendants of the Children of Israel who had walked through the Sinai Desert learning Torah from our Teacher Moses.

Our journey had now taken us through the Berkshires. Soon the elevation dropped and we moved into more heavily populated areas as we continued eastward across central Massachusetts. We saw increasing signs of urbanization: shopping centers and residential subdivisions in what had once been farmland. That meant less protective cover for us.

Thursday, July 23 was a clear, warm day; we had found a secluded spot near Sturbridge for our daytime siesta. For some reason, I felt particularly calm and relaxed. I lay down under the shade of a maple tree, staring up into its branches.

"Gavriel! Gavriel where are you?"

It is Esther Jacobson's voice.

"Gavriel is missing! He was here an hour ago, before I went to sleep!"

We all rush over. No one knows where he is. We search the woods; we call out to G-d: "Help us!"

He is gone!

The shadows lengthen. Night is coming on. To be alone in the forest is dangerous, especially for a little boy.

"Gavriel," we call again and again.

We say Psalm 20, "May G-d answer you on the day of distress... May He dispatch your help from the Sanctuary and support you from Zion. May He remember all your offerings... May He grant your heart's desires... May we sing for joy at your salvation... May the King answer on the day we call!"

"Abba, look!" says Shmuli.

I turn and see an enormous white bird rising through the underbrush. With majestic wing-strokes it ascends through the treetops in the gathering dusk, the last rays of the sun casting upon it a deep orange glow against the darkening sky. Higher and higher it glides, until it disappears over the eastern hills.

Only then do we hear a child's voice.

"Mommy! Daddy!"

"Gavriel!" shrieks Esther Jacobson, as she rushes into the underbrush.

We all run after her.

"Gavriel!"

"Can you help me with this branch, Mommy? I can't carry it."

"Gavriel, are you all right?"

"Yes, Mommy, but I can't carry this branch."

"Gavriel, what are you talking about? What branch?"

He points to the forest floor. We all stare.

"The bird gave it to me."

On the forest floor is a branch some ten feet long whose width is the girth of a man's leg. It appears to be a grapevine, but it is enormous, and heavy with what appear to be grapes, each fruit the size of a cantaloupe. Lifting the vine requires four men, two on each end, and even then it is difficult. We lug the branch into the clearing.

"What happened?"

"Everyone was asleep, and it was hot. I took a walk in the woods. Soon, I couldn't find the camp any more. I came to a clearing, and sat down under a tree and cried. Then I heard this 'whoosh' behind me, and I saw this huge, white bird with big watery eyes. The bird put its head next to mine, and suddenly I felt all better. I knew the bird would take care of me.

"The bird got down on the ground and pointed with its head. I knew that it wanted me to climb onto its back. So I climbed up, and the bird took off. We flew around for a long time. I could see for miles and miles, mountains and rivers and trees and clouds, the blue sky and the ocean, even cities far away. But after a while, I began to think about Mommy and Daddy and how everyone here must be looking for me. So I started to get sad. That's when the bird started to fly lower and brought me back. But before he flew away, he dropped this branch from his beak and pushed me toward it."

I lift one of the grapes. It must weigh a pound. I cut it from the vine with my knife's saw-blade. Then I slice off a section of the grape. It is deep red inside. I say, "Blessed are You, L-rd our G-d, King of the universe, Who has made the fruit of the tree," and eat the fruit.

The fruit is more than delicious: a feeling of peace comes over me, as if I am satisfying my hunger in a way that is not animalistic, but spiritual. We all eat from the grape. We feel elevated. We also cut a piece of the vine and some leaves. We carry them with us the way the Children of Israel carried the manna in the Ark of the Covenant.

"Yisroel, wake up. It's time for afternoon prayers."

"Huh? .... OK Leah."

Thursday night's trek was always a little easier; we knew *Shabbos* was coming. Friday afternoon, after bathing in a shady, lazy river, we felt particularly refreshed and ready for *Shabbos*, which we spent at Milepost 99.5, near a meadow dotted with wildflowers. The next morning we read the opening chapters of the Book of Deuteronomy.

As we neared the end of the Five Books of Moses, we also neared our goal. We had traveled some 280 miles since Reunion Park. We bid farewell to Interstate 90 on Sunday, July 26, spending the day in a secluded area off Interstate 495, near the small town of Stow. It had been three weeks to the day since the world had exploded.

GARRISON'S GANG

Sunday night, July 26

A S WE SET OUT FROM Stow on a sultry July night, all around us were signs that the old way of life had disappeared. Stores and homes were shuttered; roads were empty. Revolutionary landmarks, country inns and covered bridges were abandoned and would no doubt quickly disappear among spreading vines as new forests swallowed up the old evidence of what we used to call "civilization."

It was an intense time for us. *Tisha B'Av*, the most bitter date in the Jewish calendar, was three days away. On this day both Temples were destroyed in Jerusalem and the most tragic events in our history occurred. We would remain at our resting place on Wednesday night and all day Thursday for the full-day fast. We would take off our shoes, sit on the ground, crying and mourning for our lost Temples.

After traveling twenty miles, we arrived early Monday morning at a secluded spot not far from Lowell, where the Concord River passes under the roadway. As we rested in the early afternoon, we heard the sound of men's voices.

"Hey, who are you people?"

I reached for some water by my side, quickly washed my hands and rubbed the sleep out of my eyes. There were men standing around the edge of our camp. What was going on?

The more I looked, the more men I saw; fifteen or twenty were standing around us, each holding a rifle or shotgun. They were dressed like farmers, with weather-beaten overalls and jeans, some with suspenders holding up their work clothes.

"I said, who are you people?"

As I stumbled to my feet, I said a quick prayer.

G-d, here's our next test. Please let us all survive.

Looking at all those guns pointed at us was unnerving, to say the least. I tried to stand very still, hands at my sides, so it was clear I wasn't reaching for a weapon.

"Sir, we're not here to harm anyone. We're a group of families, with women and children, from New York and New Jersey. Our destination is the coast of Maine. We rest during the day because of the heat and then travel at night. All of us are victims of the attacks, like everyone else."

The man speaking was very big, maybe two hundred fifty pounds; he wore a faded work suit with suspenders.

"Yeah, sure you're 'like everyone else.'" He laughed. "If you're like everyone else, then why are you all dressed so funny, everybody in black and those little caps on your heads?"

"We're religious Jews. It's a style of dress that's centuries old and reflects Biblical law, dating back to Mount Sinai. We cover our heads to remind us that G-d is above us."

"How do I know you're not fanatics? How do I know that you're not the ones who have been blowing up this great country and destroying our lives?"

He gripped his shotgun closer to his body.

"Yeah, answer him," said another guy.

A burly guy on my right, sweating profusely despite a red bandana around his forehead, now chimed in.

"Why are we supposed to believe anything you say? You're a strange-looking bunch to me. Say Garrison, why don't we just take care of the whole gang right now? Did they ask us before they blew up America? Are we going to let them fool us again? All this talk about religion and families. They look awful weird to me. I don't trust 'em."

Garrison shook his head slowly from side to side, like he didn't want anyone hurrying him.

"C'mon now, Henry. Just hold up a minute. I'm not ready yet. Sure, they may be part a' them who destroyed America. But maybe they're not. I don't know who they are."

Garrison gestured to the rest of his group to follow him.

"Guys, come over here and let's talk."

Then he turned to us.

"All you people. Get up and put your hands in the air. No funny business. We got twenty friends here with rifles and shotguns that love to use 'em. America may be in trouble but this is still our land. As long as we're on it, you're not going to touch us or our families. And we're not letting you outta here. Not 'til we're sure who you are and what you're doin' here."

Everyone in our group was standing now, with mothers trying to hush their children and everyone else totally silent, not knowing what to do or say.

Garrison huddled with the others in a circle just beyond me, although some of them stood off to the side, watching us. I kept trying to think of something to say that would convince them to leave us alone.

After a few minutes, Garrison called out.

"Hey, you. You're the leader, right"

"I guess so," I answered.

"OK, get over here, then. Keep your hands on top of your head and walk over real slow. Everybody else, stay put. Don't move a muscle."

The first thing they did was to search me. They seemed satisfied.

"Now, who are you?"

"I told you. We're religious Jews and we're on our way to Maine."

"What are you goin' to do in Maine?"

I figured I'd have a hard time convincing them about our mission. Sometimes I still needed to convince myself! I took a deep breath and answered.

"We want to get to the coast. The Jewish homeland is Israel. Obviously, we can't fly there the way we used to, but we figure that the seacoast is the closest we can get right now. We want to avoid cities, which are dangerous. Believe me, we're victims, just like you. In fact, the people who did this hate us more than anyone else."

Garrison's expression didn't change, and he held the shotgun close.

I continued.

"We may look strange, but this kind of clothing is based on Biblical law; we didn't dream it up. Jews have been dressing like this for thousands of years. We are descendants of Abraham, Isaac and Jacob. G-d told the Biblical Patriarchs that they and their descendants would be the source of blessing for the entire world. If you let us continue on our way, I know that G-d will bless you."

He grunted. His eyes were grey and cold.

"I heard a lot a' words just now. Words are cheap. They're also phony more times than not. Those guys that bombed America are also smooth with the words. Now get back there with your people. Keep your hands on your head."

That sounded ominous. But what could I do? I hoped my words would penetrate to his heart, but I was beginning to wonder if he had a heart. He seemed more rational than Henry, but his reply was not encouraging. I watched with increasing dread as Garrison and the others conferred in whispers. Despite the heat, I was shivering. One of the group shouted angrily and drove his rifle butt into the ground.

After what seemed an endless discussion, Garrison walked over to us.

"None of us believe you. We don't trust you worth a lick."

Before I could protest, Garrison continued speaking.

"But we're not murderers. Maybe you are, but we're not. I'm not sure if you're liars or not, and I don't want to have it on my conscience that I killed people when I wasn't sure. One thing is clear: we don't want you around here. So you're leavin' right now. And we're goin' to follow you. You're not comin' back. We're walkin' behind you 'til you all are past Route 38 up ahead. Then you're goin' to keep walkin'. If we see you again in these parts, there will be no more discussions.

"Now, you have ten minutes to pack up and get out. Understand?"

"We understand. Thank you."

My heart was in my throat, but I was relieved beyond measure. G-d was watching over us.

"That's it. Ten minutes. Now move!"

We packed up as quickly as we could, with the gunmen watching us closely. No one said a word. The only sounds were zippers closing and a baby crying. If it wasn't ten minutes, it was awfully close.

At about 3 p.m. we headed out. Normally we would still have been enjoying a leisurely afternoon, but right now I couldn't wait to leave. Garrison's behavior seemed unnecessarily cruel. Naturally, a group of a hundred strangers, all dressed in black and wearing similar head coverings, would draw more than a casual glance, especially after the world had been plunged into chaos. But he seemed so heartless.

Yet, we had to be grateful they hadn't killed us. We could never have protected ourselves.

At Route 38, we kept going; they stopped and watched us walk away. Not a word was uttered. They just stood there. I dared not look at them or open my mouth. It occurred to me that there was every possibility we could all have bullets fired into our backs. Some of them would have been happy to do it. I was half expecting to hear the crack of rifle fire. But there was only silence.

Soon, we rounded a bend and they were out of sight.

A few minutes later, I suggested that we stop and make a *l'chaim* to thank G-d for his mercies, then drink some water and finish resting. Dovid spoke up.

"Abba, aren't we still a little too close to them? What would happen if they came around the bend to check on us and found us stopped here? They might think we were planning to come back or were not taking them seriously. Maybe we should walk for another hour and get way beyond their territory before we rest. These are not people to mess with."

"He's right," several in the group chimed in.

"Dovid, of course you're right. That's the safest course. Everyone agree? OK, let's push ahead then. In the meantime, thank you once again G-d for Your endless mercies and for saving us from these people."

A big "amen."

We continued on our way.

Jeff Klein walked over. He was sure that we had been in big trouble back there and was amazed at our escape.

"We may find that same reaction again," said Jeff, "especially here in New England. People generally don't like new-comers or outsiders, black clothing or not."

"You know, Jeff, I can understand their feelings. Their entire world has been turned upside down by people they don't know. They have no interest or involvement in this faraway dispute that caused people to blow up America. Their lives, the lives of their children, their communities have all suddenly been ripped to shreds by an unknown enemy from another side of the world. And then we come along, a big group of strange-looking people from far away, and what are they to think?

"Even though they're not nice people, they did release us. It was probably a close decision. I think Garrison was in favor of it, although he didn't let on. Emanations from the holy people in our group must have penetrated their shell and made them feel that we were telling the truth. So, despite everything, feelings of mercy, if not kindness, entered their hearts."

That night, we reached the northeastern tip of Massachusetts, where we picked up Interstate 95, the last major thoroughfare on our northerly pilgrimage. On Tuesday night, we made the historic crossing into New Hampshire. On Wednesday, July 29, we reached Portsmouth.

That night was *Tisha B'Av*. We fasted in a clearing outside Portsmouth, weeping for our lost Temple. We felt completely alone in the world.

"G-d: please rebuild our Holy Temple and bring us home to Jerusalem 'on wings of eagles'[40]...for how else would we make it? We're not asking because we deserve it, but out of Your mercy. We have no right to expect anything from You, but we're still Your children, and we want to come home."

That was such a deep *Tisha B'Av*. Far from other Jews and thousands of miles from Israel, with no logical grounds for hope, in a destroyed land, with no real food and no shelter, among millions of potential enemies, this was clearly Exile. How could we ever see Israel again, let alone see the Temple rebuilt and the Homecoming of our People?

And speaking of our People, where were all our families and friends! Where were our parents and grandparents, our children and grandchildren, our brothers and sisters and nephews and nieces and cousins and uncles and aunts, all the friends and family who made up the beautiful tapestry of our lives? Where were all our beloved brethren, the holy Children of Israel who keep G-d's commandments even in the midst of Exile and universal hostility? And where were all the other good people in the world, all our friends among the nations?

"From the depths I called upon G-d.[41]

All those years in the wilderness! Twenty three years of torment until I find G-d. Yes, it is America, the land of plenty. I possess everything, but my heart aches with pain. Alone in the world, I imagine myself like the dove. In the days of Noah, the dove flew over the surging waters of the endless sea as my soul had flown over the endless expanse of the world. My soul seeks a landing place, but there is nowhere for it to rest. G-d, save me from this endless emptiness!

We had been traveling for almost four weeks and had covered three hundred and sixty miles, all on foot. Every night except on *Shabbos* and two fast days, we had walked for eight hours. Every day we had managed to find a secluded area in which to rest and protect ourselves from the sun and unfriendly eyes. We had trekked up the Hudson Valley, through the Berkshire Mountains, under wilting heat and driving thunderstorms, with little food and rationed water. Everyone walked without complaint, even when sick or in pain or tired or injured. Even the children had become toughened soldiers. All of us were on a mission and it carried us forward.

We were fighting for our lives. When you fight for your life you just push on.

We were the Nation that had survived destruction and walked through flames. We were the Nation that wept on *Tisha B'Av* and we were the Nation that would sing in exultation on the glorious day when the destroyed Temple would be rebuilt in Jerusalem. We didn't know how or when it would happen, but we knew it would happen.

"While it is true that I am a redeemer, there is also another redeemer closer than I. Stay the night, then in the morning, if he will redeem you, fine! Let him redeem. But if he does not want to redeem you, then as G-d lives, I will redeem you. Lie down until the morning."[42] The words of Boaz to Ruth.

Years ago I had heard a famous rabbi speak about these words.[43] You know how sometimes the exact thought you need pops into your mind at exactly the moment you need it? You couldn't remember it five minutes after you heard it the first time, but fourteen years later, when you are walking on Interstate 95 in the middle of World War III, it suddenly pops into your head. Why? Because that is when you need it!

The Zohar says that those words of Boaz have a prophetic meaning beyond the plain meaning of the text. The "night" is our exile. G-d is telling the Jewish People, "have courage, My children. Stay the night. Don't give up. Either you will redeem yourselves through your own merit, and then — fine! — the morning of your Redemption will come! But even if you cannot redeem yourselves, I, G-d will redeem you! Do not be afraid, My children. See the night through. The morning of your Redemption will surely come!"

Tisha B'Av was over. After a quick meal, we packed up and moved on into the night. Soon we would enter the State of Maine.

The moon was waxing, and so, for some reason, were our spirits.

OCEAN PRINCE

Thursday night, July 30

A S WE PASSED NEAR PORTSMOUTH, New Hampshire, a thunderstorm lit up the sky several miles to our north. We did not feel the rain, but the lightning made a beautiful show. Was G-d telling us that He had seen our tears and heard our repentance? As I made the blessing on the lightning, I tried once again to remember that G-d directly manages all the affairs of the world, from the microscopic to the galactic.

"Blessed are You, our G-d, King of the universe, Who makes the work of Creation."

On the other side of the Piscataqua River, Maine awaited us. Illuminated by lightning flashes, we could see the Memorial Bridge. This led us to Kittery, which, according to Uncle Phil, was the oldest town in Maine. We could smell the salty air as the breeze blew in from the sea. Gulls squawked overhead. The landscape grew flatter and pine forests lined the road.

The next night was Shabbos, which we spent near the

Webhanet River on the Maine Turnpike. Everyone, men and women (separately), had taken a swim in the river the day before, and the cool clear waters seemed to wash off layers of accumulated grime as well as tension. The Torah portion this week was Va'es'chanan, in which Moses beseeches G-d with heart-rending pleas to enter the Holy Land. His pleas, of course, were rejected, and Moses was buried on Mount Nebo, across the Jordan River from the land of his dreams.

We and Moses were exiles. I felt then so strongly his greatness. All of us could understand how he poured out his heart to G-d. He was our shepherd, then and now. How could he have entered the Holy Land then, when he knew that his beloved flock, thousands of years in the future, would be in exile? Yes, he would enter with us, in the End of Days.

As we rested and prayed on that *Shabbos*, I began to think about what lay ahead. We were now within a few miles of our destination. Once in Portland, we would be standing on the promontory of the New World. We were in a position similar to our Biblical ancestors, who stood on the shores of the Red Sea with the waters in front and the Egyptians behind.

Would G-d provide a way across for us as He had for our ancestors?

But these thoughts were not appropriate for *Shabbos*. I cleared my mind, and inhaled the tranquility of the day.

In late afternoon, thick grey clouds moved in. Just after *Shabbos* ended, the skies opened up in a torrential downpour. We ran for shelter under an overpass, where we watched sheets of rain cascade non-stop.

It was unbelievable. Here we were, on the doorstep of our goal. *Shabbos* was over and we were ready to go. But the rain didn't stop; we couldn't move. For two days and nights we sat there. The men studied while the women played with the children. Fortunately, the roadway under the overpass was slightly elevated or we could have been sitting in a river. Still, it was damp and cold and I began to think we might still be sitting there when the winter snows arrived. We paced back and forth to keep warm. It was crowded, but we squeezed in.

Late Monday afternoon, I peeked out of the tunnel. At that moment, a brilliant ray of sunshine burst forth from the west. As the setting sun broke through the clouds, a double rainbow appeared in the east. The intense light immediately brought everyone running. There we all stood, wordlessly taking in the magnificent sight.

"Blessed are You, King of the Universe. Who remembers the covenant, is trustworthy in His covenant, and fulfills His word."

The blessing on a rainbow. Yes, G-d, I know that You remember the covenant. I know that You are trustworthy to fulfill Your word. I know that You will bring the Final Redemption. Yes, G-d, I do feel that it's happening right now.

A rainbow in the east and a resplendent sunset in the west; G-d was giving us hope. "Don't give up, My children. Keep pushing onward. I am with you."

As the darkness deepened, we resumed our trek. The air smelled freshly cleansed after the storm and the bright light of the moon pierced the sky. Perhaps something good was going to happen.

On Tuesday morning, August 4, our group arrived at Milepost 37.7, about five miles south of Portland on the Maine Turnpike. It would be a short journey that night. We didn't want to establish ourselves inside the city, for the usual reasons, so we set up camp near Exit 44. We spent the day resting under an overpass, instead of in the woods, because the ground was still wet from the recent rains. We were anxious to move on, but we forced ourselves to rest.

When nightfall finally arrived, a group consisting of Leah,

Dovid, Shmuli, Shlomo Jacobson, Shaul Plotsker, Jeff Klein, Uncle Phil and me followed Interstate 295 east about three miles, where we turned right onto U.S. 1. Crossing a bridge, we turned right onto Commercial Street, which fronted the harbor.

We had arrived! This was Portland, Maine.

I was excited but a little wary. The city seemed too quiet. Uncle Phil carried the gun in his pocket. We had left the Kalashnikovs behind, not wanting to look like terrorists ourselves. We walked slowly down Commercial Street, breathing the salty air in the bright moonlight.

Suddenly it hit me. Tonight was *Tu b'Av*.

Tu b'Av, the fifteenth day of the month of Av, is one of the most powerful days in the Jewish calendar.

When the Children of Israel marched in the desert, Moses reluctantly agreed to send spies into the Land. Twelve were chosen, one from each tribe. Ten spies returned with a report that sent fear into the hearts of the Children of Israel, to such an extent that they refused to enter the Land. Bitterly discouraged, they cried that night, even though G-d had promised they would enter the Land. G-d said to them, "You wept for no reason, and I shall set [this day] for you as a time of weeping throughout the generations."[44] That day, the ninth of Av, became the day of future calamities, the day upon which our two Temples were destroyed hundreds of years later, and countless other catastrophes were visited upon the Children of Israel.

G-d told our fathers in the desert that their generation would not enter the Land, but instead their children would inherit it. Each year on the ninth of Av the men of that generation dug graves in the desert and slept in them, and in the morning many did not get up. For thirty-seven years the dying continued until the generation was nearly gone.

In the fortieth year, the remaining men of that generation dug their graves on the night of Tisha B'Av once again. But in the morning they all awoke. Had the decree been lifted? Perhaps they had miscalculated the date. So they slept in their graves again that night, and the next, and the next. They continued to do so until the full moon appeared on the fifteenth of the month. When they observed the full moon, they knew that the Ninth of Av had certainly passed. They rejoiced, knowing that the decree of death had been lifted.

Since then, we celebrate the Fifteenth Day of Av as the day when G-d lifted the decree of death, the decree which stated, "You will not enter the Land." On this day we were liberated from a death sentence, and throughout history the Fifteenth of Av has been celebrated as a day of liberation from evil decrees.

As we walked along under that full moon, our hearts were lifted by the thought that on this very night, so long ago, the decree of death had been lifted from our ancestors. For us, perhaps, there would also be a way to enter the Land. Perhaps our decree of death had also been lifted.

With this hope in my heart, we rounded a curve. To our right, gleaming in the moonlight, floated an enormous white ship. Written on the bow, in bold, black letters, were the words *Ocean Prince*.

OLD BILL

Tuesday night, August 4

WE WALKED DOWN THE PIER to get a closer look. *Ocean Prince* gently swayed in the waters of Casco Bay. She was an elegant ship, all white from the waterline to her top deck and gleaming funnel. I was instantly energized by her size, beauty and the fact that she was actually there.

This is it! This is how we're going to get across the ocean.

That was my immediate reaction, but then I started to think.

Are you crazy? What do you have to do with that huge ship? How on earth did it ever occur to you that you could get across the ocean on that thing? You have no idea who owns this ship. The owner may hate Jews. And if the owner doesn't hate Jews, why would he or she even talk to you? Who are you? A weird guy who appears out of nowhere in a world that has gone nuts. Why would anyone even give you the time of day? And, by the way, how were you planning to pay for this madness?

Where would we begin? It was the middle of the night.

225

We were in a strange city during a time of chaos. Nobody knew us. And we looked pretty unusual. That famous New England reserve would be multiplied many times over since America was under attack. It would be hard enough to prove ourselves worthy of renting a car much less chartering a seafaring vessel.

I looked over at the others.

"Well, what do you think? What should we do, folks?"

There was a lot of blank staring, head-scratching and shoulder-shrugging. Nobody said a thing. I couldn't blame them. What was there to say? Besides, they were all looking to *me*. I was the one who had engineered this.

Shlomo Jacobson spoke up.

"This is certainly an ocean-going vessel. It's not the Queen Mary, but it's a very big ship. There's room for hundreds of passengers. It would definitely make it across if we could arrange it, but how do we do that? We have no idea who owns the ship. And even if we find the owner and somehow manage to get access to the ship, we'd need tons, I mean tons of money to charter it. Then there's the problem of fuel. And it would take a pretty big crew to operate it. Who's going to pay? To be honest, I can't imagine a way in the world this will ever work. Right now, getting to that moon up there looks just as likely as chartering this ship and getting across the ocean."

Of course, Shlomo was right, and we all knew it. My spirits plunged. Suddenly the euphoria became total depression. My brilliant idea was a joke. I felt like an idiot. We'd be stuck here forever, at the edge of our dream. I was crushed.

I gripped the chain-link fence that surrounded the huge loading area where hundreds of cars, trucks and tour buses had once lined up to drive on board for the voyage to Nova Scotia. In the moonlight we could make out the information posted, including when the gates opened, departure times and phone numbers for information. Of course, there were no telephones anymore. There were no tourists. Everything was dead, and that's how I felt.

Dead.

Hopeless.

The lowest of the low.

The entire area was deserted, except for a few stray cats scampering in and out of the shadows.

"Yisroel," the Bostoner Rebbe told me, "if it's not hard it's not 'emmesdik,' truthful. For sure, if it's truthful, it's going to be hard."

So many things are hard. My entire life isn't easy. Of course, materially speaking I had grown up with all the money I needed. But spiritually, I am never at peace. Even after Leah and I meet in high school, my soul has always been restless. Just trying to be a mensch, and a decent husband... It's hard!

Then my first book, FROM CENTRAL PARK TO SINAI: How I Found My Jewish Soul, is very hard to publish. Who's interested in the story of some rich Jewish kid finding his way back to Torah? I give up completely and then Rabbi Perr tells me where to get it published.

My second book is also hard.

My third book.... Oy, that's the hardest!

Everything important to me in life is so hard. I keep thinking of the words of the Bostoner Rebbe, "If it's not hard, it's not truthful." OK, at least that's something. Maybe all these things are truthful.

And what's the hardest thing of all? Bringing Mashiach into the world! Look how long we've waited! Look at all the suffering in the world, especially the suffering of the Children of Israel. Such pain, such problems! But those words at least give me hope: maybe at least I am suffering for truth.

Hard is one thing, but this looks impossible!

Standing there, utterly forlorn, all I could think of was going back to the group and going to sleep. When I ran out of strength and hope, I knew I had to go to sleep. Sometimes, in the exhaustion of the night time, one is utterly depressed, but the morning light brings relief. Your soul goes up to Heaven when you sleep, and G-d gives you spiritual oxygen and a new perspective, new ideas and new hope for the morning.

"In the evening one lies down weeping, but with dawn... a cry of joy!"[45]

"You know what, everybody...? I for one vote to go back. I am out of ideas and out of strength. Let's sleep on this problem. Perhaps G-d will send us some answers with the sunrise."

No one objected; adults are always glad for an excuse to go to sleep. We were all in a daze. Now that we were standing at the "finish line," we had no idea what to do next. We were utterly down, utterly spent, utterly hopeless.

We walked back along Commercial Street, eight people flitting through a ghost town. Of course there were no police patrols; we'd gotten used to that, but it seemed so totally empty. No sign whatsoever of human presence. Creepy.

As we passed through a wooded section, Shmuli grabbed my arm.

"Abba, somebody's in there, behind that bush."

As I have said, Shmuli has a great eye. Decades ago, when the kids were small, the family went on trips together. Shmuli was always the one who saw the animals first, the water moccasin swimming in the Everglades, the bears in the Rockies, the mountain goats in the Grand Canyon.

"There's a man over there looking at us. See him?"

Shmuli didn't exactly point, but kind of moved his head in the general direction. Everybody stopped dead and stared. I couldn't see anything, but I usually didn't see what Shmuli saw until it was running away.

"Why don't we get behind this tree and watch a few minutes. Let's see what happens.

It seemed like a good idea, but I have to admit that I was a little frightened.

We spend summers at Florival Farm in upper Westchester County. It is real country, way beyond the suburbs. On a summer night, all you hear are the crickets chirping and an occasional dog baying in the distance. It's pitch black except for a bit of light from the Milky Way filtering through the trees. We've been singing folk music at the Steins' house. From there, it's a six-minute walk down the hill, past the tennis court and then up the hill to our house. Now it's eleven o'clock and I'm walking home alone. It's deadly quiet. Mars is bright red and somehow ominous. Why am I scared? It's so irrational!

Is there something in the bushes over there?

I break out in a run, then a sprint. Why am I afraid?

"The sound of a rustling leaf will pursue them; they will flee as one flees the sword... they will stumble over one another...but there is no pursuer...."[46]

Why am I running? There's nothing to fear. At least, I don't think there is!

It was so lonely, so silent all around us. I told myself that a Jew does not become frightened. It doesn't make sense to be frightened because our soul is eternal and there is nothing another man can do to alter the nature of our eternal existence. We can mess up our own eternal existence, but no one else can. "G-d is with me; I have no fear; how can man affect me?"[47]

I tried to will myself to be calm. We stood together behind the tree, waiting. Suddenly we saw him, a bent man with disheveled hair and a flowing white beard. He appeared from around the bush, using a stick to support himself as he walked along with a peculiar limp. The man looked about eighty, gaunt and shaky.

I was holding my breath as he lurched closer. Then, he passed in front of us.

"Should we speak to him?" I whispered to Shmuli.

He stopped, whirled around and pointed his stick.

"Whazzat? Whazzat noise?" he yelled loudly. "C'mon, I hear you. I know yer there. Come on out."

Amazing. He had heard us. And he was a lively old geezer, either crazy or completely unafraid...or both. Suppose he was crazy, though. What could he really do against eight of us? Unless, of course, he wasn't alone.

Perhaps he had a weapon....

We filed out from behind the tree.

"Hello."

What else do you say to a crazy-looking man in the middle of the night in Portland, Maine?

We all stood for a long time, staring at each other in the moonlight. Finally, Shmuli tried to break the ice.

"Sorry if we frightened you. We're with a group of people who..."

"Hey Sonny," he interrupted. "Who are you guys? Yer an odd lookin' lot. Are you Jews or sumpin'?"

Shmuli didn't even blink.

"Yes, we're Jews," he said. "We've walked from New Jersey."

The man let out a whistle.

"New Jersey. Now that's a hike. Sumpin' to do with those terrorist boys down there? Them bombs? That why yer here? You bad guys or good guys?"

"Well, we think we're good guys."

Laughter. That broke the ice a bit.

"Ya probably think I'm a crazy old man," he said.

"Not at all," said Shmuli, beginning to warm up to the guy.

"Well, I probably am," he said. "But I been around these parts a long time. I seen a lot a things, enough to *make* ya crazy, really.... Did you know this whole country has practically shut down? People runnin' out a' here. Don't know where they're goin', but a lot run away. They're scared 'bout the winter. How they gonna survive a Maine winter? No 'lectricity? No water? No food? People pick up and go south. But I'm not goin'. Nope, Old Bill shur ain't runnin'."

"Bill, what are you doing out at this hour?" ventured Shmuli.

The old man put his head on the side and gave a quizzical look.

"What is there to be inside fer, sonny? I have an old house, and I'll go to bed sometime, but Old Bill wanders around at night and talks to the animals. He looks at the moon and the trees. Do you believe that Old Bill talks to the trees?"

"Yes," said Shmuli, nodding, "I do believe it."

"I know 'em all."

Nutty as it sounds, you kind of had to believe him. I could easily imagine that he *did* talk to the trees. And the way I felt then, I could almost believe that the trees talked back to *him*!

"The moon is big tonight, sonny. That's a big eye in the sky lookin' down at us. Them guys that blew up everythin'... there's a lot they don't know. G-d is watchin' everythin'. Soon the moon is goin' to fall on them. They think they own the world, but there are goin' to be surprises!"

I exchanged looks with Uncle Phil, hoping he wouldn't get impatient with Old Bill. But Phil was listening intently, with a fascinated look on his face.

"What are you guys doin' here anyway?"

"We're trying to save our lives," said Shmuli. "It's very dangerous where we came from, especially for Jews. New York is on fire; terrorists and gangs are all over. The open countryside is safer."

"But why come to Maine?"

"We came here because...look Bill, this may sound crazy, but we have this plan that maybe you'll understand."

I held my breath. Shmuli was on a roll and we were all transfixed, watching him carry the ball.

"Bill, I'm sure you know that the Jews have a homeland in Israel. Just the way Maine is your home, Israel is our home, except that it goes back thousands of years to the time of Abraham, and the title to our home is recorded in the Bible."

"Yah, I know," said Old Bill. "I know that's true."

Shmuli paused and looked relieved. Then he continued.

"Well, there's only one place we feel safe. Even though the entire world attacks us there, G-d watches over Israel, from the beginning of the year to the end of the year. When our world here fell apart, we decided there was only one place to go, and that was Israel. So we left New York City and walked about four hundred miles to get here. And why Portland? Well my father — Bill, this is my father — he knew that there's this big ferry here, big enough to cross the ocean. And we thought that maybe, well maybe, there's a way we can get that ferry to take us across."

All eyes turned to look at Old Bill. As Shmuli spoke, his eyes widened in the moonlight, in fact they seemed to reflect the moonlight and glow with a white light. Old Bill started shaking back and forth.

"Yeah, sonny, yeah. You're gonna' do it. Old Bill says you're gonna' do it!"

He banged the ground with his stick and shook his fist in the air.

Uncle Phil looked at me. I looked back at him. Uncle Phil was a tough guy, but there was something about Old Bill that had Uncle Phil impressed.

I couldn't stay silent any more.

"But how, Bill?" I asked. "How are we going to do it? I want you to know that there are another hundred people with us, families with children. Right now they're camped back near the Interstate, waiting for us. Even before we came here, I got this idea about going across to Israel on the *Ocean Prince*. I knew about the ship; that's why we came here in the first place. I had no idea how to do it, but I got this idea about taking the boat across the ocean. I know it's crazy, but in this crazy world, only crazy ideas seem to work.

"The Children of Israel didn't know how to get across the Red Sea, but G-d split the sea for us. Here we are, also the Children of Israel, standing on the shore of the ocean. We also want to get across. We want to escape from our enemies and we want to go to our Holy Land. And we're not planning to give up. That's why we're here in Portland. You wanted to know and now you know. But we really don't know what to do next."

Old Bill threw his head back and howled at the moon like an old owl in the forest. Amazingly, I just knew that he wasn't crazy. It was so strange. There was something real about Old Bill, something timeless. I shivered.

He turned and looked back at us.

"I'm goin' to help you."

Right then, on the night of *Tu b'Av*, listening to the words of a strange old man with a limp, I knew we would make it. There was something about Old Bill .... I didn't know what it was and I didn't know how he could help us, but I just knew we were going to make it.

"Bill, that's wonderful," said Uncle Phil. "Tell us, what do we need to do?"

"You're all gonna come with me now. We're goin' to see Jack Austen. Yep, we're gonna wake up Jack Austen. Just leave it to Old Bill, OK? You leave it to Old Bill. Come along now. We're gonna visit Jack Austen."

"Who's Jack Austen?" Everybody asked in unison.

"Jack Austen owns the ship, boys."

We looked at each other. I was smiling even while tears were streaming down my face.

I think this guy's for real.

"Yeah, that old shippin' company's been in his family for decades now."

"Are you sure it's OK to go now, Bill?" asked Shmuli. "It's pretty late."

"You just leave it to Old Bill. Follow me."

Old Bill took off at such a pace that we were scrambling to keep up. For an old guy with a limp, he was walking faster than most eighteen-year-olds. We followed him around corners and down winding streets for about forty minutes, his stick clacking on the pavement. The surroundings began to change. Finally, he slowed down when we reached a neighborhood that was well-tended, with big, substantial houses set back from the road with wide lawns and huge old trees.

Bill marched up to the front door of one of the houses, a stately mansion that looked a hundred and fifty years old. He raised his stick and banged on the enormous front door.

"Jack Austen, open up! It's me, Bill. Open the door, Jack."

A window creaked upstairs.

"Bill, what on earth are you doing here at this hour? What's wrong?"

"Jack, we got important visitors. We got to talk. Right now. Turn on one a' them oil lamps and get out the whiskey, Jack. We got to talk."

I was thinking that this probably wasn't the ideal way to present ourselves to Mr. Jack Austen. To be awakened at two o'clock in the morning with a door pounding by Old Bill. In fact, we may have squandered our best chance.

Then, his voice called down from the second floor.

"Only for you, Bill Jasper, would I do this. Hold on, I'll be right down."

We saw a light flickering inside the house, then watched it descend the stairs. The heavy door opened. In the light of the oil lamp we could see a man of about sixty-five, with a patrician face and abundant silver hair, dressed in a green plaid robe and leather slippers. He looked at each of us closely.

"Please...come in, everyone," said Jack Austen, displaying a level of graciousness and good manners that I imagine had been ingrained in him since childhood. "I don't usually have visitors at this hour, but these are not ordinary times. If Old Bill says it's important, I know it must be."

We walked through the front door into an entrance hall that soared three stories, topped with an elaborate stained glass skylight. A huge chandelier dangled majestically overhead that, even unlit, evoked a feeling of splendor.

Jack Austen ushered us into a spacious sitting room and lit several oil lamps.

"Please everyone, sit."

I sank into a massive stuffed chair, upholstered in a rich, velvety material. It had been nearly a month since I'd sat down on a chair. What had formerly been a simple pleasure was now an unexpected luxury.

"May I offer you some Kentucky Bourbon, gentlemen?" asked our host. "Jack Daniels, to be exact."

He was continuing to act as though he had been eagerly expecting a group of total strangers to visit him in the middle of the night. He poured whiskey into crystal glasses for us, and we all sat immobile, staring at the glasses and taking deep breaths. I gave Dovid and Shmuli an "are we allowed to drink it?" look. Jack Austen was puzzled for only an instant.

"You are kosher, I believe. Would you rather pour for yourselves from the bottle?"

This Jack Austen is an extraordinary person, I thought; so sensitive and unperturbed under such strange circumstances.

Dovid immediately took the glass that Jack Austen had offered him and said, in Hebrew, "Blessed are You, G-d, King of the universe, by Whose word all things are made."

We all drank (except Leah!), and then sat back.

"Ma'am, may I offer you something sweet?" asked Jack Austen.

Leah smiled. I knew what she'd say.

"Would you have a glass of water?"

"My pleasure," he replied, and soon returned with a crystal glass and full pitcher on a silver tray.

Relaxed by the surroundings and impressed by our host, we sat quietly for a minute, just trying to get our bearings. Jack broke the silence.

"Please tell me now what brings you to our door at this hour. From the circumstances and the state of the world, I'm sure it's a weighty matter."

His expression was a mixture of curiosity and concern. Where and how exactly should I begin? But I didn't have to begin. Old Bill did.

"Jack, this is serious stuff. You know, we been talking about what to do since the world blew up. You've got no business left. Nobody's got their business left. And the business ain't comin' back. But you got a ship. Maybe you have that ship for a reason."

Jack Austen did not reply. He was listening intently. So were we.

"What would happen if you could sail that ship to the Holy Land, Jack? And what if your family came with you and maybe Old Bill? What then? Would you say that maybe your life was worth it for that alone? 'Cause maybe you had the ship just for that, and all those years of making a big livin' were nothin' compared to this."

Now I was holding my breath and watching Jack Austen's face.

"And I don't mean to the Holy Land and turn back. I mean to the Holy Land and stay there. That's the future, Jack. I see it in the stars. There's a time to live and a time to die. There were great civilizations in the past that are no more. America was great but now it's gone. We ain't the runnin' type, Jack, but this ain't runnin' *from* somethin', it's runnin' *to* somethin'."

Old Bill was remarkable. He knew how to say what he had to say.

"You know, Jack, since they blew up America, I been thinkin' what to do and nothin' is good enough. I'm thinkin' and thinkin' and there are just no answers. Until tonight. Tonight I was out there lookin' at that full moon, wonderin' what it's seein' in this shattered world below. I was wonderin' what the future's gonna bring and in the moonlight I suddenly see these Jews. And I start talkin' to them and I see that they *are* the future! They are forever! When the world's fallin' apart, you gotta hang on to what lasts forever."

I looked over at Jack Austen. He was holding his glass in two hands, staring hard at Old Bill.

"Now they have no way to get where they're goin', and we have no life left here. You have nothing' left to do with that ship except... what? Sail it to the Holy Land! And Jack, you would not be doin' them a favor if you took them to the Holy Land, but they would be doin' you a favor. Do you understand what I'm sayin'?"

Old Bill fell silent. Jack Austen took a long sip of his drink and leaned back in the chair. Silence. In the stillness of the great room, we heard the swinging pendulum of an old grandfather clock. Shadows curled at the edges of the glow from the oil lamps. I stared at the paintings, the tapestries, the spiral staircase off in the center hall. A large calico cat strolled up and jumped on the arm of the sofa, purring loudly.

Finally, Jack Austen spoke.

"What you're saying is enormous, Bill, enormous. Of course, I would have to discuss it with Martha and the family. The logistics would be very difficult. We'd need a crew and lots of supplies. Fuel we have. We actually have a huge supply of fuel, but we don't have the electricity to pump it on board. But, that's not a discussion for now. I need to sleep on this and then talk to Martha.

"I will say this. I've been thinking along the same lines, that is, to go somewhere. But where? I didn't know. And now you have this amazing idea. I don't know any of you, but Bill doesn't bring me ideas or people who are not honest. I feel the truth of your mission. And I believe what Bill said, that we must grasp onto something that can never be destroyed. We must think about this very deeply. There's not much time left to sleep, but I must sleep on it.

"As for our new friends, here, I grant that it is totally illogical that I should feel comfortable discussing these vital, life-altering issues with you, considering that we have never met before, and considering that you are obviously from a different world and a totally different lifestyle.

"And yet, it is not so illogical.

"I want to tell you a story. When I was a young boy, my father, may he rest in peace, took me to Boston. I will never forget this trip. My father had troubles then, troubles with his health and troubles with the family business. Somehow, he had made the acquaintance of an old and revered rabbi who had a large following in Boston. We went together to visit this rabbi.

"I remember how he looked. He was regal in a long, velvet coat of beautiful deep blue material. I will never forget the look of that coat; I can see it now, perhaps some fifty years later. It had light blue stars against the deep blue background. Even the buttons were covered in blue velvet.

"The rabbi had a long, white beard and soft, blue eyes. He was drinking tea from a clear glass cup; there were sugar cubes on a china plate and he would place one or two very carefully in his tea with silver tongs. His wife offered us cake and tea. She served us.

"My father told the rabbi about our troubles. The rabbi listened to my father with such concentration that it seemed there was nothing else in his world than my father's story. His eyes were focused intently on my father. We must have been there for an hour. The room was quiet and serene.

"The room was lined from floor to ceiling with wooden bookcases, filled with old leather-bound books, each of which had been handled and read, and read again. I knew, because the books looked as if they were all the rabbi's friends.

"The rabbi took one of the books down from the shelf and consulted it silently for several minutes. Then he put his hand on my father's head and concentrated. My father was crying. The rabbi gave my father a Book of Psalms in English and told him which ones to say. He also gave me a Book of Psalms. He told me to say one psalm every day, Psalm 121. Why do I remember? Because I still say it, to this day! Here is the book the rabbi gave me."

Jack Austen lifted an old, much-used leather-bound Book of Psalms in English translation from the table beside him.

"Before we left, the rabbi said to us the following words, which remain with me as fresh as if they had just been spoken.

"'My dear friend Samuel, may G-d guide you and watch over you forever. May He ease your way through this world. May He give you health and strength until old age and may you see happiness from your family for generations to come. May your business prosper and may it be a source of pride to you and not a burden. May your name be good in the world and your word be trusted.

"'And my dear child, Jack, may G-d watch over you. Remember this day that your father brought you to me, a son of Abraham, Isaac and Jacob, a child of Israel. May the G-d of Israel watch over you and bless you to become a man of integrity like your father and his father before him, and a dear friend of the nation of Israel. If the day ever comes when trouble comes upon you — and may it never happen, but in this world many troubles do come upon us — I want you to remember the blessing I gave to you and your father. May the G-d of Israel watch over you and protect you.'

"My father's health improved after that, and the business prospered. My father told me, after we left, that if ever I have any problems in my life I must go to this holy rabbi and he would help me. And, if ever I could not do that, I should look for a blessing from the Children of Israel. Because of those words of my father and because of this message from the holy rabbi, I am not amazed that you have come here tonight. I almost think that, long ago, the holy rabbi was hinting that one day our path to survival might look something like this."

He paused, seemingly looking at his father and the great rabbi in his mind's eye.

"Now, perhaps, you can understand why I am not at all shocked to see you here. All of you are welcome to spend the night with me."

"Thank you, Mr. Austen," I replied, "we appreciate your kind invitation. But our families are waiting for us near the turnpike exit. They will be worried if we don't return tonight."

"I understand, my friend. What is your name?"

"Yisroel Neuberger."

"Yisroel, I have a van. Use it to drive your group back to your families. There is plenty of fuel. Let's meet back here to-morrow at noon. Then we'll discuss the next step. Does that sound fair?"

"Fair? How can I begin to express the gratitude I feel? G-d has introduced us to holy beings. May He always bless you and Bill for your kindness, no matter what lies ahead."

"You are very kind, Mr. Neuberger. To be honest, I feel blessed tonight. I feel that something very important is hap-pening. Bill has had quite a journey in life himself, and I'm sure you will hear about it someday. His soul touches deep currents and tonight he has gone into the deepest of waters. We may yet see happy days again. We may see more than we ever dreamed we could see."

He turned to Old Bill.

"What will you do, Bill?"

"I'll go in the van and show them the way. I'll spend the night with them so we can return together tomorrow."

"All right. Here are the keys to that gray van in the drive-way. Bill will show you the way. Goodnight all. Until tomor-row then."

"Goodnight, Mr. Austen. May G-d bless you."

We put our glasses on the oak side table, filed through the entrance hall and out into the moonlight. Certainly tonight the moon had looked down upon some interesting doings upon the face of the earth.

PIPE SMOKE

Wednesday morning, August 5

S SOON AS OUR GROUP had finished morning prayers, we briefed them on the events of the preceding night: how we had seen the *Ocean Prince* shining at her moorings in the full moon, and our dramatic encounter with Old Bill, whose presence, of course, added realism to our story. We recounted our journey to the home of Jack Austen and our late-night conference in that grand old mansion.

We tried to convey the story accurately, without raising everyone's hopes unduly, yet there was a palpable air of excitement throughout the camp as our group from the previous night once again boarded the van to return to Jack Austen's home. We rode in silence, all of us lost in thought, including Old Bill. I had the feeling that he was as anxious to board *Ocean Prince* as we were.

In the light of a clear Maine day, Jack Austen's house looked even more imposing, although with a certain New England aura of understated elegance. That same quality was apparent in its owner, who was waiting for us out front. He seemed to possess a sensitivity that sprang from deep wells of kindness and thoughtfulness. My spirits rose when I saw him.

This time he was accompanied by a dark-haired woman who stood by his side in such a way that it was immediately clear she had stood by his side for a long time. He introduced her to us as Martha, his wife.

Jack and Martha Austen ushered us into their home, and once again we returned to the venerable sitting room. Cold drinks were served in heavy crystal glasses. We settled ourselves on the deep-cushioned chairs and sofas. There were a few moments of silence; no one was in a hurry to begin. There was no tension, but everyone realized that weighty subjects were under consideration.

Jack Austen leaned forward and began to speak.

"Our family has had searching discussions since we spoke last night. Bill, you for one know how long the Austen Family has lived in this town. We are grateful for all the generations that we have lived here and for all the success and acceptance that we have had in this community. But we think we are realists. We think that we know when there is a fundamental change in circumstances, and now we are convinced that our life in this town is over, for better or for worse.

"It's not that we didn't know that before last night. We knew the world had changed forever, even our little part of the world. But we are New Englanders, and we don't jump so fast. In this case, we did not know what the alternatives were; or to put it more accurately perhaps, we didn't really think we had any viable alternatives. That was true until the middle of last night, when you arrived, Bill, with our new friends.

"My wife and children and I have considered your idea carefully. Frankly, we are intrigued; it seems to offer a way out of the maze. But I hope you will not object if we express some questions and concerns."

He paused. I saw that he was waiting for our reaction. I responded on behalf of the group.

"Mr. Austen, it would hardly be normal if you had no questions or concerns. We ourselves do not know, of course, what the future will bring. Please express your concerns, ask your questions and we will do our best to respond."

"Thank you, Yisroel.

"Say we decided to accompany you, and we were all successful. Say we actually made our way to the Holy Land. How would we fit in as non-Jews? Would we be accepted? Could we make a life there?"

No one was in a hurry to answer these weighty questions. After a few seconds, I responded.

"Let me first say, on behalf of all of us, that I have rarely met such kind and sensitive people as you. In a dangerous world, you welcome strangers in the middle of the night and make us feel at home. Our lifestyle differs from yours, but you treat us with honor and respect. We have been refugees for weeks, so our sense of gratitude is almost impossible to describe.

"Let me try to answer your question. The Children of Israel, from the time of our original Patriarch Abraham, have always welcomed into our midst those who desire to come close to G-d and who respect the nation of Israel. Such people are our friends, and such people will be blessed by G-d Who blesses us. You have already shown us your friendship. I am sure you and your family would find a welcome among our people.

"In any case, may G-d bless you and your family and our amazing friend Bill with the same kindness and compassion you have shown us."

"Thank you for those words. They help answer my question."

Jack Austen had taken out a pipe, stuffed some tobacco in it and lit a match. He took a deep draw and sat back in his chair. The smoke rose in a cloud whose pungent aroma filled the room.

"There is plenty of room in G-d's world," I continued, "and there are commandments for everyone. But whether one is a Jew or a non-Jew, it seems very clear that G-d is telling us all today, 'You cannot continue to live the old way. If you don't hang on to Me and My words, there is no survival.' Just as one is safer the closer he is to G-d, I would also say that one is safer in Israel than anywhere else. You are talking about the center of spirituality. Yes, there has been much conflict in Israel, but G-d's eyes are on the Holy Land from the beginning of the year to the end of the year. In the land that is close to G-d, there is more protection."

"What would happen if we lived in Israel as non-Jews?" asked Mrs. Austen.

"Let's take one step at a time. The first priority is for all of us to save ourselves in a physical sense. America is dangerous now. In addition, you have no more livelihood, which is in itself a sign from G-d. As for living in the Holy Land, I am sure you would be welcomed as heroes. You have been so kind to the Children of Israel.

"You have a spiritual soul. Why should you not live in the holiest place?"

Jack Austen took a deep draw on his pipe. Smoke curled up over our heads and again I was conscious of that sweet and calming aroma. The pipe tobacco somehow seemed to put one in a contemplative mood. We sat there quietly, nobody anxious to break the silence. I felt as if I were an actor in a great drama or a traveler in an epic journey.

Jack broke the silence.

"The negative part is pretty clear; we really are aware that there is no more life for us here. We are also aware that the wellsprings of our moral tradition are in the Land of the Bible. Certainly we are seeking spiritual as well as physical anchorage, the more so since we have lost our traditional moorings. The world knows that Israel has always been the location where man connected to G-d. That's why so many people have fought over it. The world may be jealous, but in a moment of candor everyone will acknowledge that the Bible gives it to you."

Jack Austen was speaking with increasing emotion now. A number of people, apparently younger family members, had entered the room. Martha listened with glistening eyes. Jack looked over and smiled at his family, then continued.

"We need to correct the pretense that has skewed most of history. It's in our interest to admit that Jews have a unique connection with G-d and the Land of Israel. Anyone who denies that the Jews have a spiritual blessing, ends up denying themselves that blessing. In this new world, only reality counts. Our own future depends on telling the truth."

I looked around. Leah, Dovid, Shmuli, Shlomo Jacobson, Shaul Plotsker, Jeff Klein, and Uncle Phil were clearly impressed with Jack Austen. Old Bill, sitting with his stick planted firmly on the floor, was swaying slowly back and forth.

Jack continued.

"This morning, my wife, our daughters and sons-in-law and I decided that we want to join you, no matter what the risks are, and they are undoubtedly great. We are ready to put our resources at your disposal and cast our lot for survival and perhaps a new level of spiritual truth. We will take the adventure with you and we will take the risks with you. I am sure there will be plenty of both."

These were heavy words. Not unexpected, but weighty.

Sometimes you feel that events in your personal life are directly emanating from the Source of all existence. That is very powerful. Here we were, sitting in an old New England living room with pipe smoke curling around our heads, involved in absolutely cosmic events. G-d was once again splitting the sea. He was saving us. He was answering our prayer.

"*Hodu l'Hashem ki tov...* give thanks to G-d, for He is good."[48]

"Mr. Austen," I said, "you are an amazing man."

"Yisroel, would you mind calling me 'Jack.'"

I walked over and extended my hand.

"Someday, perhaps, I will call you 'Yaakov.' Today I am proud to say that I am your friend. Jack, you are blessed by G-d. We have many things to decide, and much to accomplish in a short time, because we must now begin to be very logical and practical. But, before that, I would like to ask you if we could pour a little more of that good American bourbon we drank last night.

"Our Torah tells us, '*choose life.*'[49] This is a decision for life, and I believe that at such a moment we should make what we Jews call a '*l'chayim,*' an affirmation that we have chosen life in every sense of the word."

Martha Austen knew exactly what I meant. She and one of her daughters left the room. They soon returned, carrying the silver tray with the crystal decanter and the heavy glasses, gleaming now in the sunlight streaming through the great windows. Jack poured out the clear brown liquid.

We drank.

"*L'chayim! L'chayim!* May we live! May our children live! May the world be renewed!"

FAREWELL AMERICA

Wednesday afternoon, August 5

"JACK," I SAID, "NOW I think we have to get to work and plan every step. We've got a big task ahead of us. Do you think the ship can make it across the Atlantic? What happens, for example, if there is a serious storm? Can we find a crew? What about fuel and supplies? And then, what should our destination be?"

"I'm a pretty seasoned skipper," said Jack, "and my wife and children are all experienced. Salt water has been in our blood for generations. *Ocean Prince* has operated as a cruise ship in the winter, crossing the high seas. And, by the way, Novia Scotia isn't an inland trip, even though we refer to the ship as a ferry. I have no reason to doubt that we'll make it across the ocean.

"As for rough weather, that's a definite possibility, especially since it's hurricane season. For our crew, we've got able-bodied sons-in-law as well as myself. Old Bill is no youngster, but he's still a good man on a boat. And I'm sure your group has some strong men. We can teach them what to do. As for fuel and supplies, we must have provisions for months ahead in this business. We haven't been operating since the attacks began, so we have plenty in our storage facilities. I'm not saying it's going to be simple, but we should be OK.

"There are some worries, however. We'll have to prepare and leave quickly and quietly, under cover of darkness. You never know who's watching. Some strange people have been spotted around here recently. Just the other day, a plane with no markings flew very low up the coast, so we know that there are people watching us. We must be careful and not let anyone see us preparing the ship. They will undoubtedly search for us when they see that big ship gone. I'll feel better after we're on the high seas."

This was chilling news: even quaint and quiet Maine was not all that far away from trouble.

"Today is Wednesday, August 5. I estimate we'll need four days to get ready, if all your able-bodied friends can help. Let's aim for Sunday. We should try to cast off during the early part of the night.

"What do you say, Yisroel? Are you and your group OK with this?"

I glanced around: thumbs up.

"Jack, I think I can speak for everyone. We trust you and are hopeful about this entire plan. You are a sincere man. Everyone in our group will be grateful that G-d has brought us together in this miraculous way. How else would we hope to cross the ocean if we hadn't met you? And how else would you have a future for your family if you hadn't met us? G-d brings people together who need each other.

"Just one more thing: our destination. Do we sail direct to Israel? What do you suggest?"

"This is a crucial question," said Jack. "I've been giving it a great deal of thought. This morning I looked at maps. The obvious choice would be to sail for Gibraltar, enter the Mediterranean and proceed directly to Israel. But I'm not so sure about that. Gibraltar is almost certain to be heavily guarded. It's impossible to pass through the Straits if they are in hostile hands. The passage is only about eight miles wide; no ship can pass through day or night if whoever controls one or both sides wants to stop it. It would be suicidal to attempt it.

"An alternative might be to land in Portugal, but the distance from there across Europe would be tremendous. So, even though it would make the voyage longer, I was thinking that we should head for the coast of France, perhaps a port that we could enter under cover of darkness. We would still be facing a long overland route across Europe, but with the likelihood of failure at Gibraltar, I don't think there's much choice."

I hadn't considered a long journey through Europe. But Jack had a very good point. I took a deep breath and kept listening.

"I found a French port that might work. It's a small town called Paimboeuf, which has a protected anchorage near the mouth of the Loire River. I'm not certain that the water will be deep enough there for us to dock, but I think it would work. Certainly, there are major docking facilities at St. Nazaire, which is a big port city on the Atlantic Coast at the mouth of the Loire. But I would like to find as small a place as possible. The sleepier the better, as there will be fewer people to 'welcome' us.

"In any case, main roads lead from this area to Nantes and from there to Paris. From Paris, the biggest roads and most direct route would be through Munich, Vienna, Budapest, then south to Belgrade, Sofia, Istanbul, Ankara and then down the coast of Lebanon to Israel. That's my idea of a route, once we've landed. This is a major question for us to mull over. It's a long way by land, but I just don't like the idea of Gibraltar."

"Let's all think about this. Is there anything else to discuss at this point?"

"I can't think of anything. How soon can your group get here to start loading and preparing the ship?"

"We will get you your seamen as soon as we can move the group into town. If you have additional vehicles, we can move everyone very quickly and we'll get to work right away. Before we begin, however, I want to ask Bill how he feels about all this.

"Bill, look what you started!"

Bill looked at Jack and then at us.

"You are the angels that have been sent to save us. This is from heaven, and we will all go together. Not just go... we're gonna make it! Mark my words!"

Over the next four days, with the exception of *Shabbos*, we all worked together under Jack Austen's direction, loading and outfitting the *Ocean Prince* for our voyage. Fortunately, Jack had fuel, water and other supplies in his warehouses. It was hectic, hard work with a welcome bonus: our group moved onto the ship and our hardscrabble lifestyle of vagabond refugees immediately disappeared.

Beds! Electricity! Walls, ceilings and floors!

Sleeping on beds again! Right away, I felt more refreshed and energetic in the morning. We didn't have to worry about waking up under a thunderstorm. Indoor plumbing: unbelievable!

We worked as much as possible at night. At times, I found myself looking over my shoulder for strangers, but we never spotted anyone. I was too busy to worry about it, anyway.

When we realized that we would have refrigeration on

board, we called upon people in our group who knew how to slaughter animals according to Jewish law. They were able to prepare chicken and ducks, cutting them up and freezing the meat. Knowing that we would be able to eat like normal people was in itself cause for celebration, after so many weeks of deprivation. We didn't know how long it would last, but we would certainly enjoy it while we could. We could especially make use of the added strength it would give us.

Leah and a group of women made the ship's galley kosher, separating it into separate sections for meat and milk. They picked berries and other fruit for preserves, milked cows and baked bread. A massive supply of food was stored in the pantries, enough to carry our group through a long period of travel.

On Sunday, August 9, we were ready. The weather had turned stormy and the sky was dark, with a cold wind blowing in from the sea. I thought with endless gratitude about how G-d was saving us from a seemingly impossible situation. Yet, perhaps the most dangerous portion of our Exodus was now beginning.

After all, none of us, including Jack Austen, had ever piloted a ship across the Atlantic. And these were perilous times, with unsuspected dangers liable to emerge without warning, at any place. Who knew what awaited us, either on the open waters or after we landed in Europe? Who knew what enemies we might encounter? Did Jack really know his way on the high seas? Would our navigation equipment function correctly?

Jack inspired confidence through his understated New Englander demeanor, his calm, studied manner, logical reasoning and formidable leadership skills. He was thoroughly honest and didn't put on airs. If he said he would do something, you could count on it.

We had agreed on Paimboeuf as our destination. Jack's sons-in-law had located navigational charts of the area, and we were reasonably sure the harbor there would be deep enough.

Late in the afternoon of our impending departure, Leah and I watched dusk eclipse the day's lingering glow. A strong breeze blew in from the sea; the surf whipped our faces as we stood on the dock, looking past the horizon to our future. The darkening sky was overcast. Soon it would be time to get underway.

Anticipation was tinged with sadness as we prepared to leave America's shores for the last time. This had been home. America had been good to the Jews, the least hostile land of our Diaspora. Leah and I had met each other, gotten married and raised our children here. We had searched openly and widely for our religious roots, and then lived our Torah, all in America. Now, the currents of history had overwhelmed even this strong nation. Perhaps its very success had weakened it.

Our group stood together for a simple farewell ceremony. We thanked G-d for all the years of plenty. We asked Him to save our brethren and all the good people who were still here. We asked Him to save us as He had saved our brethren thousands of years before when they fled into the sea. Here, too, we were leaving the land of our exile, pursued by enemies who would stop at nothing to destroy us.

Where are Efraim Borenstein and Shmuel Gantz and their families now? Will we ever meet again?

All of us had come to the seashore with little more than an idea and a full measure of hope. Here we had found the most unexpected help in the heavenly messengers who were waiting to escort us across the sea. As we set out upon the waters, we realized how completely our fate was in G-d's hands.

A young couple on our way to Oxford, we lean against the ship's railing. Our smiling parents, still youthful, stand opposite us in a huge crowd on the dock, waving brightly-colored handkerchiefs. The scene is frozen in time, and indeed, in a photograph. Our parents are filled with pride that their darling children are going off to the world's most famous and ancient university to bask in European culture.

Buried within our luggage is a bottle of champagne, a gift from our parents. At Southampton, the customs official asks, "And what may this be?"

"Just a going-away present."

"Well, isn't that jolly! My parents never gave me a bottle of champagne! Now off you go! Don't forget, we drive on the left over here!"

Days of champagne and caviar, when life seems filled with dancing bubbles. But perhaps the memory is flawed. As the bubbles pop, something gnaws at my soul, embitters my laughter and tarnishes the veneer of culture. Something inside me cries out for truth, and I don't know where to find it.

Tonight, a group of religious Jews and their friends were sailing from Portland, Maine in absolute silence under blackout conditions on a dark and stormy night. No handkerchiefs waved; no sound was heard except for the creaking of the hawsers slipping off the bollards. Jack, with only the occasional flick of a searchlight beam, guided the ship in darkness out of the channel and into the open sea.

Standing at the railing, we watched the outline of America slip into the fog. All we could see were shadows receding into darker shadows. Moments later, even the shadows were no more, and we were on our way, sailing into the unknown, into the dark of night. In the glow of flashlights and the spray of salt-water, we recited the Traveler's Prayer.

"May it be Your will, our G-d and the G-d of our fathers, that You lead us toward peace, emplace our footsteps toward peace, guide us toward peace and make us reach our desired destination for life, gladness and peace. May you rescue us from the hand of every foe and ambush along the way, and from all manner of punishments .... May You send blessing in our handiwork and grant us grace, kindness and mercy in Your eyes and in the eyes of all who see us. May You hear the sound of our supplications, because You are G-d Who hears prayer and supplication."

SHEIK MUSTAFA AL-HARARI

Sunday night, August 9

LEAH AND I WENT UP to the bridge. Jack stood at the helm, surrounded by sons-in-law and family, Old Bill, and a few trusted crew members from the old days. We all stared out into the blackness. It would take about seven days to reach the shores of France, assuming all went according to plan.

It was exhilarating to be on the move, and yet I felt trepidation. Radar probed the night, but I imagined all sorts of shapes and unseen dangers. What if we encountered another ship? Just who was sailing on the high seas these days? How could you tell who was your friend? Were there any friends left in the world? We all desired just to keep going and avoid contact with other ships. As we plowed through the dark waters, all we could see was what our radar screen showed, and, for now, that was nothing. Despite the fuel burning below, in reality we were running on pure faith, pure prayer.

Was this not the generation to which the words applied: "Behold I send you Elijah the Prophet before the coming of the great and awesome day of G-d. And he will turn back [to G-d] the hearts of the fathers with [their] sons and the hearts of sons with their fathers."[50] Was this not the generation that had seen the children running home to G-d, bringing their parents back with them? Although many were running in the opposite direction, still the children were returning like never before, and the hearts of the parents were returning with them.

Around midnight, Leah and I left the bridge. Jack's son-in-law, Arthur Emerson, and some others stayed up on watch, while the rest of us went below. But despite the comfort of a real bed and the gentle swaying of the ship, I tossed for hours, imagining dangers lurking in those dark waters.

When the morning dawned bright and warm, I felt encouraged. "In the evening one lies down weeping, but with dawn...a cry of joy."[51] It was our first day out and I enjoyed being able to see the beauty and sheer vastness of the sea in daylight.

Around 11 a.m., I was standing on the bridge.

Jack Austen was at the helm. Pipe smoke floated around us.

"Hmmm," he said, "I wonder what that is."

Something in his tone made my heart skip. I quickly walked over and looked at the radar screen. Something was sailing directly across our path, north to south. It was far away, but unmistakably there.

My brain went into overdrive. I imagined a naval vessel from some hostile power turning toward us and firing big guns across our bow. Or a torpedo silently boring through the waters and a huge explosion blowing the ship apart.

As I stared at the radar image, my eyes began to play tricks. I kept imagining it had stopped moving from left to right. I thought it was getting larger, which would mean it was approaching us.

I found myself repeating *"ain od milvado ....ain od milvado."*

There is nothing but G-d. All reality belongs to Him, whatever happens is His will and I have nothing to fear, because He is perfect.

Then I realized that the blip was the same size, and had moved southward, off the radar screen. It was passing us!

Thank You G-d for saving us again!

Whether the other ship had seen us and was not interested, or whether it had missed us in this vast ocean, I didn't care, but the phrase came back to me, "like two ships passing in the night." Well, it was daylight, but G-d had wrapped us in darkness. The ocean was vast. Invisibility can be a blessing. "Blessed are You, our G-d, King of the universe, Who...creates day and night, removing light before darkness and darkness before light...."

Yes, G-d creates night as well as day. Darkness can be a blessing.

At night, we observed blackout rules. No lights burned in exterior cabins or on deck. Of course, on the bridge, instruments flickered and glowed. We watched the radar screen in the darkness.

The second night out, at around 10 p.m., Leah and Shmuli and I were on the bridge when we picked up another blip, directly on our course. We watched it anxiously; it seemed as though this time the blip was getting larger.

"Looks like a ship to me," said Jack Austen, "heading straight toward us. It's twelve miles away at this point. It probably picked us up on radar as soon as we picked it up."

It was nearly impossible not to panic.

Old Bill spoke up.

"Okay boys. Get down from the bridge. All you Jews off the bridge and down into the engine room, the way we worked out. Follow the plan. Grab your stuff, all your children and straighten up your rooms...and do it as quickly as you can. Then disappear and pray until we tell you it's safe. Our job is to lie and yours is to pray."

Jack Austen grabbed the microphone and spoke into the ship's PA system.

"Attention, please. Attention, please. This is Jack Austen from the bridge. All our Jewish friends immediately go to the engine room, exactly as we discussed. This is an emergency. It is not a drill. You have five minutes to clear your belongings and go with all family members to the engine room. Not one second longer. Again, this is not a drill. Remember to turn all lights off as you leave. You have five minutes to disappear into the engine room. Then pray with intensity. Ship approaching, possibly hostile. Disappear now and pray for all of us."

We bolted down darkened corridors. The adults had flashlights and we knew where to go. Mothers and fathers carried children. Uncle Phil, Aunt Bessie and the Frankels rode the elevator to the lowest level. The rest of us climbed down steps, then more steps and more steps and passageways. We had taken a test run, so we knew just how to get there.

Soon we were all assembled, or shall I say packed, in a hot room deep in the ship's interior. It had taken seven minutes for everyone to squeeze in. Shmuli read off the list of families. No one answered for the Lyons.

Missing!

Just as Shmuli opened the door to find them, they scrambled inside.

Men and women tried to stand separately as much as possible as we all began to pray. Here we were, buried deep down in the ship.

"*Min hamaitzar*...from the straits I call out to You."

"G-d save us! After all we have been through!"

"Waters encompassed me to the soul, the deep whirled around me .... I descended...yet You lifted my life from the pit, O G-d. When my soul was faint within me, I remembered G-d."[52]

Yaakov Gruenstein led us in psalms. He would say a verse and we would repeat it. Sometimes our voices cracked. I kept trying to concentrate on understanding the words. It was hard to focus, but we needed above all to attach ourselves to G-d. Our lives were literally at stake. I imagined a huge explosion: black smoke, fire, water pouring in, chaos, swallowing salt water, drowning.

"*Ain od milvado.*"

We have come such a long way and accomplished so much. G-d, would You have led us this far only to die? We are trying not only to save our families, but also to enable the Children of Israel to survive and bring about the Final Redemption.

Our eyes were flowing with tears. Children and adults were crying; no one knew what the next seconds would bring. Suddenly, the engines slowed, then stopped completely. This was it.

"*Min hameitzar,*" from the depths we prayed.

On the bridge, Jack Austen, his two sons-in-law, Old Bill, and others saw the other ship approaching in the darkness. Piercing searchlights were aimed at *Ocean Prince*, bathing it in light from top to bottom, bow to stern. As the other ship approached, the men in the bridge, shielding their eyes as best they could, saw that it was a giant warship painted in military camouflage with Arabic writing on the bow.

Suddenly the *Ocean Prince* seemed pitifully small.

A loudspeaker blared over the waters, broadcasting a voice with a Middle Eastern accent.

"Identify yourselves. Where are you from and where are you bound?"

Jack used the PA system.

"Good evening. We are bound from Portland, Maine, for Egypt. We respectfully invite your excellencies to come aboard. We are carrying a distinguished personage to Cairo."

Silence. Maybe three minutes. Then the loudspeaker blared again.

"Stand by for boarding. We warn you that we are heavily armed. Our guns are trained on you. No tricks will be tolerated. We will not hesitate to blow you instantly out of the water if we sense any hostile intent, whether or not our officers are on board your ship. As of now, you are considered an enemy vessel. Prepare for boarding."

Moments later, three dozen Arab sailors lowered themselves onto the deck. Dressed in spotless white uniforms, they were followed by an officer dressed in white trimmed in gold, whose uniform was emblazoned with colorful insignia. A leather portfolio was tucked under his arm.

The sailors carried submachine guns as well as side arms, knives and radios strapped around their waists. Some remained on the main deck while the others escorted the officer up to the bridge. The blinding searchlights continued to bear down on every surface of the *Ocean Prince*, creating a surreal sense of being on a movie set rather than the high seas in the dark of night.

A dozen sailors and the officer marched to the bridge and stood outside the door. The door opened. Escorted by four sailors, the officer strode inside and looked around. Then he gasped.

Jack Austen and his sons-in-law stood at full attention in merchant marine uniforms, flanking a man seated on cushions and dressed in the robes and *kaffiyeh* of a distinguished imam. He exuded an air of authority and the regal calmness of a desert *sheik*.

It was Old Bill Jasper.

He did not rise.

"*Salum Aleikum*, greetings," he said in perfect Egyptian Arabic.

"Greetings," said the astounded officer. "Who are you? What is your business here?"

Old Bill introduced himself as Sheik Mustafa al-Harari, the leader of a religious sect in Boston. He told the officer, with obvious pride, of leading an uprising against the infidels as part of the coordinated attacks. After leaving his two sons in charge, he was returning to Cairo and from there to Mecca in his old age. He had chartered the ship and its crew to take him there.

Speaking Egyptian Arabic perfectly and displaying a keen grasp of the Koran, Old Bill chatted easily with the officer, whose expression ranged between confusion and amazement. Bill concluded with a rousing description of the July 5th triumphs, followed by a heated diatribe against the American infidels.

The officer abruptly excused himself and stood for a few moments on the deck outside the bridge, engaged in a hushed conversation on the two-way radio. Moments later, he returned and handed the radio to Old Bill.

"My commanding officer wishes to speak to the Imam."

The two-way radio crackled loudly as the commander and Old Bill spoke for several minutes in Arabic. Then Old Bill handed the radio back to the officer, who again retired to the deck for privacy.

Returning, with a bow of respect, the officer bid Sheik Mustafa a cordial farewell and offered blessings on his safe return to Cairo and pilgrimage to Mecca. Then he withdrew with the sailors and left the ship. Soon the searchlights were extinguished. The warship pulled away and faded into the night.

Minutes of silence passed until radar confirmed that the Arab ship was far away under full speed. Then an enormous cheer arose on the bridge and everyone began talking and laughing at once.

Jack picked up the microphone.

"Attention, attention, friends in the engine room. Please report immediately to the main deck. We have some celebrating to do."

All of us began shouting at the top of our lungs as we scrambled out of our deep confinement. I doubt if it took five minutes this time for all of us to complete the upward journey.

Long after the telling and retelling of everything that had happened, while children were sleeping and adults were strolling along the deck, Leah and I sat in the bridge with Jack, Martha, Old Bill and the Austen children.

"How on earth did you do it? It seems impossible that you could pull it off."

Old Bill threw back his head and howled, just as he had the night we met him. Only tonight there was no full moon. Then he laughed softly.

"You young people think ya know all about the world, without ever having to leave your own backyard. But there's more out there than ya know. When I was a kid, it was a different world."

He was enjoying the puzzled look on our faces. He pointed his stick at me.

"Do you know where I was raised?

"My pappy was a preacher and missionary in the Upper Nile Valley. I was raised there, near Asyut in Egypt. I knew plenty of them sheiks and dervishes. I grew up speakin' their lingo and readin' their books. That Koran is somethin' I know just as well as them."

He smiled as we stood there, shaking our heads in astonishment.

"Yeah, if I do say so, I make a pretty good sheik. All I need is a few hundred wives."

Peals of laughter.

"You know, we had lots of souvenirs from them days when we moved back to Maine. Kept 'em up in the attic. After everythin' blew up, I looked up there and, yup, everythin' was there. I figured that's somethin' we might need."

Jack looked a little sheepish and admitted that at first he was mostly humoring Old Bill about bringing along all the Arab items.

"I had no idea that we'd really need a sheik aboard."

Again, more laughter.

"Yeah, I'm a regular good A-rab sheik, all right, but I doubt I'll be goin' to Mecca too soon."

I was filled with astonishment.

Blessed are You, our G-d and the G-d of our fathers, G-d of Abraham, G-d of Isaac and G-d of Jacob; the great, mighty and awesome G-d, the supreme G-d, Who bestows beneficial kindnesses and creates everything, Who recalls the kindnesses of the Patriarchs and brings a Redeemer to their children's children, for His Name's sake, with love....

"Bill, when I said you are an angel, I didn't know the half of it! Tonight, you outdid yourself, beyond what anyone could have imagined. You are an emissary sent direct from heaven to do things that no ordinary person can do."

That night, we celebrated with some "exported, duty-free" Jack Daniels.

G-d had indeed sent angels to protect us, and now it seemed they were accompanying us as we sailed across the great sea.

GATHERING OUR STRENGTH

AFTER THE ENCOUNTER WITH OUR uninvited guests, I finally began to calm down. The weather had turned beautiful, and we sailed through calm seas and warm, starry nights. At first, I kept checking the radar screen at all hours of the day and night, half-expecting to spot more potential adversaries. But we sailed on in blessed solitude.

"It's almost as if we're on a cruise," I said, as Leah and I walked the deck, drinking in the blazing colors of a spectacular sunset. "G-d is giving us a rest after our trials of the past weeks."

"Relax now, Yisroel, because there's plenty of challenge ahead. We're going to need all our strength."

We looked to the horizon, flaming with orange-red clouds. We watched the water sliding by and pondered the immensity, power and depth of the oceans which cover most of the globe. Of course, it was no cruise; we were still completely vulnerable. All the more were we grateful for the few days of rest for our weary souls and bodies.

We walked the decks and regained our strength, talking about the "old days" and the miracles that had brought us to this point. Basya Horowitz was trying to learn to live again; responsibility for her children occupied her time. But there was always that faraway look. Her mind's eye gazed upon her husband's shallow grave alongside the Garden State Parkway.

Mothers and children watched whales and the seemingly endless ocean. Whenever they weren't needed to help run the ship, the men learned Torah on deck, in the bracing North Atlantic breeze. In the evenings, we gathered in the spacious lounge, where we had set up a very nice study area. Of course, all blinds were drawn. In the lounge we also gathered for prayer services three times a day. All in all, we were getting an uninterrupted rest and gathering strength for whatever lay ahead.

Suddenly the picture of Efraim Borenstein and Shmuel Gantz and their families came before my mind's eye. How were they? Where were they? Had they made it through? Would we meet them again? I thought a lot about family members, friends, our entire Jewish Family and the many friends we had in the world. Out there, among hordes of enemies, there were many who loved and admired the Jewish People, who expressed it — sometimes in obvious and sometimes in subtle ways — and who sometimes risked their own lives to save us. I imagined for a moment that I was looking out over the endless waters and there were dozens — no, hundreds — no, THOUSANDS of ships sailing alongside us, bound for the Holy Land, bringing all G-d's Children home!

G-d, may it be Your will to bring us all home!

Jeff joined me one morning for a stroll on the deck.

"This has been the most amazing experience," he said.

"We've been saved so many times against all odds. And yet, for some reason I'm not surprised. I feel that G-d is so close to us."

"When life is routine," he continued, "who really thinks about G-d? But when you're facing danger and death, you immediately realize you've got to beg Him to save you. I guess the word is 'pray.' What else is there to do? Otherwise you would collapse. I'm sure that's nothing new for you, but for me it's huge."

"I agree, Jeff, but I don't think you go far enough. The entire Torah existence is set up to remind us constantly that G-d exists, so that we don't 'need' danger in order to keep our perspective. For example, why do I wear a *yarmulke*? Is it normal to cover one's head constantly? Sometimes that yarmulke just doesn't sit right. A puff of wind can blow it off. So, why is it there? It reminds me that G-d is above me. The more I'm conscious it's there, the better.

"The *mezuzah* on the doorpost. Why is it there? To remind me that G-d guards the house, the room, my life. It's not necessary to have near-death experiences to get close to G-d; it's necessary, however, to keep the commandments."

"It sounds crazy," said Jeff, "but the fact that Marge and I and Julie came so close to danger now is actually a source of happiness for me. If we hadn't met you and learned the reality of living a spiritual life, then we would really never have lived at all, literally. I've got to be grateful.

"The tiniest step can change a person's life. Say we had walked onto the parkway five minutes earlier or later. Say we had taken a different road or walked past you and not said a word. Anything could have changed in the most miniscule way and our lives would have been totally different. It all seems so accidental, but I don't think it is. G-d puts you in a certain place at a certain time. It seems it's up to you whether or not you're going to take advantage of it. Every decision is crucial."

"That, Jeff, is 'free will.' The person you walk next to in life is crucial. Thank G-d for us that you walked alongside us, and I do believe we can say 'thank G-d for you' that we walked alongside you. We are a beautiful team, and we have literally saved each other's lives along the way."

"What do you think is going to happen now, Yisroel?"

"I think we're going to have a lot of challenges in Europe. We have a very long way to go and I for one don't have a clue as to how we're going to get there. Of course, I didn't know how we were going to get this far either, but here we are! All I know is that we have to try. But I'm sure we're literally at the end of history, and I do believe that, if we stick to G-d with all our hearts and strength, with His help we'll make it all the way."

"What do you think the 'end of history' is going to look like?"

"I don't know, but I'll tell you what I've learned about the period before the end of history. Our prophets have told us that, before the coming of the Messiah, sons will bring their fathers back to G-d and fathers will bring their sons back to G-d. In recent decades there has been an unprecedented movement in which children who had grown up secular have returned to Torah observance. These Jews in many cases influenced their parents to become observant. In addition, these young Jews married and their own children grew up observant. This kind of thing never happened before in history, but the prophet Malachi said about twenty three hundred years ago that exactly that phenomenon would occur 'before the great and awesome day of G-d.'[53]

"I'll tell you another sign. It hasn't been long since the Arabs were desert nomads with no stature beyond their own sandy world. But our prophets and rabbis told us thousands of years ago that in the end of history the children of Ishmael would dominate the earth. Well, look around. I don't have to tell you that right now it sure looks as if those 'desert nomads' are dominating the earth."

"Yisroel, you're coming up with heavy stuff!"

We'd been walking for a long time, circling the boat perhaps ten times. Now the sun was setting. We descended to the lounge, our study hall and synagogue, just as afternoon prayers were getting underway. The water sparkled and shimmered in the sunset as the ship glided through the sea.

By evening, the clouds that had been brilliantly bathed in red and yellow began to thicken. As we finished our evening meal, a steady gale was blowing, and we could feel the ship rolling in the choppy sea. After dark, rain began to fall in sheets.

Leah and I aren't such good sailors. When a ship is rolling in a storm, it is intensely disorienting because there is nothing to hold on to. Our stomachs were tossing as the boat rocked around like a bath toy. All we could do was stagger to our room and lie on our beds. For three days, we were totally helpless. I don't know who guided the ship, but we were out of action.

Then one morning, I woke up and saw through the porthole a bright sunrise, blue sky and tranquil sea.

Thank you G-d, for calm weather.

That balmy day brought healing and relaxation, fresh air and renewed strength. Toward evening we thought we saw a little elevation on the eastern horizon. Gulls were flying around the ship. As the sky darkened, we saw tiny dots of light ahead.

Europe!

If our calculations were correct, we should be off the

coast of France near the Loire Estuary, with the port of St. Nazaire straight ahead. Jack reduced power and the *Ocean Prince* glided slowly up to the estuary entrance. Our plan was to sail past St. Nazaire and dock at Paimboeuf on the southern bank of the Estuary. We figured that, with high tide, there would be no trouble docking there if we could find an available pier.

It was a dark night. We were operating under blackout conditions except for an occasional flash of the searchlight. There were no street or harbor lights burning; only a few individual homes showed flickering flames. Using the searchlight and radar, we edged carefully into the mouth of the river and made our way steadily eastward on the flooding tide.

At about 2 a.m., we believed that we were approaching the town of Paimboeuf on our starboard side. Old Bill wielded the searchlight and soon spotted what appeared to be an empty pier. Gingerly we inched forward; the ship scraping against the dock. Some of the younger guys jumped to the pier and secured the ship's lines to the bollards. Once the winches were pulled tight, the *Ocean Prince* was secure.

Emotions of joy, relief, amazement and gratitude washed over me. We had come so far!

"Blessed are You, our G-d, King of the universe, Who is good and does good."[54]

We were in France.

DREAMS AND CHARIOTS

Early Monday morning, August 24

OUR REMARKABLE VOYAGE WAS OVER. All of us had prepared for this moment. Several days before, we had organized our supplies into bundles and knapsacks we could manage. We had studied maps to plan our trek across Europe and had pinpointed what appeared to be a wooded area to the south of Paimboeuf as our first overnight stop.

We collected our belongings, clambered down the gangways, and organized ourselves for the road. All voices were hushed and every movement was silent. To attract attention could be problematic, if not fatal to our success.

Leah and I lagged behind. We had grown fond of the *Ocean Prince*. Although inanimate like our bikes, Uncle Phil's truck, and even the roadways on which we had walked, it had nonetheless been an instrument of our salvation. I wanted to have a final pictorial memory of the ship. G-d had introduced us to the owners and the pilots and the friends who had enabled us to cross the ocean; He had lent us this

272

hunk of steel which had carried us so many thousands of miles across deep waters.

Noah and his family had been saved in a boat. Moses had been saved in a basket. In this big basket we had all been saved. We lingered on the dock, remembering the night in Portland when we had first seen *Ocean Prince* rolling gently in the moonlight. It already seemed a century ago.

Thank you G-d!

We turned and caught up with the others.

It was 3:30 a.m. The streets were dark and deserted. The moon had set hours ago. Fortunately, no one seemed to have noticed our silent arrival. We figured there were probably two hours until sunrise, enough time, I hoped, for us to reach our rest area. It was going to be a shock, after the relative luxury of Portland and a week aboard ship. We had eaten well and managed to catch up on sleep. Now we would once again be traveling on foot and living on the extremely limited supplies that we could carry on our backs.

No one in our group had questioned the decision to land in France. But now we were faced with a seemingly interminable journey to Israel, a distance seven times as long as from Perth Amboy to Portland! That trip had taken a month, but now summer was ending and cold weather approaching. How were we going to survive an overland journey of twenty-four hundred miles — across Europe and Asia Minor, then down the Mediterranean Coast to Israel — through strange and hostile countries in the frozen grip of winter? I had an awful vision of our starving and bedraggled group, huddled on some Alpine pass in the midst of a blizzard.

In the old days, travel by train across Europe was commonplace, with tourists peering through insulated windows at quaint villages, mountains, castles and "the natives." I fantasized about commandeering a train the way we had secured a ship, but I had a strong feeling that Europe had gone the way of America. I doubted that any trains would be running in our direction. Gone were the days of the Orient Express.

Not only was the distance daunting, but we were in alien lands with language and cultural barriers. Leah and a few others spoke French, but France had been hostile to our people for centuries before July 5. In addition, there were plenty of Middle Eastern types around. Could they have taken over Europe?

No matter what, we had to get started. According to the map, south of Paimboeuf there was a pastoral area off Rue des Floralies, also called Route D77, the road that would lead us eastward toward Paris. Our aim was to put as much distance as we could between ourselves and the ship. When the morning broke, a lot of questions would be asked about that ship. We didn't want to be there to answer them.

We walked through the small town's deserted streets in absolute silence. After a half mile, we reached the intersection with Rue des Floralies. We turned left and the countryside was on our right.

As we walked toward the sunrise, we saw in the first light of morning that our educated guesses had been correct. To our right was rolling countryside with plenty of shelter among groves of trees. A bright day was dawning and we were anxious to hide ourselves before the road became busy. Minutes later, we had all disappeared within a forest grove, invisible from the roadway. We prepared to settle down for the routine we had practiced in America, rest by day and move by night.

First we prayed, raising our voices to G-d, still overwhelmed at our ocean crossing. As we read from the little Torah scroll, many of us had tears of gratitude mixed with trepidation. After the Torah reading, I made the *gomel* blessing on behalf of our whole group. We say this blessing after having passed through a life-threatening experience, such as a passage across the ocean or through a desert, after sickness or release from prison. I'm sure everyone felt as if we had been through all of them.

"Blessed are You, L-rd our G-d, King of the universe, Who bestows good things upon the undeserving, Who has bestowed every goodness upon me."

The others responded, "May He Who has bestowed goodness upon you continue to bestow every goodness upon you forever."

Yes, we needed that.

Afterward, despite my worries and the brightness of the warm August morning, I immediately fell into a deep sleep.

I stand in a magnificent synagogue. Hundreds of people are praying. I am in the front row, before the Ark. It is Kol Nidrei Night, the beginning of Yom Kippur. I stand with my tallis over my head. I am blessed with a holy wife, children great in purity and love of Torah, grandchildren zealous in their passion for serving G-d.

"I have all this and who am I?"

I am crying. Under my tallis, tears are falling down my face. I feel like a piece of dust.

No, smaller.

An atom.

No, smaller.

A sub-atomic particle.

A worm, an ant is great compared to me.

Yes, the world is turbulent and chaotic, but it is the chaos within myself that tortures me. I am a creature of no discipline, no merit, no learning, no accomplishment. My greatest desire is for mundane pleasures that reflect no vision of greatness, a per-

son of selfish habits and banal existence. I cannot raise myself above the level of the animals. I am nothing.

My life is out of control. How can I merit any help from Above? How am I to hope for a blessing from G-d? Everything I have received was undeserved. In what merit will I survive? In what merit do I have such a family?

How absurd! This sub-atomic particle is trying to communicate with the Ruler of the Universe!

I am crying, which actually is a comfort because tears can open the Gates of Heaven. I have to survive, no matter what. I may have no worth, but at least I can cry. At least I am upset at being a nonentity! At least I have feelings, so perhaps G-d will pity this quivering blob of desperation. Maybe G-d will hear my prayers.

I pray in the merit of our grandchildren, passionately zealous to serve Him. I think how Leah and I grew up in our empty, secular world, and how miraculous it is that all these children exist. It is too much to comprehend. Now we all have to be together. We have to.

It was August 24, 2020, and I was lying on a forest floor in the Loire Valley in France. The sun was hanging in a dark blue sky and the day was warm. My face was wet. Yes, I had been crying. I wiped my face and looked around. I was so tired. I lay down again, nestled among the trees.

I am with Leah and all our children and grandchildren, standing on a hilltop in Israel. It is springtime; the sun is warm and the meadows are covered with wildflowers. The cousins are running over the hills. The children are happy. The world is at peace and all our troubles are over.

High on a hilltop to our south we can see the Temple shining in the sunlight. A column of smoke ascends straight upwards, like the ancient Clouds of Glory that had surrounded the

Children of Israel in the days of Moses and Aaron. The warm sun penetrates our hearts.

We are no longer afraid. We don't have to hide. Thousands of years of exile are over. We can play innocently on the mountains of Israel without fear. We feel the Presence of G-d. No one threatens us. No one can hurt us. There are no newspapers, televisions, cars, or meetings. There is no money and there are no bills. We are happy with what we have. G-d's bounty is enough. We have everything.

"When G-d will return the captivity of Zion, we will be like dreamers. Then our mouth will be filled with laughter and our tongue with glad song. Then they will declare among the nations, 'G-d has done greatly with these.'"55

Gladness fills our hearts; tears of happiness are on our cheeks.

Again my cheeks were wet.

I blinked in the hot sun. It was two in the afternoon and we had work to do.

A few feet away, Old Bill and the Austens were talking. Right away I noticed something odd; Old Bill had his Arab gear on again. He motioned to me. After I had washed my hands and face, I walked over.

"Yisroel, I was born to be a sheik, don't you think?"

We laughed.

"Bill, let me say that you're the first and only sheik I ever plan to meet. But I don't know how comfortable you'll be hiking to Paris dressed in that outfit."

"Well, I have a bit of a scheme that requires Sheik Mustafa Al-Harari's special touch. The Austen boys and I are going into town to see how it flies. Should be back in a couple of hours."

"I hope the sheik speaks French...."

"Don't worry, Yisroel. Some of us A-rabs speak a good

French, you know."

Old Bill's eyes twinkled. He had that mischievous smile; he was definitely up to something. If it had been anyone else, I'd have been worried, but somehow Old Bill inspired confidence.

"May G-d be with you."

I watched as Old Bill and Jack Austen's sons headed down the road back toward town. Anyone seeing them would probably have done a double take: an old Arab, bent over and clutching a gnarled stick, walking briskly between two young Westerners down a country road in France.

What was he up to? Clearly, he was going back to the town pretending to be a sheik, but why? Would he be in danger? As I was trying to come up with some answers, I noticed Jack Austen smiling at me, his grey eyes dancing. He knew.

"Okay, Jack. What's going on? What's Old Bill up to now?"

Jack shook his head and said, "I've been sworn to secrecy. Just pray that he and the boys stay out of trouble. But I don't think we need to worry about Old Bill. He's a step ahead of everyone else."

Old Bill did seem indomitable. It occurred to me that Jack was pretty special too. He had brought his entire family to an unknown land and had given up a fortune, a luxurious home, and decades of prominence in a New England town. That beautiful ship of his was sitting at someone else's pier in a foreign country, and would almost certainly never be seen by us again. Now he was basically penniless in this strange land with a bunch of black-suited Jews he hardly knew. Yet he seemed to be a happy man, smiling as his boys walked away with Old Bill.

I spent the afternoon studying maps and calculating how far we would likely be able to walk before the coldest part of winter arrived. Leah and the grandchildren explored the countryside.

By dusk, there was no sign of Old Bill and the Austen boys. I was beginning to worry. By the time we finished dinner, I was sure there must have been trouble. Uncle Phil, Shmuli and I decided we would go to town under cover of darkness. Just as Uncle Phil was loading his gun, we heard the sound of engines over by the road. Then we saw lights. Seconds later, the lights were extinguished. We heard the engines shut down and doors shut.

The three of us ran through the camp frantically, signaling for everyone to go silent and lay low. It could be the police or soldiers or something as innocent as people wanting the privacy of the woods. Several of us huddled behind a wide tree.

We heard the sound of movement through the tall grass. It was difficult to make out anything in the darkness, but I stuck my head around to try and see. All I could make out were shapes. Several people were approaching. Phil raised his gun.

Then I saw them.

An old Arab and two young retainers.

"Bill! It's you!"

"Yup, sonny, it's me all right. We're back with our chariots. You're gonna love 'em. So let's load up and take off. No more walkin' for us, boys. We're goin' in style. We're goin' by bus."

I turned a flashlight on Old Bill, and he was grinning from ear to ear.

"Bill, what on earth have you done now?"

We gathered around the old man to hear his story.

"Well, this is what happened. First, we loped into town. It took a while to get there, 'cause there was lots of people around and plenty of eyes staring at us. Heads were turnin' all right. You could feel those eyeballs in your back!

"I was headin' for the center of town, cause I knew there would be stuff goin' on by the docks. There was the *Ocean Prince* tied up with plenty of people crowded around, looking up close. So we head over there and I saw a lot of A-rabs in the crowd. The more we got toward the center of town, the more A-rabs. Then they laid eyes on me."

This was going to be a long story, it seemed. I wanted to know right away just what happened and what he meant about a bus, but Old Bill was a very good storyteller. So I just waited and listened, happy that he and the boys were back in good shape.

"Well, these guys came over and started speaking to me in 'Fransays.' I know a little Fransays, so I told them I prefer to speak A-rabic. They looked at me with a little nod to each other, like they were surprised and pleased, and they started talking A-rabic to me.

"So I told them my story, you know, that I chartered this boat in America and had left my sons in Boston to run things after the revolution. They knew all about what's goin' on over there. They told me that the A-rabs are very powerful here too and had taken over most of Europe. There is still fighting in Germany and a couple other places but otherwise they are in power. Right now, they are taking over the government in France and have overthrown the infidel governments.

"They were impressed with my story and how I had chartered the ship and brought my entourage with me and how these American boys were accepting Islam. They wanted to help me get to Mecca. It would be a long trip, but if you had a car you could do it in a few weeks. The roads were good and the A-rab police would let me through with no problem.

"So, I told them I had actually converted a few dozen families to Islam and we were all going to Mecca and how could we do it? They wanted to think about it, and invited me and

Jack's boys to come with them to the mosque, and we sat down there and talked. Turns out they had just the thing for us, the town school buses that they had no use for. They had shut all the French religious schools and they would give me two school buses to take the whole crowd to Mecca. They had painted A-rab letters over the name of the schools so the A-rabs in charge all over the place would let these buses go anywhere, especially with me in there."

I couldn't believe what I was hearing. My smile was growing as wide as Old Bill's.

"So we three old boys sat around with the A-rabs and smoked and prayed and they fed us a few good meals and we drank tea and talked about America and Europe and how 'we' were takin' over the whole world, and they were very happy and glad to help me.

"I happened to have some nice presents for them. I had these old daggers from when I was a kid in Egypt, beautiful daggers with jewels on the handles. I took them with me, just in case. Well, they loved the presents. And they couldn't do enough for this old man with the white beard who was going to Mecca and bringing converts with him.

"So we went to see the buses, and they were perfect. They are powered by hydrogen fuel cells so you don't need gas, and there's some extra hydrogen tanks for us, so that we could really go anywhere.

"They wanted to come to see you all out here, but I said everyone was very tired and disheveled and all, and the babies might be cryin,' and it wasn't a good time. Besides, we wanted to be on our way. So I got maps and instructions for all the way to Mecca, how we could get there and all the big cities we should go through. Plus I got papers from them saying who we are and where these buses came from, all in A-rabic writing. So now we have papers for the borders and for the A-rab police.

"Boys, we have these two beautiful buses and we're going in the DIRECTION of Mecca, but we're gonna get a little 'lost,' and we're goin' to end up in JEROOSALEM!"

Then Old Bill let out a whoop and a yell and everyone else started screaming and jumping up and down. Such joy and excitement; you couldn't believe it!

I think we all felt something very strong. I for one felt that a cloud of angels was protecting us. It seemed to me that not only might we make it to the Holy Land, but that the biggest miracles in history were about to happen all around us.

I was still afraid, even afraid to hope, but I thought… maybe.

Maybe….

In the midst of darkness, amazing things were happening.

"Blessed are You, G-d, King of the Universe, Who…creates day and night, removing light before darkness and darkness before light…."

Everyone was anxious to see the buses, so we walked over to inspect them. They had been well used for many years, but were big, with room for us and our supplies. Old Bill was right; they would be our chariots, sent by G-d to carry us forward on our great odyssey. Our hearts were lighter as we packed our belongings.

Then we climbed aboard and sat down. The engines started; the buses vibrated with power, and we headed down the road towards Paris, the first destination on the last leg of our trip home to Israel, to Jerusalem, the Holy City.

VALLEY OF DEATH

Monday night, August 24

THE NIGHT WAS MOONLESS. The road was dark and there were virtually no lights in the countryside. Here and there a candle or oil light flickered in a window, but it was apparent that the electrical grid had been knocked out here in France just as it had been in the U.S.

Our journey began with hope, as everyone was buoyed by the unexpected luxury of our modest but serviceable buses. Maybe we wouldn't have to slog over the Alps through mounds of snow after all. Still, for some reason, I felt a nagging wariness that I couldn't shake. As soon as we started off down those dark roads, a kind of ominous presence seemed to surround us.

We had to drive slowly due not only to the darkness but because the roadbed had not been maintained. Often we had to dodge abandoned cars, rusty axels and enormous potholes. Sometimes we smelled smoke. In the distance I could see flames; perhaps fields were burning.

After traveling a few miles, we came to a large intersection with a makeshift roadblock and a crude floodlight powered by a generator. The bus came to an abrupt stop and several men in Arab clothing approached, carrying submachine guns. Without any greeting or pleasantries, they pounded on the door. Once inside, they walked slowly from front to back, shining a flashlight into our faces.

The adults were visibly frightened; children were crying. Things were getting scary again.

Ain od milvado. Ain od milvado.

Old Bill jumped up and began to speak with them. He showed absolutely no fear and wasn't fazed by their questions. Although they were speaking Arabic, it was obvious what they wanted to know.

"Who are these people with you? They all look like Jews."

Old Bill seemed to relish the situation.

"They ARE Jews. But they have all accepted Islam and we are on a journey to Mecca."

It was an incredibly bold statement and it was helpful that I didn't understand Arabic because I don't think my face could have hidden my reaction. Bill had this uncanny knack for exactly the right words. We WERE Jews. He deflected our interrogators by telling them the truth!

The combination of Bill's forthright manner, his fluency in Arabic, the papers he carried and the Arabic markings on the bus convinced the interrogators. They slowly got off the bus, as if half convinced, then stood on the side of the road, looking somberly after us.

It had been a close call. Would our entire trip across Europe and Asia Minor be a series of heart-stopping encounters, at any one of which we could be dispatched into the Next World? The strain was almost unbearable.

G-d, please help Your children. We are only flesh and blood. How much can we take?

We soon discovered that roadblocks were indeed set up at every important intersection. Over and over, we were stopped and harassed. Over and over, Old Bill was able to get us through. Soon, all of us were drained, wondering how soon we would encounter the next roadblock, and whether Bill would be able to continue his magic. No longer was this a pleasant ride. Heavy silence fell over us.

"Even though I walk through the valley overshadowed by death... You are with me."[56] We could see death on every side. He stared into our faces, shined lights in our eyes and carried big guns which he would happily use.

I always sleep with my room door open and the light on in the hallway outside. Sometimes I look under my bed; I am petrified that something is there. I feel safe if my parents are home at night. Just to hear their voices is reassuring. If they go out for the evening, I am afraid.

Much later, I learn that, before going to sleep, one says "Shema Yisroel...Hear O' Israel, the L-rd our G-d, the L-rd is One.... Whoever sits in the refuge of the Most High, he shall dwell in the shadow of the Al-mighty. I will say of G-d, 'He is my refuge and my fortress' .... You shall not be afraid of the terror of the night."

We call out to "the angel who redeems me from all evil.... Behold, the Guardian of Israel never slumbers nor sleeps...."

We kept getting through!

Did we merit this protection? I worried about that. We were in danger not only from the Moslems, who were apparently in control, but also from the French, who might think from the markings on the bus that we were Moslems.

This seemed an endless night, bumping along the roads of France through the darkness. About five hours after leaving Paimboeuf, we passed just south of Paris. Was the Eiffel

Tower still standing? Did Paris still look like Paris? We had no idea; we were not sightseers. We wanted to bypass every city, every obstacle... just move fast. Village after village looked like a war zone, even in the darkness. Countless churches had been gutted, their spires toppled.

Some time after dawn we passed through Reims, a town renowned in the old days as the capital of the French champagne region. Leah had spent a summer there as a teenager, living with a French family and learning the language. She had taken a long bicycle trip with her French and American friends along these same roads, now littered with mounds of rubble.

Shortly after dawn, we stopped just south of Verdun, the site of a World War I battle in which seven-hundred-and-fifty-thousand people had been killed or wounded during the course of nearly a year. What had they accomplished? Verdun was once again a war zone.

We found a secluded spot at the end of a rural road near the United States military cemetery. We hid the buses and ourselves. Although it seemed that our hideout was protected from prying eyes, we could hear the sounds of gunfire and smell smoke drifting our way from a battle somewhere nearby.

It was good to walk around, stretching our legs and breathing in the early-morning air. The children immediately began to run, play tag and explore. It seemed wise to evaluate our strategy, so we held an impromptu meeting, sitting on fallen tree trunks and large rocks.

There was really no reason to restrict ourselves any more to night-time travel. Our Arab papers, the specially-marked buses and our secret weapon, Old Bill, seemed to be getting us through. If French resistance fighters saw us, however, we would face a different danger.

Moshe Greenberg still thought it was better to travel at night and be less conspicuous. But others wondered if the headlights made us more rather than less visible. At night people might think we were heavily armed fighters. The discussion ended with everyone agreeing we really didn't know which course was best. We put off a final decision.

We slept nervously a few hours, had something to eat and finally decided it was just too nerve-wracking to wait there until dark. We didn't like the sound of battle nearby. There was a sense that we needed to keep moving. As long as we had the buses, we decided to push on with all possible speed.

"Besides," said Yaakov Gruenstein, "we can see the roadway better in daylight."

We had just ended afternoon prayers, and Leah and I were packing our knapsacks, when we heard twigs crackling somewhere off in the woods. Everyone froze. Tsemach Jacobson, Gavriel's younger brother, began to cry; his mother quickly picked him up and quieted him.

Jack Austen's sons-in-law and a few yeshiva guys moved stealthily into the woods. Seconds later, we heard a scuffle. This was followed by pops of gunfire, then the sound of moans. Phil handed me the gun; I crouched low and headed toward the sound of the gunfire. Jack Austen was also moving into the woods. Everyone else lay on the ground. We hadn't gotten far when the Austen boys appeared, walking behind two guys who looked French. Jack's boys had apparently disarmed the pair. They were sullen and silent. Leah tried to question them in French and Old Bill in Arabic, but they wouldn't open their mouths.

After tying them up with strips of cloth from their shirts, we put gags in their mouths and threw their shoes into the woods. One was wounded, and Jeff bandaged his leg. Whoever they were, they were clearly hostile.

It seemed a signal to hit the road. We loaded the buses quickly and everyone scrambled aboard. We left the two guys tied up on the ground. By the time they got loose, we would be far away.

Minutes later, we were roaring up the country road, then back to the main highway, A4, headed for Metz and the border at Strasburg. We made good time, despite several roadblocks, and by nightfall we had arrived at the Rhine River border crossing.

We are returning to America from Israel on El Al. We are sleeping when the loudspeaker crackles. "This is your captain speaking. If there is a doctor on the plane, please report to aisle 25 immediately."

Within seconds, several shapes rush past in the semi-darkness.

About ten minutes later, the captain comes on again. "I am sorry to inform you that we must make an emergency landing. We are currently about twenty minutes from Berlin Airport and we will be stopping there for a medical emergency. We are sorry if this causes any inconvenience to our passengers, but we are sure that you all understand the necessity for this diversion."

The plane immediately began its descent and soon we touch down on German soil. On the tarmac I see the blue and red lights of an ambulance and several police cars. Much frantic activity; then they speed off into the night. We are on the ground for a while as we take on fuel and prepare for takeoff.

It looks like a normal country: the people, the cars. But we are in Germany!

It is a mission of mercy. I appreciate their help.

But we are in Germany! I don't like it here!

Please G-d, let us leave quickly!

I was not happy about stepping onto German soil, saturated as it was with Jewish blood. This really did seem like the Valley of Death. All my life I had gone out of my way to avoid it. It was ironic that we needed to pass through this macabre land to reach our beautiful homeland, but we had no choice. Our buses crossed the highway bridge over the Rhine River. Half way across, we were already in Germany. Once over the bridge, we pulled up to the border station. My stomach ached with tension.

Soon a pair of Moslem militiamen boarded the bus. They walked through slowly, as usual shining lights in our faces and looking at us with cold eyes. No, not just "cold"; they were filled with hatred. Old Bill was his usual unflustered self. His negotiations seemed to be proceeding as they had a dozen times before.

Suddenly, everything changed; the conversation turned serious. The Moslems motioned to Bill to leave the bus, and the three of them entered a hut by the side of the road. Through the windows I could see that a very heated discussion was taking place, with Old Bill speaking forcefully and gesturing emphatically. The Moslems kept pointing at the bus, shaking their fists and banging on the table. Soon other Moslems joined them.

Bill looked cool as ever, but I felt anxious. Something was going wrong. After a few harrowing minutes, Old Bill walked out of the hut. He looked through the bus door and motioned for me to get off. I squeezed Leah's hand and said a short prayer. I'm sure she did too. I'm sure a lot of people did.

"Look, they want to talk to you," said Bill. "They asked for the leader of the Jews. Just tell the truth, up to a point. You are all Jews and everything was falling apart in America and you were trying to escape when you found me. If you want to say that I converted you, that's fine, but I'm going to leave that up to you. They will probably ask you whether you accepted their religion. I can't tell you what to say."

This was very difficult. Now I needed deep wisdom and help from G-d. It would be an abomination to say that we had converted. Of course, my words could condemn two busloads of men, women and children, including my own family. Who was I to decide their fate?

Ana Hashem hoshia na! Please Almighty G-d save us now! *Ana Hashem hoshia na!*

I took a deep breath and followed Bill into the guard shack. Although I wasn't exactly trembling, I felt overwhelmed. It was a hot night. The sticky, heavy air of Germany seemed to envelope me. Cars were lined up behind us, their drivers honking, but the Moslems didn't care. They had plenty of time.

Eight or nine Moslems with traditional head covering stared at me. Their eyes were full of loathing. Old Bill looked completely relaxed, and this had a calming effect. Still, underneath I was raw nerves.

Ain od milvado.

One of them, tall and thin with drooping eyelids, started speaking in accented English.

"Who are you?"

"Yisroel Neuberger."

"You are a Jew?"

"Yes."

"What are you doing here?"

"Trying to escape from death."

"That's not an answer. What are you doing here?"

"My group and I met ..."

I froze. I simply couldn't remember Old Bill's Moslem

name. I coughed and cleared my throat and then—it must have been the angel that saved me again—because I suddenly remembered.

".... Sheik Mustafa on our way out of America, and we sailed across the ocean with him."

"But you are Jews, yes?"

His eyes narrowed and he leaned closer.

"WELL?"

I couldn't disgrace G-d. I wanted to save everyone, but I couldn't say that we had converted. I couldn't lie. I couldn't do it.

"SPEAK."

His eyes looked as if they would pop out of his head. His neck muscles were taut and bulging. My ears were ringing. I couldn't think.

"Yes. We are Jews."

He screamed something in Arabic.

"You lying Jews. The Sheik said all of you are converts. We will kill you. Every one!"

He started banging on the table in a furious rage.

'JEWS! YOU ARE ALL LIARS!"

Old Bill, still composed, started to speak. I clearly remember seeing his mouth open, almost in slow motion, but before any words came out there was a thunderous explosion.

BOOM!

The little house shook. Plaster fell on my head and the lights went out. I felt a hand grab mine with iron strength and Bill was pulling me away and out the door.

BOOM!

Again, an explosion.

Then "tat-tat-tat-tat...."

Machine gun fire. The Arabs dove for the floor as Bill and I ran for the buses.

Just as I stepped onto the bus I felt another hand grab mine. I had no time to turn around, but it seemed all right. The hand was not pulling me back; it seemed as if it was trying to get me to pull it in. We fell into the bus, the hand coming in behind me.

"GET OUT OF HERE! STEP ON IT!"

Jack Austen's sons hit the accelerators. We were roaring down the road before I got to my seat. Quickly the Rhine and the Moslems were way behind us. They were too busy fighting for their lives to think about us. There was a furious firefight underway, and more explosions lit up the sky.

I fell into a seat. Old Bill was already sitting. Whoever had followed me onto the bus had been thrown to the floor by the lurching start. I pulled out my flashlight and shined it in his face.

An Arab!

Before I could say a word he was buried in a pile of Jews. Two guys pinned his arms to the side. The bus was careening wildly down the road and we were piled on top of this Arab!

Old Bill started shooting questions at him. We could hardly hear through the deafening roar of the bus, but Old Bill seemed after a while to understand him.

"What are you doing here?" he yelled.

"I hate those guys! I hate those guys," he was screaming. "Let me come with you. Search me. I threw my gun down by the door. I promise I have no plot against you. I want to get away from them. They're crazy!

"You can trust me. I'm telling you right now: I'm wearing an explosive belt. You can hold on to my hands and take it off me. You don't have to worry; I can't detonate it if you are holding my hands. I don't hate you. I admire Jews! You are fighters! You are survivors! You are stronger than my people because you believe in peace. Take off the belt. It won't detonate. The detonator is locked."

We were all holding our breath, but maybe this guy was for real. Shaul Plotsker, who wasn't afraid of anything, unstrapped the explosive belt and took the detonator. He handed it over to Old Bill, who examined it carefully and then put it away in his sack.

"What's your name?"

"Ahmed bin Azul."

"Where are you from?"

"Al Batrun in Lebanon, north of Beirut, on the sea."

"Why did you come with us?"

"I'm telling you I'm afraid for my life. Those guys are crazy. All they want to do is blow up infidels and churches; the whole world is their enemy. Their own wives are their enemies! This is not the Moslem way, at least not the way I was raised. But they have taken over, and you can't survive if you don't join them. I would rather die with Jews than live with them. It's hell with them! They already began to suspect that my heart wasn't with them."

"What do you want to do?" said Old Bill.

"I want to come with you. I can help you. And you can help me."

"All right," said Old Bill. "Take a seat over there."

All this time we had been speeding at breakneck speed on German Route E52. If only we could simply keep going, nonstop, until we reached Israel! We kept racing ahead. No one was following, but we kept up the speed as if a thousand hornets were flying behind us. We turned left from E52 onto A5, heading north towards Karlsruhe.

Just south of Karlsruhe, the A5 intersected the A8. This was another big road and we were off on a tear eastward. The miles were piling up and I was beginning to breathe normally again. I worried about the Arab, but, if Bill said he was all right…. Maybe we would make it after all. We were traveling very fast southeast toward Munich.

Munich.

That name triggered horrible thoughts. So many tragedies had occurred here, including a blood libel 800 years ago and the Olympic tragedy of 1972. Not far from Munich is Dachau. This was indeed the Valley of Death, but it was the only way to reach the Land of the Living.

Old Bill, who was sitting behind me, leaned forward and put his hand on my shoulder.

"That was kinda close, huh sonny?"

"Bill, I don't know what's going to happen next, but you are amazing."

He leaned closer.

"I grabbed some papers there. They warn that conditions in Germany are very dangerous. The Moslems are not in control here yet and anyone entering Germany needs to proceed with caution. It's considered an active military area with heavy fighting in some locations. Notice that we haven't passed a Moslem checkpoint for a long time, and it's been a lot of miles since the border. We may have different problems coming up."

The intensity of pressure was ratcheting up. It just seemed impossible to deal with. It was all too big for me! It had been crazy enough up to now, but this seemed totally beyond our capacity.

G-d, protect us! Save us! *Ana Hashem hoshia na!*

I shut my eyes and tried to think.

Onward we sped through the night, two buses full of Jews and our friends. We passed Stuttgart, then Augsburg, and still no checkpoints. Then, around 2 a.m. the pavement began to get rough. The ride became very bumpy and we had to slow down to about twenty miles per hour, then fifteen.

We had hundreds of miles ahead of us and we were traveling at fifteen miles an hour. The minutes ticked by but the road didn't improve. It felt as if we were riding over cobblestones. I was feeling impatient and anxious, wondering how long we'd be stuck at a crawl, when bright flashes appeared in the sky to the north and then the south. The smell of smoke drifted through the air.

Then it happened.

BANG!

I was in the first bus. I was slammed forward in my seat; baggage went flying.

BANG!

The bus stopped abruptly, then lunged forward for an instant and fell back.

Behind us, the second bus screeched on its brakes; miraculously it had just missed rear-ending us.

Chaos. People were screaming and wailing. Babies were crying and even some of the parents. Everyone was groaning with pain. Baggage was all over the place.

What had happened?

Fortunately, everyone had been strapped in with seat belts on or else there would have been serious injuries. We tried to feel through the darkness and retrieve glasses, handbags and other belongings in the mess.

Tim Gatling, Jack Austen's son-in-law, who had been driving our bus, opened the door. Heading toward the front felt as if I were walking downhill. I grabbed a flashlight from my knapsack and climbed out. The bus was pitched forward at a steep angle.

I took a few steps and then I saw it in the flashlight's beam. Across the entire length of the Autobahn was a huge ditch, like an anti-tank obstacle, at least five feet wide and three feet deep. It must have taken special equipment to construct such an enormous ditch. I doubted that even a tank could make it across. Obviously it was meant to stop traffic.

It worked. We were finished.

Just minutes before, our buses had been roaring through the darkness like unfettered stallions. Now, bus number one was leaning into the ditch, its front wheels out of sight. Bus number two couldn't hold all of us, and, besides, there was no way to maneuver around the ditch.

I had no idea what to do next. I looked back at the bus, at Leah, our children and grandchildren, Uncle Phil and Aunt Bessie and our friends. Everyone was waiting for some kind of signal from me. I just shook my head. How were we going to walk hundreds of miles through battlefields to the Holy Land?

"OK, folks, it looks like the end of the line for these buses. Let's unload everything."

People wearily emerged from the buses. I felt totally defeated. We had made it across the ocean and seen miracle after miracle as G-d had rescued us time after time. But now, it was all over.

Long Island to Munich.

I wanted to cry. I was out of ideas and out of hope.

And then it got worse.

A Field Near
Munich

Early morning, Wednesday August 26

T WAS THREE A.M. AS we huddled together at the edge of a large meadow next to the Autobahn. A chilly wind was blowing, hinting at the approaching winter.

I was already cold, inside and out, shivering from fear, despair and fatigue. Everyone was exhausted. We were physically bruised from the impact of the sudden stop and emotionally shaken from our harrowing experience at the border. Standing in this forlorn field, close to Munich and Dachau, a region infamous for its crimes against our people, I had absolutely no idea what to do next. How would we get through this brutal country with no transportation, especially in the grip of the coming winter? How would adults survive, much less children?

Then, I looked around and realized that everyone was waiting for me to do something. I guessed there was nothing to do except to try and move forward as best we could.

We started walking, a little apprehensively, more like

zombies. Everyone was silent, some holding their children's hands and some wheeling strollers. Leah and I were at the front and I was waving my flashlight from side to side.

Then we saw them: a line of men in dark uniforms, standing in front of us, blocking the way.

We stopped and stared. These men had no expression on their faces.

My stomach knotted.

Silence.

One of the men, taller than the rest, stepped forward. He spoke English with a heavy German accent.

"You are Yuden, yes? We have been expecting you. Our observers down the road saw your camouflaged French buses and alerted us. Our radio transmitters still work. The Islamists have not succeeded in taking over our country and they never will. In fact, I see that you have one of them with you! Collaborating with the enemy, eh?"

Ahmed was speaking quietly with Old Bill back by the buses. I saw them bending over something. Old Bill was opening his sack and handing something to Ahmed. Meanwhile, the Germans were surveying all of us with their searchlights.

"I invite our Islamic friend to join us right up front. Come over here. What is your name?"

"Ahmed."

"Well, a good Islamic name! You are very welcome here with your Jewish cousins!"

"Now, where are your other Islamic friends? Are they following you? That's okay; we'll just wait for them. In the meantime, please follow me over here to the left, the large field. We have prepared a personal welcome for all of you."

There were dozens, perhaps a hundred men waiting. Moving in and surrounding us, they seemed very calm.

I began to pray. Leah walked next to me as we moved in the direction they indicated.

"Just where were you intending to go?" asked the leader.

"We are heading eastward, with G-d's help. We've come from America."

"And who gave you permission to enter Germany?"

"Actually, there seemed to be confusion at the border. We got the idea that national borders, at least for the time being, have ceased to exist as they did in the past."

He laughed a hollow laugh, without smiling.

"Yes, you are right, some things have indeed changed. But not everything. Not everything has changed."

He stroked his chin and looked at the men around him.

"You have not answered my question yet. What was your destination? Are you simply traveling eastward or did you have a specific destination in mind?"

"Well, yes, we are intending to go to Israel."

"Oh, how interesting. Israel. We refer to it as 'Palestine.' Isn't that a long way off? And you are on foot now, I believe, since you have apparently just lost your means of motorized transport. In addition, you are not so warmly dressed. It will be a cold winter. Just how were you planning to get there?"

I had no choice but to answer his questions.

"When the United States was attacked, we escaped miraculously and were fortunate to have been able to sail to France. We have had G-d's help wherever we went, and we hope to continue to have it. Perhaps you will help us with clothing, food and transportation. The Bible says that those who bless the Children of Abraham...."

"Enough! No preaching!"

He looked past me, casting his gaze over the entire group.

"I regret to inform you that your journey is over. We don't like your kind. Our leaders once made a very good start toward ridding the world of all of you. Unfortunately, they were not able to complete the job. They left that legacy to us. The world may be in turmoil, but perhaps this is a special opportunity, from G-d, as you say, to complete their work. Now will you all please be so kind as to step over here, to this area of the field, where the men stand with the torches."

I looked toward the field, where that large group of uniformed men stood. They all carried weapons and were obviously well trained. As we walked, I managed to confer in a whisper with several others. But no one in our group, not even Old Bill, had any idea how we might escape. If we ran for it, they would shoot us. But they were going to shoot us anyway. And who would run? Entire families? Just men? Just children?

"You there! Stop talking!"

He wasn't pretending to be polite any more.

"We will not tolerate anyone speaking. We can see everyone. Anyone who talks will be shot. That includes talking to children."

"*Shema Yisroel*," cried someone.

"*Hashem Elokainu, Hashem Echad*," others answered.

"I warn you! I will not tolerate this! If you pray, pray to yourself. If we hear anything, we just shoot in that direction. Someone will die."

From the back of our group, a voice cried out.

"What will you gain from this? We are not your enemies. We mean no harm to you."

One of the men to the leader's right raised his arm and pointed a pistol.

BANG!

A bullet whistled past my ear.

"You are lucky now, but maybe not next time. I advise you to take me seriously. No more words. No plots. No schemes.

You are under a sentence of death. It will be carried out."

Ahmed stepped forward toward the leader.

"I want to talk to you," he said.

"Raise your hands," said the leader.

Ahmed stepped closer. He started to scream.

"What are you doing to these people? What have they done to you? Your Hitler was a failure and you are nothing! Don't you realize you lost that war? And you'll lose this war! You're living in the dead past!"

A circle of Germans was steadily closing in on Ahmed, guns at the ready, waiting for the right moment, but he didn't care. He kept screaming and gesticulating, waving his arms up and down.

"Put your hands up," said the leader, "or you will be shot."

"What do I care?" said Ahmed. "You're all cowards. You know that in the end you can't defeat the Jews. Give up now, before it's too late."

The leader laughed derisively.

"You're surrounded, you filthy Arab. Silence!"

"Silence?" Ahmed screamed. "SILENCE?"

Ahmed's voice shook with such intensity that every face turned.

"I will teach you sons of idolatry about silence!"

At that very moment a deafening roar and tower of flame shot upward and outward from Ahmed, a wall of fire engulfing the circle of men surrounding him.

The explosive belt!

Screams reverberated; bodies disintegrated before our eyes! I turned away, but the cries of the wounded sounded like the wailing from those who suffer eternal torture in the depths of hell.

Ahmed had tried to save us! I couldn't believe my eyes! He had used his last strength and passion to try to save our lives! May G-d have mercy on him! I was moved to the depths of my heart.

But quickly I saw that it was not going to work. The Germans were nothing if not efficient.

"*Achtung!*"

A new leader stepped forward.

"You will not get away so easily, Jews. In war there are always those who fall, but the army goes on. We are many. We will not let this Islamic assassin succeed in his evil plot. Very clever of you to bring him with you, my dear friends, but it will not save you! My men have you surrounded.

"Now. All women come forward. If you have children, bring them with you."

A chorus of anguished wails, louder even than the crying of the wounded.

"No."

BANG!

"Ayy."

Someone behind me had been shot. There was a commotion.

"Order! *Achtung!* No more sounds!"

"I'm okay," someone said. "Don't worry."

Baruch Hashem!

How foolish! In a few minutes none of us would be okay, G-d forbid.

"Have mercy on us!" a woman called out.

The leader ignored her.

"Women come forward with your children. Now!"

Nobody moved.

One of the uniformed men strode forward into our midst. He tried to grab the hand of Ayelet Gruenstein. She looked him in the eye.

"Take your hand off me. I will go with my children, and

we will live forever because we are under G-d's eternal protection. But you will die forever like the swine that you are."

Applause. What courage!

"Silence!"

I was choked up. Sobbing.

Ayelet walked forward, her head held high, clutching her children's hands.

Everyone began crying. Leah squeezed my hand and walked forward with Ayelet. Other women followed, with their children.

So this is how it was going to end. All our wives, our holy children and families, our hopes, the promise of living in the Holy Land. All gone.

I first see Leah when we are teenagers at the Fox Ridge School. She is all sunshine, full of hope and goodness, caring and understanding, and even more so every day of her life. She is all anyone could be, bringing only happiness into other people's lives.

It is such a miracle and blessing to go through life with Leah, to raise a family and see generations of holy children come from that first meeting of two naive kids so long ago. Now everything is coming to an end. I know we will meet again, in another world. I know G-d will continue to watch over us in death as He has in life. If there was one thing I had learned, it is that G-d is above all of creation, beyond time, beyond birth and death.

Even so, I am just flesh and blood. I can't remember when I existed as a soul only. All I remember is this world. I have lived my entire adult life in this world with Leah. We have built everything together, with the blessings of G-d. To see it all end! It is all too much, but it is really happening.

We all stood there, men, women and children, tears

streaming down our faces. We were powerless. It was happening so quickly; there was nothing we could do.

They lined the women and children up, telling them to stand close to each other in the center. The leader issued an order in German and men with rifles formed a circle around the women and children.

Crying and shrieking.

The men raised their rifles. There was no escape, no way to stop them.

"Goodbye Abba."

"Goodbye Ima."

"May G-d watch over you until we meet again."

"*Shema Yisroel, Hashem Elokainu, Hashem Echad.*"

"*Baruch Shaim kavod malchuso l'olam va-ed.*"

"Goodbye Chaim."

"Goodbye Rachel."

"Goodbye Miriam."

"SILENCE!"

Crying and shrieking.

"SILENCE!"

The leader gave a command in German and the men raised their rifles.

Crying and shrieking.

This was it.

Ana Hashem hoshia na! Ana Hashem hoshia na!

G-D SAVE US!

Time seemed to stand still.

There was utter silence.

Then I heard it.

A tiny sound.

What I would call a thin sound.

First I thought it was a baby crying, a very thin sound.
The crying and shrieking stopped.
Everybody was listening.

But then it was clear that it was not a baby crying, because it continued without any pause whatsoever, and it was sustained and became louder. It was very steady. It became more intense, like a siren, but not painful.

Perhaps it is the Shabbos siren in Jerusalem. Oh, I am hallucinating!

It did not stop.

But everything else stopped.

The men with the rifles stood frozen. No one moved.

The sound did not come from one place; it came from every place, from all around. You couldn't ignore it. The sound got louder, and the men with the guns began to tremble; the guns were shaking in their hands. We started looking around, everyone looking at each other. No one spoke.

The sound was getting continually louder, a strong sound now, but absolutely pure, a pure sound with no harshness in it, one very pure tone. It came from everywhere, from around us on all sides, from above us and even below us. The sound became even stronger, but as strong as it became, it never became too strong. It was one note, loud but never painful. It seemed to enter you and give you a feeling of peace. It was a sound more powerful than anything I had ever heard before.

Then something flashed across the sky.

Something white, luminescent in the night sky, something leaving a white phosphorescent trail, like snow crystals.

White forms streaking across the sky. You could hear the "swish."

They looked as if they were going with a purpose, a destination. There were more and more of them.

Now they were coming from every direction.

The men with the guns were frozen.

The sound was continuing.

A siren, louder and louder. Yes, it WAS like the *Shabbos* siren in Jerusalem, very pure.

A white shape swished past very close to us. It was powerful; you could feel the energy.

The men with the guns were shaking. Something was happening. Guns began to drop on the ground. The men tried to run, but they couldn't, as if their shoes were nailed to the ground. They were shaking.

A huge white shape swished directly overhead. Someone like a man, maybe twenty feet tall, white and luminescent, was standing in front of us. We were all shaking now.

We were all crying now.

We were crying with happiness!

We knew!

We were jumping up and down, shouting. Everyone was jumping, jumping. Even the old ones. Ed Frankel, whose back had hurt so much yesterday that he couldn't walk, was jumping up and down. And it wasn't cold anymore. Or at least we didn't feel the cold. The children were jumping. The mothers were screaming with happiness. We were all jumping and shouting.

"*Shema Yisroel, Hashem Elokainu, Hashem Echad.*"

Jumping and shouting.

"*Baruch shaim kavod malchuso l'olam va-ed.*"

Now the shape spoke, and we all trembled.

The voice was so powerful that it literally knocked me over.

"My Children, you are saved by the Almighty. This is the end of history. *Mashiach ben Dovid* has entered the world. The loyal children are saved.

"Enemies of Israel, this is the message of the Almighty G-d

to you: '*Arise to your fate. You are powerless and your weapons are powerless. Arise to your fate. Arise to your judgment. You have persecuted My Children. I warned you time and again. I wrote in My books and spoke through the mouth of My prophets. Those who have persecuted My children will receive the fate they intended for My children. As My servant Ovadiah said: As you did, so will be done to you, your recompense shall return upon your head .... For your violence to your brother Jacob, shame will cover you, and you will be cut down forever.*[57]

"Children of G-d, you are going home to Jerusalem, but first you will see the punishment of your enemies. Look at the top of the hill ahead of you."

We all looked.

There, accompanied by huge white angels, was a man with a little moustache, shaking and groveling. They walked toward us, down into the meadow.

The Germans were in a circle now in the center of the field. Around them were hundreds of angels, all huge in stature and glowing white in the black night. The angels illuminated the night. Warmth emanated from them. From every direction more angels were appearing, and with them were pathetic, cringing figures, trembling and shaking. They were being gathered into the center of the field.

The angels from the top of the hill were approaching now, and a way was cleared for them. They approached the tallest angel, who stood in the center.

"Shickelgruber,[58] we have removed you from your grave because you are summoned to appear in Jerusalem."

"GGGGGG," he tried to scream, but words did not come out. Instead, from his nose, mouth and ears slid ribbons of slimy worms, and he was choking on them. The worms covered his face in slime. Other worms slid into his clothing. He was writhing and struggling, gurgling and groveling.

"Shickelgruber, the Almighty addresses you: 'WHAT DID YOU DO TO MY CHILDREN?'

"WHAT IS YOUR ANSWER?"

Groveling and shaking, he fell to the ground, trying to speak, but no words came out, only twisting worms and slime.

"Take him away to Jerusalem."

"And now, my children," said the Angel, "You will also go to Jerusalem, but you will go in honor and dignity."

He pointed to the horizon. From over the hilltops came more luminescent forms, but these were huge birds, their wings glowing silver in the night sky. There were dozens and dozens of birds, and they flew gracefully to where we stood. The children were screaming with delight and happiness. Somehow all the pain had been forgotten.

The birds landed near us and the Angel instructed us to sit upon their backs, family by family, for each family a bird and for each bird a family. The youngest children and their parents went first; each bird had an indented area in its back that was large enough for each family, like a soft bowl covered in feathers. The parents would slide their children down into the bowl and then they would follow, and there was just enough room for each family. Within the indented area were warm drinks and delicious cakes; the birds made cooing sounds that soothed us.

As each family sat together, the bird would get to its feet, unfold its wings and jump off into the air, circling around us and then flying off to the southeast. No one was afraid. Everyone was filled with happiness beyond the power of speech to convey.

The Austens and Old Bill stood off to the side, watching the families and children soaring off into the air. I worried for them; they seemed to feel out of place, but suddenly the Angel addressed them.

"Our dear friends, brothers and sisters of the Children of Israel, come. Take your places. This eagle is meant for you. Come to Jerusalem, where you will be honored forever among the Great Ones of the World. Your reward is boundless, for you have listened to the Voice of G-d and you have brought blessing to the world. Those who bless the Children of Israel will be blessed, and you have blessed the Children of Israel. Come, our friends, to Jerusalem. You have nothing to fear. All your troubles are over."

The Austens helped Old Bill as they climbed over the enormous bird's back. In the glow, I saw Old Bill smiling at me, thumbs up.

"Thank you, Bill. Thank you, Jack. Thanks to all of you," I shouted. "We will see you soon, with G-d's help, in Jerusalem."

They looked at us with wide smiles, and then their bird jumped up and flew off into the night sky. Before long, the glow of its giant wings disappeared over the eastern horizon.

And then, there was no one else left but Leah and me, the children and grandchildren. We were bathed in the angels' silvery light. One more huge bird flew over and alighted on the ground. All the children climbed in and then I helped Leah.

I had no words. Our hearts were overflowing with emotion. I paused a moment and thought to myself, "I want to feel the earth of Exile for the last time."

I stood there for a moment on that alien soil, soaked with Jewish blood. I rejoiced in my deepest soul that I would never again have to stand there. Never again would I breathe the air that reeked of hatred of G-d and His Children, never again would I be forced to swallow the poison of Exile.

I untied my shoes; I would go home in purity. I placed my hand upon the bird's wing. It was soft and strong. I didn't have to climb, because something lifted me. I found myself sliding out of my shoes and down a soft embankment into what seemed like a feather bed. There was enough room for all, and our little compartment was filled with food and drink to revive and sustain us. Then the giant bird leapt up, as if it were lighter than air, and the ground fell away beneath us. The Angel stood there, a silver beacon, fading into the distance, finishing the work that remained, and we knew we would see him once again in the Holy City.

As the breeze passed over our faces, I became aware of a beautiful aroma. I realized that never before, even in the heights of the Rocky Mountains, had I breathed pure air. There had always been some mixture of bitter poison. I had become so used to it that I had ceased to realize it. But now the air was absolutely pure, invigorating the soul. I knew I was inhaling the aroma that our Father Abraham had inhaled when he discovered the Cave of Machpela in Hebron. That cave is the entrance to the Garden of Eden, where mankind existed in perfection until our rebellion poisoned the wine.

And now we were returning to the Holy Land, the Holy City, and G-d would allow us once more to savor the primeval purity of the world as it had existed at its first Creation. As we soared through the sky, the sun was rising in the east, and in the west the moon was setting. The moon was as bright as the sun, and the world was filled with light.

EPILOGUE

THE BREEZE BLEW OUR HAIR. The blue-green sea was below us. I yelled out at the top of my voice.

"*Hodu l'Hashem ki tov, ki l'olam chasdo.* Give Thanks to G-d, for He is good; His kindness endures forever."[59]

"*B'shuv Hashem es shivas Tzion hayinu k'cholmim...* When G-d will return the captivity of Zion we will be like dreamers."[60]

"WE ARE LIVING THE DREAM!"

"Yisroel, you're hurting my ears," said Leah.

"Oh, sorry," I said. "I'm just excited."

"I am also," said Leah. "But maybe a little quieter."

"Okay Leah."

We looked down upon the blue-green sea. Ahead was the coastline of the Holy Land. All around I saw eagles like ours, hundreds, perhaps thousands of powerful, pure white birds with huge outstretched wings gracefully undulating against a dark blue sky. They were coming in from all sides, headed for the gleaming hills on the horizon, the Holy City, Jerusalem.

We gasped as we crossed the coastline. We were home!

In the old days, before innocence had deserted us, El Al

passengers used to clap and sing as they reached the border. Now we started singing *shalom aleichem*...peace to you, as we crossed over into the Holy Land.

Peace to G-d, Who had brought His children home.

Your children have returned!

Peace to our brothers and sisters.

Peace to the Land of Israel.

Peace to the entire world.

We soared over the coast and up to Jerusalem, landing on the Mount of Olives, across the Valley from the Temple Mount.

We slid down the eagle's giant wing. Our feet touched the warm earth and we stooped to kiss the soil of Israel.

I heard a soft noise and turned. The great bird's giant, watery eyes were looking at us. One by one we embraced his neck. We could feel the pulsing blood and the beating of his powerful heart.

We turned west to look across the Valley of Kidron to the Temple Mount. We had an unobstructed view of a sight that took our breath away. The Temple stood in golden glory before our eyes, as countless thousands, clad in white, made their way upward toward its entrances. We could see across the eastern wall of the Old City into the Temple itself. It was filled with people, and we could hear from inside the most beautiful music we had ever heard, sounds of perfect harmony reaching to the heavens. An aroma of perfect purity entered our nostrils, reviving our souls after two thousand years.

The day was bright, but the light was soothing. A warm breeze caressed us. I looked around, and there, coming toward us, were our children from Israel and our children from New York, who had been in Israel when the world had exploded. We were all together now. How long had it been!

"Rachel, Shira, Aliza, Shmuli, Ruchoma, all the families, all the children." Leah and I were ecstatic. Everyone was safe. Everyone was together...forever.

We looked around, too overcome to speak. What a sight. How could you begin to describe it? A day of perfect happiness we knew would never end. Our troubles would never return and our tears would be wiped away forever.

Jeff, Marge and little Julie walked over.

"Yisroel, Leah ...." Jeff was sobbing with happiness, "How can we say 'thank you'? What can ...."

He couldn't continue. We embraced for a long time.

"Look, over there," someone said. "Old Bill and the Austens!"

They waved and started walking in our direction.

I couldn't keep my eyes off Old Bill. He looked different. How can I describe it? He still looked like Old Bill, but he was glowing like a torch! Light radiated from every feature. His eyes sparkled like the sun. He was not old, but rather ageless. He moved like a lion, walking in grandeur. He looked taller than before, and was dressed all in white, his head wrapped in a turban, like the pictures I had seen of the priests, the children of Aaron in ancient days of glory, when the Presence of G-d hovered upon the Holy Temple and the children of Israel served Him in purity and unity.

"Bill."

That's all I said. I couldn't get anything more out of my mouth.

"Bill."

"Yisroel," he said, "I have something for you. I am going to return two of your possessions. They really belong to your wife, but I am going to let you give them to her."

He reached inside his robes. As he drew out his hand, I saw light emanating from his skin. On his open palm lay Leah's diamond ring and a small, tear-stained Book of

Psalms. I looked up at him. He seemed to tower above us.

"Bill...Bill, who are you?"

We knew that angels walked the earth. We had seen angels ourselves only a few hours earlier. Our Father Abraham had been visited by angels, and every Friday night we had welcomed angels to our homes in the brilliant light of the Shabbos candles. When I sang "Shalom Aleichem" I had always tried to imagine the reality of the angels entering our home, blessing and sustaining us. As a young married student, worlds ago in Ann Arbor, Michigan, I am sure that an angel had come to me on the awesome day that I had first dared to believe in the Existence of G-d.

Or was Bill a prophet, an exalted servant of G-d? We all knew that Elijah walked the earth, that he was present at every bris and sat with every Jewish family at the Passover table.

It almost didn't matter who he was. What mattered was that G-d had now begun to reveal His Presence to the world. We were surrounded by sanctity and sanctified beings. Whoever Bill was, G-d had sent him to guide and help us through the birth pangs of Mashiach.

"Come with me," said Bill, "to greet *Mashiach ben Dovid*. The Day has come, the Day we have been awaiting since our Father Abraham was first summoned by the Master of the Universe. Even more! The Day we have been awaiting since our Ancient Parents, Adam and Eve, were expelled from the Primeval Garden. In Exile, all that was holy was hidden, and everything visible was corrupt. Now it is over. Evil has been removed from the world. *Gog* and his armies have vanished; our enemies are no more. Our fight is over. *Mashiach ben Dovid* is our king and he is awaiting us. Will you allow me to bring you to him?"

I dropped upon the ground and bowed toward the Temple, to the G-d of Israel, Ruler of Heaven and Earth. My heart was overflowing with joy, and there were no more questions. I felt complete peace for the first time in my life.

I looked at our precious children and grandchildren, raised in sanctity and steeped in Torah, with eyes always looking toward eternity, and I saw that everything we had lived for had now become reality. All secrets were revealed and all evil had vanished like a wisp of smoke.

The one who had called himself Old Bill took my hand, and we walked with our family and friends toward the Holy Temple upon Mount Zion. There, King Messiah ruled and the Sanhedrin sat. There the Priests officiated in sanctity. There the aroma of incense filled our entire beings and the songs of the Levites elevated our souls, upward toward the throne of G-d. Goodness ruled the world. Peace was proclaimed; all our troubles and fears were over. The world was filled with the knowledge of G-d as the sea fills the ocean bed.[61]

NOTES

1. Deuteronomy 11:12
2. Ethics of the Fathers Chapter 3, Mishna 2
3. Deuteronomy 4:35
4. Psalm 91
5. Isaiah 40:31
6. Genesis 48:16
7. Talmud Tractate Brachos 32b
8. Ecclesiastes/Koheles 3:4
9. Book of Daniel 2:31-35
10. Psalm 91
11. Malachi 3:19-20
12. Genesis 12:1
13. Psalm 118
14. Talmud Tractate Pesachim 64b
15. Psalm 113
16. Genesis 37:25
17. Genesis 12:1
18. Isaiah 6:8
19. Psalm 116
20. Rashi's famous comment on Exodus 19;2
21. Rashi on Genesis 15:5. Bereishis Rabbah 44:12.
22. Psalm 19

23. Koheles/Ecclesiastes 3:1-3
24. Deuteronomy 32:2
25. In Jewish law, an eruv delineates an enclosed area within which one is allowed to carry items on Shabbos. Some communities have a special telephone number (the "eruv hotline") so that residents may check whether the eruv is intact that Shabbos.
26. Psalm 95
27. From the High Holiday prayers
28. Talmud Tractate Shabbos 119b
29. Proverbs Chapter 31
30. Psalm 126
31. Numbers 25:10 ff
32. Psalm 92
33. Lamentations/Eichah by the Prophet Jeremiah/Yirmiahu haNavi
34. Psalm 91
35. Genesis 37:3-4
36. Exodus 13:17-18
37. Talmud Tractates Gittin 6b, Eruvin 13b
38. Psalm 126
39. Exodus 11:7. This Biblical sentence is sometimes said as a means of trying to invoke Divine help against the attack of wild animals.
40. Exodus 19:4
41. Psalm 118
42. Book of Ruth, 3:12-13
43. Rabbi Yisroel Reisman. This thought I also found in the writings of the Ben Ish Chai, published by Yeshivat Ahavat Shalom.
44. Talmud Tractate Taanis 29b
45. Psalm 30
46. Leviticus 26:36-37
47. Psalm 118
48. Psalm 118
49. Deuteronomy 30:19

50. Malachi 3:23-24
51. Psalm 30
52. Jonah 2:6-8
53. Malachi 3:23-24
54. A blessing made when a particularly good event occurs in which many people share the benefit.
55. Psalm 126
56. Psalm 23
57. Ovadiah 1:15; 1:10
58. The actual name of Adolf Hitler, may all his names as well as his memory be erased forever.
59. Psalm 118
60. Psalm 126
61. Isaiah 11:9

ACKNOWLEDGEMENTS

s the world nears the Final Redemption, I want to express gratitude that I have found G-d and His Torah, that He has given me life and the desire to glorify His Name, an exalted family, trustworthy guides and friends. In the words of our Father Jacob, *"yesh li kol,"* I have everything. Now I ask that He permit me to use the powers He has given me to sanctify His Name.

I don't know how to praise my wife sufficiently. Suffice it to say that we are partners in everything, and it seems clear it was planned that way from the beginning of time. May G-d bless her and our righteous children, whose loving help and Torah wisdom are always with us.

Rebbetzin Esther Jungreis introduced us to Torah some thirty four years ago. We cannot sufficiently express our gratitude. The story is told in *From Central Park to Sinai: How I Found My Jewish Soul.*

Both my exalted parents contributed unique qualities to me which have molded my life. I am blessed with loving siblings.

It is our privilege to know and receive guidance from Rabbi Naftali Jaeger and his rebbetzin, Rabbis Yaakov Hillel, Binyomin Forst, Yeshaya Klor, Yisroel Belsky, Dovid Cohen, Nate Segal, Naftali Weinberg, Reuven Cohen and Dovid Gelber, Avraham Jacobovitz and his rebbetzin, Zev Kahn and his rebbetzin, and many others who have warmed us at the fires of their Torah greatness.

My Torah study partner for over a decade is a *talmid chacham* and *tzaddik* named Rabbi Moshe Grossman. I am forever grateful for the Torah he teaches me with endless patience.

Finding a publisher is no easy matter; finding *tzaddikim* to publish one's book is a blessing beyond measure. The entire Feldheim family, including Reb Yaakov Feldheim, Reb Yitzchak Feldheim and Reb Eli Meir Hollander, are holy Jews whose kindness and high standards are an ever-flowing source of *chizuk*.

Reb Amos Bunim provided the amazing quote from the Malbim that introduces this book. I want to thank Don Softness, my long-time public relations consultant, Karen P. Lane, Stuart Schnee, Yael Landa, and Fern Sidman for their devoted work. Deenee Cohen and Henshy Barash designed the brilliant cover. Professor Lewis Burke Frumkes was of constant help and encouragement. The Hon. Arnold I. Burns wrote a beautiful endorsement.

I am grateful to Naftali Hirsch, Jim Kaufman, Michael Sacofsky, Rabbi Moshe Greenbaum, Stanley Blumenstein, Ragan Roth, Gavriel Aryeh Sanders, Tehilla Lancry, Mrs. Henni Becker, Jason Allen Ashlock, Gene Mastropieri III and the astronomer who told me the Milky Way gives off enough light to cast a shadow.

Countless people have given me blessings, ideas and encouragement. I apologize to all whose names I have neglected to mention. May G-d soon bless us all with the coming of *Moshiach ben Dovid*, the rebuilding of the Holy Temple and the Final Redemption of the Children of Israel, well before 2020! May we arrive in peace!

Roy Yisroel Neuberger
Sefira 5768

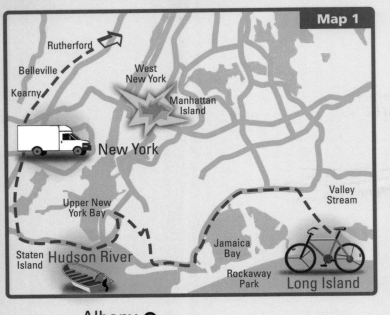

Map 1

Rutherford
Belleville
Kearny
West New York
Manhattan Island
New York
Valley Stream
Upper New York Bay
Jamaica Bay
Staten Island
Hudson River
Rockaway Park
Long Island

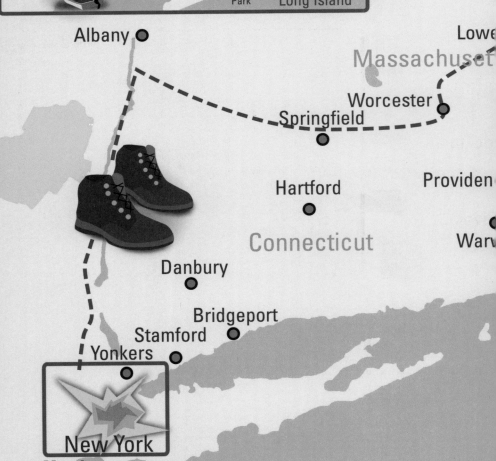

Albany

New Hampsh

Manche

Lowe

Massachuset

Worcester
Springfield

Hartford

Providen

Connecticut

Warv

Danbury

Bridgeport
Stamford

Yonkers

New York

Map 1